GOLD SQUAD

M.V. VILTCH

aethonbooks.com

GOLD SQUAD
©2023 M.V. Viltch

Aethon Books
www.aethonbooks.com

Typography, Print and eBook formatting by Steve Beaulieu. Artwork provided by Vivid Covers.

Published by Aethon Books LLC.

Aethon Books is not responsible for websites (or their content) that are not owned by the publisher.

ALSO IN SERIES

The die is cast.
—JULIUS CAESAR

CHAPTER
ONE

I t was *that* kind of night. Feeling like there should be a projection of 'denied' beaming on my forehead, I stumbled into my room and flumped into my chair. I savored the cool air on my clammy skin. Summers in the southern North America sector were no joke, and since cabs weren't allowed to enter Evans Joint Ops, the walk to my barracks had been a brutal one—a hike through what felt like a rainforest, complete with the savage insects that threatened to bleed you dry.

I had half a mind to tell the cabbie to gun the air-car and fly over the security station altogether, but that would've been suicide. The automated point-defense turrets and the armed guards would've shredded us into confetti. Not to mention the mechs. These towering, deadly machines would have incinerated us without a qualm. They were Legion property and a relatively new addition to our otherwise low-key Space Force installation. Courtesy of the Galactic Senate, they were brought in as extra security for the secretive R&D labs they had on base.

My buddy, Reeds, a stocky trooper with an almost maniacal love for weapons, shuffled in behind me, laughing.

"Way to go, Jake, you ladies' man. She talked to you like, what, one time all night?"

He barked another laugh as he settled his sweaty ass against my dresser. "Wasn't she the one who invited you to the party, though?"

I leaned my head back with a loud exhale as the room spun around me in a drunken daze.

"Yeah," I muttered. "She sure did."

The woman Reeds was referring to and had relentlessly teased me about for the past hour was Anna, a hot civilian office assistant I'd set my sights on. I'd been after this girl for months, and yesterday, she'd finally caved. She invited me to a small gathering off base. Even though most of my brilliant jokes strangely caused her to cringe, I jumped at the opportunity. In fact, like a dumbass, I blurted, "I'll be there!" before she finished extending the invitation.

A smile played over my face as I thought back to the low-cut outfit she had on tonight and the three-minute conversation she graced me with.

I shrugged at Reeds. "Ehh… at least the view wasn't something to scoff at, right?"

I did a victorious spin in my chair to highlight my point, only to quickly realize that was a bad idea. The room continued to spin after the chair stopped.

Reeds snorted and shook his head. "No, sir! But I hope it was worth it, man. It would suck if you blew your exam, on top of blowing it with the chick, huh?"

I straightened, confused. "Say what?"

For a few seconds, I just stupidly blinked at him. Then it hit me. My qualification exam for the Force's logistics specialist program was today. I had to report to the test hall in three hours.

"Damn!"

I flung my head back as a slew of colorful profanity escaped my lips. Sure, a logistics specialist wasn't the most exciting of positions, but that was exactly what I liked about it and the whole reason I'd enlisted in the Space Force. It had the most extensive array of Earth-side clerical specialties, and all I needed to make me happy was an office, a computer, my favorite coffee mug, and a never-ending pile of requisitions.

"You forgot, didn't you?" Reeds chided.

"No," I huffed but rushed to reach for a bottle of water.

I chugged it like a castaway on a deserted island. My mission to fly a desk hinged on qualifying for the specialty, and I needed to sober up. Because the alternative wasn't pretty, not when there was an endless war raging throughout this dumpster-fire of a galaxy.

"Chug! Chug! Chug!" Reeds boomed through bouts of laughter, watching me attack a second water.

He gave my back a hard slap, making me choke and spray a fountain over my desk. "Just like those tequila shots, right?"

I shoved him away, sending him stumbling back with a stupid smirk on his face.

"You could've reminded me sooner, you know."

"Where's the fun in that?" he mocked, only to almost topple over the other chair in my room.

Cursing up a storm, he caught himself on the desk, but it was too late for the padded nemesis that had gotten in his way. The chair clattered to the floor with an explosive bang. I winced, having no desire to wake the entire barracks. If I did, I'd surely pay for it in punches and unwelcomed wrestling matches when morning came around.

"At least that pansy clerical specialty you're gunning for gets two chances to pass, right? Maybe you won't strike out at *everything*."

I swatted at him, but he jumped out of the way, chuckling. Thankfully, he was right. Clerical specialties did get two chances to pass. Hence, I'd chosen to go out instead of studying. I figured since I only had one shot at Anna and two with the exam, going after the girl first was the logical thing to do.

Reeds righted the chair and neatly tucked it under the desk. "I'm gonna head out, man. It's zero four hundred, and I got PT in two hours. The Force still needs grunts, you know. Someone has to do all the killing."

A second later, the door clicked shut behind him. Probably for the best. That left me with three hours to catch a nap. I didn't have tedious PT to get to as Reeds did, but something told me the exam was going to be just as brutal. Especially with the amount of alcohol sloshing in my gut.

Deciding not to waste any more time, I chugged more water, set my alarm, then collapsed onto my desk. Climbing up to my bunk was out of the question. The ladder might as well have been a mountain.

A heavy sigh escaped me as my head hit the crook of my arm. For all the slacking I did, I had enough sense to know the test was no joking matter. Not only did I not have much else going for me after the debacle at my last job, an underpaid civilian gig, but I was nothing like Reeds. I had zero lust for battle. Zero desire to spill alien blood in the name of Earth or the Galactic Senate on some forsaken planet, floating who knew where amongst the stars.

Truth be told, the vast, merciless darkness beyond the green and blue ball we called home kind of scared me.

———

Two days later, the moment of truth arrived. I nervously chewed my lip as I sat down in front of my computer and stared at the blank screen. Needless to say, the exam hadn't gone as smoothly as I'd hoped. Even though the questions had been on the easier side, I'd run into the teensy problem of not being able to focus. As with a mind of their own, the letters had all blurred into a giant pixelated blob after the first few words or so.

Since staring at the dormant laptop got me nowhere, I decided to quit dragging out the inevitable and swiveled a finger on the touch-pad. The thing hummed and beeped, taunting me as it booted. I wanted to give myself *some* credit, but the heavy weight in the pit of my stomach wasn't a promising sensation.

I clicked the Test Results tab—then groaned. A giant red all-caps "FAIL" blazed beside my name.

"Fuck!" I slammed a fist down on the table, causing my computer and scattered knickknacks to clatter and jump.

This sucked! Not a complete surprise, but still a punch in the gut. Part of me had hoped that I'd skidded through, but it looked like the universe had other ideas.

Allowing myself a few minutes to wallow in self-pity, I then pulled it together. This wasn't the end of the world—or my career. I still had another crack.

Resigned, I directed my browser to the Logistics specialty application and scrolled through the pages of small-print blather to the one page that actually mattered. I suppressed a flare of irritation. Who the hell bothered reading the small print anyways?

Hurriedly filling it out, I swiped the page to my tablet. It beeped, popping up the infuriating spinning 'wait' circle as it processed the information. Subduing my urge to bash it to smithereens, I turned my attention to the holo-cube on my desk. You'd think with humanity charting the stars with the same ease oceans were once charted, the military would issue us something with better processing speed.

I flicked the holo-cube to check the time as much as for a distraction. I'd broken its neural transmitter ages ago, a thin piece of metal, plastic, and some kind of alien tech that looped over the ear. Now the thing was a fancy paperweight. Yet I liked the cyclone of colors swimming withing its crystalline walls and its peculiar glow, so I kept it. It made me wonder about the unknown, about all the mysteries contained in the eerie nether of the cosmos. After the Rap-Wars and the sabotage of Earth-Net, the Senate took censorship to a whole new level, leaving info about the galaxy and its species, both foe and ally, nearly impossible to come by.

The small device dinged and rolled, stopping with a flickering green projection of "1630." I cursed under my breath as my eyes darted between the twinkling display and my inferior tablet. My re-enrollment request had to go through the company officer, and he normally didn't stick around past 1700. Catching him tomorrow was always an option, but did I really want to screw around with something like this and risk ending up a ground trooper dying somewhere among the stars?

I didn't. Grabbing my tablet, I bolted for the door. With any luck, the CO would have me re-registered by today.

Thinking of where I went wrong with Anna, I hightailed it down the hall. Maybe I hadn't worn enough cologne, or my hair was too messy. Or perhaps I'd said something untoward, but I couldn't remember reciting one of my more questionable jokes. Not in the three-minute conversation we'd had. I finally concluded that women were a puzzle I had no hopes of solving and left it at that. I had more pressing concerns before me.

With a squeak of my boots, I skidded to a stop in front of the CO's office. I breathed a sigh of relief. The door was ajar, and he was behind his desk. Steadying my breaths, I smoothed out my hair and uniform, then knocked.

"Enter!" the CO barked without looking up from his tablet.

I ventured in but paused after a step. A strange atmosphere hung in the air. The CO wasn't in his usual good spirits, sitting ramrod straight behind his desk, his elbows planted firmly on the wooden surface scattered with holo-cubes, phones, tablets, and e-papers. His eyes were kind of squinted, and his finger jabbed at his tablet as if the thing had just insulted his mother.

Rubbing his chin slowly, he finally looked up to acknowledge me and gestured for me to sit. I groaned internally, anticipating a lecture, but nevertheless, shuffled over. Giving him a pasted smile, I glanced around the office in search of a clue to his peculiar mood. Surely it wasn't the qualification exams. Plenty of troops failed. Hence the rule about retakes.

My eyes roved over a bookshelf, a window, and a half-dead droopy plant on the sill. Its crinkled brown leaves were barely hanging on, and most had fallen off to litter the checkered floor. The light outside was now fading, and a bright beam from the lowering sun cut through the auto shades. It shined onto the only curious items I was able to spot—a row of boxes lined on chairs.

I stretched my neck to peek inside but failed to get a good look. They appeared to be filled with uniforms but not the correct color for the Space Force. Maybe our barracks were getting recruits from another service, and the CO simply didn't know where to put them all, nor wanted to deal with the hassle. Seeing as such matters were above my paygrade and frankly none of my business, I returned my attention to him.

"That qualification exam… I failed," I said with a heavy exhale, plastering on the most remorseful expression I could muster.

"I honestly have no idea what happened. I knew everything on that test. I swear I did."

I lowered my head and rubbed my forehead in feigned shame. To my surprise, out of the corner of my eyes, I glimpsed no improvement to the CO's somber demeanor. I wanted to scoff but held it back. In my opinion, my act was going well. I'd give myself a second chance in a heartbeat.

"I'm not giving up or anything," I quickly added.

Leaning forward, I slid my tablet across the desk, to where the signature box was under his nose.

"I'm ready to apply again, and this time I'm not going to fail. I'll study all night if I have to. All weekend, if that's what it takes. This second time around will be the one, I swear."

Unfortunately, the CO still didn't bite. I'd expected him to grab the tablet, sign off, scold me, then send me on my way, everything wrapped up in a neat little bow. Yet the man didn't even glance at my application, and his frown deepened.

I squirmed under the strange gaze.

"Hmmph," he snorted after what felt like an eternity.

He shook his head. "No. I don't think you're retaking that test, trooper."

My eyes flicked to the tablet, then back at him in confusion. "What do you mean, sir? When did they change the rules about retakes?"

Damn! I really didn't want the hassle of selecting another specialty.

"They didn't. The Force's regs are still the same. They just don't apply to you anymore, now that you've been transferred."

"Whaa—?"

Now, I was utterly lost. Where could I possibly be transferred to? The base I was currently on was Space Force's largest, and where those wanting to qualify for a clerical specialty resided.

The CO released a heavy sigh. "Look, Adlar, there's no easy way to say this, so I'm just going to cut to the chase. You've been transferred out of the Force and into the Legions. I don't get any pleasure telling you this, but it is what it is."

He raised his hands in surrender. "I had absolutely no say in the matter."

My jaw dropped. For a few seconds, maybe even a full minute, I blankly stared at him. I think I blinked a few times but that was it. I sat as still as a statue listening to the antique analog clock on the wall tick away the seconds. The CO leaned back in his chair, saying nothing.

"Uh… this is a joke… right?" I finally managed, half-curious, half-amused. "I mean, it has to be. I didn't enlist in the Legions."

I wanted to raise my voice but controlled myself.

The CO shifted in his chair with discomfort or possibly pity. "I'm afraid this is no joke, trooper. There's a troop pick-up scheduled at the airfield tomorrow, and they decided to requisition additional personnel. And since you're not technically enrolled in qualifying for a specialty at the moment," he narrowed his eyes at me, "due to failing that exam, you were fair game. You were added to the transfer list this morning."

I glanced down at my untouched tablet, the application for logistics glowing brightly on the screen, then back at the CO. Surely, this had to be some huge misunderstanding. I knew Space Fleet sometimes commandeered Space Force personnel, but had no idea the Legions did too. Wouldn't they be better off conscripting troops from the Marines or the Army? After all, the Legions were all about ground combat, the brutal and bloody kind. The kind portrayed in the bestselling VR games—the ones I sucked at.

The CO noticed my stumped, deer-in-headlights expression. "You didn't read the fine print when you signed up, did you?"

"I… I guess not," I stammered. "But I'm not even remotely qualified. I don't know anything about the Legions!"

"Not many people do," he casually shrugged, tapping away on his tablet. "Back in the day, during the Rap-Wars, the Legions were all the hype, but not anymore. Now that the war is out *there*," he pointed a finger at the ceiling, "out in the galaxy, away from Earth, many people don't know much about it, even some here in the service. Everything's classified, but that doesn't mean the Legions don't need bodies, trooper, and it doesn't take much for someone to qualify. You're young, fit, and perfectly capable of donning heavy-gear. So there, you're qualified."

The CO stretched his neck to glance over my person.

He gave me a weak smile. "In fact, someone of your shape and size is a prime candidate for the job as far as the Legions are concerned."

My throat tightened at the mention of heavy-gear. Not too long ago, curiosity had gotten the better of me and I'd ventured into one of the stadium-sized R&D labs. To no surprise, most everything was classified and hidden away behind doors flashing the emblem of the Galactic Senate, a golden Earth, and Mars with a Viper-class fighter streaking past. Even the majority of the lab personnel weren't granted access.

However, not everything had been top-secret. Basic weapons, rudimentary robotics, and other everyday gear was out in the open, and amongst it all were the jet-black heavy-gear suits. They'd hung in their supports like towering mechs, popping out holo-projections of targeting data and lines of code. I'd felt small and insignificant next to the creepy armor as I wondered about the men dying in the deadly get-up at that very moment. I had thanked my lucky stars that day for choosing to enlist in the Force and not the Legions, and now...

The CO finished tapping and slid his tablet across the desk. "Confirm that's you, then sign."

I looked down at the picture of the dirty-blond, blue-eyed man staring back at me. Yup that was me all right, Jake Adlar, 6'1, 22 years old, date of enlistment... The stats kept going, but I stopped reading. Was this terse description what had earned me this transfer? Was this what some stranger saw and said, *"Oh hey, what about this docfus?"* Or did a computer make the selections? Did some AI run through thousands of troop profiles and decide to add me to the pile? My fists balled. I yearned to stab that AI in its circuits for this freaking honor.

The analog clock ticked away. *Click, click, click...*

Finally, I closed my hanging jaw. Not seeing any other option, I placed a shaky finger on the signature box. It beeped a confirmation, and the screen flashed to text. I blinked, trying to make sense of it all. The tiny text was transfer orders, pages of them. Frowning and still struggling to accept the situation, I began to read. Well, tried to read, intending to thoroughly absorb every line, but my eyes refused to comply. They skipped over the first few paragraphs and jumped to a number—and I about shit myself.

"Ten years!" I exclaimed, looking back at the CO in disbelief.

"They're extending my service term by ten years? That's bullshit, sir! They can't do that!" I no longer gave a damn about raising my voice.

"Sure, they can," he countered, giving me one of those patented *are-you-an-idiot* looks.

"You're about to become a Legionnaire, and the Legions—*the Senate*—can do whatever they want with you. This was all in your initial contract. But if it makes you feel any better, they aren't extending your service for ten years, per se. The orders are a standard

Legion contract, and as such, simply informing you there's a possibility of such an extension." He snorted. "We're talking about light-years here, after all, depending on what ship and what outfit you're sent to."

Suspecting there might be some cruel lesson in what was currently happening, I again willed my eyes to read every last word only to fail. Blood pounded in my ears, and I wanted to be anywhere but here. That left me with no choice but to do my usual. I scrolled to the bottom and stared at the blank fingerprint area where I was expected to sign.

My finger hovered over the box. The CO took a deep breath and exhaled slowly, his expression softening.

He sighed. "Look, kid. I'm not thrilled about this either. I don't enjoy telling young men like yourself that they're being sent light-years away from Earth, and I still have about twenty of these conversations to get through. But as I said, it is what it is. We go where we're told to go, where we're needed; that's what we all signed up for, right? So just sign your transfer, and let's get on with this."

Easy for you to say. I fumed internally but remained silent. He wasn't the one who'd just been handed over to the freaking Legions like some lamb to slaughter, about to be shipped out into the unforgiving cosmos. What about my plans for a specialty? What about meeting someone or starting a family? I was in no way ready or interested in something like that, but still, I wanted to have the option.

"What's your size?" he asked, getting up and walking towards the boxes lining the chairs.

"Extra Large," I muttered.

Grimacing, I dropped my finger onto the tablet, the screen cool under my touch. What choice did I have? What life could I possibly hope to have here on Earth after a court-martial or a dishonorable discharge?

The CO was still talking, but the dull ringing in my head blocked him out. The tablet beeped a haunting confirmation, and my heart skipped a beat. This was it; there was no turning back. I was now a ground trooper in the Legions and had just accepted orders directing me to go light-years away from Earth for up to a decade.

Satisfied, the CO shoved an all-black uniform into my trembling hands, and, giving me a firm handshake, ushered me to the door.

"Don't worry about packing up your room. We'll ship your stuff back to your address on record. Just report to the airfield tomorrow morning, zero six hundred."

Right as I was almost out in the hall, I whirled to face him. "Am I going to Camp Red, to Mars?"

With its harsh environment and rough terrain, Mars provided a great training ground for Legionnaires while also housing the majority of the Galactic Senate. I supposed it wouldn't be too bad to dive into my new life, starting with Mars.

The CO blinked in confusion.

"Ahh..." he said a moment later, then chuckled. "Camp Juno, you mean?"

He shook his head, patting me on the back. "I don't think so, kid. From what I understand, the transports aren't coming from Mars."

I frowned.

"Don't worry, Leege." He gave my back another hard clap and smirked. "I'm sure you'll be provided with all the training you need. On the job, that is."

He then roughly shoved me into the hall. I jumped as the door slammed shut behind me. In a daze, clutching my new uniform with still-trembling hands, I ambled away from his office. My life had just derailed in a blink of an eye, and I felt... stunned. Tomorrow, I was leaving Earth. Just like that, I was going to be blasted off into space —to *war*.

I didn't know whether to scream or punch something once I was back in my room. Instead of doing either, I sat with the new uniform neatly folded on my lap and stared off into nothing. What in the living hell had I gotten myself into?

After who knew how long, my eyes slid to the small picture of my parents on the shelf above my desk. I had to call them, but how? How was I supposed to tell my mom her only son was going away to possibly die on some strange alien world?

Taking in a steadying breath, I reached for the phone—and scowled. A message shined in my face. It was from Anna. She apologized for not spending more time with me at the party and wanted a do-over, just the two of us.

"Aww, hell," I groaned, flinging the phone onto my table.

It clattered, bumping into the holo-cube and sending a wavering 1800 to illuminate the underside of my bunk in a greenish glow. Go figure. The day I land an actual date with Anna, I get sent off-planet.

Collecting my phone, I swiped away her text. What else could I do? Tell her I'm all of a sudden going away at a moment's notice? She wasn't going to want to hear that age-old tale. *We go where we're told to go, where we're needed.* I sighed. It was best to leave it alone for now. Plus, she wasn't who I was worried about.

I dialed my parents. The call was as grim as I had anticipated. My mom cried and yet somehow still managed to bring up the topic of grandkids while my dad attempted to retain his composure.

I heard him swallow audibly. "Just... don't lose yourself out there, son," he finally managed. "The Legions... they're... different. I've heard stories, you know."

Between his service in the Navy and his current job with the local police, my dad had worked security at a small research branch for the Galactic Senate, so I didn't doubt he'd heard stories. He'd never mentioned them before, though.

"I won't, Dad," I mumbled. "I'll be okay, I promise."

I then took a few more minutes to reassure them that everything will be fine and that I'd be back in one piece. I knew that was what they wanted to hear—whether it was true or not. Ultimately, we had no choice but to say our goodbyes, and I was again left with only the silence around me.

A lump still in my throat, I made a few more parting phone calls informing my friends of my fate, then reached for my computer. It was time to research where I was going. Unfortunately, after much typing and clicking, the only semi-useful thing I was able to find were the Legions' recruitment pages, information on the Galactic Senate, and some history about Rap-Wars. How the ancient, humanoid aliens we called the Synths invaded Earth, believing us to be their slaves, and how with the help of a snake species called the sleeks, we chased them off, in the process forming the Legions and the Senate. Now the Legions were bringing the fight to the Synths. Liberating other planets in the name of humanity, Earth, and the Senate in an endless conflict that spanned the galaxy.

Besides the short history excerpts, profiles of what I assumed were important people, and gallant pictures of heavy-geared troops, I couldn't find much else. After all, Rap-Wars took place decades ago, and the Legion ships, which were only briefly described on the recruitment sites, were rarely Earth-side—a fact that in no way made me feel better about my current predicament.

I intently studied page after page. *Become a hero—become a Legionnaire,* read the pretty words to the backdrop of armored troops in action. *No one quits; everyone fights...* The plethora of slogans was endless, but what was that trooper running from, the one on the home screen? Sure, he looked like an all-powerful badass in his glistening armor, but what was chasing him? What bloodthirsty alien monster was right on his heels, wanting nothing more than to shoot him down or rip him apart?

I slammed my computer shut. I was no longer numb or pissed, just vaguely disgruntled. *How the hell had I managed to get myself into this?* Sure, I could hold my own in a fight, but battling aliens wasn't exactly a behind-the-barracks tussle with some recruit. Damn that small print and my inattentive brain.

With a deep breath, I shook off pointlessly kicking myself. It no longer mattered how I'd gotten here. It was time to man up and accept the situation. This wasn't what I'd envisioned for my future when I'd enlisted, no desk or coffee cup was coming my way, but pouting wasn't going to accomplish squat. I was heading to the stars.

Resigned to my fate, I removed the flimsy e-picture of my parents out of the frame and shoved it into my backpack. Then I turned to my dresser to pack. I looked at my civvies, trying to decide what to take, knowing I had limited room. As I stared at the clothes, my gaze wandered to my window. I froze as if in a trance, one outstretched hand still clutching a T-shirt. I was suddenly mesmerized by the smears of brilliant purple and red clouds slowly crawling across the twilight sky. What the hell was I doing?

Grabbing the first things my hands landed on in the dresser, I stuffed them into my bag. Then, I went to spend my last day on Earth outside.

CHAPTER
TWO

It was still dark when my alarm jolted me awake. Reluctantly, I pawed for my phone and silenced it, then dragged myself out of my bunk. I didn't want to imagine what would happen if I missed the transports—a fate worse than the Legions, perhaps.

Throwing on my new, all-black Legion uniform, which felt stiff and uncomfortable on my skin, I ambled for the door. I paused when I caught a glimpse of my reflection. The messy hair wasn't going to be a problem, but my pained expression might. Looking like I was on the verge of a panic attack wasn't going to help me fit in with *actual* Legionnaires. With much effort, I forced my face to straighten, then at last walked out.

I arrived at the airfield during one of my most favorite times of the morning. The sky was just beginning to brighten with oranges and reds, and the cool predawn crispness had yet to be replaced by the day's humidity. I made it a point to savor the scene. I had never been much of a nature watcher but having no idea when or if I was coming back added a certain beauty to every dried-up shrub and rock in my vicinity. Even the dusty road and the gray, dreary buildings seemed to have an otherworldly glow about them.

Taking a mental snapshot, I headed to the security gate and checked in. The airfield's regulars had been moved out of their usual spots, and a row of unfamiliar black vessels sat in their place. They were large and ugly, their unpainted hulls dinged and scuffed, and the bows charred from atmospheric re-entry. The daunting trio loomed hauntingly over the smaller planes like vultures among a herd of pigeons.

The drab sight sent a shiver down my spine, but I shook it off and marched up to the first transport in my path.

"Which one do I board?" I asked a Space Fleet soldier in the process of directing a loading-mech.

The boxy forklift on legs whirred and clanged as it loaded crates into the back of the transport.

"Doesn't matter," he replied. "They're all going to the same troop carrier. As long as the stairs are still next to the ship, it has room."

I thanked him with a nod, then walked around to the side of the vessel, stopping at the gangway. I contemplated if this was the one I should take.

"Excuse me," said a female voice as a smallish woman in a Fleet uniform rushed past me and up the stairs, her shoulder-length brown hair bobbing as she went.

She greeted the Lieutenant at the top and darted inside. Grinning, I took a deep whiff of her lingering perfume. Something flowery with a hint of spice. This was precisely the ship I wanted to be on.

One hand grasping the stairway's railing, I gave the airfield's desert-like landscape a parting scan. The cacti and the scraggly shrubs weren't the customary flora for this area, but those were the only plants that tended to survive the nano-chems dumped on the field to keep the weeds, greenery, and snakes at bay.

Under the golden glow of the impending sunrise, the dusty field suddenly looked picturesque.

"Getting on, trooper?" came a shout in my direction.

I glanced at the LT at the top of the stairs, then towards the back of the ship. The cargo hold was now closed, and the low hum emanating from the engines increased in pitch. Without answering him, I turned back to the brightening horizon, hoping to catch one last sunrise before departing for who knew how long. I just needed a few more minutes.

"You'd be the last one on, so if you're boarding, hurry up."

Fidgeting, I considered dragging it out a bit longer but then noticed more men walk through the security gate and angle towards the transports. All were wearing the Legions' black uniforms. Not wanting to forfeit a spot on this particular ship, I relented and rushed up the stairs.

"Check-in right here," the LT instructed, shoving a tablet in my direction as his head gestured towards the box in his other arm. "And anything electronic, or anything with any kind of recording capabilities goes in here."

He narrowed his eyes. "That includes personal drones or any other such devices. They're all against regs."

I placed my index finger on his tablet's screen without qualm but hesitated when I looked inside the box. I grimaced at the collection of phones amidst the other gadgets.

"Uh… what if I deactivate the camera option and—"

"Seriously?" the LT cut me off. "Do you see any Legion insignia on me? Do you think I have a say?"

He made a show of glancing at the Fleet pilot's badge pinned to his uniform, then rudely rammed the box at my chest.

"Now hand over any contraband and get on, so we can go." He shook his head. "And you better leave that snark at the door. That won't get you far where you're going."

I grumbled under my breath but knew it was pointless to argue further. With a scowl, I reached for my phone, moving as slowly as I dared while keeping an eye on the horizon. Just maybe, I'd glimpse the yellow ball making its appearance.

The LT shuffled irritably.

"Fine," I mumbled and tossed my phone in.

I didn't want to press my luck. Who knew how long I'd have to endure this man? Even though Fleet brass had minimal authority over Legion troops, being part of the flight crew made him in charge.

Inhaling one last breath of Earth's air, I stepped inside the transport.

A slew of heads jerked up and fixated in my direction as all the occupants gave me a curious once-over. Some eyes were stone-cold, while others were as wide as saucers. I stared right back. It was easy to tell which troops were the add-ons, the transfers. Compared to the actual Legionnaires, we looked like fish out of water, and I suddenly felt very self-conscious about not having a single tattoo. A moment later, everyone lost interest in the 'new addition' and went back to chatting.

"Make way." The LT shoved past, startling me out of my trance.

He threw a glance over the troops now in his charge and rushed up the stairs to the flight deck.

"Two minutes!" he shouted a warning over his shoulder, one that was mostly ignored.

Only a few troops dropped what they were doing and lumbered to strap in with weary groans.

My eyes followed the LT as he disappeared, and the door behind me began to close. The narrow beam of natural light from the sunrise vanished. I swallowed hard, subduing my urge to bang on it and shout to be let out.

Right as I turned away from the door and from everything I'd ever known, the transport came to life. The engine's low hum spun up to a loud whine, and the deck thrummed under my boots. The vessel lurched, then lifted, swaying like a boat rocking on the water.

"Sorry," I mumbled as I tried to keep my balance while rushing to an empty bunk, bumping knees and stepping on toes.

The accommodations were anything but luxurious. Stacked bunks lined the outside bulkheads with two rows of back-to-back bucket seats running down the middle. About fifty troops were stuffed into the confined space. I hoped the trip wasn't going to be a long one; these crowded conditions were going to get old fast.

Stowing my bag in a bin attached to a bunk's frame, I tried to sit, but to no avail. The bunks were stacked too closely together, and being as big as I was, my shoulders pressed up uncomfortably against the metal frame above me. Sighing in frustration, I was about to stretch out instead when my gut churned, then sank. I forgot all about claiming a bunk and joined the other troops in rushing for the seats, as we'd all had the same premonition.

Right as my belt clicked into place, with impressive speed and absolutely no regard for its occupants, the transport tilted up and shot off into the atmosphere. Just as that happened, I reached out and grabbed a trooper who was a second too slow getting to a seat. I yanked the girl onto my lap in a bear hug as the troops who were unfortunate enough not to be secured went flying towards the stern.

The cabin erupted with shouts and profanity as they tumbled over each other in a tangle of arms and legs.

"Thanks," she chuckled.

I held on to her for the minute it took the ship to exit the atmosphere, level out, and kick on the gravity. There was a strange feeling of weightlessness, but then the cabin returned to normal. Well, *almost* normal, because even buckled, there was an odd sensation of being slightly lighter.

"You can let go now," the woman said, to the backdrop of crude, loud protests coming from the stern.

The troops thrown there were now busy untangling themselves.

I unwrapped my arms. "Oh... yeah. Sorry."

Hopping off my lap, she spun to face me, flinging her hands to her hips. Her uniform jacket was off, and my eyes were drawn to a tattoo of an open-mouthed serpent that wrapped around her arm. The woman was short but muscular, with black spiky hair, and seemed a bit rough around the edges. That surprised me, considering she didn't look to be much older than me.

"I'm Nessmine Lopez, but you can call me Ness," she said, giving me a crooked smile. "I guess the adventure begins, huh?"

She glanced towards the grumbling troops making their way back to the seats and bunks, rubbing their bodies and casually wiping bloody scrapes with their sleeves.

I chuckled. "Yeah, I suppose it does. I'm Jake Adlar; nice to meet you."

She extended her hand, and we exchanged a firm handshake.

"So, what brings you to this particular party, Jake? I don't know what it is, but you don't look like the rough-'em-up type."

Her dark eyes scanned over me in a probing fashion. "You're big and all, but there's just something about that pretty face of yours that doesn't scream Legionnaire, you know?"

I shrugged at her accurate assessment. "Stupidity, I suppose."

She barked a laugh and shook her head, then suddenly looked puzzled. "I don't remember seeing you mustering up for the ride out here, and I would've remembered you. Where did you do your basic? Camp Juno?"

It was my turn to laugh. "Nope. Never been anywhere besides Evans Joint Ops. Just got yanked from the Force yesterday."

Ness let out a low whistle and settled onto the bunk across from me. "They pulled you out just like that, huh? I didn't know that was possible. Isn't the Force basically desk-jockey support roles nowadays, research and such?"

Yes! I wanted to shout, *that was my thinking exactly!* Nobody signs up for the Space Force with aspirations of going into actual combat. So far, every recruitment poster I'd seen had people working over computers and holo-projections or in labs, smiling wide smiles like their lives depended on it. *Take part in inventing the future,* the slogans had read. Damn, how I wanted to be one of those smiling people right about now, instead of crammed into a metal canister full of mostly men.

I was about to agree with her feverishly, but movement on my right grabbed my attention. A few seats down, a trooper craned his neck in a very obvious fashion, trying to get a better look at me. Our eyes met, and I guess he took that as an invitation. He hastily unbuckled, and a second later, his butt hit the bunk next to Ness.

"I couldn't help but overhear." He leaned forward, elbows on his knees.

He was a lanky, toothpick-like fellow and was also having trouble sitting in the cramped space. Even though he didn't look very comfortable, he appeared intent on hanging out. Ness gave the guy a welcoming smile.

"I was also transferred, just like that," he said. "I mean, I knew I was going up, being from the Fleet, but not like this. I thought I'd be going to some station or doing my time on some ship, but then *bam!*"

He clapped his hands together loudly. "They tell me I'm an add-on to the freaking *Legions.*"

He shook his head in disbelief, losing his grin. "I don't know anything about ground combat, man, or what the fuck is going on out there." He pointed at the overhead.

Before I could reply, a malicious chuckle sounded from a bunk on my left as a rough-looking trooper leaned his head to the side to be in our line of view.

"It's because a bunch of the troopers managed to get dusted," he scoffed. "That's why the cohorts are filling the ranks with add-ons. They must have a campaign coming up and need ground troops...."

He propped his head up with one arm to where he could meet my eyes.

"...and *bait*," he added with an evil smirk.

I recognized the man. Not personally, but I had spotted him prior to take off. He was one of the few buckled in as if he'd known what to expect, unlike the newbs or the lazies. I didn't much care for his snarky, know-it-all tone, but after giving him a quick once-over, I concluded the odds weren't in my favor.

"Hmmm..." Ness stood and glanced around the cabin as if seeing everyone for the first time.

"This is a pretty large pick-up. Three transports just for one troop carrier, for three cohorts. That is a lot."

"Hell yeah, it's a lot!" the prone man chided, once again jumping in uninvited. "They do that on purpose, you know. Split up a Legion's cohorts onto different carriers. That way, if something takes out a troop carrier, the whole Legion isn't wiped in an instant."

I swallowed the lump in my throat as I processed his words. After all, he looked like he knew what he was talking about. So, not only were we going to be thrown into combat, but there was also a chance of being blown to bits?

Trying not to fidget, I attempted to retain a neutral expression, not wanting anyone to see me frazzled, but judging by Ness's softened glance, I'd failed. She gave the gruff man a stern, disapproving look.

"You're just a ray of sunshine, aren't you? Maybe they're swapping out troops."

The man snorted loudly as if Ness had just suggested something along the lines of *"pigs can fly."*

"Sure they are, and I'll run the Galactic Senate one day. They don't send troops home unless they're in a body bag. Figuratively speaking, that is, since you just get shot off into space if you're killed, and that's only if there's enough of your body left to—"

"*Aaanyway!*" Ness loudly interrupted him, probably for my benefit. "What do you think they're gonna feed us on this ride?"

She spun her head around as if looking for a clue. I smiled weakly, appreciating her effort. We all knew we were getting meal bars, a nutrient-packed chalky substance flavored with what could only be described as plastic. Maybe they'd throw in a few ration packs if we were lucky.

"Wait a minute," the skinny kid jumped in, a concerned look crossing over his face as he glanced over at negative nancy. "So, you're not just coming back from leave, then?"

Ness rolled her eyes and lightly punched the guy on the shoulder. "Don't encourage that one," she whispered.

But it was too late, the gruff man caught the question, and since there wasn't much else for us to do, he was more than happy to continue showering us with disheartening information.

"Hell, no!" he snorted, rolling off his bunk and moving to sit a few seats away from us. "I just came off another troop carrier. I'm from the sixth cohort. As I said, the cohorts we're going to must've had a bunch of troops dusted all at once, so here we are."

He nodded towards the lanky kid and me, baring his teeth. "Add-ons and all."

I wanted to ask how long he'd been in, now that I knew he was a seasoned Leege, but I wasn't so sure I wanted to hear the answer. Instead, there was something else I was curious about, something the recruitment sites had chosen to leave out.

"So, what's out there? What kind of aliens are we fighting?"

The guy suddenly brightened, a genuine smile spreading over his rugged face.

"Oh man!" he exclaimed, roughly shoving another trooper out of his way and hopping a seat closer.

"There are all kinds out there, but the main ones the Synths use for their ground troops these days are these large cyclops monsters they buy from the sleeks. I once shot one, point-blank, right through its massive eyeball. The moron got disconnected from the bot who leads the formations, and I caught it just then. You should've seen that thing pop! It was like a damn water balloon. My whole suit was gunked!"

The man reminded me of Reeds, zealously recounting combat as if death on some forsaken planet, chewed up by enemy fire or aliens, was something to aspire for.

His grin vanished a second later. "The bots are kind of a pain, though. They aren't drooling dummies like their troops. They hide, then shoot when you're not looking. They got my squaddies."

Confusion crept over his face as if he were thinking back to some distant memory, the events of which still puzzled him to this day. "That's why I was transferred. I didn't have a squad anymore."

We grew silent at his sudden turn of mood. "I'm Bishop, by the way." He extended a hand. "Sorry I came on so strong. Sometimes, I can't help it, but there's no need for bad blood, right? We might be fighting side by side in the same cohort or squad in the upcoming days; who knows?"

I shook the man's hand with hesitation while pondering an appropriate response. I considered offering condolences or asking for more details about his fallen teammates but changed my mind. There was no need to dredge that up or sour his mood.

"It's all good," I said instead. "I'm Adlar, this is Ness, and…" I trailed off, realizing I didn't know the skinny kid's name.

Our nondescript, Legion-issued uniforms weren't outfitted with name tags just yet.

"Foster," the skinny kid chimed.

Bishop flashed a genuine smile. "And hopefully, none of ya become *bait*."

He playfully punched the side of my arm with a meaty fist, making me grimace.

"No worries," I said, forcing a chuckle to hide my nerves.

I felt a tinge of sweat. I had no idea what *bait* meant in the context of his comments, but I had yet to encounter bait that jumped off the hook to live happily ever after.

CHAPTER
THREE

T t turned out that our rough take-off was an extremely accurate intro to how shitty the rest of the trip was going to be. Since high-tech jump drives capable of prolonged hyperspace travel were pricey, they were reserved for fancy space-yachts and the like. A standard Fleet transport wasn't worthy of such a luxury. Thus, we had to jump out intermittently to allow the cheaper drive time to recharge, and the transitions were anything but smooth. Now, on any short voyage, traveling in such a way didn't pose a problem; what were a few lurches here and there? However, ours was not a short voyage. Not even close.

"How much more of this do you think we have left?" I asked Bishop when it was safe to peek out from my bunk after another jarring jump out of hyperspace.

He sat a few seats away, buckled and pouting. The uncomfortable conditions hadn't helped soften the man's rough demeanor.

A few groans and moans echoed through the cabin as those who'd been thrown righted themselves. A faint ding provided a warning, but it only gave us seconds. We'd spent the first few days of the trip trying to work around the problem by timing the jump intervals, and even made it into a game of sorts, but there seemed to be no consistency, so we gave up.

"How the fuck should I know?" Bishop grumbled, unbuckling

and bulldozing through people without a care on his way to his bunk. "Just pray this circus trick holds up, and we're not all incinerated."

Exchanging confused glances with Ness, we both shrugged. There was no point in asking the pain-in-the-ass to elaborate. The man was as aggravating as a head full of lice, but given his large size and hot-tempered demeanor no one dared to tell him that. Though I'm sure, he was aware. You don't go around all your life being an ass without eventually realizing it, he just didn't care.

Topping off the discomfort of being rattled like a maraca was the fact that the transport wasn't outfitted with fitness equipment. This surprised me initially since being in prime shape was in a Legionnaire's job description, but not as much after I slammed my head against various bulkheads and bunks during the jumps. Not to mention the unfortunate incident I had on the john. Still, not getting much physical activity in, other than a few push-ups here and there, was pure torture, leaving my body to feel increasingly sluggish with each passing day. Then, on what I think was the second week of travel, we finally got a break in our tedious routine.

I was stretched out on my bunk, counting the number of screws above me for probably the millionth time, when a sudden silence swept over the cabin. Even Ness, who was sitting by my feet and chattering about something I wasn't paying attention to, cut short mid-sentence. Mouth agape, she fixed her gaze towards the front of the cabin. Curious, I swung my head around to see what had finally shut everyone up. Walking down the stairs from the flight deck was the short-haired woman I'd seen when I first arrived at this particular transport, and *damn*, was she cute. I rushed to sit up, shoving Ness out of the way, trying to get a better view of the mysterious lady.

"Seriously, Jake?" Ness complained, rolling her eyes with exaggerated disapproval.

I didn't care. There was something about the woman's round face and green eyes that had me staring up at her like a dumbass. A moment later, Ness stopped scowling to do her share of possibly inappropriate ogling.

The woman, whom I could now tell was a Space Fleet LT, stopped halfway down the stairs and scrunched her nose. I couldn't blame her. Workout equipment wasn't the only thing considered unnecessary on this type of transport; showers were too, and the sanitary wipes only did so much.

The LT had a tablet and a notepad in one hand, a box in the other, and was straining to keep a straight face. I smiled, appreciating her efforts, no matter how futile.

"I'm going to give you a quick briefing and let you know where you've been assigned," she said in a monotone, no doubt having given this identical speech hundreds of times before.

"I'll also be issuing phones and tact-watches. They'll receive service and link to the ship's net once inside the troop carrier. For the newbies here, the watches are to be worn at all times; consider them part of your uniform."

She paused, allowing the chatter that followed her phone-and-watch announcement to settle, then continued.

"You're all joining the first, second, or third cohort of Legion Invictus, which are currently onboard the troop carrier *Venator*. When we get there, all decks beside the Legion decks and rec areas are off-limits, so head straight to your assigned spot. Your squad leader will fill you in from there."

With that, she descended into the cabin and proceeded to speak with the closest trooper. Brimming with anticipation, I watched her make her way down the line until, finally, she was in front of me. I grinned, inhaling her pleasant scent. The flowery spice momentarily chased away the cabin's stale stench of old socks and sweat.

Raising a questioning eyebrow, she sat down across from me. Still grinning, I scooted a tad closer. My butt was on the edge of my bunk, and my back pressed uncomfortably into the metal frame above, but I didn't care. I placed my elbows on my knees and leaned towards the girl. I think she said something, but I just kept smiling.

Ness slapped my arm. "She asked you your name, you idiot."

"Oh!" I exclaimed, straightening. "It's Jake Adlar, ma'am. What's yours?"

The LT gave me another raised eyebrow. She flicked her pen to point at the name tag on her chest, then glanced at her tablet.

"Oh yeah, duh." I felt my cheeks warm.

Unlike the rest of us, she was wearing a standard black and gray camo SF uniform, and the name tag on her chest was as plain as daylight.

"Nice to meet you, Lieutenant Wagner. What brings you here?"

Ness let out a dramatic snort.

"Sorry," she chuckled. "He's usually a lot more normal than this."

I cringed. What I'd meant to ask was how she'd ended up flying the transports or joining Space Fleet, but for some reason, my words hadn't come out as I'd intended. Not that I was surprised, considering this was about how well most of my conversations went with the ladies.

I half expected the LT to roll her eyes or become frustrated, but she didn't. Instead, after writing something on a piece of *actual* paper, she flashed me a genuine smile. And it wasn't one of those *"I'm just being polite while trying to get away from you as fast as possible"* smiles either, but a real one. One that reached her eyes.

"Second cohort, fourth unit, tenth squad," she said, extending the paper, phone, and a watch towards me.

"What's this?" I asked enthusiastically, glancing at the paper, the boyish part of me hoping it was her number or soldier ID.

"It's where you're assigned, where you need to go when we land."

She leaned towards me as she spoke, her eyes intently studying mine. I felt my cheeks warm again at her gaze, then even more as I worried about her seeing me blush.

"I used to just tell the troops their assignments," she continued, "but that resulted in a bunch of them running around, claiming they forgot where to go. Some even ended up on the officers' decks, which blew back on the Fleet crews. Now, I write it down."

She shrugged. "It's old-fashioned, I know. But it's easier than sending it to your phones. You'd be surprised how much stuff is still not automated. Budgets and all."

Smart and beautiful, I thought to myself with a grin. Was it just my imagination, or had she spent a little more time talking to me than the other troops? I sure hadn't seen her smile at them the way she was at me.

"See you around, Adlar," Wagner said, standing.

I opened my mouth to say bye, but her watch caught my eye. The entire screen flashed crimson. Raising a finger to point, I was about to ask what that meant, but didn't get the chance as my body flew up and my head slammed into the bunk above. The ship's stern had lurched up as if kicked, and a warbling vibration passed through the hull. Bouncing off with a painful thud, I toppled to the deck with Wagner on top of me. Her box flew out of her hands in a shower of phones and watches.

Before I could regain my bearings, an electrical whine shrieked through the cabin as the ship accelerated like a bat out of hell. It then banked at an almost a ninety-degree angle, sending anyone who'd managed to remain standing flying in all directions. The cabin erupted with curses and panicked shouts. For a split second, everything went pitch-black, then strobed red, as alarms blared from the overhead.

"Wagner!" sounded a shout over the intercom. "Get up here! Everyone, buckle up and brace for impact and evasive maneuvers!"

I opened my mouth to ask what was happening, but an elbow jammed painfully into the back of my neck as Wagner pounced off me. Like a damn gazelle ,she leaped over the rows of seats and high-tailed it to the flight deck. I was too scared to enjoy the view as she vanished. Grunting, I sat up and rubbed the bump on my head and the knot in my neck.

"Ness—" I began.

The ship shot straight up, nearly sending me flying. I lashed out a hand and caught an armrest just in time. Yanking myself up, I jumped into a seat. Screams rang out over the emergency alarm as everyone scrambled to secure themselves.

Fastening my belt with shaky fingers, I searched for Ness amidst the chaos, my chest tight with fear. Before I could spot her, the ship dove, sending my stomach into my throat and my legs flying up into the air. It then swerved in zigzags like some guppy trying to evade a shark.

"*Bzzt, bzzt, bzzt…*" a hailstorm of something peppered the hull.

Each hit shuddered the vessel and sent a shower of glitter-like sparks from the power conduits on the bulkheads. Wisps of smoke wafted into the strobing red emergency lights, and the cabin reeked of electrical burn. With gut-wrenching dread, I realized we were under attack. Probably by the Synths if I had to guess. A rogue ship lying in wait must've locked in on us.

The transport veered erratically to evade the fire, but the enemy was determined. Bolt after bolt hammered the vessel. The shield deflected for the moment being, keeping us alive, but it was easy to tell it was weakening. With each hit, the hull's shudder became more prevalent, and the flicker of the lights from the power surges more frequent.

My heart jumped into my throat, and I squeezed my eyes shut. I would've also covered my ears, but my hands were busy clutching my belts in a death grip. My mind could envision nothing but morbid outcomes. I wondered if death would be quick. If one of those bolts pierced through the shield and we blew, would my demise be instant, or would I feel the flames.

"Fuck!" Ness' bark tore me away from my doom and gloom as she flopped over the backrests; teeth bared and hands clawing at the seat. She pulled herself over as I grabbed onto her and yanked her straight.

"Guess our circus trick didn't hold up!" Bishop shouted through bouts of unsteady laughter. It was coming out in spurts and starts as we jostled. He didn't appear to give a damn and beamed like a crazed kid on a roller coaster.

Huffing with exertion, Ness clicked her belts in and grabbed onto them with white knuckles. I snagged her hand in an attempt to subdue my panic. The ship was swerving like a damaged air-car. My teeth rattled and my head flopped.

With some effort, I managed to turn enough to look at Ness and check for injuries.

"You okay?" I asked.

"I-I-think—" Her teeth clattered.

"Breeep, breeep, breeep..." Yet another alarm sounded, followed by an automated mechanical voice.

"Re-set man-datory," it crackled, interrupted by the power surges. "Reset man-datory—" The warning continued on a loop.

My stomach cinched. I had no idea what a reset entailed, but it didn't sound promising. Nor did it appear to be a common occurrence. Everyone else was as confused as I, shouting, cursing, and exchanging fearful glances. Even Bishop stopped beaming his crazy grin. He was wide-eyed, head swiveling in confusion.

CHAPTER
FOUR

The ship banked sharply to starboard, engines screeching, then accelerated hard, making my stomach flip-flop. It lurched into hyperspace, but only for a moment, jumping out with another jarring jolt. The cabin reigned with panic. Emergency lights strobed over ashen faces, and shouts intermingled with the alarms.

I barely registered the mayhem, too busy clutching Ness' hand and breathing hard. My mind was stuck in a world of impending doom. I knew we'd jumped, but I also knew the shield was spent. Smoke filled the cabin and most of the conduits looked like burned toast. If the Synths were capable of tracking us through hyperspace, we were done for.

As I pondered our uncertain fate, a sudden strange sensation overcame me. I felt myself growing lighter. My stomach lurched as my body attempted to float up like an inflated balloon with the restraints holding me in.

I spun to Ness for answers, for what to do, for *anything*… only to see she wasn't going to be much help. Her eyelids fluttered shut as her head sagged limply one way then the other, and her free hand floated up and to the side all of its own.

"Ness?" I squeezed her hand, not sure if I'd managed actual words.

For some reason, my mind felt fuzzy and it was hard to breathe.

My lungs expanded, I felt that much, but something told me I wasn't actually getting air.

Ness didn't respond to my squeeze, nor my words.

"Bishop?" I called for him next as I looked around, trying to make sense of things.

The ship had steadied, and the power surges had ceased, but something wasn't right. Painted in the red emergency lights, the cabin was eerily quiet, veiled in a numb, empty kind of silence. As if a magician had waved a wand, pillows, packs, and anything not secured began to slowly levitate. So did my gut as I tried not to hurl.

Through blurring sight, I picked up flashes of movement. I could feel my eyelids growing heavy as tunnel vision threatened to yank me into unconsciousness. Troops all around me had unbuckled and were kicking towards the overhead. I looked up, blinking feverishly to remain lucid in the thinning atmosphere. A slew of white face masks with small silver boxes attached had deployed, with troops torpedoing towards them.

Sides heaving with desperation, I mimicked everyone else. I unclipped my belts and pushed off, aiming an outstretched hand for salvation. My fingers closed around a mask just as my head bonked on the ceiling. A jolt traveled down my spine. Wincing, I ignored the throbbing and rushed to strap the mask around my face and inhaled.

With a faint click, a wave of blissful oxygen flowed into my lungs. I didn't savor the moment. As the haze in my mind cleared, panic gripped me. I had no idea if Ness was okay. She hadn't passed out from being shaken by the evasive maneuvers as I'd first thought, but from lack of oxygen. Snagging another mask, I flipped as if in water and kicked off the overhead. I shot towards the deck, shoving floating junk and troopers out of my way.

Clutching onto the backrests next to Ness, I flipped right side up and fumbled with the mask while trying not to float away. I paused when a body caught my eye. It was Bishop, levitating mid-air as if possessed, red light strobing over his pasty skin. Blood stained his forehead. It broke off in tiny droplets to sail around the cabin. I didn't know if he'd smacked his head trying to get to a mask and passed out or if he hadn't gotten to air fast enough. I gritted my teeth in frustration and returned my attention to Ness. I wanted to help him also, but she came first.

Wedging my knees underneath the seat for leverage, I wrapped the mask around her head.

"Come on, Ness. Come on," I pleaded, shaking her by the shoulders. "Wake up!"

I wasn't ready to see anyone die, especially not her.

The mask jerked, then squeezed as her chest heaved like it was about to pop, and her eyes flew wide. She attempted to speak, but I couldn't hear her. With no air in the cabin, the silence was deafening.

Relief flooded over me. Smiling, I patted her knee and pushed off with my legs, aiming towards Bishop. The man was a pain, but no one else was trying to save him. The conscious troops were buzzing around collecting and masking the unconscious ones they actually liked. Well, the vets were, at least. The newbs were just like I had been a minute ago, frozen with fear, clutching to masks and anything stationary as if it were their mommas.

Pushing down my own clamoring panic, I moved on autopilot. Bishop had been without oxygen for far too long, and he didn't have much time. That is if he was still alive. Even if he wasn't, I still had to try.

Grabbing fistfuls of uniforms and corners of bunks, I used floating men and anything else my hands landed on to propel myself. Everyone had started slacking after the initial days of our trip, and nothing was properly stowed. Phones, watches, packs, and even boots pelted me. I did my best to avoid the greenish-brownish globs that I suspected were vomit.

Plowing into Bishop, I grabbed onto him with one arm as my other caught a bunk and jerked us to a stop. Twisting around, I shoved him into the narrow space between the bunks so he wouldn't float away, then scanned the silent mayhem for a mask. Most had been claimed already, while others had snagged on bulkheads, seats, and exposed wiring. Finally, amidst a tangle of floating uniform jackets, a glimmer caught my eye. Grappling at the bundle, I ripped out the mask, then dove back to Bishop where I attempted to wrestle it onto his face. Maneuvering in null gravity wasn't an easy feat for someone with no experience.

"Come on. W-ak-e up," I mumbled through a rattling jaw.

The cabin around me was starting to grow cold, and not the kind of cold that made you want to reach for a cup of coco and a toasty jacket, but the kind only the nightmare of space could evoke. My teeth chattered uncontrollably, and my body shivered of its own accord. Maybe this was worse than I thought, and we had a breach.

I shook him, but that didn't do squat with both of us floating in zero-g. He just kind of wobbled as the force of my shake moved me as much as it did him. I was about to resort to slapping him across the face and even pulled my arm back when, suddenly, the disco rave of emergency lights ceased, and a loud *whoosh* resounded through the cabin.

"Reset complete," announced a mechanical voice, this time smoothly without a single stutter.

Bishop and I crashed down like rocks, along with everything else that had been gliding about. In a cacophony of clatter and chaos, cursing troops, pillows, boots, phones, and vomit rained onto the deck.

Stumbling over the clutter, I jumped off the bunk and yanked Bishop off by one leg. His head loudly slammed against the deck plates as his large mass thunked to the floor. Figuring that was the least of his worries, I pounced on top of him and, with all my might, slammed a fist down onto his chest. Being the large man that I was, my fist came down hard.

"Whaaaaaa!" he rasped in a deep breath, popping up into a sitting position and flinging me off in the process.

His wide eyes swept over the confusion, then zeroed in on me. Pulling off my mask, I gave him a weak half-grin through chattering teeth. The cabin was now warmer, but I still shook. Now that no more shots peppered the hull and there was air, gravity, and warmth, my adrenaline was giving way to panic and confusion.

Struggling to my feet, I reached out a shaky hand to help Bishop. He clasped it with a firm grip and staggered up, wiping blood out of his eyes. A nasty gash crossed his forehead.

"Thanks, man," he mumbled through the mask, then yanked it off and chucked it to the deck.

He gave my back a hard slap. "I owe you one."

"Wha-what was… that?" I trembled.

Bishop scowled, looking like one of his smart-ass comments was right on the tip of his tongue, but then his expression softened.

"Unlucky jump, that's all. Synth ships are all over the galaxy, just waiting for easy pickings."

I nodded slowly in understanding. It now made sense why the transport jumped in random patterns and why trying to time the jumps hadn't worked. I thought about that then stared at Bishop. He'd known all along. No wonder the vets had been snickering and jeering when we were attempting to figure it out. I wanted to say something but a "that sucked," was all I managed.

"Ha!" Bishop barked a laugh. "Tell me about it; at least they didn't get their pound of flesh this time, right?"

I didn't return his grin, rooted in place like a stump, even as troops bumped into me as they rushed about. People were getting out med-kits and helping the injured. I, however, wasn't sure I could move.

Bishop rolled his eyes. "Come on," he said.

Grabbing my shoulders, he forcefully turned me around, yanking a trooper out of our way.

"Move!" he yelled, sending him to cartwheeled over the backrests.

The man yelped but didn't retaliate. Bishop walked me to Ness, who was busy applying a skin patch to a man's bleeding cheek.

"Brought your boy back," he boomed, shoving me towards her.

"Jake!" She jumped up, grabbing me up in a tight hug. "Are you okay? Are you injured?"

Holding me at arm's length, she scanned me over with concern. I shook my head in small jerks but didn't unwrap my arms from hugging myself. I couldn't seem to shake my jitters. This was my first taste of combat, and I wanted to crap myself.

CHAPTER
FIVE

Ness gripped me by my shoulders and shook me. "Snap out of it, man!"

I only blinked in reply, stiff as a board. With a strained exhale and seeing I needed a minute, or twenty, or *forever*, she stopped jostling me like a bobblehead and shoved me into a seat. Guess she figured I'd just flop over onto the deck like one of those startled goats in the vids if I wasn't restrained. I didn't protest and let her buckle me. Satisfied I wouldn't escape, she gave my shoulder a final reaffirming squeeze.

"Deep breaths, Jake, deep breaths," she said, then went back to helping the injured.

As she pushed by Bishop, she gave him a reprimanding, narrow-eyed look as one would a child. I watched her disappear into the mass of clamoring troops, feeling left behind. Internally, I wanted nothing more than to also help. Some hadn't been as lucky as us, and the cabin was filled with pained moans. Though my mind wanted to help, my body refused. *This couldn't be my life now, could it?*

Heeding Ness' unspoken command to babysit, Bishop continued to loiter near me, his deer-in-the-headlights expression not hiding the fact he had no idea how to deal with someone in shock. He fidgeted as if standing on hot coals and meticulously picked at his uniform with two meaty fingers, doing everything possible to avoid my eyes.

Perhaps where he'd come from, men simply smacked their heads together and pounded their chests like gorillas after a close call.

After about a minute and a shifty glance at Ness, who was a few seats away wiping blood off a trooper's arm, Bishop deflated with a loud sigh and slumped into the seat next to me.

He nudged me with an elbow and grunted. "You did well. We made it."

He then turned away, concluding the pep-talk. We sat in silence after that; me staring straight ahead in a daze, and Bishop pouting, arms crossed.

A metallic click, audible over the chatter, broke me out of my thousand-yard stare. The sound of boots rushing down the stairs came next. Glancing over my shoulder, I saw a frazzled Wagner bolt into the cabin. She had a glowing med-wand in one hand and a tablet in the other. Her chest heaved with panic, and her hair was no longer a smooth bob but more of a tangled nest.

"Is everyone okay?" She surveyed the mess with wide eyes.

No one answered, but all heads turned to the stern as people shuffled out of the way to form a tunnel. Two men hadn't gotten up. Other troopers were straddled over them, performing CPR and cursing for them to awaken.

Breathing heavily, Wagner rushed to the prone troops and dropped to her knees. She shooed away the men on top of them. The cabin hushed, and the atmosphere grew heavy as everyone edged in to gather around her. I remained in my seat but watched. The bodies were cast in a bluish glow as she ran the med-wand over them while intently studying the readouts on her tablet.

With a loud sigh, she slumped back onto her heels in defeat. I guessed the tablet hadn't painted a pretty picture. Unlike the larger ships, transports weren't equipped with advanced medical tech, and there wasn't much that could be done for broken backs or grave internal injuries.

Seeing the defeat on her face, most of the gathered bystanders groaned with disappointment and dispersed. The few that remained dropped down next to the dead men that must have been their buddies. Eyeing the morbid scene, I realized I felt relief that the casualties weren't Ness, Bishop, or Foster. I didn't take pride in the selfish thought, but there it was. Perhaps there were worse things than your own demise.

Rising, Wagner moved out of the way, giving the troops time with the departed. Two other men were already extracting black body bags from a compartment in the bulkhead like they knew the drill.

With hands on her hips and a surly frown, Wagner moved her attention to the upturned cabin. Her nose crinkled in disgust. What had come up, had come down, and what had come out of some people was greenish-brown, wet, chunky, and very unpleasant.

Judging by her revulsion, I suspected the pilots were responsible for the cleanup at the end of each voyage. They were going to have a hell of a time getting the puke out of the nooks and crannies.

I almost cracked a smile at her scrunched expression, but then, her eyes slid to my row. Our gaze met. I quickly looked away as my cheeks flushed and my heart raced. I had stopped trembling, but I was still shaken, and I didn't want her to see the panic in my eyes.

"Super smooth, Adlar," Bishop cooed in monotone when he saw me jerk my head away from the LT.

He didn't appear at all unnerved by his bout with death or the fact there were bodies lying no more than ten steps away from us.

"How… how do I find her on the carrier?" I asked, ignoring his mocking chuckles.

He would know all the tricks since he'd been onboard troop carriers before.

Bishop pulled back and looked at me like I was crazy, then shook his head, jabbing a large finger into my chest.

"Nah, man, you don't find her… she'll find you." He paused. "Well, maybe. But if that one doesn't, don't worry. There's plenty of fish on the carriers. SF girls *love* us troopers."

He waved a thumb in Foster's direction, who'd ambled to the bunk across from us, a skin patch on one side of his head.

"I mean, how could they not? Look what they get on the Fleet side." Bishop grinned.

"Hey!" Foster shot back with a pained grimace as he rubbed his torso. "I'm a Leege now, too."

He paused, then mumbled. "At least kind of, I guess."

Bishop barked a laugh, patting Foster on the back as he got up.

"Sure you are, buddy, sure you are. I'm gonna find a med-kit." He winced, touching the gash on his forehead.

It had stopped bleeding but definitely needed attention.

He kicked my boot. "You aren't going to faint, are you?"

I rolled my eyes for a reply and slumped lower in my chair, crossing my arms. It was my turn to pout. The man would've probably teased me relentlessly if he weren't worried about Ness. No matter her small size, she was a trooper through and through and had taken me under her wing. To be honest, I kind of felt like teasing myself at the moment. I wasn't too proud of almost falling to pieces. Sure, I'd held my own when bucketloads of adrenaline pumped through my veins and determination had pushed me forward, but afterward, I had turned into a puddle of mush. I didn't foresee that being an attribute that would help me survive.

Bishop chuckled at my pouty expression, then lumbered away, pushing through the crowded cabin in his usual rough-handed manner. Toes were smashed and ribs elbowed, but nobody dared to lash back, even though some contemplated the idea, judging by their disdainful snarls. I made a mental note not to get on his bad side.

Ness rejoined me after everything had been somewhat put back together and handed me my phone and watch. I had no idea how she'd found them amidst the mess, but somehow, she'd managed.

"Want to be roommates?" she asked. "Bishop and Foster aren't in our cohort; they're both going to first, but it looks like you and I are going to the same cohort, unit, and squad. How cool is that?"

"Huh?" I replied, her unusual request catching me off guard.

I'd been busy watching Wagner in my peripheral vision as she finished passing out duty assignments and helping with what limited medical care the transport had to offer.

I blinked at her. "Are we allowed to be roommates?"

"Sure, why not?" Ness shrugged. "The Legions don't give a damn about Earth's military regs. They don't answer to Earth-gov. A buddy of mine who was in told me it's two people per room, and you just pick any room that's available or is a man down."

"Well…" I rubbed my chin in thought, uncertain. "Even if it's allowed, is it a good idea?"

I wasn't sure it was. I liked Ness and all, but I was hesitant to share a room with her. The only woman I'd ever lived with, so far, was my mom.

"Yeah, I'm sure." She chuckled and shoved my shoulder. "Don't worry about the boy/girl thing. I won't be crawling into your bed at night if that's what you're thinking. Unless you suddenly sprout a pair of jugs, that is."

She cupped her hands in front of her chest and groped the air, laughing and hooting like we were in a bar. "Then I might come join you."

After a few more seconds of indecision and looking at her mischievous grin, I relented. "All right, why not?"

Not only had we survived almost being incinerated, but we'd now spent days upon days cooped up in this metal can without getting on each other's nerves. If that wasn't a sign of a perfect roommate, I didn't know what was. Plus, I was sure she'd smell a lot better than any of the other Neanderthals I could hope to find in this bunch.

"Great, then it's settled!"

"So, what happened to that buddy you had? Which Legion is he in?" I asked, truly curious.

I, myself, didn't know a single soul outside of this transport who'd been a Leege.

Ness shrugged. "Don't know. He just disappeared, probably died."

She glanced around the cabin as her tone lowered. "Not hard to do around here."

I threw her a pained glance. Like Bishop, she didn't appear shaken by the attack, nor bothered by what fate possibly had in store for us. I couldn't understand why. How had tumbling head over heels and almost turning into cosmic dust not fazed either of them?

CHAPTER
SIX

Fortunately, the rest of the trip was uneventful, and the landing on *Venator* was a lot smoother than our takeoff. We landed with a gentle bump, ferried out of the airlock, and lurched to a stop. No one moved; no one spoke. We all just sat there, tightly sealed away from whatever awaited us. I'd lost count of the days, but if I had to guess, the voyage had taken almost a month. A fact I tried not to think about, not wanting to imagine how far from Earth I now was.

The opening of the flight deck's hatch brought the cabin back to life. Groans of elation and sighs of relief rang through the stale air as we all dragged ourselves up and grabbed our meager personal bags, then lined up between the rows of seats. Everyone was chomping at the bit to exit. I was no exception. Under the nerves, there was a twitch of excitement. This time last year, I was... well, I couldn't remember what I was doing, but it wasn't walking onto a troop carrier.

I stretched my neck over the other troops to see if it was LT Wagner who'd opened the hatch, but it wasn't—it was that other guy, the prick who'd checked me in and made me miss the sunrise.

With a sour expression, he rushed to unload us.

Doing my best to shake out my sore muscles, I fell in with the ambling crowd. I raised both my arms over my head in a long, pleasant stretch right as someone bumped into me from behind. I snorted and shoved the guy. I didn't see the need to crowd. It wasn't as if we'd arrived at some beach vacation.

A moment later, it was my turn to exit, and I stepped out onto the gangway. A cavernous hangar greeted my eyes, and I couldn't help but marvel at the size. I knew troop carriers were massive, easily a mile long with twenty decks or more, but knowing and actually experiencing it firsthand were two very different things. The three transports, which had towered over the planes back on the airfield, were now mere flies in the belly of this giant.

I descended, savoring the fresh air. Even though it was also recirculated, it was great to finally escape the cabin's stale stench. Not to mention the lingering hints of vomit that had insisted on hanging around. Instead, something like ozone, oil, and burnt electronics tickled my nostrils. Probably from the rows upon rows of Vipers lining the bay.

They were crafts designed for space combat, with light hulls, missiles, and rail guns. They couldn't withstand repeated atmospheric re-entry, thus I'd never seen any in person before. As I eyed the sleek hulls, I wondered if the other hangars were also lined with combat craft. If they were, this ship sure was packing.

Now if that was a good thing or not, I didn't know. Large-scale space battles were rare, not unless some species laid a trap and were sure of a victory. No side wanted to risk the vast losses that would result otherwise. No sir. Why lose thousands of personnel and expensive equipment when you could deploy ground-pounders to whichever hellhole of a planet was the host of the most recent conflict and let them battle it out?

Intrigued, I wanted to take a closer look at the Vipers, but I resisted. *Keep your head down,* I told myself, closely following the trooper in front of me as if he were the momma duck. After all, that mantra had worked for me back on Earth. Well, *mostly,* I suppose, considering I was on a freakin' troop carrier, and not in a comfy office chair behind a desk, nursing a cup of coffee.

As my eyes roved over the bay, some of my tension eased. Besides the Vipers, everything else was reminiscent of a standard airfield. Space Fleet personnel scurried about, chatting and laughing as they attended to the ships and their tasks. Equipment beeped and clanged in the background. Maybe this wasn't going to be so bad after all.

"Troopers!" boomed a loud voice.

It came from the direction of three men standing next to a row of cargo elevators, three of which were open. One man was impatiently waving us over. I couldn't help but throw one last, longing glance at the transport, hoping to catch a glimpse of LT Wagner. I knew she'd probably be trouble, but there was just something about her I couldn't shake.

"First cohort!" shouted the impatient man, sweeping his arms towards the open elevator in an exaggerated gesture.

I shivered with irritation. I never liked Fleet stuck-ups like that; men that treated the infantry ranks like mere cattle.

"Well, this is it," Bishop said, as he and Foster gave Ness and me a firm handshake.

"Don't be bait out there, okay? And don't get dusted!" he shouted over his shoulder as they piled into the open elevator.

I breathed a heavy sigh as the two men disappeared behind the closing doors. I hadn't gotten to know either one of them too personally since neither were big talkers, but the idea of never seeing them again unnerved me. What if they died during this campaign? What if *I* did?

"Second cohort?" asked another, more patient, Fleet soldier looking over the group.

A crowd of unfamiliar faces had joined us, probably from the other transports. Some of us nodded at the man and squeezed into the elevator he directed us into. Ness and I were among the last to enter, so I was next to the doors and the control panel. My heart sank. The floors were labeled by service type. That meant, Wagner and I weren't on the same deck.

The elevator slid to a stop at C-2 and spat us out to a completely different scene than the one we'd left. Unlike the SF deck above, there were no chattering and laughing men in the second cohort's hangar bay. Instead, serious-looking troopers in heavy-gear suits loitered around the dropships. Even the air was different here, the metallic tang and the ozone-charged aroma of blaster rifles almost overpowering.

"Good luck, troopers," said the Fleet soldier as we piled out, his tone grave and in no way a reassuring sign.

The man sounded like he was wishing farewell to someone permanently moving away.

Begrudgingly, I followed everyone into the bay, weaving between the dropships, which were lined in three perfect rows, ten ships per row. A cold shiver ran down my spine when I got a closer look at the jet-black vessels. They weren't all nice and spiffy like the fighters on the Fleet deck. Charred burn marks scarred their smooth exteriors.

Pausing next to a ship, I extend a cautious finger to graze a scar, the words from the Legion recruitment site, *No one quits, everyone fights,* surfacing to the front of my mind.

"Beautiful, aren't they?" Ness said.

"Hmm…" I snorted, retracting my hand right as a Fleet mechanic popped out from around an engine pod and fixed me with a disapproving stare.

"I think we have different ideas of what passes as beautiful, Ness. *Very* different."

Some of the singed streaks were as wide around as my thigh. Whatever heavy weaponry had nicked them hadn't been messing around, and it was nothing I wanted to encounter.

Ness laughed and slapped my arm, amused by my unease. "You're funny, Jake. But don't you worry, we'll make a Leege out of you yet. Soon, you'll be looking forward to that hot hum of your blaster rifle powering up. There's no better sound. Just watch."

I arched an eyebrow at her. Dozens of *hot* sounds instantly jumped to my mind and none of them had anything to do with weaponry. Ignoring my skepticism, Ness stretched tall on her tiptoes to scan over the row of ships then glanced at the white numbers stenciled on the deck next to each one.

"We better find where we need to be. I'm sure whatever brass is giving us our welcome tour is shitting themselves with impatience by now."

I chuckled in agreement and let her guide me. Each dropship's parking spot was numbered, with the numbers ascending further into the bay at the back of which massive white numbers were painted onto the bulkhead. Those labeled the units. I tailed Ness towards fourth, taking in my new digs as we went.

Metal bulkheads, dropships, armored troops, a lift-mech, and more ships. Nothing to write home about. Then, as my head twisted this way and that, something above caught my eye. A long, rectangular window of what I presumed was the control room over-looked the hangar bay. People milled inside, but it wasn't them who'd garnered my attention, but the single man standing apart, almost against the glass, arms crossed over his chest. I didn't recog-nize his insignia, but his all-black uniform pinned him as a Legionnaire.

From my vantage point, I judged him to be on the smaller side. Yet, I felt a chill. Something about his disposition and gaunt, narrow face bade caution. I wouldn't poke a scorpion no matter its smaller size. He stood glacially still, observing the new arrivals. Then, his eyes landed on me.

I snapped my gaze away. "Hey, Ness. Don't make it obvious that you're looking, but who's the man in the control room, the one staring at all of us?"

Ness, of course, ignored my instructions and bluntly fixated on the window. She quickly jerked her head down.

"See the shields on his collar?" She edged closer as if he might somehow hear us. "That means he's a Prefect. They're the logistics officers. He and a few Primus ranks run each cohort, but they don't drop with the troops. Thankfully. They're supposedly royal jackasses with a god complex. It's best to stay away from them. The Centurions will be the ones dropping with us. They command each unit. Hope we get a good one."

I nodded back a confirmation in the now almost silent hangar. The current occupants had all stopped what they were doing to eye the new arrivals entering their ranks. Ignoring the troopers' burning stares, I followed Ness down the row of ships that was fourth unit until we arrived at a ship with a "10" beside it.

A large, dark-skinned man in a heavy-gear suit, one hand on his hip and the other wrapped around a menacing helmet, stood next to the battle-worn vessel. A small silver Earth emblem glinted on the left side of his armor, over his heart. I figured he was the welcoming committee. The man's face spread into a creepy grin as he watched us approach.

I considered greeting him, but one glance into his steely eyes made me reconsider. Instead, Ness and I quietly massed with the other troopers already there. The man scanned us with a predatory expression, like a wolf looking over a herd of sheep, as more troops joined the group. He quietly chuckled when the deck lurched under our feet, and we all glanced around in confusion. The ship thrummed as a light vibration passed through my boots.

"Welcome to your new life, maggots!" he suddenly boomed, startling me and causing me to jump.

I'd been busy looking around, hopelessly trying to get a clue about where we were headed.

"I'm Squad Leader Gundy. Now drop your bags and fall in, it's time to make Leeges out of you!"

I wanted to ask the man where we were going. I knew the ship had jumped, but something about his expression told me this wasn't time for Q&A. Everyone else was already hustling to follow his instructions. They dropped their bags to the deck and rushed into formation as Gundy continued to bark regs at us.

"I suggest you keep your filthy selves off the living quarter's elevator. The brass don't like that. There are elevators in the hangar bay and around the rec area—"

He kept going, but I stopped paying attention. Concern gnawed at me as I carried out the man's request. How were we supposed to settle into our rooms without our bags?

Turned out getting us settled wasn't at all what the SL had on his agenda, and not even an hour into my arrival, I found myself being stuffed into a heavy-gear suit. We were all herded into an equipment room where some attendant, who right off made it clear he wasn't in a chatty mood, scanned my measurements, slapped a neural transmitter over my ear, then—very rudely—shoved me into armor. Everything was done swiftly with zero concern for my comfort. I wasn't even allowed questions.

Within minutes I was encased in the rugged suit like an exoskeleton of a bug, with me being the squishy insides. Heart racing, I slowly moved my arms and legs. The suit's servos whirred gently, and I sensed it trying to work in tandem with my body. It was an unnerving sensation, to say the least.

Then the helmet was slammed over my head. The smell of neoprene, plastic, and electronics filled my nostrils as everything went pitch-black, and the outside world ceased to exist. I was fully encapsulated. An uncontrollable feeling of claustrophobia overcame me, and I had to do everything in my power to subdue my panic.

"Keep your head down," I whispered to myself, trying to calm my rapid breathing.

The numbing silence inside the helmet was overwhelming.

The suit clicked, and the world returned. A slew of diagnostics streamed in my HUD. I blinked at the flashing text, understanding none of it, then tried to ignore it. My head spun, and I found the armor to be tight, ungainly, and overbearing. It hadn't been a minute and I already wanted to escape it. I sighed. As uncomfortable and miserable as I was, I needed to get used to this. The suit was now my second skin, meant to protect me.

With SL Gundy shouting at us, the suited squad was then ushered to *Venator*'s massive training arena and onto a six-lane track skirting the periphery. The training area looked like a cross between a paint-ball course and a monster truck arena. Mounds of sand formed hills, ditches, and foxholes, while anything and everything, ranging from sandbags to giant boulders and half-destroyed dropships created hideouts throughout the field.

The pops and zaps of blaster fire and explosive rounds echoed somewhere amidst the props. I shuffled nervously. There was no partition between the arena and the track, nothing protecting us from the live exercise currently taking place.

"Move it!" Gundy's voice shouted in my helmet as a hard shove landed on my back.

"Double time!"

Reluctantly, I fell in with the jogging squad, but it wasn't pretty. Having never worn heavy-gear before, I found myself struggling to integrate with my suit, and as everyone sprinted ahead, I clunked after them like some stilted bear. It appeared I was the only 'add-on.' Everyone else had gone through basic. To make matters worse, my HUD had yet to stop dousing me with information. There was targeting data—to what, I wasn't sure—twisting grids, a bouncing reticle, and countless other overlays I had no clue how to deactivate. I was certain the lines spiking on overdrive were my heartbeat.

All in all, I was quickly growing frustrated. We'd yet to do one loop around the arena and already my muscles ached, and twinges of a headache crept into my forehead. For some reason, the darn SL wouldn't stop yapping. I was sure what he screamed over comms was pertinent, but my utter discomfort made it hard to care. My hands itched to unclasp and throw off the helmet altogether. Groaning, I knew that wasn't an option.

As a distraction, I decided to try and get a handle on my HUD and directed my attention to finding the elusive volume controls first. Toggling options with only your eyes and thoughts wasn't exactly an easy feat, and it took me a few tries to access the desired function. Relief flooded over me when I succeeded, and SL Gundy's annoying voice extinguished. It was now just me and my ragged breaths in the blissful silence of my helmet.

When I directed my attention back to the track, I realized I had truly fallen behind. The rest of the squad was now two hundred feet ahead, and for some reason, they weren't moving. The two lines of troops were stopped, their helmeted heads turned in my direction.

"Shit," I mouthed, picking up my pace to catch up, my thighs burning as I sprinted.

So much for keeping my head down. Oddly, when I reached them, the group remained stationary, with SL Gundy standing at the head of the formation, his faceless, jet-black visor pointing my way. My head swiveled in confusion as the rest of the troopers shuffled back, forming a tunnel between the SL and me.

"What's going on?" I asked.

What kind of nonsense was this? I was about to repeat my question when the large man pounced. Next thing I knew, a huge fist slammed into my visor, sending me sprawling back onto the track, my head rattling in my helmet. Heart racing, I pushed up, trying to make sense of things. Had the SL just punched me, an hour into training?

As I scrambled back to my feet, panting, I glimpsed something speeding towards me out of the corner of my display. Before I could protest—or dodge—the SL's oversized suit-powered boot slammed into my chest.

I landed on my back, hard, in the sand of the arena, air exploding out of my lungs.

"You gonna try and mute me, boy?" the SL roared in my comm.

Hurrying to my feet, I shuffled back as the realization of what had happened dawned on me. The SL hadn't stopped yapping those last few blissfully silent minutes of the jog. Instead, I'd inadvertently muted the guy.

"I didn't mean to, sir, I swear!" I staggered back, dust billowing around my ankles.

The SL wasn't having it. He kept advancing—lumbering towards me like some angry beast. How far back could I go? The pops and zaps of explosive rounds were getting louder. My helmet's audio picked them up, displaying probable locations of the fire's origin. There was no mistaking it, I was about to be smack-dab in the midst of the exercise.

"It was an accident, sir," I called, still retreating.

He didn't answer, and the pounding of his determined boots echoed in my audio. We were at least two hundred feet into the arena by now. Not knowing what else to do, I picked up my pace of retreat, weaving around stacked barrels and boulders.

Then, the SL suddenly stopped. I tried not to audibly sigh with relief, figuring he'd take that as another invitation to attack. What the hell did he want, anyway? Was he expecting us to brawl? Was that how the training was done around here, pummel each other at every opportunity?

I was about to call the misunderstanding at its end and ask to rejoin the squad when a giant mass smashed into me and sent me spinning into the dirt.

"Watch it!" an unfamiliar voice shouted as the trooper who'd knocked me down dove into a foxhole.

"*Pop, pop, pop.*" Fire rained around me.

Dust clouds billowed as the rounds slammed into the dirt, exploding on impact.

Acting on pure instinct, I scrambled on all fours and leaped for cover behind the barrels. When the slew of pops subsided, I hazarded a peek. The SL's massive form loomed about fifty feet away. He stood statue-still, arms crossed, watching the show. I swear I could sense the prick grinning inside his helmet.

"Pax!" SL Gundy shouted. "Hand me your weapon."

The live rounds stopped flying, and the suited figure that had previously knocked me over reappeared. The man's suit was of heavier build than mine or Gundy's, and with a gold Earth emblem stamped over the heart. Was he another squad leader? I slowly edged out from behind the barrels, unsure how to proceed.

The gold-emblem trooper threw me a glance but without hesitation, handed Gundy his weapon. I reflexively backstepped. Was I supposed to run?

Gundy didn't give me much time to decide. He swiftly leveled the gun and squeezed the trigger. A snap sounded. My display flashed red as the round nailed me square in my chest and sent me crashing to the sand in a cloud of dust.

With panicked hands and gasping for breath, I frantically pawed my torso for injuries. There weren't any, just a charred mark on my breastplate where the bullet had burst. It hadn't penetrated my gear. Still, in no way did it not hurt. My entire chest throbbed like I'd been bashed with a hammer.

"I feel better now, maggot!" Gundy's voice barked inside my helmet.

I no longer cared how loud it was.

CHAPTER
SEVEN

I surprised myself when I somehow managed to power through the five-mile jog that followed my adventures in the arena. As I got the hang of working with my suit, instead of against it, it became easier to keep up with the rest of the squad. Not to say that the experience was a pleasant one. Quite the opposite, in fact. The suit had done its job and protected me against serious injuries, but there wasn't much it could do against the effects of being tossed around like a ragdoll and then shot. Every muscle ached, and my sore chest pounded like a drum.

Shortly after I rejoined the squad, Ness fell in step beside me.

"Well, that was something, huh?" she said over private chat. "I thought about jumping in and helping you out, but you know, didn't feel like getting my ass whooped."

She laughed, playfully punching me.

I rolled my eyes in the privacy of my helmet. "Thanks for the thought… I guess."

I figured this was just the beginning of getting my ass handed to me and it was pointless to get butthurt over each and every occurrence.

"But here, let's go over your display," Ness offered.

She then explained how to navigate my HUD and operate the elusive comm options. Slowly but surely, I mastered it, and a tad of confidence trickled into me. Just maybe I'd manage to become an actual Legionnaire and stay alive. Unfortunately, my elation was short-lived, because then the next exercise arrived, and shockingly it didn't comprise of Gundy sitting us down in a share circle to hear our problems.

See, the Legions couldn't use parachutes to drop troops on their targets. That would result in a bunch of dead bodies floating down to the ground. Parachutes gave the enemy's defensive batteries too much time to take everyone out. Furthermore, they made for an unacceptable landing radius, especially on planets with turbulent atmospheres. It wasn't like the Legions were going to wait for a sunny day to deploy.

So, instead of parachutes, we used air packs. The air packs worked in tandem with our suits to slow a trooper's descent after plummeting through the enemy's defensive fire. The problem being, as you dropped, you had to get yourself at least a few degrees past a prone horizontal position for your armor's jets to kick in and fully right you. For someone like me, who had zero experience with skydiving, that wasn't as easy as it sounded.

"Let me show you how this is done!" Gundy shouted as we gathered at the gaping mouth of the air tunnel.

Even though my suit was pressurized, and incoming audio set to the lowest level, the whooshing in the chute sounded like I was standing behind a massive turbine. Slowly, I stuck my head into the daunting opening and peered into the endless expanse below. My pulse quickened. Huge blades whirled underneath a metal grate as air howled around my helmet.

All my confidence vanished in a flash.

Donning an air pack and clasping a magnetic retractor to his forearm, SL Gundy marched up to the ledge, all the while instructing us on how to secure the equipment and connect it to our suits. Then, without hesitation, he leaped into the howling air, still blathering on. Now, about how to handle ourselves. As the air caught him, Gundy effortlessly maneuvered into an arch position, front to the wind, arms out, and legs bent at the knees. He then twisted into a dive, head down, arms at his sides, explaining that this bullet drop was the safest way to fall. It gave the enemy that much less time to blast you out of the sky.

A loud buzzer sounded. In company to the alarm, the power of the air in the tunnel decreased, then stopped completely. Like a rocket, Gundy plummeted into the void, only to twist up at the last second, fire off his air pack, and land smoothly on his feet. He then slapped a panel on the wall, bringing the fans back to life, and a moment later was again across from us, floating like a bird soaring on an updraft. Using the retractor to shoot out a cable which magnetized to the wall, he reeled himself in and leapt out to stand before us.

"You're next, Adlar!" he shouted, throwing me the air pack and the retractor.

My heart raced as I caught the items. Sure, he'd just walked us through this step-by-step, but something told me this wasn't going to be as easy as he made it look. Reluctantly, I donned the air pack and secured the retractor, then ambled to the ledge on wobbly legs, trying to work up the nerve to jump.

"We don't have all day!" Gundy barked, slamming a boot into my back.

Yelping, I toppled forward. The air punched into me like a cannonball as I flailed helplessly in the torrent. Instinctively, I tried to grab onto something—anything—only for my panicked fingers to close on nothing. Steadying my breathing, I concentrated on imitating Gundy's maneuver, hips forward, arms to the side, legs bent, but it wasn't happening. Every time I leveled out, I somehow teetered too far forward, back, or to either side, resulting in the air spinning me around like a tumbleweed.

I swear, it was as if my body had decided to work against me for the time being. I flipped and flopped, ping-ponging off the metal walls with loud clangs.

"What the fuck do you think you're doing?" Gundy roared to the backdrop of everyone's snickers.

"I'm gonna rip you a—" he cut off abruptly as the blare of the buzzer pierced the sound of the whooshing air. "Shit!"

Suddenly, everyone's roaring laughter became the least of my worries.

I plummeted down, screaming and flailing as the grate flew

towards my head. Right as I was about to splat, a wall of air slammed into me, and I again tumbled head over heels. The world around me spun in a blur of gray as I was lifted back up to the entrance.

"Get the hell out!" Gundy roared.

Wanting nothing more than to do just that, and trying not to hurl from all the spinning, I did my best to aim the retractor at the wall next to the opening, just like Gundy had done, but once again, failure was imminent. The dang thing shot right into the hall instead, causing Gundy to duck, lose his footing, and nearly topple into the tunnel. Since I was flopping whichever way, I only glimpsed him trying to climb back onto the deck, but my squadmates' gasps and his curses told me everything I needed to know.

I was in a pile of shit. What topped the cake at that moment was that unlike everybody else, whom I assumed darted back from my shooting retractor, Gundy couldn't. He was still busy climbing out of the tunnel. The magnet popped him right over the head as it reeled back in. Judging by his enraged roar, I guessed it nailed him good. At that point, I considered just staying in the tunnel for as long as possible. Maybe permanently moving in. Nothing nice was going to take place once I made it out.

Unfortunately, I had no choice but to attempt another exit. It wasn't going to be long until the buzzer sounded, and I really didn't feel like going for another downward plunge. Especially now that it was fair to suspect Gundy might not rush to restart the air. I shot the retractor again, this time semi-correctly.

Magnetizing to the wall, the line jerked taught then reeled me. I almost dared to breathe with relief. However, as I stretched a hand to grab the railing lining the opening, I failed to find it.

"Shit," I muttered in realization.

The darn magnet hadn't landed close enough to the exit, and the most I was able to do was graze the railing with my fingertips. Still, I kept trying. Floundering upside-down like a leaf in the wind, I thrashed and pawed with all my might.

I probably would've flopped about endlessly, but a large hand reached into the tunnel and caught my outstretched arm. It forcefully yanked me out and flung me onto the deck. I didn't fight and let my body skid as far as it wanted. Then, I just lay there, huffing and staring at the bright overhead lights, relieved to be on solid ground.

The rest of the squad took no pity on my mishap. A chorus of roaring laughter erupted, even as Gundy cursed and cuffed troops over their helmets. They didn't care. They howled like hyenas, slumping against the bulkheads as they clutched their gut. I couldn't blame them; I'd put on one hell of a show.

What concerned me more than their booming laughter was Gundy. To my complete surprise, he made no move in my direction. Instead, yanking a cackling trooper straight, he slapped him a good one upside his head, then began fitting him with an air pack.

Taking measure of the situation, I dared to think in a positive fashion. Maybe the SL wasn't overly pissed. If anything, he, too, was to blame—for thinking I'd get this right on my first try. The man should've known better.

I was wrong. Being understanding wasn't one of SL Gundy's personality traits. No sooner had I rejoined the squad, then a hard blow to the back of my head almost knocked me over. Dazed but managing to stay on my feet, I twisted around to see the SL towering over me, fists clenched like he was about to swing again.

Steeling myself, I balled my fists. Heat flushed my cheeks. I'd had enough of being beaten. Then, my eyes gleaned the howling tunnel. I hesitated. Perhaps this wasn't the time for anything drastic. Gundy could easily toss me in. This time with no air pack. With some effort, I scrapped the idea of fighting back and braced for the inevitable. If he was going to punch me, so be it. At least there weren't any weapons around, so there was that.

The anticipated punch never came. The man slammed me back against the bulkhead instead, bringing his visor an inch from mine. Both of our visors were set on clear, and our gaze locked. His was full of rage without a hint of understanding.

Alarmed, I considered an apology but didn't think it would matter. He swung, and I flinched, but his fist missed my head. It bashed into the wall, sending a loud metal-on-metal clang to echo down the hall and vibrations to tickle my back. The commotion garnered us curious glances, but everyone quickly turned away. None wanted to get involved in my current predicament.

"You think this is a joke?" Gundy roared into my face.

I blinked at him, breathing faster. Was that rhetorical? Because I didn't remember laughing. I'd almost pissed myself, I'd been so scared.

"Uh… no sir, of course not," I at last broke the awkward silence.

Gundy poked a large finger into my chest. "You're Legion property now, boy! And if you die from dropping, that's a waste! The least you can do is live long enough to be *bait* for those drooling alien freaks. You get that?"

"Yes, sir." I gave my head a quick nod as confused as I was.

Damn. So much for staying under the radar—again. If anything, it looked like I was now the SL's favorite, and not in a good way.

"I don't want to see you treat an exercise like a game ever again. Is that clear, trooper? Or I'll break your neck myself. At least that way we won't risk lives to retrieve your equipment."

"Yes, sir." I nodded again, then froze.

My face scrunched. He truly *was* under the impression I'd been messing around. Maybe I was so bad that he couldn't help but think that.

Huffing angrily, the SL turned to walk away, but I reached out and grabbed his arm. Stopping, he slowly lowered his head to look at my fingers, his eyes screaming he wanted to break each one. Wanting to keep my fingers, I smartly retracted my hand.

I fidgeted, unsure how to tell him that he'd gotten it wrong. That my incompetence wasn't an act. Bluntly, I supposed. I wasn't a warrior—a Legionnaire. I had no business fighting anyone. Our visors were still on clear, and my lost expression must have told him everything he needed to know.

He stepped back, placing his hands on his hips, a quizzical look veiling his face. "You weren't messing around in there, were you, maggot? How the hell did you get through basic? Don't they teach anything back on Earth nowadays?"

I hesitated, but then figured it was best to be honest. "I didn't go through basic, sir. At least not Legion Basic. I was an add-on. I'm actually in the Force… I mean, I *was* in the Force."

"Aww, hell… you're from the desk jockey brigade? I thought there was something funny about you."

I shrugged weakly.

"Chum for the waters, huh?" He chuckled, shaking his head.

My brow arched. What was all this talk about being *bait*?

"I want to learn, though," I quickly offered. "I don't want to be chum, sir. Nor do I want to break my neck."

I had never wanted any of this, but now that I was here, I intended to stay alive.

Gundy chuckled again, but this time in a less menacing fashion.

"Ain't that the truth. Those beasts will tear you up quick. Look, kid, go to the rec area tonight and practice diving in the pool. Even if I dared to give you clearance to use the air tunnel unsupervised, it's not available. We have a drop coming up, so it's all booked. The pool is all you're gonna get. Sure, you're gonna walk away with some bruises, but it's better than ending up dead, right?"

I nodded. "Yes, sir."

"Falling is a big part of your new life, boy. Don't be afraid to fall, just learn how to do it right."

With that piece of advice, Gundy stalked away to hassle the rest of the squad. After watching them, it became clear why the SL had presumed I was messing around. Nobody else flailed as I had. Sure, it took some people a minute to straighten out, then reposition correctly in the strong wind, but overall, everyone landed successfully. By successful, I mean no one else plummeted towards the ground, head-first, with absolutely no hope of righting themselves.

My worry escalated. Gundy said we had a drop coming up. How soon was that? Was I going to have to drop with the rest of the squad whether I learned to land or not?

I spent the remainder of training in a glum mood. Thankfully, there weren't any more complicated exercises. After the air tunnel, Gundy tortured us with yet another jog around the training arena, followed by some sort of scavenging drill, retrieving weapons, helmets, and extremely heavy mannequins scattered throughout the props and dunes while under light fire.

It surprised me how well Ness did. She loped around with ease, avoiding bullets and collecting items. I, on the other hand, did just enough for Gundy to stay off my ass.

I spent most of the exercise behind cover, out of his sight, fiddling with my hover-cart. It was a pretty nifty contraption that unfurled to form a large hovering bin. They weren't the sturdiest of things but held a lot of weight while extremely easy to push. Overall, my head wasn't in the game. All I could think about was that pool. I was going to fall tonight, and I was going to do it right.

CHAPTER
EIGHT

After the scavenging exercise, we did a short stint at the firing range, popping down a bunch of disgusting-looking holographic projections. There weren't any cyclopes, but the purplish seal-sized snakes weren't a pretty sight.

"At least you don't suck at everything," Gundy growled, giving my back a hard slap.

As my dad was a cop, I wasn't a novice when it came to firearms. Sure, we were shooting blaster rifles instead of pistols, but I successfully popped that sleek with every shot, even at long-range.

Shortly after bestowing me with the half-hearted praise, Gundy, very rudely, shouted he'd had enough of us for the day and dismissed us. His words were music to my ears. Even though I'd somehow survived the training, I felt like I'd been put through the meat grinder, run over by a dump truck, then chucked off a cliff. Which wasn't far from the truth, I supposed, considering the amount of falling and tumbling I had done. We were then issued a laundry sack full of essentials like T-shirts, extra uniforms, and such and released to find rooms.

Ness had been correct about the bunking situation. Once we made our way to the living quarters on our cohort's deck, troops split up into pairs and went into any room with an open door, with no one directing our selections. As Ness and I walked down the hall, a pang of concern stabbed at me every time we passed a room with a single occupant. Their somber expressions and sidelong glances hinted at their previous roommates' dire fates.

"How's this one?" Ness asked, finally veering into a room.

"Sure." I shrugged, following her in.

I had no idea what mental checklist she was using. To me, all the rooms looked the same. Metal boxes without a view.

They were oddly similar to the ones back in the barracks, at least as far as the layout. A bunk bed on each side with a desk underneath and a drawer next to the desk. Size-wise, however, the room was maybe half of what I was used to. Ground troops sure didn't live in luxury aboard *Venator*.

"Are you coming to eat?" Ness asked, dropping her bag onto one of the desks. "Man, I could sure use some grub after all that."

I hesitated as I glanced at my watch, which had automatically set to ship's time. It was already nearing 2000, and I still had to get to that pool, but since we hadn't been fed all day, my stomach decided for me.

"Sure," I replied. "But let's make it quick, there's something I need to do."

Ness cocked her head in confusion, but then a knowing smile crossed her face. "You're going to look for that lieutenant, aren't you? I saw you ogling her and drooling."

She pursed her lips, suppressing laughter. "Between the panic attacks, that is."

"Ha! Got jokes, huh?" I rolled my eyes as I grabbed her, turned her, and shoved her into the hall. "But no, that's not it. I'm going to the pool to practice that *falling* thing I managed to fuck up today."

"Whatever you want to call it, man."

Ness, of course, completely ignored my request to hurry and stopped to chat up every woman that happened to pass by. As annoying as it was, I obliged her and used it as an opportunity to find the pool's location. So far, besides the silver placards posted by the stairwell and the quarter's elevator, I hadn't seen any directional markers.

On our overly lengthy walk, I learned that while each cohort's deck had its own gym, other rec stuff like the movies, VR rooms, and, unfortunately, the pool were shared by all the services, with the pool being just one deck below the officers'. After acquiring the needed information, I no longer tolerated Ness' loitering and dragged her along to the galley.

There, I rushed through the buffet-style line, loaded my tray with a sandwich and three cups of coffee, then hurriedly shoveled everything into my mouth. I hardly tasted the imitation meat that I think was supposed to be ham. Five minutes later, I dumped my tray and rushed to the door, leaving Ness to hit on the ladies all by herself.

"You're a shitty wingman, you know that!" she shouted to my back.

I threw her a dismissive wave over my shoulder. The idea of conquering my fear had been festering within me ever since Gundy had suggested the pool. Or maybe it was just the desire to live that was the motivator. You know, that pesky want *not* to slam down, headfirst, into unyielding earth after plummeting through thousands of feet of atmo. At least head-first would make the demise quick, but still, not desirable.

Being that the quarter's elevator was off-limits, it took me longer than I liked to get to the pool, but I stayed on task. I even resisted exploring the rec rooms. I figured I'd check them out later, as a possible place to invite Wagner to once I found her.

For a few minutes, as the elevator hummed upward, all thoughts of the pool went out the window, or the airlock, I suppose, as I contemplated how to find the girl. Maybe I'd roam the SF decks and claim ignorance if anyone caught me. Or perhaps I'd find out what deck she worked on and then—

The elevator eased to a stop and spat me out into an almost identical yet unfamiliar hall. An uninterrupted metal bulkhead ran down one side with what looked to be living quarters on the other. Thankfully, the hall was empty. The only other occupant was a cleaning bot. The boxy thing hummed and beeped, slowly making its way down the deck with a mechanical determination, brushes swishing under its chassis.

Noting a placard with a blue puddle and an arrow pointing to the right, I rushed to follow the instructions. With any luck, just maybe I'd get a few hours of shuteye tonight. However, my resolve was fleeting. My eyes bulged, and my jaw dropped. The water-filled hole in front of me appeared to be bottomless. Just a long, unforgiving chute like the air tunnel, waiting to swallow me whole.

Nor did my mood improve when my eyes slid to the diving board. I winced as my neck craned. Apparently, the Legion had a very different idea than most people, or any sane species for that matter, of what was acceptable. The distant white plank was at least two, even three, times higher than what one would find at a rec pool. All my previous bravado vanished, and I found my feet refusing to move. What was the SL thinking?

Seeing as I still had no desire to splat on the first drop, I gritted my teeth and got on with it, changing into my swim trunks. Gundy was right, what were a few bruises when weighed with death? My bare footsteps echoed in the vast room as I marched up to the ladder and climbed. My heart pounded faster and faster with each rung. By the time I reached the top, it felt like it was beating in my throat, each heartbeat thumping in my ears. Maybe having three cups of coffee wasn't the best of ideas.

With slow steps, I eased towards the end of the board. I could feel the thing bow under my weight. Cursing in anticipation of the impending hurt, I contemplated scrapping the entire endeavor. The pool was a mere puddle below me, its glassy, still surface glimmering in the white overhead lights. How was I not supposed to fear falling, when falling was terrifying?

I sucked in a strained breath, resigned for agony.

"No one quits, everyone fights," I whispered, then jumped.

CHAPTER
NINE

The water slammed into me like a brick wall, and my loud shriek changed to gurgles as I choked on the liquid. I don't even know what part of me hit first, since pain exploded over my entire body. Initially, I'd done a pretty good job of holding a diver's pose, but then panic overcame me and I reverted to screaming and flailing.

I would have gladly taken a few more of Gundy's punches, or even a couple of explosive rounds to the chest in lieu of this. The entire left side of my body stung and throbbed. What was exponentially worse was that this was only the beginning. I couldn't give up. Wincing and coughing up water, I swam to the edge of the pool, rolled up onto the plaster overlay, and flopped onto my back. There, I remained, motionless, listening to the lapping of the now-disturbed water echo around the room. I could've lay there forever, avoiding the pain of the next jump, but the pounding of quickly approaching footsteps grabbed my attention.

I let my head roll to the side as a small figure dashed through the doors and bolted to the edge of the pool. After throwing a glance at the water, she darted to stand over me.

"Are you okay?" asked a very familiar, pleasant voice. "What happened?"

"Uh-huh," I murmured, a smile inching onto my face.

The bright overhead lights framed Wagner's face just right, adding a nice glisten to her brown hair.

I grinned wide, propping up to a seated position. She took a step back, panting with a worried look on her face.

"I could've sworn I heard a woman's scream." She threw a glance at the pool. "I thought someone was drowning."

My smile fell as my eyes darted around the room with concern. My mind raced. There was no way I was going to admit the wild shrieks came from me.

"Uh…" I said, as she stared at me expectantly, her giant green eyes demanding an explanation.

Thinking fast, I pointed at the door. "They just left! Yeah, there were a few ladies messing around in here, but they weren't drowning or anything. They were just having fun."

"Oh…" Wagner relaxed, dropping her hands from her hips. "Well, that's good. It's kind of late for that, but to each is own, I suppose."

Her brows scrunched. "What happened to you?"

"Huh?"

Crap. Had she seen through my BS?

"What'd you mean?"

She gestured at my shoulder. "What happened there?"

My eyes roved to where she was looking. The skin was bright red like a nasty sunburn.

"Oh, that. It's nothing." I tried not to visibly wince. "Just getting some diving in, that's all."

I glanced at the diving board and Wagner mimicked.

"Insane height, huh?" she said, with a shake of her head. "You Legion boys are a crazy bunch, that's for sure."

When she looked back at me, her worry was gone. A smile now played on her pretty face and her eyes danced. I grinned back, not making a move to get off the floor. The water had settled, and the room was veiled in silence, with only the tapping of a few drips echoing somewhere behind me.

After thirty seconds or so, Wagner fidgeted and ran a hand through her hair, pushing it off her face. "Well, uhm… I guess I better go. See you around, Adlar."

With that, she headed to the door. "It's Jake," I called to her back, watching her go.

The uniforms weren't designed to accentuate the female form whatsoever, but somehow, they fit Wagner just right. I admired every second of her walking away.

After she disappeared, I reluctantly directed my attention back to the task at hand. I threw a wary glance at the distant diving board. I had no idea why that girl turned me into a stuttering fool, but the possibility of getting to know her made me want to live that much more. Seeing as how staying alive hinged on not cracking my skull on the first drop, I gritted my teeth, got up, and marched to the ladder. Then I jumped. Over and over again.

After some absurd amount of jumps, I grew even more eager to conquer my fear and stopped wasting time waiting for the pain to subside before climbing back up the ladder. The darn thing wasn't going to win. I was going to conquer the pool, the air tunnel, and whatever other *insane* thing the Legion expected of me.

Gradually, with each jump, my panic receded, and I no longer flailed like an injured bird. My brain processed actual thought during the fall instead of just rampantly freaking. I even dared to try a flip, like a professional pool diver, but after one failed attempt, gave up. I doubted troopers were expected to do acrobatics while hurtling to possible death.

Sore and exhausted, I finally decided to call it quits and get some much-needed rest. I took a quick rinse and changed into my old, wrinkled uniform. Kicking myself for not bringing a fresh one, I bolted into the dimmed hall. There was now only four hours left until the start of another fun-filled day of Legion training.

To my dismay, the closest elevator happened to be the one in the quarter's hall, the one troops were discouraged from using, because, god forbid, some brass got stuck riding with the likes of us. I hesitated, weighing my options. On one hand, I'd had enough prancing in the spotlight, but on the other, my body ached, and I wanted my bunk.

Ultimately, the decision was a simple one. Gundy's instructions had been more of a *suggestion* rather than explicit orders. Therefore, this particular ride was fair game. Inspecting the hall like a burglar on the prowl, I pressed the control panel. To my relief, the place was deserted. Not even a cleaning bot was in sight.

The elevator's gentle hum grew louder as it neared, then came to a stop. That's when a horrible sound greeted my ears. Muffled chatter and laughter came from behind the closed doors.

"You have to be kidding me," I growled, glancing around for an escape.

Even though I'd been eager to break the 'suggested' rules not even a minute ago, in actuality, I wasn't raring to piss off anyone else just yet. Being on Gundy's shit-list was enough.

Just as the doors cracked open, I ducked into the stairwell. I held the door a few extra seconds as it closed to make sure it wasn't going to slam. Then with a long exhale of defeat, I dropped my head against it, welcoming the coolness of the metal on my tired forehead. This hell of a day just wasn't going to end.

Rolling off the door, I slumped against the bulkhead and listened to the confusion in the hall; two men asking each other who'd pressed the button and why the elevator had stopped. A few seconds later, everything returned to silence.

Defeated, I was about to trot down the stairs, even if my body loathed the idea, when a strange noise caught my attention. A voice echoed from a few decks above me, and from the sound of it, not a happy one.

Curious, I edged up to the landing between the decks, stopping and crouching when I realized the sound was descending. I could now tell it was a woman's voice, and it was cursing up a storm. A strange echoing thumping accompanied her song of displeasure. Wanting to know more, I peeked through the inside of the stairwell, but to no avail. The mystery was out of my view.

The slew of profanity and heavy thuds gradually approached. I stepped down a step, not wanting to be seen, and craned my neck around the bend of the staircase. The rear of a woman in tight jeans emerged into view a deck above me. She was bent over, waddling backward, dragging something towards the hallway door. I stretched my neck farther until I was finally able to see her cargo.

It was an unconscious man, also dressed in civvies, his navy-blue collar shirt partially untucked from his pressed slacks. I didn't know whether to be worried or laugh. Judging from their outfits, the pair weren't on their way back from the training arena, and it appeared the man might have had one too many.

"Fuck this! That worthless—" the woman hissed through pants of exertion.

Straightening, she stretched her back, letting out a loud sigh as her eyes scanned the limp man with disdain. The dude was completely out. Not a finger flinched.

Swishing black hair out of her face, she flung open the hallway door and braced it with a leg. She then proceeded to drag the man through, huffing and grunting with each pull.

I chuckled at the amusing situation. Someone dragging their passed-out, intoxicated buddy back to their room at the crack of dawn wasn't anything new. It was a common occurrence back at the barracks. I wanted to plain laugh but choked it down. That would be rude. What I had to do was help. What kind of man would I be if I didn't? Bounding up the stairs two steps at a time, I darted after her, into the hall.

I grinned. "Need a hand?"

Freezing in place, the woman's head jerked up from her hunched position, hands still clamped under the man's arms. Shocked brown eyes gaped at me as her top lip curled up in a snarl.

I shuffled uncomfortably as her somewhat attractive slender face became anything but. I'd expected her to laugh and accept my gracious offer of assistance, but for some reason, she was glaring at me like I'd just pissed on her favorite shoes.

With a heavy slap, she dropped the man to the deck and pounced over him, landing to stand between me and the prone body, and forcing me a step back in surprise.

The woman was petite with a strange witchy kind of appearance. It's not that she was hideous, far from it, but something about her slender face and straight black hair had me thinking of black cats and such. Maybe a cauldron or two.

I leaned around her to look at the man. "Is he okay?"

The woman leaned just as quick to block my view.

"What makes you think I need help?" she snapped.

I shuffled, fiddling with my fingers. I couldn't understand the hostility. "It just seemed you were struggling, that's all."

Scanning over my wrinkled uniform, the scowl on her face deepened. "Are you a trooper?"

"Yes, ma'am, I am. Trooper Jake Adlar from fourth unit."

Her eyes narrowed to slits as her hands flew to her hips. "What the *fuck* are you doing on the officer's deck, then? You're not supposed to be up here."

"Uh…" I glanced around my surroundings in confusion.

Was I on the officer's deck? I hadn't even considered what deck I'd entered when I rushed to help her, but since the officer's deck was right above the pool, I supposed her accusation made sense.

Releasing a low growl, the woman's head spun as she gave the hall a hasty inspection. "Just get out of here! I don't need any help, he's just drunk. Now go!"

She made a frantic wave at the door.

Irritation bubbled within me. I snorted and flung my arms over my chest. It was my turn to scowl. Here I was, thoroughly beat, still taking the time to offer the lady a hand only for her to eye me like I was no better than dung.

"Fine. Suit yourself," I said.

With a snarl of my own, I gave her another loud snort, making sure she knew full well what I thought of her, then sauntered through the door and down the stairs. This time, I didn't hesitate to use the elevator. If there was someone in there who disapproved, they could be the ones to get their asses out.

This was only my first day on *Venator*, but I'd already had just about enough of this fucked-up Legion and everyone in it. I wasn't in the mood to deal with further bullshit. I was determined to take the shortest possible route back to my bunk, no matter whose judgment I had to endure.

Maybe I was just talking big before chickening out once more, but I'd never know. The elevator slid open to an empty compartment, and I rushed in, hurrying to select my deck before my luck turned. My anger about the strange encounter slowly subsided as I began to dread tomorrow's training.

Who cared about some chick's crazed behavior, anyway? It seemed like everyone here was a few coils short of a functional jump drive. Or, perhaps, she was just a mean drunk. Who knew? Besides, I had bigger things to worry about, like surviving Gundy on almost no sleep.

CHAPTER
TEN

Ness' whisper cut through my sleep as a hand clasped my shoulder and gently shook me.

"Wake up."

I groaned in reply. *Was it that time already?* I was dead tired, and my muscles ached as if I had run a marathon. Now I had to do it all over again.

"Just a bit longer," I mumbled, swatting her away and yanking the blanket over my head.

"Hmhm!" A loud cough sounded from somewhere below.

It was a man's cough.

Slowly, I pulled the blanket off and cracked open one eye. Two figures, neither of which were Ness, stood in our room. Cautiously, I opened the second eye. Two MPs were next to my bunk, glaring up at me.

"Uh..." I propped up on my elbows to get a better look. "What's... going on?"

"Are you Trooper Adlar?" one of the men asked.

"Yes sir, I am."

"Your Centurion wants to see you. We're here to escort you. Hurry up and get dressed, we don't have all day."

They turned and marched out, leaving Ness and me exchanging baffled glances.

"What the hell did you do?" Ness asked, eyes darting between me and the door.

"I'm not sure." I shrugged, sitting up.

My body still hurt, but all sleepiness had been chased right out of me. This was only my second day on the ship. What could the Centurion, the officer in charge of the entire unit, possibly want from me?

Heart rate spiking, I rushed off my bunk and threw on my uniform, then splashed water on my face and messed-up hair, trying to smooth it out. Maybe he wanted to discuss my shitty performance in the air tunnel. Or maybe Gundy had complained that I'd been messing around.

I grimaced at the sight of my reflection. The cowlicks and my groggy face didn't pin me as an exemplary trooper, but it would have to do. The MPs didn't seem of the patient sort, and I sure as shit didn't want to keep the Centurion waiting. In less than two minutes, I was out of my room and nervously tailing the MPs down the hall.

As we walked into the elevator, I turned to the heavier MP with a freckled round face and a gut to match.

"What's this about?" I asked.

"You'll find out when you get there," the guy replied without glancing my way.

I frowned but saw no point in questioning him further. Maybe he was as in the dark as I was and simply playing the escort. Instead, I nervously watched the ascending numbers on the control panel flash past all the lower decks. I suspected I was now only a deck or so away from the Tribune himself, the man in charge of every Legionnaire aboard this vessel.

What the hell had I done?

We exited the elevator into a brightly lit hall, and I was surprised to feel the springy softness of carpet under my boots. The entire fancy hall was carpeted, and the walls adorned with *actual* paintings. Not holographic projections or photos, but actual framed art, oil perhaps. They were all of massive ships in front of even more massive planets. I couldn't help but wonder if one of those giant ships was *Venator*.

The MPs led me to what I presumed was the Centurion's office. Not daring to venture in without an invitation, I remained in the hall and peeked inside. A tall man with broad shoulders, a square jaw, and piercing blue eyes stood behind a desk, talking with someone. He paused mid-sentence when he spotted me loitering in the doorway.

"Trooper Adlar?" he asked.

His voice was stern but not angry. Maybe this wasn't about some violation.

"Yes, sir."

"Come in," the man said, taking a seat behind his desk and gesturing to a chair across from him. "Shut the door."

Doing as told, I entered the office and swiped the door shut. The room was as lavish as the hall, except the décor here was Roman themed. Paintings of armies in ancient armor and victorious men on horseback brandishing swords adorned the walls. Squinting, I attempted to get a closer look at one, only to almost trip over my feet. A small, skinny figure had moved to stand beside the Centurion—one I instantly recognized.

It was none other than the woman I'd encountered the night before. The rude, witchy lady. Except now, she wasn't wearing the tight jeans and top I'd previously seen, and her black hair no longer swept freely around her shoulders. Instead, it was pulled back into a sleek bun, and she was dressed in an Earth Legion uniform—complete with giant gold earth emblems adorning both sides of her collar.

Holy shit! She was a freaking Centurion. My stomach flip-flopped as I took a seat. I must've sounded so stupid, prying into her business and snarking at her. If that wasn't already a long enough list of unacceptable behavior, I suddenly realized I had no idea if my eyes had wandered. In my tired state, had I unknowingly scanned her form in an inappropriate fashion? *Fuck, of course I had.* I remembered her lack of cleavage vividly.

After giving me a moment to fester in dread and probably turn sheet white, the Centurion placed his elbows on his desk and leaned towards me.

"I'm Centurion Paxton." He gestured towards the woman behind him. "This is Centurion Fallon. But I believe you two have already met."

My mouth went dry as I stupidly blinked at him. I wanted to squirm but controlled the urge. The tiny woman crossed her arms over her narrow chest and glowered at me. She seemed much less jumpy than last night but no happier.

Her face twisted into a scowl. "Yes. As a matter of fact, we have. Yesterday—"

A sudden clatter of glass behind me interrupted her and made me jump. We all turned to look. Another man was in the office, whom I'd missed seeing before, sitting in a chair backed against a wall and pouring himself a drink from a glass decanter. The sharp aroma of whiskey wafted through the air as the brownish liquid splashed into his glass. Like Paxton, he was also built like a dump truck, except rougher around the edges, and had Centurion insignia glimmering on his collar.

The man stopped pouring when he realized the room had grown quiet and looked up. He placed the decanter on the table next to him, swishing the liquor in his glass in a leisurely fashion.

"Keep going, keep going." He gestured with a hand. "Don't mind me."

He had a light Australian accent and a brimming grin on his face. He didn't appear at all concerned by the fact it was early morning, and he was clutching a drink.

I looked back at Fallon, right as her eyes narrowed to slits.

"Why are you even here, Braves?"

The man Fallon had referred to as Braves leaned back in his chair and calmly sipped his drink, casually crossing one leg over his knee. He didn't seem bothered by Fallon's obvious dislike of him, nor was he trying to hide his amusement.

"Ehh… the VR rooms were all booked, sooo…."

He gestured over us with a slow sweep of one hand. "I thought I would join `ya for whatever this is. Pretend I'm not even here. Keep on with your stories."

I turned back to the two Centurions. Paxton retained an impassive expression while Fallon bared her teeth, and an eye kind of twitched. She looked like she wanted to detonate.

"Fine," she hissed. "Let's just get on with this. As I was saying, last night, I discovered one of your troopers," she glared at me, "this one right here, lurking around the officers' decks. I feel such a blatant violation must be addressed *immediately*."

My heart hammered faster as the wheels in my head turned. This was about me being on an officer's deck? *Seriously?* Sure, I'd broken the "suggested" rules, but I couldn't have taken more than two steps past the stairwell entrance, and it was only to see if she needed a hand. There was no way I was about to get in trouble for that. *Was I?*

My palms grew clammy, and I squirmed as if sitting on hot coals. Punishments in the Legions were no joke. They didn't consist of cooling your heels in the brig or extra duty assignments, but of floggings and power-bolts to the chest. Was that what was coming my way?

I studied Paxton intently, trying to gauge his expression, but the man's stony face was unreadable. Nodding slowly, he appeared to mull over the woman's words.

"I see, Centurion Fallon," he spoke at last, leaning back in his chair and rubbing his chin in a way that reminded me of my CO back on Earth.

"Are you aware, trooper Adlar, that you are not to be on the officers' decks unless requested?"

"Uh..." My mind raced, figuring out if I should be honest or feign ignorance.

After all, this was only my second day on the ship. Perhaps claiming I didn't know any better would get me a pass on any physical punishment. Then again, lying, especially to commanding officers, carried with it even a harsher sentence.

I decided to do a bit of both.

"I am, sir. I was just looking around and got lost. I apologize."

"There, he admitted it!" Fallon jabbed a bony finger in my direction triumphantly. "He was in fact on an officer's deck, where he wasn't supposed to be."

Paxton pulled back, seemingly surprised by her exuberance.

He eyed Fallon sidelong then turned to me. "Can you promise us you're not going to be on the officers' decks again without an invitation, trooper?"

"Yes sir, I can!" I said, trying not to sound too enthusiastic.

The man seemed reasonable, so just maybe he'd give me a pass and this whole horrid encounter would conclude. Unfortunately for me, Centurion Paxton might've been reasonable, but Centurion Fallon wasn't. The woman was a freaking psycho. On a flip of a dime, she reverted back to the spastic demeanor I'd witnessed the night before.

"Are you serious, Paxton?" She rounded on him, hands on her hips and voice almost shouting. "That's all you have to say? We discussed this already!"

My face scrunched at her brashness. *What a bitch,* I thought internally. She wasn't going to let this go.

Concentrating on my Centurion, I silently hoped he wasn't as crazy. The man blinked, looking baffled. I didn't know what it was they'd discussed, but apparently, he'd missed each and every word.

Glass clinked behind me as Braves chuckled, but I was too scared to look. *Was this woman about to have me flogged, or worse?*

A moment later, I realized why Braves was enjoying this particular show. As Paxton, Fallon, and I blinked at each other in bewilderment, I couldn't help but recognize an all too-familiar look in Paxton's eyes. It was one of a man who had no idea what he'd done wrong and why his lady was mad at him, but knew that she was.

An involuntary smile tugged at my lips, but knowing what was good for me, I stifled it. Paxton looked lost, trying to figure out how to smooth out the situation. His eyes darted between Fallon and me, momentarily even landing on Braves.

"I mean…" he began with a shrug.

He froze mid-sentence when his eyes met Fallon's. The woman was pissed.

Shifting in his seat, Paxton smartly reconsidered finishing.

"What would *you* recommend we do, Fallon?" he said instead.

The witchy woman stuck her nose up at me victoriously. "I say we ship him back to Earth immediately and be done with him."

Centurion Paxton appeared stunned by the drastic suggestion. Even Braves let out a low whistle. For my part, I perked up with hope and excitement. Here I was, expecting to be sentenced to pain, only to receive a punishment that was a godsend. I wanted nothing more than to go back to Earth.

"Isn't that a bit extreme, Centurion?" Paxton asked.

I groaned internally with disappointment.

"No, not at all. It's paramount we maintain discipline on the ship, and I'm certain that is something this trooper does not possess, or will *ever* possess. We'll all be better off if he's sent back to Earth. The sooner, the better. On the next scheduled transport, perhaps."

She leaned a fraction closer to Paxton's ear. "We talked about this."

Paxton hesitated for a breath, perhaps again attempting to recall the mysterious conversation, but then determination crossed over his steely eyes. I resisted an audible sigh as all hope drained from me. I could tell he was composing himself to deny Fallon her wishes, and that both his girlfriend and I were about to be extremely disappointed.

Taking in a deep breath, Paxton stood and faced Centurion Fallon, squarely.

"I'm sorry, Centurion, I just can't do that. My unit needs bodies, and I can't send a man away for such a minor infraction. Not this close to a drop. Now, trooper Adlar said he'll be more careful in the future and seeing as he's still new to this ship, I don't see the need to pursue this matter any further."

Fallon's eyes narrowed, and her lips pursed as she stared daggers at Paxton. But the man didn't budge. I resisted narrowing my own eyes. This pain-in-the-ass woman was really starting to irk me. What the fuck was her problem, anyway? All I did was offer her help.

Then, something inside my slow brain clicked.

I straightened, throwing Fallon a wide-eyed glance. Could it be that Centurion Paxton knew nothing about her "drunk" friend if that's what the man even was? Who knew what story the crazy bitch had woven in my absence? Perhaps there was even foul play involved. What if she'd been dragging a corpse? Thinking back, I couldn't recall smelling alcohol, then again, I *was* pretty tired.

Fallon didn't miss my sudden change of expression and divined my thoughts. A flash of uncertainty crossed her face. I could see the wheels in her head also turning as she debated how to proceed.

"Fine!" She threw up her hands in defeat. "If you're not going to enforce discipline in your unit, so be it!"

With that, she rushed out the door, but not before tossing each one of us a dirty glance. Paxton held his stoic expression.

When she disappeared, he turned to me. "You're dismissed, trooper. Go join your squad in training. We have a drop coming up."

I didn't have to be told twice and jumped out of my chair, aimed at the door.

Braves chuckled, lifting his glass in a toast. "Better than VR, ehh?"

Having no words for the man, I rushed past him and into the hall.

"Hey! You need an escort!" sounded a shout behind me as I made for the stairs.

It was the burly MP from earlier, but I ignored him. My mind reeled. The woman's nasty attitude had me replaying every moment of last night in search of an explanation, why she was so eager to be rid of me. Had I just stumbled into some lover's triangle, and she wanted me off the ship so my Centurion wouldn't find out?

Mulling over my newest misfortune, I rushed down the stairs, absentmindedly shoving past chattering people. Whatever had just happened, I was sure of one thing. I had zero desire to get further involved in any of it. The brass' personal matters were none of my business. Yet, something about the woman's last glance twisted my gut. It had been cold and calculating, like some dead-eyed reptile taking measure.

A heavy sigh escaped me as I reached my deck. As if being on SL Gundy's shit-list wasn't enough, I was now smack-dab in the crosshairs of some crazed Centurion.

CHAPTER
ELEVEN

S hoving my newest mishap out of my mind, I hustled to rejoin my squad. I had no idea what just happened, but I figured I'd keep my mouth shut and let the brass sort out their own personal issues. What kind of ass-kicking my tardiness was about to earn me was of greater concern.

After getting into my heavy-gear and a good bit of searching through the labyrinth of passageways, I finally located my squad. They happened to be at my most favorite place on the ship, the darn air tunnel. Everyone was leaning over the opening, observing whoever was flailing around in there. I slowly approached, keeping a close eye on Gundy's fists.

"If it isn't the man of the hour!" Gundy exclaimed when he noticed me.

His visor was set to clear, and an egging glint danced in his eyes. "Brown-nosing the brass already, huh?"

As one, all heads popped away from the tunnel and spun to me. The aggravating man was on squad-chat. Shuffling nervously, I only shrugged in reply. I wasn't about to go into details with the likes of him.

An uncomfortable silence followed as the squad stared at me and I at them. The sour bunch was like a gaggle of old ladies awaiting some juicy gossip. With a shake of his head, Gundy at last dropped the topic.

"Here." He threw me an air pack and a retractor. "Don't want the drop to kill you before the brass does."

He chuckled menacingly. I caught the pack mid-air, but the retractor clattered to the floor.

Ness picked it up for me.

"What did the Centurion want?" she asked over private chat.

"Nothin'," I dismissed, taking it from her and rushing to the tunnel. I had no desire to recount my visit.

As I geared, I kept an eye on Gundy, wondering how much he knew and why his fist wasn't slamming into any part of me. The man enjoyed hassling me too much to pass up this opportunity, yet all I'd gotten was a snarky comment. Perhaps he was saving my punishment for after I made a fool of myself again, but that too didn't jibe. He didn't strike me as being reserved.

The air loudly whooshed past me as I again found myself face-to-face with the gaping entrance, but this time, I didn't wait for Gundy's boot to provide me the necessary motivation. Picturing the pool on the bottom of the chute, I sucked in a steadying breath, then leaped. The SL had been right; it was all about not fearing the fall. As the air lifted me up, I stretched out my arms and legs, bent at the knees, and actually balanced.

A moment later, the buzzer blared its horrific cry, but unlike last time, I didn't panic. Instead, as gravity had its way, I smoothly maneuvered out of the arch position, then tipped up. With a hard kick of the thrusters, the suit righted me and the air pack hissed, slowing my descent.

Regretfully, the landing didn't go as smoothly. Right as my boots clattered onto the grate, I somehow pitched backward, causing the last burst of propellant to send me skidding, head-first, into the wall. Squad-chat erupted with bouts of howling laughter, but I didn't care. Rubbing my helmet, even though that did nothing for my head, I grinned victoriously. I now knew I at least had a chance of making it down to the ground in one piece when the time came. That was a win in my book. Last night's training at the pool was worth every lingering bruise.

Unfortunately, the Legion, and possibly the universe at this point, had no intention of allowing my joy to continue. When the entire cohort was first herded into a chilled, theater-style auditorium, I felt great. Not only because class time meant no PT time, or in my case, less having the shit kicked out of me time, but also because I was looking forward to getting a nap while the brass blathered. Even if I did have to do it with one eye open while leaning on my hand to hide the closed one. Sure, it wasn't the most comfortable of positions, but I'd take what I could get.

Switching hands, I was about to let the other eye have some rest, while some clerical higher-up droned about water usage and what-not, when an unexpected sight perked me up. Three very familiar Centurions marched onto the stage, following the sharp-faced man who'd watched our arrival from the control room window. The man, who I now knew to be Prefect Neero, proceeded to the podium as the three Centurions rushed to line up in parade rest at his back. All appeared wary of the Prefect.

I then discovered what Gundy meant by "we have a drop coming up," and it had a lightning bolt shoot through my body. The drop was the day after tomorrow.

I forgot all about taking a nap. I didn't think I was ready. Wide-eyed, I glanced at the troops around me to see if anyone else was shocked by the ridiculous timeline, but I couldn't tell. Everyone sat motionless, eyes front and center, locked on the Prefect. Was I the only one worried about this, or were the rest of the troops just better at hiding their concern?

A light rustling and hushed whispers sounded behind me, but before I could investigate, a hard slap landed across the back of my swiveling head. A shadow fell over me as a large figure leaned over my shoulder, so close that warmth radiated onto the side of my neck and face.

"How was your nap, boy?" SL Gundy growled into my ear.

I gulped. I guess Gundy was up to date on trooper nap tactics even if we weren't on Earth.

"Now that you got your beauty sleep, princess, hows about you pay attention. If you want, I can stand right here and point your head forward. Does that sound like something you'd like, boy?"

I shook my head, but only slightly. I didn't want to imagine what would happen if I accidentally grazed his cheek.

"No sir. I'll point my head forward myself, sir."

"See to it that you do. I don't think you want the Prefect seeing you're in need of some extra motivation, do you? Neero loves himself some fresh meat."

Gundy chuckled, his hot breath tickling my ear. I did everything in my power to resist scratching the itch, as I was sure that wouldn't bode well for me, and I wanted this encounter to end before the Prefect noticed a disturbance in the audience. *Venator* swarmed with tales of him dolling out harsh punishments for the most minor of infractions.

Neero was our cohort's interim Prefect. A field promotion of sorts, after the cohorts original Prefect and two Primus' all mysteriously vanished during the last campaign. Rumors claimed that it was Neeros' doing. Then, when he didn't receive the coveted promotion that he was all too sure was his, permanently, he was less than thrilled. Since shit rolled downhill, it promptly rolled right on top of the ground troops.

It turned out Gundy was right to incentivize me to pay attention, even if I wasn't a fan of the delivery method. The Prefect wasn't up on the stage to discuss water concerns or whatever else the other speakers had prattled on about during my nap. He was up there to brief us on the upcoming drop.

By now, thanks to Gundy's screaming run sessions, I knew the gist of the Legion's tactics. Eradicating the Synths wasn't as easy as dropping a bomb. Domed, force-field type shields covered their outposts, and even with improvements from our alien allies, our weapons weren't capable of penetrating. Or if they did, when delivered at slow speeds, most simply deactivated due to some kind of electrical interference or some such.

Not that Earth had the option of sending in a nuke snail-mail anyhow, even if the weapon would successfully neutralize the target. See, unlike the Synths, Earth had to worry about a giant inconvenience called civilians. The Legions couldn't just bomb the hell out of every planet the Synths infested. That would create enemies of the local inhabitants and possibly drag Earth into yet another war—or *worse*.

An even darker entity lurked in the nether—the ancients. They were our overlords, *everyone's* overlords, and they weren't keen on their subjects nuking planets. We hadn't actually met them yet as they ruled though their proxies, the sleeks, and that was fine by us. There was an unspoken consensus amongst species that it was best not to stir them from the shadows.

As such, the Legions employed guerilla-type tactics to target only the Synths. We were annihilating Earth's enemy while also liberating the locals. At least that was the propaganda drilled into the troops. From the tales floating around the ship, I wasn't sure the locals viewed our military actions as humanitarian as the Senate tried to portray them, but nobody was asking the opinion of the rank-and-file.

"Listen up, troops!" Prefect Neero's bark echoed around the dead-silent auditorium as he swiped a picture off his tablet to the wall behind him.

The plain wall shimmered and transformed into a screen. An aerial snapshot of a jungle with a massive mountain formation cutting through the middle materialized. By now, I'd learned that the Synths liked to set up shop on planets similar to their original home world, which was comparable to Earth, so I wasn't surprised that besides the purple hues in the canopy, the jungle scene was reminiscent of the Amazon. A large red circle overlaid a chunk of the mountain, with three blue lines converging on it from different directions. Two approached the target on one side and a third from the other.

Wide-eyed, I fixated on the line with a four next to it, pointing towards the red circle at an eight o'clock angle. That was us, fourth unit. In one day and a wake up, I was going to nosedive into that jungle along the course laid out before us. Suddenly, the air tunnel, the pool, the shooting range, and the tiresome arena exercises became all the more real. I hoped all the bruises I'd so far earned weren't for nothing.

The Prefect threw a cold glance at the image as he spoke. "We've designated this planet Atlas. It's the third planet in a single star system and though it's in the middle of nowhere, it's now a priority target. So far, we've tracked a single outpost."

He aimed a finger at the image. "There. And the Senate wants it leveled before the Synths dig in or get any ideas about expanding.

That being said, since this is our first interaction with the local inhabitants, the Senate wants it to be known we *care*."

The way he'd growled *care* made it very obvious that he, himself, didn't.

"Campaign's been designated green. Use of beam weapons isn't authorized," he finished.

The rest of the auditorium echoed the disapproval. Groans erupted and arms flew up. I thought about it and understood both angles. Beam weapons, or beamers, operated by a heavy specialist, were similar to an RPG. Except instead of firing missiles, they fired a five-second beam of concentrated energy laced with rads. They were able to cut through almost anything. Stone, metal, aliens, you name it. They'd slice right through, making our job that much easier. However, they had a drawback. They left residual radiation in their wake. Now on planets the Senate couldn't care less about, the campaigns were marked red. Meaning anything and everything in a trooper's path was to be mowed down. No one cared about poisoning the planet in the process.

The Prefect gave his disgruntled audience a few seconds to let out their frustration, then raised a hand, palm forward. The auditorium silenced in an instant.

"The gravity is about eighty-five percent of Earth's normal, and oxygen content is at nineteen percent. Weather patterns…"

He cut off with a horse bark, and looked up from the podium.

"You don't need to worry about the weather patterns. I don't give a damn if a tornado suddenly sprouts; every trooper is to stay on mission. Clear the area as you advance towards the target. Kill as many of them as you can. Kill everything and get it done. Is that understood?"

"Yes, sir!" erupted a unified chorus, right as a lanky man in a lab coat bolted onto the stage, stopping to the left of the Prefect.

Slowly, with tiny steps, he edged forward to where he was in the Prefect's peripheral vision and raised a shaky finger to get Neero's attention. Pushing up his thick-rimmed glasses, he shuffled uncomfortably, mumbling under his breath. The Prefect rewarded the lab-coat with a deep scowl but yielded the stage, retreating to stand by the statue-still Centurions. The three hadn't flinched a muscle the entire presentation.

The lab-coat rushed to the podium. "No, no, don't kill everything! Please don't do that."

He threw a nervous glance at the Prefect, then turned back to us, fidgeting with a shimmering holo-cube while mumbling something about anomalous radiation readings in orbit and other sciency explanations on why this planet was so important. I strained to listen, curious, but it was fruitless.

"Ahh, here!" he spoke clearly at last as a hologram of a moth-like creature popped into the air. I grimaced in disgust. It looked to be the size of a large house cat, with patterned grayish wings and six spiky insect legs. Three black marble-sized eyeballs bulged from its fuzzy head.

"These are the local inhabitants," the lab-coat explained, gazing up at the image with reverence. "And it is in their honor that we've designated the planet Atlas after one of the largest lepidopterans back on Earth, native to Asia with a wingspan of—"

The Prefect loudly cleared his throat.

The lab-coat shuffled fearfully and quickly decided to give us the bullet point version of whatever speech he'd prepared, constantly reiterating the importance of us being careful not to harm the freaky creatures. Apparently, the things displayed a hive-like insect mentality, and pissing off one could prompt the rest to attack. Something like that wouldn't exactly shine a holy light on the Legion. Nor would it aid in furthering interspecies cooperation if such a thing was even possible. We had no idea what opinions the moths harbored about our invasion—or humans in general.

The next thing to project into the air was what the lab-coats presumed to be the moth's natural predator, and shockingly, it too wasn't a looker. The scruffy boar-like creature had a head similar to a pig's but with the sharp fangs of a saber tooth tiger. I suspected the scientist, who seemed extremely fascinated with the planet and the locals, had much more he wanted to say, but the Prefect finally had enough. Taking two long strides towards the man, he grabbed him by the back of his collar and yanked him away from the podium. A loud squeal escaped the stumbling lab-coat as he flailed his arms, trying to catch his footing. A second later, his rushed footsteps echoed around the auditorium as he hightailed it to the exit.

Shortly after the theatrics, we were dismissed and all looking forward to a late lunch, which unfortunately wasn't to be. Instead, to the dismay of the entire squad, Gundy tortured us with what he referred to as the "Adlar jog." Not sure why he called it a jog, though, since it turned out to be a fast-paced five-mile run in full kit.

"Listen up," Gundy shouted as we cleared our third loop around the track.

Most of us were huffing by then, starting to sweat in our suits even with the temp regulators. Pops and zaps echoed from somewhere in the arena, but my attention jerked from the live fire as I dodged yet another flying fist from a pissed-off teammate. Everyone was grumbling and cursing, blaming me for the experience.

"Let me fill you in on tenth squad's mission, the one and only reason you gnats exist," Gundy boomed.

"We're the clean-up squad. None of you wastes of suits have enough field experience to be of any better use. We're gonna be the last to drop, then trail behind the actual fighters, troopers worth a damn, picking up equipment such as air packs and evacuating the injured."

The scavenger hunt exercise, along with the hover-carts and gurneys, now made sense.

"When possible, you're also to retrieve the dead. If there's enough of them left to collect that is. If not, you're to retrieve the most expensive part of the heavy-gear get-up, the helmet."

He tapped a finger on his head, which sounded a muffled *thud, thud, thud,* over comms.

"This bucket right here costs pretty penny and is to be salvaged whatever possible."

I gulped, mulling over Gundy's instructions. Prior to the transport, I'd yet to see a dead body, and now I was about to see many. I thanked my lucky stars I was in tenth squad. Pulling helmets off of left-over chunks of people was going to be gruesome for sure, but it was better than turning into said chunks myself.

Following the run, Gundy dragged us to the shooting range, but shortly after getting there, was called away to join the brass for meetings, and we were dismissed. Bone-tired, I took a quick shower and dragged myself to my bunk, half-waving at Ness, who was perched on top of her desk, chatting and giggling with some chick pressed up on her arm.

"Wake me up for dinner," I mumbled, climbing up and pulling up the covers.

Inhaling a long, pleasant whiff of whatever lavender products the girls had used, I slept the sleep of the dead.

CHAPTER
TWELVE

The blare of a horn jolted me awake. It screeched on a loop in three blast intervals. Panicked, I jumped out of my bunk and threw on my uniform like a toddler learning to dress. I almost did a facer while trying to don my pants. At last dressed, I charged the door in fear for my life.

"What are you up to now, Adlar?" came Ness's groggy voice. "Are the MPs here to drag you away again?"

Turning, I saw her sleepy face with partially closed eyes looking down at me from her bunk. She chuckled.

"Isn't there some sort of an emergency?" I asked.

What if *Venator* was under attack or venting air? My mind raced with the thousands of possibilities of what could go wrong in space.

Ness laughed, rubbing the sleep out of her eyes, and with a loud sigh, began getting out of her bunk.

"You didn't pay attention to Gundy at all, did you, Jake?"

"Uh... sure I did," I lied.

Well, semi-lied. I'd caught some stuff between the exhaustion, discomfort, the beatings, and my very short attention span.

Ness climbed down and plopped onto her chair, doing a spin. "That's not an alarm. It's the pre-deployment horn. Three blasts mean we have two hours until we need to be at the dropships, but feel free to go gear up now."

She pointed at the door, grinning. "I'm sure Gundy will commend your eagerness."

Leaning back, she did another spin. My tension slightly subsided, and my panting eased. However, I must've still looked confused because Ness elaborated.

"They don't want anyone sleeping through the drop, that's all. It's not like anyone's going to walk down the hall herding our asses."

"I didn't even know we'd reached Atlas," I mumbled, finally feeling safe enough to part with the door.

I made my way to my chair and sat. "Or that we came out of hyperspace."

Ness shrugged. "I didn't wake up either, but we must've been here for at least four hours or more. First cohort must be almost back from their drop since they're getting us ready. They can't drop all of us at once, or else the Synths won't bother deploying troops. They'll just obliterate us all with heavy weapons."

Jumping out of her chair, Ness made her way to the mirror and proceeded to spike her hair. I watched her get each spike just right, having no idea why. She was about to spend who knew how long in a helmet. Enjoying her gel's fruity scent, I decided not to point that out.

Instead, as she continued to chatter, worry again impinged on my mind. Sure, we weren't in any immediate danger, but about two hours from now, I was going to be shoved out of a perfectly flight-worthy ship to fall through thousands of feet of atmo onto an *actual* alien planet. It was daunting.

"Jake!"

I glanced up to see that Ness had finished her needless beauty routine and was now wiping her goopy fingers on her uniform.

She jerked her head towards the door. "Come on. Let's go grab a bite, then head to gear up."

I followed Ness to breakfast where all I managed was an egg, I was so queasy, then we headed to the equipment room. Even though we were early, second cohort's hangar bay was hopping with activity. Hordes of Space Fleet personnel rushed around the dropships, completing their final checks and securing containers and equipment to the decks with cargo straps and magnetic clamps.

I threw a glance at the far end of the hangar. The inner airlock doors were now retracted, leaving only the outer door between us and the unforgiving, endless void beyond. During a full cohort deployment, the entire bay was vented, instead of vessels taking the time to use the airlock.

A fully suited Gundy was already by our dropship, hunched over the air packs, as Ness and I walked up. Standing, he zeroed in on me and released a frustrated growl. Not in the mood to deal with his crap, I veered away and beelined for the bow of the ship.

"Where do you think you're going, maggot!" he barked to my back.

Ness chuckled as my head dropped in defeat. With a deep inhale, I turned and shuffled to stand before him. I had no clue what his problem was, but he didn't waste any time and bit right into me.

"I don't know what you did, and I don't want to know," he barked, "but thanks for showing up early and saving me the trouble of having to buzz your watch, those things just annoy the crap out of me."

He scowled as I silently waited for him to get to the point, to tell me what I'd done wrong this time. Hopefully his lecture wasn't going to drag.

"All right, down to business."

He loudly clapped his gloved hands, then stuck a large finger right up to my nose.

"You've been transferred, boy. Now, take that gear off," he poked me in the chest, "and go gear up in Gold Squad's equipment room."

Not budging, my eyes jumped between the SL's finger and his scowling face. *Did he just say something about Gold Squad?* The Gold Squads were each unit's first three squads, the cream of the crop as far as everyone was concerned.

Gundy shook his head at my confused stare, placing his hands on his hips.

"This just figures. I have to deal with training your ass, and just like that, the Centurion pulls you. I tried telling him you're no good for first squad. Hell, I'm not certain you would've lasted a single drop on the clean-up brigade. But the Centurion wasn't having it. For whatever reason, he's dead set on moving you. So that's where you're going."

"But that's—" I tried to protest, only for Gundy to cut me off.

"You're in first squad now, boy." He clapped a heavy hand onto my shoulder, a wolfish grin on his face and glee sparkling in his mocking eyes.

Befuddled, I threw a wary glance in the direction of Gold Squad's equipment room then back at him. His words weren't registering. The Gold Squads were the best of the best, the most experienced of the troops. What could they want with me?

Ness jumped to my aid. "How is that possible, SL? It doesn't make sense. Don't those squads drop the closest to the target? You yourself said we aren't good for shit!"

Gundy barked a hearty laugh, not bothering to hide the fact he was savoring every second of this.

"You aint! And you're right about that, the Gold Squads drop right in the middle of those drooling beasts! I have no idea what Adlar did to make this happen, but after three days of dealing with him, I sure as hell can believe it."

His smirk vanished as he grabbed my arm and roughly shoved me away. "Now stop wasting my time and get!"

I stumbled but caught my footing, locking Ness' gaze. Concern veiled her eyes, but this was out of our hands. Not knowing what else to do, I turned away and started walking. My mind reeled. How the hell had I been transferred to a Gold Squad, and not just any Gold Squad, but first squad?

When I arrived at Gold Squad's equipment room, I was no closer to solving the mystery, but I ambled inside, nonetheless. I feebly greeted the men working there. They were checking equipment and fumbling with helmets and suit parts.

"What's up, trooper?" one asked, acknowledging my arrival with a nod.

He was sitting behind a projection table, sifting through lines of code that danced in the air. A half-disassembled helmet lay on the screen beside him. It flashed and beeped in response to his waggling fingers.

"I was told to come here and get suited," I said.

The guy's fingers froze as he stared at me with a flat expression. Then, exchanging glances with the other men, they all busted out laughing. I felt my cheeks flush. Was it that obvious I didn't belong?

"Wrong equipment room, dude," a voice grabbed my attention.

Spinning towards it, I saw a lanky man grinning at me from next to the blaster racks. He had a surfer drawl to his tone and one hell of a peculiar haircut. The bottom half of his head was shaved, and the rest of his blond hair was pulled back in a stubby ponytail. Completely against regs as far as I knew.

His eyes gave me a slow once over. "Plus, it looks like you already have your suit on, man, so you better skedaddle to whatever light squad you're in."

He waved a hand at the door.

"I'm... being sent to first squad. SL Gundy said to change suits."

At my statement, a guy sitting over another holo-desk perked up with interest and narrowed his eyes at me in suspicion. He was a stocky fellow with a buzz cut and a mischievous face.

"SL Gundy? That's tenth squad, isn't it?" he said. "And all of a sudden you're moved to first? Just like that?"

I nodded, shuffling uncomfortably under their strange stares. Their blatant amusement at the possibility of me being some lost fool who'd wandered in here by accident had given way to a shifty vibe. Fists flew over mouths as some stifled laughter and odd looks were exchanged. For some reason, they were now acting like they were in on some joke I wasn't in on.

"So, just to be clear." The man next to buzz-cut leaned towards me, also smirking. "You were in tenth squad, then, *poof*." He made an explosive motion with his fingers. "Just like that, you're in first?"

I shrugged. "Looks like it, I guess."

More shifty glances were thrown about, and one man plain laughed. My concern intensified just like my confusion, but I opted to keep my mouth shut and let them get it out of their system. It took them a whole minute, but they at last simmered down.

Huffing, buzz-cut hauled himself from his chair. "Fine, enough wasting time. You must be the new arrival we were notified of. You weren't what we'd expected, but orders are orders, so let's get you suited."

Donning a transmitter, he humped to stand before me and extended a holo-cube in my direction. I pulled back as a wide beam of green light scanned over me, squinting when the blinding glow hit my eyes. It vanished after getting through with my head. When that happened, the man tossed the cube onto his table's holo-screen.

"Maybe it's a mistake," I offered, hopeful. "You sure the notice was about me and not someone else?"

"Unfortunately not." He scowled at the holo-table. "The computer just pinged you as it, and now that we know your basic dimensions, your issued suit will adjust for the details."

Turning to the table, I eyed the scrolling redouts dubiously. I supposed it had been wishful thinking that Gundy had gotten it wrong. The cube's glow intensified as the myriad of colors inside it spun, transferring data. When it beeped, the man headed towards the racks of heavy-gear suits, cursing and grumbling all the while.

"Waste of equipment, that's what this is. Don't they know how much stuff we already refurbish? We're practically patching these back together with tape and tact-glue!"

Lugging over a heavy-gear suit, he began checking the helmet and the unfamiliar boxy contraptions mounted to the forearms.

Not wanting to be a pain, I followed their instructions without comment. I stuffed my arms and legs where they told me to stuff them and turned when they told me to turn. Within minutes they had me in a heavy-gear suit that wasn't at all like my last. Sure, it was the same basic design, but it felt different. Different to the extent I couldn't help but wonder why the other suits weren't called light-gear.

"It's a bit tight," I complained, raising my arms.

Even though *a bit tight* was an understatement. It felt like my chest was in a vice.

"It's fine!" The man slapped my hands away from my breastplate. I was yanking on it, trying to pull it away from my chest.

"The computer said this was your size, so this is your size. These aren't like the ones lower squads get where the padding simply expands. These are *all* laced with smart material. The nanites are in both the padding and the metal composite, so the suit will slowly adjust, then save your settings."

"So the next time you drop," he tossed an amused glance at his buddies, "we'll have a suit ready for you."

I frowned, both at his goading attitude and at my total discomfort.

"Here." He shoved a helmet into my arms. "I guess we won't be seeing this ever again. I might as well mark it out of inventory now."

I accepted the helmet absentmindedly, watching the surfer guy by the blaster racks. Unlike that of his asshole companion, the crooked grin on his face wasn't dripping with malice. There was a shred of understanding and possibly concern in his careworn gaze.

Noting me staring at him, he clicked the blaster he was holding into a charging port, released a small sigh, then walked my way. Or more accurately, waddled. A strange limp accompanied each of his steps. I side-eyed his leg discreetly, not wanting to be rude. Nowadays, anything besides death or total dismemberment was reparable. Yet, oddly, the man was limping.

Coming to stand beside me, he clapped a hand onto back. I jerked in surprise. What I'd felt wasn't simply a *thump* on the shell of my suit, but his entire hand, every one of his fingers as if on bare skin.

"Surprised you felt that, right?" he said.

I nodded, both confused and worried. If I could feel that, how was this get-up supposed to protect me?

He grinned at my concerned expression. "Don't worry, the pressure-relaying strands only work when there's no substantial force, like with touch. So it'll still protect you from being shot, blown up, and what-not. It's similar to tenth squad gear in that regard, only better."

I nodded again, grateful that at least *someone* was considerate enough to explain something to me.

"And don't listen to Hughes, man," he continued, beaming at buzz-cut. "He's just pissed his leave was denied... *again*. And no woman on the ship gives him a second look."

"Whaa—" Hughes glowered, then flipped him off. "Screw you, Cavelli."

"That'd make one of us," Cavelli retorted before turning back to me. "Good luck out there, okay? I mean it."

He gave my back another hard slap then gestured at the door. I got the hint.

Sighing and feeling like I was now encapsulated in a freaking tank, I exited the equipment room and trudged back to the dropships, the very much undeserved golden earth insignia sparkling bright on my breastplate.

CHAPTER
THIRTEEN

"Ahh… finally," greeted a burley, dark-haired man as I approached.

He lumbered towards me, opening his arms wide in a welcome. "Finally, we get another trooper. We've been short for ages."

I slowed my steps and hesitated. Sure enough, unlike the usual eight to ten troops per squad, only three milled around first squad's dropship. A shiver ran down my spine at the fact. I doubted their other squadmates were simply on leave.

"Let him breathe." A man broke away from the dropship and strode over to me. He had a dominating presence that seemed to take over the bay. "You must be Adlar. I was just notified of the transfer, but that's the Legion for you, right?"

His chiseled features, piercing blue eyes, and sandy hair looked strangely familiar.

Resisting my very strong urge to fidget and shy away, I raised my arm to meet his. He grabbed it before it was fully lifted and gave me a firm shake.

"Welcome to first squad. I'm SL Paxton, but you can call me Pax, and we're sure glad to finally get another man. Mills here especially."

He slapped the burly man on his back. "Mills is our heavy. Well, usually, for the missions that allow it."

Turning, he pointed at an Asian man near the dropship, hunched over an air pack. "That's Lee over there, our tech specialist."

He looked around, then back at me. "And I don't know where Somner is, but you'll meet him soon enough. Now, I know we didn't get to train together, but I'm guessing you know the drill by now. What cohort did you transfer from, anyway? First or third? I haven't seen you around second."

I sucked in a strained breath, deciding there was no point in lying. There was going to be no hiding my inexperience. With my luck, I'd trip over my own feet in the next minute or so.

"I'm actually not from another cohort. I was transferred from tenth squad."

Taking a step back, the two men exchanged concerned glances, then both turned to Lee, who had stopped fidgeting with the equipment to also stare at me.

Then, both Mills and Lee groaned in unison.

"Awww… man." Mills waved a dismissive hand at me. "It's just another *poof*."

"A what?" I asked, confused. The guy in the equipment room had used the exact same word but hadn't elaborated.

"A *poof*," Lee shouted over his shoulder, scooting over to another air pack. "You pissed someone off, didn't you? Some officer or some connected civilian employee. Maybe hit on someone's girlfriend or something?"

"Uh… I don't think so," I replied as my gaze dropped to the deck in thought.

His peculiar comment had me scratch my head. Then, slowly but surely, as I stared at my boots, unfocused, an unsavory premonition began to come to light. I suddenly realized what had brought on this odd turn of events, or more precisely *who*.

Breaking away from the dropship, Lee came to stand next to the SL, crossing his arms. "You're not the first one we've gotten." He scanned me over with a smirk. "A *poof* is what we call someone who gets sent here to disappear. You know what I mean?"

Unfortunately, by now, the picture was clear enough, and it wasn't pretty.

Lee's eyes fixated on my waist. He barked a loud laugh and nudged the SL. "Actually, Pax, we should call this one fireball."

"Aww… come on Lee," the SL said. "Give the guy a break, I think he's freaked out enough already. Go finish getting the gear ready, the double bell is heading our way."

Lee mumbled something under his breath and shook his head, but obeyed and retreated to the dropship. I, however, didn't budge. I was too busy seething internally and running out of creative curses for who I thought was responsible. Plus, it's not as if I had any idea on what to do anyhow.

Saying nothing and with a smirk still on his face, the SL stepped towards me and reached for my waist. He then yanked off the four egg-shaped devices attached there, one by one, like he was plucking grapes. I shook off my anger and paid attention. I'd noticed the strange gizmos when I was gearing up, but, having no idea what they were, hadn't messed with them.

"I think I'll take the frags from you, for now," he said, reattaching them to his own suit. "Unless you can guarantee that you're going to land on your feet when you drop?"

His eyes locked with mine. I'd had no idea that the black eggs were explosives. They looked nothing like regular grenades and had no markings. There wasn't even a safety pin.

I fidgeted, then concluded that the question wasn't rhetorical. I quickly shook my head *no*.

"I highly doubt I'd land on my feet even on my tenth drop," I said.

If I happened to still be alive by then, I silently thought to myself.

The SL chuckled. "Here." He waved me towards the dropship. "Let's at least give you a fighting chance. We'll go over your suit and check your gear."

Inhaling a deep breath, I warily followed, grateful that at least the SL wasn't treating my life as some joke. As I walked, a new realization suddenly dawned on me. Inhaling that deep breath hadn't been a struggle, and my suit no longer squeezed me like a vice. I hadn't noticed that the nanites had adjusted, but they had. The armor still felt snug, a fully encapsulating shell, but at least I no longer had to strain to breathe.

The SL went over every little detail of the suit, patiently

explaining everything. Not only was Gold Squad's armor of a heavier build, but it came with an extra battery, allowing the armor to withstand enemy fire that much longer. A fact I was both happy and not happy to learn about. Just yesterday, I was hoping to see zero action collecting corpses, and now I needed *two* damn batteries to keep me kicking?

"Watch this," Pax said, after instructing me to don my helmet, and stepping behind me.

Grabbing my forearm, he pulled it up and pointed my arm away from him. "Find the option for the energy blade."

By now, I was fairly proficient with navigating my display and I had no problem finding the option and toggling it on. A three-foot beam of sizzling blue light shot out of the box mounted on my forearm. The blade buzzed and crackled as I sliced through the air.

"Make sure you're not toggling the blade to training mode when you need to kill something," Pax said, taking a step away from me.

My grin lingered as I deactivated the blade and removed my helmet. Maybe this wouldn't be so bad. The Gold Squad equipment was some nice stuff, and I felt safer in the heavier gear.

"Attention on deck!" boomed a voice, loud enough to be heard over everyone's chatter and the banging of tools.

We snapped to attention, and the bay quieted, with only a few Fleet officers still going about their business. I glanced towards the entrance right as second cohort's Centurions sauntered in. All three were in gear like mine, gold emblems shining on their chests and helmets tucked under their arms.

"At ease!" thundered Centurion Paxton's familiar voice as the three dispersed to their units.

Paxton veered for mine, Fallon to fifth, and Braves headed towards sixth.

The troops relaxed and went back to checking and rechecking gear. Unlike everyone else, I didn't budge. I was now more than certain that my dire transfer to first squad wasn't some random personnel shuffle with me drawing the short straw.

Son-of-a-bitch!

Gritting my jaw, I turned to fifth unit. There she was, the scrawny witch, clasping forearms with the squad leaders and chatting away.

She must've spotted my ashen face staring at her because she paused greeting her men and turned to me. Her thin lips twisted up into a victorious, wicked grin.

My throat closed. Unable to oust me from the ship, the woman now wanted me *dead*.

I silently cursed Centurion Paxton, since he was the one ultimately in charge of my unit. Apparently, he wasn't the one wearing the pants in whatever lunatic relationship the two had going.

A double blast of a horn jolted me from my brooding.

"Stand-by for deployment," crackled an announcement from the intercoms, right as the cargo elevators slid open and released a flood of Space Fleet pilots to disperse amongst the dropships.

"Load up!" my SL shouted, waving an arm towards our ship.

But I didn't budge and, just for a moment, I forgot all about my troubles. I craned my neck hoping to see Wagner. Maybe she piloted both the transports and dropships.

However, I didn't get much time to search for her. A quickly approaching Centurion Paxton grabbed my attention as he rushed towards our group like a honed in missile. I had half a mind to stop him and protest my situation, but the man didn't as much as glance in my direction. Shouldering past the entire squad, he beelined to the SL. Standing no more than a foot apart, the two men clasped forearms and locked eyes.

Then it hit me. With a *duh*, I realized why the SL looked so familiar, and my slow brain finally made the connection of them having the same last name. Since the SL didn't look anywhere old enough to be the Centurion's brother, I figured he must be his son.

Heaving a sigh, I turned away from them and slipped my helmet over my head. It beeped and ran diagnostics as my suit synched with the squad.

"Adlar, load up!" Lee's voice shouted over comms, right as a single, loud blast blared from the speakers, its echo lingering hauntingly in the air.

It was time. With a deep breath and trying not to stumble over my wobbling legs, I clanged up the ramp and into the dropship.

CHAPTER
FOURTEEN

There were many models of dropships, but the ones commonly used to deploy troops, the one we were currently on, were anything but roomy. The narrow, cylindrical fuselage provided the enemy with the smallest possible target, and the ships were protected with deflector shields. As long as they weren't hit directly on the centerline, they spun off the immense energy with motion. Now, any ship that was unfortunate enough to be hit right down the middle and not able to redirect the force, was toast. A detail that didn't give me the warm fuzzies.

Pushing past Mills' and Lee's knees, which were almost touching as the men sat facing each other, I made my way towards the bow. I pushed past another trooper to an empty seat furthest away from the ramp, right next to the cockpit. I didn't want to be the first to drop once that ramp opened. Hell, I didn't want to drop at all, but it wasn't like I had much choice in the matter.

Right as I finished strapping in, the ramp clanged shut, and the dropship's engines spun up with a low whine. It rose with a gentle sway, then taxied, rocking as air forcefully whooshed around us like a tornado. Metal groaned with strain and the ship trembled. Vapors hissed somewhere overhead and something in the hull rattled.

I grabbed onto my belts with both hands and tried to steady my erratic breathing.

"Don't wet your pants yet, Adlar!" Mills barked a laugh to the backdrop of everyone's snickers. "They're just venting the hangar. We haven't even lifted off yet."

"*Poof.*" Lee mimicked an explosion with his hands.

Gritting my teeth, I turned away from their teasing and double-checked my outgoing comms were set on mute. I didn't want the squad to hear me panting like a racehorse in the confines of my helmet.

A moment later, the ship steadied.

"Hangar's depressurized. Prepare for blast-off," announced our pilot.

I could see him fiddling with the electronics. He too didn't appear fazed, working his forward display with mechanical precision. I chose to take that as a promising sign. That meant this particular pilot, and his ship, had survived.

After the announcement, we lurched forward, gaining speed, then blasted away from the carrier.

"You can let go now," sounded an unfamiliar voice in my helmet as the trooper I'd yet to meet extended an arm in my direction. "I'm Somner, and ignore the jack-asses, they're just messing with you."

He gave a telling nod towards Mills. "He'll cool down after he gets it out of his system."

To the backdrop of Mill's derisive snort, I hesitantly unwrapped my hands from my belt and reciprocated the man's greeting, giving his arm a firm shake.

"You know what you need to do?" He placed his elbows on his knees and leaned towards me. "You need to survive."

Groans erupted over comms.

"Here goes Somner, taking in the strays again," Mills chided. "Do I need to remind you of what happened to the last man you coddled? Or wait," he paused, rubbing his helmet's chin in thought. "Or was the last one that chick that smacked right into a bot." He let out a low whistle. "That was gnarly, even by *my* standards."

"Pfft," Lee scoffed and tried to swat at Mills, who dodged. "You're an idiot, you don't remember shit. That chick was like three newbs ago, and she—"

I stopped listening and turned to Somner.

"Do I even want to know?" I asked on private chat.

He barked a laugh. "You sure don't, man, you sure don't. But check it, if you make it, think how badly that'll piss off whoever wanted to turn you into roadkill? Think about it."

He leaned back and nodded his massive helmet as if he'd just stumbled upon some epiphany. I had no idea how to reply, so I chose to say nothing.

Instead, my mind wandered. I was fully aware of my surroundings and felt the ship's thrum through my armor, but I still wanted to pinch myself to make sure this wasn't all some horrible nightmare.

Somner turned away and joined the others in casual chatter.

I remained quiet, listening. For the life of me, I couldn't understand how they were all so relaxed. Here we were, outfitted in armor, strapped with weapons, soon to be jumping out of a dropship to clash with monsters and be shot at by bots, and they didn't show a shred of concern. They chatted away like we were heading to a Sunday brunch, discussing every day topics ranging from how crappy the new coffee in the galley was to how Pax needed to find a girlfriend.

"You'll be fine," Somner said over private chat, placing a large, gloved hand on my bouncing knee. I hadn't been aware I was moving it, but the guy must've seen it and figured I'd reverted back to panicking.

"This is just the first drop, so we're not that close to the shield yet. We advance in stages, mowing the droolers to more manageable numbers as we go, and as far away from the shield as we're dropping today, we might encounter two formations at most. Maybe three. Plus, first cohort just scoured this area and second squad is right behind us. Just do what we say, and we'll get you to the safe zone and back up to *Venator* in no time, okay?"

He paused, then patted my knee. "Well, maybe do what most of us say. Don't listen to Mills so much. He might get you killed just for the fun of it, so double-check with Pax before doing anything he asks. I know this isn't what you want to hear, but most newbs don't survive, so keep your head on a swivel, got it?"

Just as Somner finished reassuring me, and I was about to attempt relaxing at least one muscle, an explosive bang slammed into the belly of the ship, sending warbling vibrations throughout the hull. An electrical crackle followed as the ship banked sharply then flipped and proceeded to spin.

Gripped with fear, I screamed and grabbed onto my belts for dear life. My jaw rattled as I jarred about in the restraints, but I still managed to keep on screaming. The vessel twirled like a ribbon in the wind, engines screeching. I don't even know how many times it flipped before leveling out again, but my head and stomach were still spinning when it finally did.

"Shut up!" came a loud shout.

I hadn't realized I was still hollering. I slammed my mouth shut and did a double-take of my surroundings, trying not to hurl from the nausea. I was still in one piece, and the giant ball of flame I'd anticipated never came. The ship had leveled out and the horrific screech of the engines was now again a methodical thrum.

"Hey, Adlar," Mills barked with a snarky tone. "I'll make a deal with you. I'll keep you alive if you promise to warn us next time you plan on screaming like a little girl!"

"Ughm…" was all I managed to mumble. My head still spun as if I were in a carnival's fun house, and my gut flip-flopped. I was sure I was about to hurl my breakfast all over my visor.

A buzzer rang through the cabin as a bulb near the rear ramp began to flash.

"Go time!" Pax shouted as the clicks of releasing belts filled the cabin.

Taking in a shaky breath, I remained glued to my seat and made no move to release my own. After the ship was hit, my mortality seemed that much more real and I felt numb.

Rising from his seat, Somner leaned over me, and two clicks sounded as the belts slid off my chest. He grabbed my arm and yanked me up, turning me to face the stern. I didn't fight him and let him shove me forward against Mills. My still-spinning head flopped down onto Mills' shoulder.

"Hey! This isn't that kind of squad!" Mills elbowed me away from him.

My display beeped a proximity warning as a hand whacked me over my head.

"Get it together!" Somner snapped.

I attempted to do just that. Grabbing onto the overhead railing for balance, I breathed in and out, until everything around me steadied. That's when another buzzer rang and the ramp began to open. A narrow beam of natural light appeared, growing larger as it lowered, and the scream of the wind intensified.

"Go, go, go!" Pax shouted, stepping forward.

Without hesitation, he leaped and vanished into the bluish-purple void of the planet's atmosphere. My grip around the overhead railing tightened as I fought to remain upright on legs that suddenly felt like Jell-O.

"Remember your training," Somner instructed, pushing me forward.

Lee disappeared next, then Mills, both hurling themselves into the void. Then it was my turn. My entire body trembled inside my suit, but I edged towards the opening nonetheless. The air and engine's whine were deafening, and the jungle flashed below us in a blur of greens and purples.

Taking in a deep breath, I closed my eyes and envisioned the diving board back on *Venator*. I wasn't jumping into an alien atmosphere, just the pool, that's all.

A hard shove landed on my back, and the deck below me ceased to exist.

My eyes flew open as a wall of air punched into me, and my ragged breaths momentarily fogged my display. Three black silhouettes plunged towards the ground below me, far enough to where they were almost dots. Then Somner shot past.

Forcing my mind to go blank, I steadied my breathing and concentrated on stabilizing into an arch position, hips forward, head back, and legs bent at the knees.

After I succeeded, I took a moment to glance around. Troops rained onto the planet like a hailstorm, and a slew of contrails from the evading dropships decorated the sky above. One after the other, they pulled up, aiming for the relative safety of space, a barrage of massive bolts hot on their tails. They veered and dodged, trying to avoid the maelstrom of incoming fire. One ship wasn't as fortunate as the rest. With a thunderous boom, it exploded in a shower of fire and slag. The leftovers spiraled down in trailing plumes of fire and smoke.

The ships weren't the only casualties in the chaos filling the sky. The Synths' defensive fire was also picking off random troops. Most were in the bullet drop, screaming towards the thick canopy at maximum speed, but not everyone was making it to the ground. My breath caught as a crackling beam slammed into a falling trooper in a momentary flare of white light and sparks. What remained of the trooper flipped and flopped, smashing lifelessly into the trees.

I yelped, as a bolt whizzed past my helmet and glitched my display. The sky was aglow with them. My heart pounded in over-drive, and I had to do everything in my power to resist flailing about from pure panic.

"Hurry up, Adlar!" Somner prompted in my comm.

He'd shot past me earlier, but I just wasn't ready for a nosedive. Even if it got me to the ground faster, and away from the barrage of fire, I didn't see myself successfully pulling off the maneuver.

I twisted my body, wanting to see the source of the fire. There, in the distance, shimmered a shield. The giant bubble-like dome was set over a section of the mountain with a slew of massive bolts spewing out of it in all directions.

I then noticed the jungle rushing up at me with impressive speed. Trying to remain calm, I blocked out the fire, telling myself that for the moment, it didn't exist. Either I was going to make it, or it suddenly wasn't going to be my problem anymore.

Mimicking my training, I tilted my body up and activated my suit's deceleration protocol. It jerked as it took control. The jets on the breastplate hissed, punching me back and upright as the air pack rumbled out propellant to slow my descent.

I landed semi-upright. At least initially. My boots slammed on a giant leaf which, needless to say, didn't support my weight. The suit clicked control back to me. Screaming at the top of my lungs, I tumbled head over heels, crashing through branches and foliage. My screams cut short when I smashed onto the ground, and all air exploded out of my lungs. If I had any breath left, I would've probably kept on screaming. Groaning and splayed out like a starfish, I now understood why Pax had relieved me of my frags and, boy, was I thankful.

"Seriously, Adlar!" came Mills' voice. "What fucking deal did we just make, not a minute ago? You know how annoying it is to toggle you in and out of mute? Plus, how do we know if something is actually wrong? We can't come running just 'cause Adlar saw a teeny spider!"

"Lock it up," Pax barked. "Drop your air packs and gather up." He paused. "On second thought, Adlar, you stay put and we'll come to you. Everyone, gather on Adlar."

I had no complaints about that. I was still busy huffing and trying to scramble up from the dirt. Grimacing, I wiped at my visor. I'd smashed some unlucky bug when I'd crashed, and my visor was coated in red goop and crunchy bits. At least I hadn't landed on one of those saber-toothed pigs, I considered. Or some whale-sized alien beast.

No damage warnings popped up in my display, but as I rose, I still patted down my armor to check. I then momentarily forgot all about my fear as I glanced around. It was quiet down here and tranquil as if the chaos in the sky didn't exist.

I took a careful, awe-filled step forward. Twigs crunched under my boots as giant feathered leaves swished over my suit. Some were as wide as an air-car with purple veins webbed through the green.

I craned my neck, studying the lush canopy above. The trees were hundreds of feet tall, a hard thing to grasp, considering I'd sustained no injuries from my fall. Golf-ball-sized red and yellow fruit grew in pendulous clumps on some of the branches, and massive overlapping leaves blocked out most of the sky and light—except in one spot. A bright beam from Atlas' sun illuminated the human-shaped imprint I'd left in the grass. It shone through a narrow tunnel of torn leaves and limply dangling branches. The rest of the area was cast in gloom, shadows overlapping shadows.

I did a few small hops, testing out the lower gravity. I felt lighter, though not to the point where I could spring off the ground and sail in long leaps like on Earth's moon. Maybe that was why I hadn't cracked my suit when I'd cannonballed onto my face.

Picking up a rustling, my head jerked to look, and I tensed. A few squeaks followed. A slow breath of relief escaped me, and I redirected my attention back to my teammates' locators. The scenery around me was captivating, but this wasn't the time for sightseeing. This wasn't a vacation. This was a war zone.

Glancing around the ocean of green, I tried to get my bearings. The trees were tightly clustered together, and their odd purple and green trunks made it impossible to see more than fifty feet in any direction. The bark was oddly smooth in appearance.

Moving a large leaf out of the way, I curiously inspected the ground. My eyes were greeted by more leaves and a thick carpet of purplish grass.

"Where the hell is your weapon?"

Startled, I jumped, releasing the leaf in my grasp. It snapped back into place with a rustle. The shape of a black heavy-gear suit emerged into view and rushed towards me. It was Pax.

"Oh." I pulled out my blaster to the disapproving shake of his head.

All of us were armed with only the basic blasters. Unlike the heavier blaster rifles these held a charge without requiring charge packs. I considered that a blessing, not knowing how troops managed to drop with the larger weapons, or how heavies pulled off landings with beamers in tow.

Pax rounded us up into a huddle behind a trunk with giant leaves sweeping over our heads.

"It looks like we're going to be facing the usual down here," Pax said. "First cohort finished sifting through suit cam data and sent out the intel. So far, no reports of anything besides the usual droolers and bots, so that's good, I suppose."

My display flickered and a ghastly image popped up. I recalled Gundy mentioning the creatures. The bear-like beast was huge, both in height and girth. Tufts of thick brownish fur dotted its grayish flesh which sagged in folds around the massive gut. A single enormous eyeball sat in the middle of the bulbous head. It was hard to tell the beast's exact height from the snapshot, since it was taken from someone looking up and over their shoulder, but my suit estimated it to be at least seven feet.

I couldn't help but wonder about what trooper's camera had snapped the picture, and if they'd survived the dance.

CHAPTER
FIFTEEN

"That's just gross!" Mills exclaimed. "I'll never get used to the sight of those ugly mugs. Aren't the Synths running out of them yet? How many planets have we mowed them down at, ten, twenty?"

He rubbed his helmet's chin in thought. "Thirty? I can't even keep track anymore."

Pax shook his head. "They'll probably never run out. Those damn sleeks from the Rigel system mass-produce them in test tubes, then sell them to the Synths or whatever other race is in the market. They have whole planets devoted to breeding. They just don't sell the females. That way none of their customers get any ideas about making their own product if you know what I mean."

I nodded along, remembering Gundy mentioning it was illegal to own the females. That all we'd face down here are the males.

"That's just fucked!" Mills spat. "I've been saying for years, we need to start taking out those slithering snakes, even if we do depend on their tech. They're advanced as shit, but it's not like they can fight…."

I let him go on for a few more seconds as I stared at the image, then cut in.

"How is it possible to *create* something like this?" I asked. I must have zoned out when that was covered.

Mills forgot all about finishing his rant, and along with everyone else, burst out laughing.

"*How is this possible,*" he mimicked in a teasing whine. "You are fresh from Earth, aren't you, *newb?*"

Somner's fist slammed into Mills, causing the crouching man to topple over into the bushel of leaves behind him. The giant stems groaned and snapped under his weight.

Somner turned to me. "You'd be surprised what's possible out here, Adlar. Most people just don't get to hear about it, it's all classified, just like the Senate and Earth-gov need it to be. Those idiotic, underground drooler hugging groups are a problem enough as it is."

"I say we off those idiots also," Mills piped in, righting himself and swishing grass off his suit. "The damn things are manufactured to kill us, and those fucks want to save them? Like they're some sort of puppy dogs. I say they deserve the same fate as their precious pets—our blades. The Senate needs to start doing something about those fools, and soon, before we have droolers running around Earth, ripping people apart."

I cleared the gruesome image out of my display and interrupted Mills before he got too wound up again. "How do the Synths organize them? Training?"

I didn't know if that was a stupid question, but I just couldn't pin the hulking beast as capable of strategy; it didn't even look like it was advanced enough to bathe.

"Nah," Mills said. "The Synths are masters in neural interphase. They use machines to fight. A bot to control a formation of whatever species they purchased and enslaved. Watch, you'll see. I'm sure we'll take down a bot soon. That'll cause its group of droolers to turn into a disorganized mess, at least for a few minutes, until some other bot in the vicinity connects to them."

"But remember, newb, just because the bot is down doesn't mean you're safe," Lee jumped in with a matter-of-fact tone. "The creatures are created to be predatory, and, like Mills mentioned, designed to kill us. So, don't be fooled into thinking they won't attack when disconnected."

I fidgeted, now understanding why the Legion's recruitment site lacked detail, and why no personal electronic devices were allowed aboard Legion ships. Even though it was common knowledge back home that the galaxy was teeming with different species, most Legion operations were classified. The Galactic Senate especially was famous for keeping everything under wraps, only releasing very carefully worded, propaganda-like statements about the Legions and their overall plans for the galaxy.

All chatter and laughter died in a blink when a shot whizzed over our heads. Trunks splintered and crashed as every frond around us trembled from the impact. My helmet automatically dampened the deafening noise, allowing only muffled rustles to reach my ears.

"Too big to be from a bot," Pax said, just as another massive bolt of crackling electricity cut through the trees. "The Synths must be shooting blindly where they saw troops land, or they might be going after the aerial drones. Either way, enough chit-chat. It's time to move. If there's droolers around here, they'll converge on the noise."

Still crouching, blaster in hand, Pax turned to me. For a second, I wondered if he was able to see the wide-eyed, stumped expression I had plastered over my face. I quickly double-checked that my visor was still on tint.

"There's one more thing you need to know, Adlar," he said. "Your suit won't be able to pick up the enemy targets so don't rely on your display to tell you where the contacts are. The Synth troops have some sort of jamming capability."

I nodded, my heart pounding in my ears.

"Game time!" Pax said, looking over his squad. "Let's push towards the shield and snag us a formation or two."

Everyone whooped in reply. Well, almost everyone. I stayed dead silent, trying not to barf from my knotted stomach.

Popping up from the leaves, the squad proceeded to zigzag through the trunks. Having no idea of what they were doing, I tailed Pax, mouth shut. Thankfully, he filled me in on their tactics. Even though the Synths changed out the slaves they used for ground troops—they'd utilized dino-type creatures during Rap-Wars—their strategy remained more or less the same. No matter how advanced their tech was, there was only so much control a machine was able to have over flesh and bone beasts, and the bot was our primary target.

Our goal was to trap and take out the droolers first, then disperse and go after the elusive machine.

"Another thing," Pax continued, pushing through a cluster of mega-ferns. "Never bunch up with too many other squads when under fire from the bots. Same reason all the cohorts don't deploy at once. It's all about ratios. The machines are programmed with very linear reasoning. If the number of Leeges in a certain location surpasses the number of droolers, they'll blast the hell out of everything. They don't give a damn about killing their own."

He froze, raising a fist to stop us, and signaled us to crouch. Only our heads peeked over the swaying leaves.

"Targets in front. A drone just glimpsed a disturbance in the jungle and it's heading our way. Only one thing it could be, boys!"

Mills whooped like a wild coyote, pumping a fist.

"Oh shit!" He cut short as we all ducked from an onslaught of fire.

Trees again groaned and splintered as dirt gysered skyward.

"Drone's down," Pax reported. "We're on our own. Let's get this show on the road and make sure tenth squad is only picking up air packs."

Then, without any further instructions, they dispersed, leaving me twisting my head in confusion. Not knowing what else to do, and having not received any instruction, I remained rooted amongst the rustling plants, watching everyone in my HUD. Like actors on a stage, preparing for a performance they'd acted out many times before, they took up positions. The hairs on my arms tingled as a wave of nerves washed over me. I was all alone in a jungle teeming with monsters.

Tightening my grip on my blaster, I turned this way and that, wanting to dart after someone, anyone, when a hand grabbed my arm and yanked me back. I shouted a curse, almost jumping out of my skin before realizing it was Pax.

A low growl sounded over comms. "I swear, Adlar—"

"Lock it up, Mills." Pax pulled me along for a few steps, then shoved me behind a trunk. "You're with me. Stay close and do as you're told, got that?"

I nodded in confirmation, pressing myself flat against the trunk.

Maybe if I pressed hard enough, I'd merge with the bark and disappear.

In silence, I studied the rest of the squad. It appeared they'd advanced north, then dispersed to either side of Pax and me. Lee was on our two, Somner on our ten, and Mills directly across from us to our left. We'd semi-encircled where the disturbance had been reported. I wanted to ask what the plan was but decided not to interrupt and just watch, not wanting to be a distraction.

Once everyone was in position, Pax signaled me to follow. Slowly, we edged in, until Pax stopped and pushed me behind a tree again. I remained there for a beat, but then curiosity got the better of me. I poked my head out and scanned in front of me, only to see nothing but swaying leaves. My HUD showed everyone's locators but not a single enemy contact.

Pax also swung out from behind the trunk. I jumped, startled, when he suddenly fired aimlessly at the ground and trees in front of us, splintering their fronds and sending charred leaves and bark to spray up like confetti.

Not even a second later, a roar, the likes of which I'd never heard before, trembled the air. A giant drooler erupted out of the leaves and barreled towards where Pax's shots had landed. Like a rabid dog, he attacked the blast-riddled flora, pummeling at the fronds and yanking whole plants out of the ground with roots still attached. A moment later he seemed to calm. Tossing the bushel of leaves he was holding back to the ground, he then turned in baffled circles, scanning the area. There was a wild look in his one swiveling eye.

Both amazed and terrified, I leaned out further from behind the tree to get a better glimpse of the beast. He was now hunched over and grunting, pawing through the underbrush as if looking for something he'd lost.

Then, it suddenly hit me what Bishop and many others had meant by *bait* and, yup, everyone was a fucking asshole!

"Target in sight." Pax leveled his blaster.

He fired three precise shots into the drooler's gargantuan back. Howling mad, the beast reared up as bloodied holes blew from his flesh, but instead of collapsing, he turned and charged, trampling shrubs and saplings alike. I staggered back, my pulse pounding in my throat. Drool rained out of his maw and his bulk jiggled with each thundering step.

Unlike me, Pax didn't retreat. He held cool and steady, blaster leveled. As the drooler neared, he fired a single shot with practiced precision. The beast jerked back as his head blew apart in a spray of brains and gore, then crumpled and vanished beneath the leaves.

Exhaling a shaky breath, I fixated on where the thing had fallen until a hard tug on my arm broke me out of my trance. Pax signaled me to follow with a crook of his finger and jogged into the leaves. I darted after him, right as a chorus of enraged roars converged on where he'd put down the drooler.

"First off, Adlar," Pax said as we ran. "You need to be aware that when one of those things sees you or knows where you're at, they all do, at least the ones in the same formation. They're all connected. Second, you should probably consider using that blaster you're clutching. Standing there, gawking, isn't going to keep you alive."

Swallowing hard, I glanced at the blaster in my hand as the roars behind us intensified. The droolers had abandoned the location of their fallen teammate and were now stampeding after us.

"I know," I mumbled quietly, my cheeks growing hot.

Why hadn't I shot? The snarling monstrosity had been coming right at us, and I'd just shuffled back like a dumbass. I hadn't even raised my blaster. Setting my jaw with resolve, I tightened my grip on my weapon. Pax wasn't always going to be there to take the shot.

"All yours, Mills," Pax said, his voice still unnervingly calm, as he swished through the leaves effortlessly, carrying out this long-practiced routine.

Studying my HUD, I saw Mills had crept up, and we'd led our pursuers right to him. Zagging through trunks behind my SL like a tail, I made sure to keep track of everyone's movements. I was determined to learn their tactics and stay alive. I wasn't going to freeze again.

A small smile crossed my lips at the thought. I needed to survive, if only to see that bitch of a Centurion detonate when I sauntered back to *Venator* as if it were nothing.

Blaster fire shrieked behind us, and the roars of rage on our tail changed to wails and howls of pain. The death cries pierced through the jungle, dissipating into echoes and startling what unseen wildlife still remained in the area. Bizarre alien hoots and squawks yanked me from my daydreams of aggravating Fallon.

I diverted my attention back to my display. After killing the droolers that we'd led to him, Mills relocated directly south of Lee, who hadn't budged from his initial position.

Leaves slapped at me from all sides as I pushed myself to keep up with Pax. His glimmering suit kept vanishing out of my sight amidst the stew of plants. Thankfully, my HUD kept track of him. I almost screamed again when, after a feathery leaf swept past my visor, Pax snagged me and shoved me behind a trunk.

Panting, I checked my display. Pax and I had done exactly what Mills had, just on the other side, and we were now positioned directly south of Somner. Both had edged towards us. The squad now formed a kind of tunnel through the jungle with the location of Mills' last kill between the rows. We were boxing them in.

I gripped my blaster with both hands, determined not to freeze. As soon as one of those things charged into our trap, I was going to be the one to send a bolt through his eyeball.

But nothing came. All I picked up was the light rustling of plants and everyone's labored breathing. At times, a few distant squawks and chirps found their way into my audio.

"Where's the rest of them?" Mills said after a few minutes. "It never takes them this long to attack."

I slumped against the trunk as gently swaying leaves swished against my helmet. I swiped at a bright red beetle that landed on my visor, being careful not to crush the bug as I'd done before. The disgusting thing was the size of a walnut with way more spiny insect legs than I wanted to have this close to my face. The legs must've been lined with spikes because they scratched and scraped on my visor as I swiped it off.

"No idea where they are," Pax replied, stepping out from behind the tree.

He turned in circles, scanning the area. Everything was eerily still. No droolers charged the site of the previous kill, nor had they followed Pax and me. Even to a newbie like myself, the situation seemed odd. Judging by the loud roars I'd previously heard, the beasts were pissed. Yet, none charged.

"What the hell?" came Lee's shout as blue power-bolts showered into the middle of our trap where the droolers were supposed to attack, sending up splintering explosions.

"That was the bot, Pax! Why is he showing himself already, where are the rest of the morons? Didn't we only take down three to five of them?"

"Yeah," Mills seconded. "There should be at least ten more. Maybe the Synths *are* running out of their dumbass slaves."

"I doubt it," Pax countered, his tone tense. "Something isn't right."

The slew of fire hadn't fazed him at all, and he continued to ruffle through the brush. I jumped when a few more beams slammed into the same spot, turning that area into a blackened mess.

"Can you tell where the fire is coming from, Somner?" Pax asked.

"Nah, just from somewhere north of Lee and me."

"Well, crap. That's no good. We're separated, and they aren't rushing into our trap like they usually do. Everyone, stay put. Give me a sec."

Pax rejoined me behind our hideout and stared off into the distance.

"Okay," he clicked back to squad-chat. "I talked to second and third squad, they're having the same issue. The droolers aren't charging in their usual style. Our orders haven't changed, though. We're still to advance and take out anything in our path, to clear the area, so that's exactly what we're going to do. Everyone hold where you're at, second squad is going to join us."

It didn't take long until five jet-black suits glided into our view and swiftly moved to join Pax and me. In my display, I saw that Mills was also joined by additional locators. Clutching my blaster, I kept watch, while Pax conferred with the other squad leader.

I observed them with a wary eye. Internally, I was hoping that since the Synths were doing something funky the SLs would conclude we needed to retreat towards the safe zones and regroup. Their probable locations were already starting to pop up on my display whenever I zoomed out, miles away from the danger. However, to my complete disappointment, Pax gave the order to advance.

So, that's what our combined squads did. Separated by about thirty or forty feet in case the bot pinned one of us, we all moved in a line, towards Somner's position. Unlike everyone else, I didn't separate. I stayed tight on Pax's side like a shadow, my heart pounding in my throat. Everything was unnervingly quiet.

"Arghh!" A shout blared over comms.

I twisted around right as the trooper behind me became a squeeze toy. A towering drooler had popped out of nowhere and grabbed the man, one massive arm holding him in a bear hug as the other fumbled over the helmet, trying to rip it off. Pax fired, only for his shots to slam uselessly into trunks—the grappling duo was gone.

Fighting the urge to retreat, I rushed with everyone towards the fallen trooper and drooler. I didn't make it. Movement flashed in my peripheral vision. Rounding about, I saw the rear trooper tackled by another drooler. The two flew into the grass as more screams rang over comms.

Acting on impulse, I charged to help, right as the beast pounced onto the man's back. Energy blades shot out from the trooper's arms, mowing down the grass in a crackling shower of light as he thrashed. But the man was pinned face down, the drooler on top of him, and his blades failed to reach the beast. Two massive paws slapped onto the man's helmet and yanked.

With an ear-splitting *"crack"* of rending metal the helmet popped off.

By then, I was blasting away, burning hole after hole in the drooler's lumbering back. Gore splattered the grass, but it was too late. The man's exposed head was in the drooler's paws, and as the beast toppled over and died, he twisted and pulled. With a gruesome crunch and a wet ripping sound, the man's head tore from his body.

The sight knocked all the air out of my lungs. Staggering to a stop, I pitched back to fall on my butt. My mind struggled to process. There was the drooler, stone-dead, dark maroon blood pooling onto the grass. It was thick like oil, almost black. Then, there was the headless trooper, gushing a pool of red.

Right about then, the drooler's lifeless arm shifted. It flopped limply to the side, releasing the man's severed head to bounce and roll, then vanish into the underbrush.

I tried to control myself but failed. Ripping my helmet off, I puked onto the grass.

"Adlar!" Pax's voice shouted from my helmet. "Get over here!"

Alarmed all over again, I slapped my helmet back onto my head and jumped to my feet. I didn't dare to turn around even though I knew I could never unsee the ghastly scene behind me. Guilt pounded at my head. The man had died because I wasn't fast enough. I should've been faster. Faster than a drooling, idiotic beast. Now a Leege was dead. *How was I here?* I clasped my helmet again, fighting the urge to rip it off, as another wave of nausea overcame me.

"Adlar!" Pax shouted, louder this time.

My whole body trembled, but I forced myself to move and shambled to rejoin the squad.

"They got 'em," I panted, pointing behind me. "T-the thing… it—"

"I know." Pax clapped my shoulder. "Don't worry about that right now, we need to run, the bot's still out there."

The words barely escaped his lips as a power-bolt pierced through the trees and plowed him down. He flew backward as two additional shots nailed the men beside him. Twisting about, I threw myself flat to return fire. Yet again, I wasn't quick enough. I was shot and sent into a tumbling spin.

CHAPTER
SIXTEEN

Electricity wracked my body. My muscles spasmed, and my skin blazed. It was as if a thousand fire ants had bitten into me all at once, and no matter how much I thrashed, I couldn't escape them. Even though my entire world at the moment consisted of nothing but hurt, I was still lucid enough to note that I was the only one screaming.

"Shake it off, Adlar!" Pax shouted as a form skidded to tower over my twitching body.

Hands grabbed onto me and hauled me to my feet.

"You'll get used to it. Now let's get the fuck outta here before we get zapped a second time."

I followed after him, trying not to trip over my shaky legs as the jungle lit up around us. Bolt after bolt whizzed by, smashing into trees with brilliant explosions of bark and leaves. The hailstorm of debris pelted me, dinging off my suit.

Not being able to see the bot that was trying to snuff us out through the mix of plants, we fired blindly behind us as we ran. Finally, the fire gradually let up. I don't know if we'd actually hit the bot, or if it was just biding its time, but we used the reprieve to gain some distance.

As I weaved behind Pax, my gaze drifted to the canopy above, taking in the sight of this peculiar planet. Its similarity to Earth was uncanny. The broad leaves swished over each other lazily in the breeze that must've been blowing, allowing sparse beams of dancing light through the cracks. I couldn't feel it through my gear but imagined it to be muggy and hot.

Remembering my not-so-smooth arrival on Atlas, a kernel of an idea popped into my head.

I sped up to fall in step with Pax and grabbed his attention.

"What if we trap it? Kind of like you guys did with the droolers."

"Nah," Pax huffed, hopping over a downed log like a professional hurdle jumper.

I almost tripped trying to mimic.

"It's not that stupid. It won't fall for a trap. It calculates our position based on the origin of our fire, so it's not going to charge. It's going to keep coming after us from a distance until we encircle it. I just wish I knew where the rest of his dumb-ass droolers were, that's what I'm worried about. We can't split up until we take them out, or they'll pick us off one by one. This drop is just strange. First cohort didn't report this kind of unusual activity."

"Yeah, but what if it doesn't know it's a trap?" I pointed up at the canopy above, then at the surrounding trees. "Those massive leaves can provide plenty of cover."

Pax slid to a stop and did a quick spin, glancing around. "You might be onto something."

He dropped flat on the ground and disappeared. The dense vegetation had swallowed him out of view as if he'd dove under water. Without question, everyone else followed suit and ducked under the carpet of leafy growths. Since our armor was designed to completely mitigate our infra-red signature, as far as the bot was concerned, we'd simply vanished. The machine didn't appreciate that very much and lit up the jungle with fresh determination.

As the bot aimlessly bombarded the area, trying to flush us out, Pax filled everyone in on the plan. A heavy hand clapped onto my back.

"Adlar, sorry to do this to you buddy, but we're going to need you to… Uh…" He hesitated, giving me a pat. "You know… take one for the team."

"Huh?" My face scrunched in confusion.

I hadn't paid attention to anything he'd said, too busy trying to determine if the clamor of splintering trees was closing in, hoping the bot wouldn't get lucky and win this game of battleship.

"If the bot takes the bait, every one of our shots needs to count," Pax said, giving my back a few more pats.

His visor was set on clear, and his piercing eyes bore into mine. "I'm going to venture a guess that you're the worst shot out of all of us, but I'm sure you can run."

"Say what?" I jerked my head around to look at the other troops who were laid out flat next to us.

Snickers sounded over the comm, Mills being the loudest.

"Aww… hell," I groaned, letting my visor smack down into the crook of my arm in defeat.

I actually was a *great* shot, but there was no point in protesting. Everyone's minds were already made up.

"Give us some time and I'll tell you when we're ready. Then you lead that bastard towards us, and we'll get him, okay?"

Pax gave my helmet a reassuring shake, then broke off, slithering into the foliage like a lizard zeroing in on a bug. One by one, the rest of the troops followed. A sinking sensation formed in my gut as they disappeared. I knew what was coming my way. Even if the plan worked without a hitch, I was about to be lit up like a goddamn light bulb. Not only that, but I was about to become something that I'd been trying so hard to avoid—freaking *bait*. If I ever did run into Bishop again, this was one story I wasn't going to share.

"Okay, we're ready," Pax announced.

At that, a jolt of adrenaline surged through my body. It seemed like only a second had passed since they'd disappeared. Hesitating, I couldn't help but think of Earth as a pang of homesickness impinged on my mind.

"Adlar?" Pax prompted.

He now sounded kind of testy. I figured he was watching me on his display and saw I hadn't moved.

With a deep exhale, I decided to stop dragging out the inevitable and slowly pushed up to my knees, then my feet. I wasn't exactly in a hurry. As the top of my head emerged from the grass, my helmet beeped. I ducked as a sizzling bolt missed me by inches, streaking into the jungle with a charred trail of shredded green. My display flickered, then stabilized.

Mouthing "Here goes nothing," I shot out of the grass.

Using every bit of the mechanical help my suit offered, I ran like the hounds of hell were hot on my heels. Whatever machine was after us was apparently done messing around because it unloaded. I weaved and swerved, yelping and sliding every time flying debris threatened to knock me down.

I couldn't allow myself to get hit before reaching the clustered locators in my display or the plan would be a bust—or. top of me getting fried. Even if my suit could withstand multiple shots, if I fell to the ground before reaching my squadmates, the bot would undoubtedly nail me with enough fire to snuff me out.

Thankfully, I didn't let down my squad, or Pax. With plenty of charge left in my suit, I burst into the center of their locators. In my HUD, they had me surrounded, but all I saw when I looked up into the trees were branches and sprawling, purple-streaked leaves. The troopers had done a great job concealing themselves in the canopy. Pushing away some tall leafy thing that had toppled over me, half of it blasted to shreds, I sighed. I knew it was time.

Inhaling a deep breath, I spun about to face the machine.

"Go further, you idiot!" Lee shouted in my comm. "We need the bot in the middle of the trap, not you!"

"Oh crap!" I turned in a circle, quickly seeing the wisdom in his words.

I ran about eighty more feet past the squad, then stopped and turned, ready to face my fate. Through the trees, I spotted flashes of silver. The bot was quickly approaching. Then, its glistening, humanoid frame emerged into view, red light shining brightly out of the single slit running across its oval head. The machine wasted no time. It fired from a cannon mounted on its forearm.

Like a caged rabbit, I hopped back and forth in the bot's view, putting on the show of a lifetime, trying to lure him into the trap. The bot missed me with its initial volley of blasts, but then there was just no avoiding the inevitable. My ass was zapped. Gritting my teeth, I fought to remain standing as a million pins stabbed at my skin. I needed the bot closer. I slumped against a trunk for support and did my best to remain a target.

The machine closed in quicker and quicker, all too sure I was his. Raising its other arm, the muzzles of its cannons burning a hot, electrical blue, it fired from both. I pushed off the trunk and tried to dodge, but I was still sluggish from the previous hit. Bolt after bolt slammed into me, sending me spinning to the dirt in a tangle of spasming limbs. I screamed and twitched as my HUD lit up like a Christmas tree.

Multiple warnings flashed and a piercing *"breep, breep"* bounced around my helmet.

Ignoring the light show, I bit down on my lip and tried to breathe. Thankfully, the bot didn't get off any more shots because my suit's battery was done for. It didn't even have enough juice to dampen the din of my squadmates' fire and victorious cheers as they annihilated the unsuspecting machine from above.

CHAPTER
SEVENTEEN

"Pax!" Mills boomed as the separated troops jogged out of the brush to rejoin us. "You're gonna have to send me the cam footage from whoever had the clearest view of our little jackrabbit, here."

He draped a large arm over my shoulders, bellowing a loud laugh, and jabbed a fist into my side. His armored hand clanged loudly against my suit.

"I bet it's priceless. I should've bet credits on how many times you were going to scream today. What do you think, Adlar? Ten credits every time you squeal like a stuck pig?"

Frustrated, sore, and in a plain sour mood, I angrily swung his arm off and shoved the jackass away from me.

"Wow, wow." Mills chuckled, staggering back, palms raised. "Don't get your panties in a bunch."

Still laughing, he retreated a few steps, right as a hand landed on my arm and someone spun me around. Having had enough of just about everyone, I raised a fist to lash out at whoever dared to bother me next, but stopped myself when I saw it was Somner.

"Good job out there, newbie." A genuine smile beamed in his eyes. "Let me show you how to change out your battery. I'm fairly sure we're not done getting fried just yet."

My suit had stopped blaring the emergency alarm, but the slew of flashing warnings in the corner of my display was hard to ignore.

Fortunately, the Gold Squads received a replacement battery, and I watched intently as Somner switched his out. I mimicked, discarding the spent battery into the grass, and re-inserted the fresh one. After seeing the damage that one formation and a bot were capable of, the fact I was now out of backups didn't fill me with confidence.

"That's the gist of it," Somner stated, clapping me on the shoulder.

I then noticed that Mills was still loitering next to us like some parasite I couldn't seem to shake. He shuffled around, throwing me careful side-eyed glances. When Somner finished his lesson, the prick didn't waste any time and stomped in my direction.

Letting out an exasperated groan, I considered decking him right then, and even balled a fist, but Somner side-stepped to block his approach. Grabbing him by the arms, he spun Mills around and shoved him towards everyone else.

He threw me a wink. "Let's give Adlar some space for now, how about that?"

Mills scoffed and grumbled with disappointment, but ultimately humped away to join Pax, Lee, and the second squad's troops. I gave Somner a weak smile, thankful for the assist. Besides him and perhaps Pax, no one else seemed to have a problem with inexperienced troops getting sent to their squad to vanish. Mills, Lee, and even the attendants in the equipment room all acted as if the idea of me getting killed off was simply a hilarious joke. The Legions truly weren't for the faint of heart.

Pax wandered over, giving Somner and me a congratulatory pat on the back.

"Fried that bastard, huh?" he said, then yanked a frag off his waist.

He gestured towards the downed bot. "Ready to find out how this works?"

I shrugged, cocking my head in doubt at the small shiny object in his hand. The munition sure didn't look like much but after being thrown out of a ship, running for my life, and getting electrocuted, blowing something up with just about anything seemed appealing.

"Plasma frag," Pax explained, noting my skepticism.

He rolled the frag around in his palm, caressing it as if it were a stress ball. "Some sort of plasma reaction that packs one hell of a punch. It's alien tech, from the sleeks."

Mills scoffed, carefully circumventing Somner as he ventured over.

"Those fucks play all sides, you see. The cowards serve as intermediaries between all the species on behalf of the ancients, and they make themselves invaluable to both the Legions and our enemies, but I still say we need to dust 'em all."

He snorted, pointing a finger at the frag. "They don't sell those things to us cheap either. That's why only the Gold Squads get them. That, right there, is probably worth just as much as an air-car back home, and we have no choice but to buy them. Those fucks made it a violation of Galactic Law for us to replicate their tech or their codes."

I frowned in thought. I'd only been vaguely aware that some of our weapons and equipment was alien-made.

"How do we pay for them?" I asked out of curiosity. "If we have to buy them from the sleeks, what do they get in return?"

I couldn't envision an advanced alien race being interested in Earth's currency.

Pax and Mills both laughed.

"Endless debt," Mills snarked.

"And perpetual *servitude*," Pax added with an implied *duh*. He gestured towards the group of loitering Leeges behind us.

"*We* pay for all this." He thunked an armored fist against his breastplate. "For our gear, our weapons, and for those fancy space-yachts all the Galactic Senate Reps seem to own. The ones where you can barely feel the jumps."

He glanced at Mills and Somner with a somber expression, then again at the rest of the troops. "Our *lives* pay for this."

I blinked at him, not quite catching on. Naturally, I'd heard very little of what Gundy had been going on about during our lengthy jogs, so I didn't recall if any of this was covered.

Mills caught on to my confusion. "The Senate rents us out, man. Rents out the Legions. Not all the campaigns we're assigned involve our grudge against the Synths. Some are just plain mercenary contracts, depending on what the sleeks need done. The sleeks themselves don't fight, you see, they're cowards, diplomats and such. Even their so-called military tucks tail and runs from most engagements. So, they use other species for hired guns whenever they need it, and boy do they."

He shook his head, sucking in a strained breath. "It seems like we're dusting whatever species they have a gripe with for the month as much as we're fighting the Synths, especially since that's where the payday's at. Mercenary contracts earn some serious credits. Credits that we need to pay back our debts to them and purchase their tech. They have us by our balls."

My brows scrunched as I processed that tidbit of unexpected info. I knew Earth collaborated with other species, and the Sleeks had helped us out with tech, but in a million years, I wouldn't have guessed we were for sale. That our lives were for sale. *The Legions, mercenaries?* I wasn't sure how that sat with me. Not that a ground trooper's opinion held any weight.

"Well, enough chit-chat." Pax veered towards the bot. "You'll learn all the ins-and-outs soon enough. All the nit and grit."

As he walked away, he spun back to face me and opened his arms wide, raising them to the sky as if worshiping a god. "Welcome to Legion Invictus, man!" he bellowed on open-chat.

"To victory!" came a unified cheer as fists pumped into the air and men whooped, chanting the Legion creed.

Feeling a bit more reserved than the enthralled masses, I quietly echoed "to victory," under my breath, then jogged after Pax.

Standing side by side, we stared at the downed machine. It was sprawled out on its back in a bed of grass burnt to a crisp. I was surprised to see it was still intact. The bot must've taken near fifty blasts, and yet, it looked merely deactivated. No red light shined out of the slit in its head. For a second, I wondered if the sleeks had a hand in designing these things, providing both sides of the less advanced species with pointy sticks to skewer each other with.

After instructing me on how to operate the explosive, Pax threw me the frag. "You get the honors."

I snatched it mid-air, my large, gloved palm completely wrapping around the small device. The moment I made contact with the shiny egg, my suit registered its presence and popped up an activation option on my display. That was a failsafe so it didn't detonate the owner if they happened to smash it flat during a fall or tumble.

Toggling to activate, I slowly applied pressure to the exterior until the shell cracked. A blue glow radiated out of the web of hairline fractures, illuminating my glove with a wavering light. I stared, mesmerized by its ethereal alien quality. The glow intensified, and even through my gauntlet, I felt my palm fill with heat.

"Throw it, dumbass!" Pax shouted, shoving me and spinning to run.

"Oh, shit!" I flung the frag on top of the bot and veered after Pax.

Pax and I hadn't made it five steps when a concussive *"whoomp"* sounded behind us. I was flung up and forwards as if rammed in the ass. This time, I didn't scream. When I got done bumping and tumbling under a shower of dirt, I laughed. I couldn't help it.

Maybe this was the beginning of me becoming as crazy as everyone else, I considered, as I struggled to breathe, tears rimming my eyes. Maybe this was the path to becoming an actual Leege. As our comms exploded with whoops and cheers from the rest of the troops, additional chuckles joined mine. They were Pax's. He was laid out flat beside me.

He face-palmed his visor, slowly shaking his head. "Lee had it right, we're calling you fireball."

"Did you dudes hit your head or something?" Mills asked quizzically, coming to tower over Pax and extending him a hand.

"We're fine, Mills." Pax chuckled as Mills pulled him up.

As the two chatted, I decided to inspect the fruits of my labor. On still wobbly legs, I ambled over to the smoking crater and peered inside. All that remained of the bot were jagged silver bits and wiring.

Pax, being a Leege through and through, didn't let us savor our victory for too long and called for us to continue our advance as per our orders. I groaned internally. I'd been ready to dust my hands off with a job well done and call it good, but apparently, wrecking this single bot hadn't won the campaign.

Sore and unsteady, I turned away from the crater and rejoined the group. Just as we were about to move out, a loud rustling sounded from the depths of the trees. We all froze and stared in the direction of the quickly approaching sound. Something big was coming our way, and it wasn't concerned with being detected.

"Take cover!" someone shouted, and we headed.

Scrambling into our respective squads, we ducked behind whatever we could. For me, it was a yellowish-barked trunk, wide enough to conceal a car. I swung out, leveling my blaster at a section of the foliage that had begun to tremble and quake.

A drooler burst into view. Roaring, it spun about in frantic circles.

I almost pulled my trigger right then, as I'd expected the beast to charge, but he didn't. Calming, he fell onto all fours and proceeded to shuffle about aimlessly, grunting and mumbling incoherently. He even took a moment to stop and scratch as if searching for fleas. A grunt of satisfaction sounded when the itch was quenched. He then lumbered towards the crater and fixated on what remained of the bot.

I had no idea what to do. My blaster was leveled, but I couldn't bring myself to pull the trigger. The creatures were, after all, slaves. Without his master, the thing looked harmless, a clueless oomph.

Pax, on the other hand, had no reservations and shot him right through the goopy eye, which burst in a spray of liquid. The drooler's surprised squeal cut short as he teetered, then pitched forward into the crater, landing onto the remnants of his master with a heavy plop.

Lowering my blaster, I processed the slaying with a hanging jaw. Bishop was right—the eyeballs did pop like overfilled water balloons. Waving off the untimely interruption with disinterest, troops returned to business and began gathering up. I didn't join. Another idea had jumped into my wayward mind. I wanted to get an up-close look at the beast.

Being very sure there was no way it survived a bolt through the eye, I slid into the crater without a care. I cringed. The thing was even nastier up close. Hulking, with folds of thick grayish skin and tufts of fur in what seemed to be random places. Crouching, I extended a careful finger to touch him, because after all, what else does one do when presented with something new.

However, my finger stopped short of the leathery flesh. Something glinted on the drooler's temple. Standing, I used my boot to turn what was left of the oozing skull, exposing a metal, coin-sized device to the sunlight. I had no idea what it was, but it was easy to tell the puzzle piece didn't belong, all nice and shiny amidst the grossness of the primitive head.

Flitting my eyes about to make sure I was alone, I grabbed the device and pulled. At first nothing happened, it was stuck in the meat. But then, right as I was about to give up and rejoin the squad, with a wet sucking sound, it popped off, leaving behind a circle of tiny punctures on the drooler's temple. I knew it was against regs for troops to remove anything off the planets we were on unless ordered, but it wasn't as if anyone was going to find out.

Turning the gadget over in my hand, I inspected it wonderingly. Bits of flesh clung to the tiny needles protruding from its surface and it was sticky with black blood. Grimacing, I almost dropped the gory thing, but then changed my mind and pocketed the souvenir.

CHAPTER
EIGHTEEN

We were all in fairly good spirits as we pushed on towards the Synths' compound, ready to put down another formation of droolers.

Mills couldn't cut me a break. Not two minutes into our march a heavy arm slung over my shoulders.

"Those alien freaks think they'll get us with something new," he boomed, yanking me closer with a clang of our suits, "but we're not worried, we got something new too."

He cackled like a damn circus clown. "You aren't a one trick pony, are you, newb?"

"Fuck off." I shoved him away from me with all my might. The dude was grinding on my nerves something fierce.

Mills staggered back, laughing, but unfortunately wasn't deterred. "Don't make me put you out to pasture, now! How else are you gonna pull your weight around here? Next time, we can even slap a bell on you."

My jaw set, and I had to work hard not to swing. I didn't know the man well enough to know if he was kidding or not, and I didn't want to encourage his ideas. My muscles still ached, and I couldn't get my fingers to stop randomly twitching.

Since admitting getting shot hurt like a bitch wasn't an option, I decided to try a different approach.

"I'm all out of batteries, man, so someone else can play bait next," I said.

Mills chuckled again, this time deep and low. "That's even better. We can use your corpse, then. Tie a string to it and *yank*!"

The fucker accented *yank* as he mimicked reeling in a fish. He'd even secured his blaster momentarily just so he could perform the theatrics. He then prattled on with all the different ways he'd turn my corpse into chum.

Sucking air through my nose, my eyes searched for a solution. I was about thirty seconds away from a fist fight, and that wasn't the impression I wanted to make on Pax my first day on the job. I spotted it five troops up, but first, I had an idea. I wasn't about to let Mill's goading go unanswered.

Plastering on a broad grin that I knew he'd see in the crinkle of my eyes, I rounded on Mills and flipped him the one finger salute.

Yup, that did it.

Cutting off mid-sentence, the oaf jerked back as if I'd just slapped him across his yapping mug, but the surprise didn't last. Releasing an animalistic roar, Mills lunged, arms flung wide like one of the droolers.

Cursing and stumbling, his grip closed on nothing. I was already gone and shoulder to shoulder with Somner. I'd yet to figure out the squad's dynamic, but it appeared the SL and Somner were the only ones able to muzzle the beast.

"What's up?" I greeted Somner, to the backdrop of Mill's profanity and colorful threats. Evidently, he wasn't a fan of my brazen move. I had suspected as much. I deemed not many newbs flipped off the Gold Squad troops and especially not him.

Somner startled back at my sudden appearance and reflexively trained his blaster. His visor was on clear, and large green eyes blinked at me in confusion. They rolled when they noticed Mills loitering five steps away as if a dog afraid of a shock-rod.

Somner lowered his weapon and chuckled.

"Don't let 'em get to you, man," he said over private chat. "He's really just a big teddy bear once you get to know him, and as dumb as one too. Watch, you'll see."

"Figured out the dumb part already," I replied as we squeezed through a leafy grove. Purple-veined fronds slapped over my visor and snapped under my boots. "It's the big fists that kinda worry me."

Somner shrugged, nonchalant. "Guess you'll just have to grow a pair and take a few lickings, but you'll get there."

I could tell he found the whole thing amusing, but still, his eyes shone with authenticity. That provided me a shred of reassurance that one day I might come into my own.

We moved on to small talk after that as we trudged.

Twenty minutes later, the mood turned. We were now about half a mile away from the shield itself and yet there was nothing in our vicinity, just rustling plants and massive trees casting shadows over each other. The lack of contacts was eerily unsettling. We even tried flushing them out by shooting into the brush, but there was nothing. The area was deserted, and no one knew why. Normally, Pax said, they'd have encountered enough trouble by now to justify a retreat.

"Stop!" Pax suddenly shouted, extending an arm.

Heads turned in confusion as everyone halted and waited with heavy anticipation. A few troops shuffled, while others instinctively took up defensive positions. We knew both second squad's SL and Pax were talking with the other squads and units. To keep the chatter down on deployment, line troops weren't able to chat with the other squads unless their SL patched them through, was killed, or the suits were within a certain range of each other, at which point one had the option to talk to any troops around them who weren't speaking on private chat.

Pax turned to face us. Saying nothing, he scanned slowly over our antsy group. The tension he radiated was palpable.

Mills shuffled impatiently. "What is it, SL?"

"The Synths… they're flanking the rear squads."

Heads spun as a chorus of *whats* and *huhs* erupted.

Pax quickly composed himself then set off at a jog back from where we'd come, signaling us to follow as he briefed.

"The bots must've been reprogrammed. The advance is scrubbed. We've been given orders to fall back and join the other squads in holding the Synths off long enough for the lower ranks to retreat. New safe zones are being set up."

A chill ran down my spine and our jog quickly escalated into a suit-powered run. I think Pax kept talking, but I couldn't focus. All I could think about was Ness. She was inexperienced, just like me and the rest of her squad. Except, unlike me, she didn't have a Gold Squad heavy-gear suit with an extra battery and a team of Gold Squad troops watching her back.

All she had was Gundy, and as fierce and experienced as he was, I wasn't sure he was capable of organizing the new troops enough to withstand a full-force attack after only three days of training.

Setting my suit to proximity comms, I hustled to keep up with everyone as we raced toward the lower squads. We encountered no resistance, and it wasn't long until comms crackled with noise. My nerves jangled. It was the sounds of screaming and dying.

Other squads had joined our charge and about thirty of us jumped into the dogfight. Centurion Paxton was in our group, shouting for the lower squads to retreat. Except they couldn't. Hordes of droolers grappled with the troops, tackling them amidst the blaster fire raining over the field. I wanted nothing more than to dash into the mayhem and look for Ness, but Pax veered away from the fight.

"This way!" he shouted, commandeering second squad. "We're going to fan right. Drone reported incoming."

Not slowing, he leaped over the remains of a blaster-riddled carcass lying in a puddle of gore and continued.

"Orders are to hold them off until ninth and tenth squads retreat."

Gritting my teeth in frustration, I had no choice but to follow.

"Ness!" I kept trying, but there was no reply.

Holding back panic, I reasoned she might not have proximity comms toggled on, or maybe she was simply out of range. Unlike the SL's gear, my HUD didn't give me the option to scroll through everyone's designators.

Fanning away from the main battle, it didn't take us long to find the enemy, or more like they found us. Like a sea demon lurching from the deep, about twenty roaring droolers stormed out of the foliage as one. They stumbled over their own writhing and dying teammates but weren't deterred. Right off, we shot down a good number of them, but not all. Soon, they were on top of us.

A pair of massive arms flew at me. I dodged and shot, toppling backwards. Red holes sprouted in the drooler's gut, but it didn't slow.

Roaring and gushing blood and torn innards out of its wounds, it pounced. Throwing myself out of the way, I jumped to my feet and leveled my blaster to put it down for good, only to be tackled by another beast.

Air exploded from my lungs and my blaster flew from my grip. I could feel the weight on top of me, crushing, as the paws wrapped around my helmet with lethal intent. My head bonked as the drooler jerked and pulled, attempting to wrench it off. Metal ground and creaked in protest. Gasping for air, I squirmed like a worm under the massive beast. I knew I had only seconds before the metal gave and my head was torn off my shoulders to roll like the other troopers.

Fortunately, unlike the other trooper, I was pinned on my back and not my belly. Toggling on both energy blades, I blindly swung at the enormous beast. The crackling beams found no resistance and drooler guts spilled over my armor. The thunderous roars changed to gurgling howls, then ceased as the beast pitched forward on top of me.

Attempting to catch my breath, I lay still under the carcass, my mind paralyzed. Another few seconds and I would've been dead. I could've laid there for days, but it was impossible to ignore the human screams filling the comms.

No one quits, everyone fights.

With a heave, I shoved the carcass off me and wiped my visor with shaky fingers. The thick blood smeared as if I were playing with paint, but I managed to get enough off to where I could see. Troops and droolers were tangled up in a brawl all around me. The Gold Squads hacked away with their blades while the lower ranks, with the less advanced suits, struggled to untangle from their attackers long enough to get off a shot.

Mutilated remains of both droolers and troopers littered the field. A heavy dread crept over me. I felt no joy that the number of beasts surpassed the troops. Even one dead human was too many. I shook it off. If I concentrated on the task at hand, I wouldn't have to think.

Determined, I rushed to aid the nearest trooper. A drooler had him in a bear hug as he thrashed and screamed, bicycling the air as the beast attempted to wrestle him to the ground. Activating my blades, I came to a skidding stop and skewered the drooler through his side like a kabob. With one swift yank, I sliced him in two. My blade sizzled and crackled as it carried out its lethal task, and vibrations traveled up my arm. In a mess of guts, the carcass dropped.

"Th... thanks," the trooper panted, scampering to his feet.

As he rushed away, I moved on to the next bundle of man and beast, then the next. My mind was blank as I hacked, intermittently wiping my hand over my visor to clear the blood.

I noticed another Leege working their way through the field. Except, unlike my half-ass, inexperienced thrusts, there was a deadly beauty to his well-coordinated movements. Leaping onto the drooler's backs, he rolled with them in tandem as his blades carried out their task. As one collapsed, he jumped off, deftly pouncing on to the next. A large gold earth emblem peeked out from under the gore smearing his breastplate. I knew who the man was.

I could have watched Centurion Paxton all day, but in my second of distraction, a large inhuman fist punched into my helmet and knocked me to the dirt. A numb ringing filled my head from the force. Without waiting to regain clarity, I acted on instinct. Flipping onto my back, I bent my arms at the elbow and extended my blades. The drooler's roar changed to a squeal as the thoughtless animal lunged on top of them and skewered himself. Waiting a second for the ringing in my head to subside and for the white stars to clear from my vision, I pushed the carcass off and jumped back to my feet.

We were winning this melee, and troops all around were beginning to whoop and cheer. Unfortunately, the concealed bots that must've been watching also arrived at that conclusion, because they started blasting. They didn't give a damn about hitting their own, and bolts rained hot on everyone's heels. They shot down the droolers as much as us.

"Retreat!" Centurion Paxton roared in our comms. "Disperse and retreat!"

The bots were shooting fish in a barrel.

"Come on, Adlar!" Pax shouted as men scattered into the jungle. "Squad one and two, you're with me!"

Since our orders to assist ninth and tenth squad's retreat still stood, that's exactly what Pax intended to do. We had bought them ample time to break away from this particular brawl, but they hadn't managed to get far before running into more trouble.

"Squad nine and ten, retreat! Retreat!" Pax roared repeatedly as the clash taking place ahead of us came into view.

I knew Pax was feverishly yelling at the squads to tuck tail and run not only because we were ordered to secure their safe escape but also because once we joined the fight, the humans would outnumber the droolers. That would result in only one thing. The damn bots would blast the crap out of all of us.

Ninth and tenth squads heeded and any trooper who was able ran. Some paused to pull helmets off the dead and help the injured into hover-carts.

Roaring at the top of his lungs, Pax clashed into the mayhem, shooting down any monster not attached to a trooper. He then extended his blades and hacked away with a skill on par with his father's.

I trailed at the very rear, slicing at the beasts with not nearly the same enthusiasm.

"Ness!" I continued trying to reach her over private chat.

There was no question we were now in range and no answer meant only one thing. My chest squeezed as I hoped for a response.

"I'm fine, Jake," her voice rang out in my helmet, right as I was knocked off my feet and tumbled to the ground with a drooler lunging onto my chest.

My heart skipped with relief.

"I'm bugging out. Kick some ass and see you soon!"

Smiling wide, I decapitated the beast on top of me with one swipe, then rejoined the fight with newfound energy.

As the number of enemies on the field thinned, just like clockwork, bolts began to pepper here and there. I was expecting the battlefield to become a disorganized mess again as troops rushed over each to scatter, but instead, cheers reached my ears.

Spinning to face a charging drooler, I dove to the ground and slid on my side, severing his legs with my blades, then lunged up and cleaved it in half from behind. Wiping my visor clean, I glanced to see what had everyone excited. Black suits flashed through the trees, approaching. The fifth unit was rushing to join in on the fight.

I momentarily worried about our growing numbers, but as they neared, the jungle behind them rumbled. There were substantial enemy forces hot on their heels, both bot and droolers if I had to guess. The bots showered the running men with bolts while some of the troops flung frags aimlessly over their shoulders. Trees crashed in deafening explosions as the ground shook and plumes of dirt and debris geysered skyward. Leeges flew off their feet like carnival pop-ups, some from the blast force and others from bolts slamming into their backs.

The concealed bots ceased their fire as our two groups converged and the ratio of drooler to man again became two to one. The drawn-out engagement was starting to take its toll. I was breathing hard, and my eyes were wild. The jungle around me was decimated and littered with the dead, the dying, and the injured. Troops screamed and writhed in the mud. Some hobbled away the best they could, others crawled grotesquely with missing limbs and torn armor.

Right as I put down yet another drooler, after barely avoiding a deadly bear hug from another, a Centurion's form caught my eye. The Earth emblem on their gear was grimed, but still visible. With artful precision, their blades streaked through the air as they lunged at two charging droolers, but they weren't watching their flank. Another one charged their way. Before I could yell out a warning, the Centurion spun and gutted the flanking beast with one blade while the other was still in the process of finishing off the first two.

I didn't need to look at the locator to know whose narrow figure danced before me. It was none other than my very own personal admirer, Centurion Fallon. Right as her kills fell at her feet, another drooler jumped from the brush. This time, she failed to evade, and two massive arms wrapped around her tiny body with binding force.

I sucked air through my teeth. Notwithstanding my sour opinion of the vile woman, I knew I couldn't just idly stand there. As such, I rushed to help, only for my head to meet a swinging arm. It hit with enough force that I almost did a backflip. I gutted the drooler absent-mindedly, determined to aid the Centurion.

Hopefully, her head was still attached to her body. As despicable as she was, I couldn't let another Leege die, especially not like that.

As I dashed towards her, Centurion Paxton beat me to the punch.

Pouncing onto the drooler's back, he hacked away like a madman as the beast bucked and howled, trying to shake him off. Gore spewed and tufts of fur flew. In the process, as the drooler thrashed and twisted, he flung Fallon high into the air. Shrieking, the woman flew like a Frisbee and vanished into the trees.

"Break off!" shouted Pax's voice in my comm. "All squads, head to the safe zones! Now!"

I wanted to do just that, except I'd yet to see Fallon reemerge from the trees. I spun to Centurion Paxton, hoping he'd also noted her journey of flight, only to see the man being rushed by two additional droolers. Against my better judgment, but feeling it was something I had to do, I charged into the trees after Fallon. I knew the bots were lurking out there, observing the fight and itching to kill. She didn't have much time.

Pushing through man-sized leaves, I soon gleaned her onyx armor. That's when I realized I was too late. My breath caught, and I dropped like a rock.

CHAPTER
NINETEEN

What I'd witnessed before face-planting to the dirt had not been a hopeful sight; a seven-foot-tall metallic frame of a bot towered over Centurion Fallon, who was backed against a tree and frozen. Still flat on the ground, I tightened my grip on my blaster. I knew full well that it would take at least three precise hits to bring down the machine, giving it plenty of time to shoot Fallon, but I didn't see another option. Nor was there time to think of anything better. I'd just have to take the chance. Hopefully, her suit had enough juice left to withstand a few point-blank hits.

Slowly pushing through the broad leaves over my head, I rose and leveled my blaster. I was about to pull the trigger but paused. Something wasn't right. I quickly dropped flat again. The robot had Fallon dead in its sights and yet, she was still standing. Not only was she still standing, but the bot's weaponized forearms hadn't been raised. This was only my first drop, and I was in no way an expert, but I'd yet to see the machines hesitate.

My skin prickled with goosebumps. Something wasn't adding up.

Cautiously, I hazarded another peek, only to see the image hadn't improved. There was the bot, and there was Fallon, still pressed flat against the trunk, still alive. Her head was craned up while the bot's was lowered as if the two were looking at each other. My unease intensified. The red light in the bot's head pulsed as if taking readings, strobing over Fallon's visor.

Then, things got even stranger. Turning, the bot walked away. With three long strides, it vanished into the trees. I gawked, confused, but quickly hit the dirt again when Fallon pushed off the trunk and rounded in my direction. I had no idea what I'd just witnessed, but I was sure of one thing—whatever it was, wasn't good.

Not daring to twitch a muscle, I intently watched Fallon in my display. I couldn't help but worry about my locator right then. I had no way to deactivate the signal, and if she happened to be paying attention to her visuals, I was dead.

As she neared, my finger slid to my trigger. Dark thoughts stewed in my head. Was I capable of killing her if it came to that? Hell, before today, I'd never killed anything, much less a person.

Then again, *she* wouldn't hesitate.

A moment later my mind was made up. She'd skewer me like a roast pig without a qualm, so it was only fair I'd return the favor. Tensing, I eyed her locator, ready to get the beat on her if she veered my way. I wondered how many shots it would take. Maybe I'd just stun her and run, I reasoned. Payback would feel damn good, sure, but was it worth my life? I'd be executed for killing an officer. She wasn't worth having my inside melted by lethal nanites.

Thankfully, my strategizing was for naught. Slowly but surely, the dot that was her moved on. Heaving a huge sigh of relief, I let my head drop to the dirt. My entire body tingled with tension.

When I deemed Fallon was far enough, I toggled the volume up on my comms. They crackled with some broken chatter, no longer ringing with screams and shouted orders. The clash was over, and my cohort was on the retreat.

Relieved, I pushed up, about to rise, when a beep sounded, and a contact popped up on top of me. Acting on instinct, I flipped onto my back, my blaster up and finger on the trigger. Yet, all I saw above me was green. Massive, feathered leaves swayed over each other as bits of purplish-blue sky peeked in between.

My suit beeped again warning me of the contact. With jerky, panicked movements, I swung my blaster to the left then right, but saw only plants. Nor were there any unnatural noises in my audio. Not that I knew what passed for natural or unnatural around here, but I was sure nothing was charging. Perhaps it was a malfunction, I considered, as I continued to aim at the swaying canopy. Who knew how many times my helmet had been bashed by an angry, feral fist or slammed against the ground? Not to mention the numerous electrocutions it had endured.

Slowly, I sat up enough to where my head was over the brush and scanned the area. The contact was still up on my display, but all my eyes saw were leaves and trunks. The jungle around me was unnervingly still.

A sudden burst of adrenaline shot through me, and I jumped to my feet, scanning above me with the barrel of my blaster. What if something was in the trees? Some ghastly creature we hadn't been briefed about. Unfortunately, I couldn't see squat through the patchwork of leaves. I couldn't even make out the trunks in most places. If something was hiding up there, I wasn't going to spot it. It was time to go.

I spun and ran. The safe zones had now been marked and confirmed and slews of locators were rushing towards the awaiting dropships. Since the bots only ventured so far from the base they were charged with protecting, the Legion always had an egress. But in no way was it convenient. The safe zones were miles away. Turned out SL Gundy hadn't tortured us with his grueling runs simply for his enjoyment.

I broke out of the trees and onto the now quiet battleground just as the last of the black-suited figures disappeared into the jungle across the field from me. I slowed my pace, astounded by the devastation. It looked like both a wildfire and a tornado had scoured the area. Most of the trees were uprooted, and those that weren't had been reduced to stumps. The ground still smoked in places.

The number of drooler corpses greatly outnumbered the dead troops, but my chest still squeezed. Too many motionless black suits littered the field. It was obvious we had won the battle, but I wasn't sure to what end? The Synths were probably gathering more troops, same as the Legion was gathering more men. Third cohort, back on *Venator*, was preparing to deploy.

A metallic shimmer of a bot's torso lurched me away from my brooding. The bright beam from the sun had hit it just right to where the light bounced into my eyes. It reminded me that I was completely exposed. I picked up my pace, bounding over fallen trees and hustling around craters and corpses. My doom and gloom thoughts were useless distractions anyway. A Leege's job wasn't to rationalize the conflict but to simply do as told.

Clearing my head, I did my best not to look at anything except where my feet were stepping, as the decimated terrain wasn't completely still. The local wildlife had sniffed out the buffet, and the boars were helping themselves to a feast. Snorting and grunting, they ripped at the corpses with their massive fangs, devouring both droolers and men alike. Some momentarily paused to squeal at me as I passed. My gut churned as I swerved to avoid them.

As I ran, my display continued to incessantly flash a contact almost on top of me, but I ignored it. The suit was definitely in need of some R&R whenever I got back to the ship. Not only was it malfunctioning, but it was also completely filthy. The blood I had spilled had dried and my exterior was an abstract painting of disgusting colors. One that had me grateful the suits were encapsulating and pressurized. I didn't want to imagine how badly I stunk on the outside. Not that I was any fresher inside the suit, either. Sure, there were cooling gels and internal temp regulators but there was only so much they could do against the sweltering jungle heat and constant strenuous physical activity.

Next, my thoughts rebounded to Fallon. I still couldn't make heads or tails of what I'd seen, or how Fallon had survived—

"Argrghh!" I skidded to a stop, flapping my arms like a bird to catch my balance.

Something strange had cut me off and almost caused me to pitch to my butt. Squinting, I focused on the being hovering before my visor. I quickly recognized it to be the moth creature the scientist had gone on about during the briefing.

The bug looked just like the hologram, but up close, a lot nastier. It was mushy and gross. Its fuzz-covered grayish torso was about the size of a cat, and it hovered up-right, its daggered insect legs facing me. Three black eyeballs rotated, taking me in. At least I think it was looking me over as its eyes rolled in its head, but since there weren't any visible pupils, I couldn't be certain.

The briefing had instructed us to stay away from the locals, that much I remembered, but for the life of me, I couldn't recall what the scientist had said to do if we were face-to-face with one. Or had he gotten that far before Neero threw him off the stage? *Fuck...* I couldn't recall.

Meeting its glassy eyeballs, I contemplated what the thing possibly wanted. Hopefully, it wasn't anything important, because then it was shit-out-of-luck, as I couldn't as much as negotiate a civil living relationship with a house cat. My mom's insipid pet had the run of the house. He slept where he wanted to sleep and climbed into any drawer he pleased. I'd long grown accustomed to inspecting myself for furballs before setting out to prowl the local bars.

As unsure as I was, I decided to talk to the bug and toggled on my external speakers.

"Uh, sorry about the mess," I said, glancing behind me at tornado alley.

I figured the commotion was perhaps why the native decided to grace me with its presence. We'd just obliterated a decent chunk of their land and I doubted their opinion had been taken into consideration.

The bug didn't respond, not that I had expected it to. I knew it was very unlikely it had understood me. It continued to hover before me in silence, wings fluttering like a butterfly's. Deciding it was best to let it be, I moved to walk around it when a second moth zoomed up to the scene. I stumbled back in surprise.

My suit wasn't malfunctioning. Two contacts glowed before me. The locals weren't equipped with whatever the Synths had to conceal themselves from our sensors. I was about to try doing a wide loop around the two, hoping my movement wouldn't prompt the arrival of a third when a trooper darted out of the trees. I felt a chill thinking Fallon had returned to finish me only to realized it was Pax.

"Wooww..." he said, fixating on what was drifting next to my head. "Not to crash your party with the locals here, but it's time to go. Everyone's retreating and we need to get the hell out before the bots deem it worth their time to come back and finish us off..."

He paused and looked around as if seeing where we were for the first time.

"How the hell are you still back here anyways? I ordered a retreat almost twenty minutes ago. Never mind... who cares... let's go!"

He spun away and waved for me to follow.

Obliging, I dodged around the bugs, careful to not head-butt them with my helmet and tailed Pax into the trees. I was now glad we'd spent what little training we received running in full kit. My muscles burned and my body was fatigued, but I wasn't drop-dead exhausted. I was able to keep up with Pax and had enough experience with my gear to allow the suit to do most of the work in the lower gravity.

All the while, I kept an eye on my HUD. It showed that the two contacts were still there, dutifully following. Glancing back, I saw that was true. They tailed about twenty feet behind us. Mildly concerned, I decided to inform Pax of the fact, in case this was somehow important, when my gaze locked on something odd. About two hundred feet north-west of us glowed three trooper locators. Perhaps injured men who couldn't keep running.

"Pax," I called out, figuring he wasn't monitoring his display since he showed no signs of slowing to check on them. "There might be injured ahead of us."

"What?" He slowed as he too checked his overlays. "There were no reports of stragglers, why the hell aren't they moving to evac?"

As irritated as Pax seemed, he changed course in their direction. "I don't know what they're still doing out here, but we can't leave them if they're still alive. The dead, we'll worry about later."

He shook his head. "This drop is just damn strange!"

I couldn't help but agree. I thought of Fallon and the peculiar machine that had seen fit to spare her. Figuring Pax might be able to shed some light on the mystery, I was about to tell him the sordid tale, but right then, two power-bolts punched through the trees. One hit Pax square in the chest, sending him spinning. The other missed me by mere inches as I threw myself prone.

"Pax!" I shouted as my nerves rattled with panic.

With it being only him and me out here, the only chance we had against the bot was to run. Making sure to remain concealed under the leaves, I wormed my way to him, grabbed his arm, and tried to yank him up.

"We gotta go!" I urged.

However, instead of rising, Pax's large hand clamped onto me and pulled me down.

I slapped the dirt next to him.

"Why aren't we running?" I protested, confused. "That bot knows where we are. We need to go!"

I pushed up again, trying to get to my feet.

"Mills, there's a bot!" I called.

Like before, Pax yanked me down.

"That's not fire from a bot, Adlar," he said with a heavy exhale.

"What?" I said, fighting my very strong urge to run.

I turned to look at him. "For fuck's sake, there's something else out here that wants to kill us?"

Zooming out my display, I scanned the area.

"Is it the locals? I wouldn't have guessed them to have firepower. How would they even hold a weapon in those... legs, or arms, or... whatever they are," I rambled as my heart pounded in overdrive.

Maybe they shot bolts out of their eyeballs, what did I know?

Pax chuckled, shaking his head. "No, you dumbass. Those bugs don't have weapons, at least not that we know of."

"Then who, or *what*?" I asked, eyeballing my HUD.

I wasn't having any luck pinpointing our ill-timed foe. All I saw in our vicinity were the two locals, the three injured men, and Mills, Lee, and Somner who'd all changed course and were rushing back to our position. I had to do a double-take when I realized I couldn't tell who the strangers were. Their locators were closing in on us, but their designators were blank.

Pax heaved a sigh and rolled onto his back, letting the hand with his blaster rest on his breastplate.

"It's not the bots or the locals, Adlar, it's something else. Well, someone else. But don't worry, they're not shooting at you, just at me. I guess those vultures couldn't pass up the opportunity since it's just us out here."

"Uh, shouldn't we still run?" I was in the dark about why troopers were shooting at us but figured those questions could wait for later. "They know where we're at, they're going to come finish the job."

The three assailants had slowed but were still edging in our direction. Pax turned to look at me, setting his visor to clear. There was no panic on the man's face, just calm and determination.

"I can't run," he said. "That was the last hit my suit could take. I'm surprised it even took that one. Warnings had been flashing for the last hour. We just have to wait it out and hope Mills and the boys get here before that posse of ass-hats braves a charge."

Tensing, I studied everyone's locators. Our squad was getting closer, but unfortunately, so were the three unknown troopers.

"They're edging towards us," I whispered.

"I know, I'm watching. Don't worry, Adlar, I'm not going to make it that easy for those fucks."

With a charged kind of excitement, Pax flipped onto his chest and snaked into the grass. Not knowing what else to do, I followed.

"Hey, Adlar," Pax called at me over his shoulder. "If they get here before Mills does and shoot me down, you run, okay? At least some of them must have enough charge in their suits for a few more hits since they braved trying this shit. So, if they catch up, you run and head for the dropships, got it?"

"What?" I countered in surprise.

I didn't know who the bastards were, but I knew they had no intention of letting Pax live. You don't start shooting at a Gold Squad Leege if you didn't plan on finishing the job.

"Pax… they're going to kill you."

Another sigh over comms. "If you don't run, they're just going to kill you, too. Then there will be two of us left to rot out here. They're after me, not you."

I didn't answer but knew the situation wasn't looking good for us. The three assailants were getting braver, and I audibly picked up their hasty approach. Foliage rustled and popped behind us.

"Mills!" Pax called. "Where're you getting to? The Boyer bunch are about to have us pinned."

"Almost there, SL, almost there!" Mills shouted, though puffs of exertion. "Just a few more minutes."

By his ragged breaths, I could tell Mills was going as fast as his suit-powered legs would carry him, but it wasn't going to be fast enough. Especially since it appeared that our assailant had noticed the approaching locators. They gave up taking their time. One rushed towards our position while the other two fanned to encircle.

"Shit!" Pax said, echoing my thoughts. "We're not going to make it, and I'm not going down like a rat on my belly. On three, we run. Copy?"

"Copy," I replied, breathing through shallow pants.

I knew what I had to do.

CHAPTER
TWENTY

"Three, two—"

Before Pax could finish, I jumped up.

"Run, Pax!" I shouted as I charged the closest assailant. The surprised man jerked to a sliding stop at the sight of me and my trained blaster. I didn't bother talking or giving him time to react and shot him square in the chest.

It was my turn to be surprised. Instead of flying off his feet, he merely staggered.

"What the—?"

His blaster lifted. I shot again and this time, he almost fell. I was about to go for a third and hopefully final shot, but he decided to return the favor. A bolt of sizzling energy slammed into me and sent me sprawling. My blaster flew out of my grasp as a searing burn consumed me.

Pushing past it, I jumped up and hurled myself at the trooper. It was a brazen move, I knew that, but I couldn't let him get a shot at Pax. Plus, as long as we were locked together, his buddies weren't going to shoot me. My suit wasn't beeping frantic alarms just yet, but a faint low-battery warning flashed in the corner of my HUD.

"Run, Pax!" I shouted as I grappled with the man.

There truly didn't need to be two of us frying out here.

The man I was embattled with was huge, a gorilla of a Leege, and judging by the way he moved, highly experienced. At first, I tried to wrestle him down but quickly realized that wasn't happening. I pulled my arm back and planted a fist into his visor with everything I had.

Not flinching at my punch, he countered with a hook of his own. It appeared he had more than I did. A cannonball of a fist nailed the side of my head and knocked me down. Before I could get back up, he charged, releasing a roar loud enough to be heard through his helmet. I felt it fair to say he didn't approve of me interfering. I couldn't see his face, but I imagined him to be snarling behind that tinted visor.

Right as he was practically on top of me, hands outstretched like an enraged drooler going in for the kill, he was shot in the head in a spray of sparks. That did it and he finally flew to the dirt.

Regrettably, the behemoth still wasn't deterred. Jumping to his feet, he rounded on me, smoke wafting from his helmet.

My gut plummeted all the way to my toes. I was unarmed and about to be *dead*. Yet right as he was almost on me, Pax sped past, a slew of blaster fire flying in his wake. The assailant's buddies were firing from a distance, looking like a pair of paranoid squirrels. They were working hard on not catching a bolt themselves.

Releasing a rage-filled roar of his own, Pax lunged at the monstrous trooper. Their powered suits slammed into each other with a thunderous clap, and they tumbled to the ground in a heap of arms and legs. Fists flew and roars blared as they tried to pound each other to dust.

Dropping to my hands and knees, I searched for my blaster. I couldn't understand why Pax hadn't just shot the guy and fried him.

At last, finding my weapon, I attempted to aim, but a clean shot was out of the question. The two men were a tumbleweed of powered fists bashing on armor. Not daring to accidentally hit Pax, I turned my blaster on the assailant's flunkies. Neither had made a move to approach. They cowered in the brush and pointed shaky blasters at the fight. Noticing me, the scumbags whirled and took off into the jungle like skittering rats. A volley of unexpected blaster fire rained hot on their heels.

"That's what I fucking thought!" Mills roared, charging out of the trees with Somner and Lee behind him. We all rushed towards Pax.

"Don't shoot!" Pax ordered.

Noting everyone's arrival, the assailant broke away from Pax and hopped back, but unlike his buddies, he didn't run.

"Don't shoot," Pax repeated.

"Seriously?" Mills griped, his blaster aimed, point-blank, on the assailant's head.

Even though Pax's order made absolutely no sense to me, I also obeyed and didn't fire. Killing the man wasn't my call. Instead, I bunched up with the rest of the squad as we all gawked at the two large, suited figures before us. Neither Pax nor the stranger lunged. Separated by a few feet, they slowly circled each other like two boxers in a ring. A strange vibe hung in the air, permeated with an essence of hate.

The hairs on my arms tingled from the tense energy as Mills shuffled nervously next to me. My mind reeled, only a month ago, my biggest worry had been passing tests and chasing skirts. Now, after being electrocuted, pummeled, and covered in alien gore, I was watching two experienced killers circle each other like dueling lions.

"Next time…" boomed a menacing crackle of external speakers as the mysterious trooper slowly backed away.

However, he didn't follow his cronies, but moved towards his weapon. In a stifling silence, Pax allowed it to happen while holding back an edgy Mills with an extended arm.

Keeping his gaze locked on Pax, the unidentified man reached down and picked up his blaster, then slowly backed towards the trees. Large leaves slid over his suit, swallowing him out of view bit by bit. Just when he was almost out of sight, he lifted his weapon and aimed. We all shuffled and tensed, tightening our grip on our blasters, but he wasn't aiming at Pax.

Unlike us, Pax didn't flinch. He remained as steady as a mountain, facing the man.

Two quick shots flashed through the air as the brute vanished into the green. A nasty laugh sounded in his wake.

Jerking my head to look, I realized what he'd shot. Screaming a piercing whine, two moths spun to the ground. My gut cinched, and my legs acted of their own accord. Falling to my knees, I ruffled through the grass with panicked hands in search of the bugs. I scooped up the first moth I found and stared at it with a hanging jaw. It dangled limply in my arms with a smoking hole blown out of its torso. Blood streamed down my armor. It was red, like ours.

A slew of strange, unexpected sensations cascaded over me— disbelief, pain, and rage—I wasn't exactly sure. We'd been slaughtering beasts all day and many corpses littered the field. Yet, the sight of the dead civilian, seeping innards and wings singed to a crisp, elicited emotions I didn't know I had.

Why hadn't Pax just shot that asshole?

No matter how unsightly the moths were, they didn't deserve this. They hadn't raised arms against us. They were just bystanders whose planet was caught in the crossfire.

"Why can't you just let me kill him already, Pax?" Mills boomed. "This shit's just gonna keep happening! You don't even have to watch. Just let me off the fucker! I won't even tell you about it. It's not like he'd be the first person to disappear on the ship."

I gently laid the moth back on the ground, double-checked my visor was on tint, then rejoined the group.

"We don't kill humans, Mills," Pax snapped in response.

He was hunched over, ruffling through the brush for his blaster.

"Even idiots like that one." He gestured to where the man had vanished. "That dumb-ass is still a trooper, a Leege, and I will never give you permission to kill him."

Collecting his blaster, he gave Mills a reassuring pat on the arm. "Thanks for the thought, though. I'm sure we're not the only ones who'd appreciate it if that fucker simply vanished."

Mills loudly sighed with exasperation, then glanced at Lee and Somner.

"You wanna give it a try?" He gestured at Pax.

Both shook their heads *no*.

Mills flung his arms high. "Ugh! Fine! Whatever!"

He then turned to me. "Hurry your ass up, you fuck! This is all your fault!"

Before I could oblige Mills, Pax was before me. Two heavy hands clapped down on my shoulders as he stared into my visor.

"You crazy fool." He chuckled. "But thanks for that, as stupid as it was. I mean it. And I'm sorry you were dragged into the mess."

"No problem." I shrugged as a smile tugged at my lips.

My muscles still twitched uncontrollably, and my insides ached as much as my battered body, but I found myself grinning. I was glad I'd done what I had, not only for Pax but for myself. Only a few hours ago I'd been pissing myself with fear, and now its hold over me was weakened.

With that thought, came another. That there was something else I feared more than droolers or electrocution—the possibility of losing a teammate. I knew right then I'd jump in front of a mech for Pax. Hell, I'd probably even take a bolt or two for Mills—depending on my mood.

We set off at an easy jog towards the few remaining dropships waiting for the stragglers, then eagerly boarded and secured ourselves. As the pilots prepared for lift-off and the ramp whined shut, something kicked my boot. I looked down to see it was Mills.

He saw me staring at his boot.

"Don't get any ideas, newb," he snorted, then clicked over to private chat. "But thanks for that back there, with the SL. Thanks for saving Pax."

I rushed to toggled my own comms to private. "Who was that? Why are other troopers trying to kill him?"

"It's not *other* troopers, it's just Boyer, fourths squad's SL, and two of his lackeys. He's been after Pax ever since his promotion to first squad's SL, with the next promotion being to Centurion. Boyer thinks Pax only got it because of his dad, but that's a pile of horse shit. Pax deserves to be where he's at. Not that you could explain that to Boyer. The guy is fucked in the head."

I thought back to the limp moth in my arms, suppressing a shudder. "Why did he shoot the locals?"

"Because he's just a shit, that's why." Mills scoffed. "A bet or some sick competition, who knows. He's probably been popping them off left and right the entire drop. *Pfft...* That fuck! He never gets in trouble for anything. Riding some officer's dick if I had to guess."

Mills flung back in his seat and threw his arms over his chest in a huffy manner. "I'd been raring to take him out for ages, but Pax won't budge. He says there's too much in the galaxy already trying to kill us and we can't turn on each other and all that crap. I don't understand it."

He shook his head. "But orders are orders. That's just Pax for you. So, it's up to the rest of us to watch his back. Up to you now, too."

Mills leaned forward, landing a punch on my shoulder. "You're one of us now, Adlar. As crazy as it sounds, you're part of Gold Squad, part of first squad, and we watch each other's backs, both on the ground and on the ship. I'll even promise to stop calling you a *poof*, how's that sound?"

I barked a genuine laugh and leaned my head back. "I'll take you up on that, Mills."

The man was grating as hell and kind of whiney, but perhaps, he'd grow on me.

A few minutes later the pilot announced we'd cleared Atlas' atmosphere and for the first time in who knew how many hours, we were able to remove our helmets. The cool air that rushed over my hot face felt like heaven, and I eagerly wiped away the sweat stinging my eyes. I took in a deep, pleasant breath that wasn't laced with my own personal funk and savored it.

Glancing at the men around me, at their exhausted faces, matted hair, and gore-covered suits, I couldn't help but reflect. Lee closed his eyes while Pax and Mills leaned back with forlorn stares. Somehow, I'd survived, and not only had I survived, but I was now part of Gold Squad. My hand slid over my breastplate to touch the gold earth insignia over my heart, and I grinned like a fool. The desire to leave the Legions, to leave this whole damned shit-show, no longer burned within me like an inferno.

CHAPTER
TWENTY-ONE

We were one of the last dropships to return to *Venator*. Most of the other ships had already ferried from the airlock and were lined up in their usual spots, with SF personnel buzzing around them like bees. Beeps and clangs echoed throughout the hangar as they rummaged through tool-filled carts and fretted over charred hulls, and smoking engines. The entire place reeked of singed metal and something comparable to wet dog and vomit.

Before my teammates could stop me, I shouldered past them and jogged down the line of ships. They all shouted at my back for me to help clear out the dropship.

"Give me a sec," I said over my shoulder, untensing when tenth squad's ship came into view through the suited bodies in my way.

Ness was there, in one piece, laughing and joking as she rifled through a hover-cart full of items she'd retrieved. Spotting a few bloodied helmets in the cart, I tried not to dwell on their previous owners' dire fates.

"I'll be damned!" boomed SL Gundy's familiar voice.

He stomped over, clasping my forearm. "How the hell did you make it out, boy?"

Spinning about at Gundy's greeting, Ness charged me and embraced me in a tight hug. She broke away, giving my chest a slap, one arm still wrapped around my waist.

"Adlar wasn't going to die just yet! He's Gold Squad now!" she stated proudly, albeit with a hint of concern glistening in her eyes. I'd survived this drop, but we both knew there was still the next.

I squeezed her again and gave her a reassuring grin.

"Got lucky I guess," I answered Gundy.

Honestly, I could've even hugged him right about now, but I decided I'd already pushed my luck enough for the day.

Feeling comfortable enough around Ness and the troops I'd trained with, I decided to inquire about the strange incident I'd witnessed in that eerie tangle of trees. I was sure Gundy had encountered plenty of bots.

"Sir," I said. "Have you ever noticed the bots act strange? Hesitate to kill?"

I still wasn't sure if my eyes hadn't simply been playing tricks on me. Maybe the machine was damaged, and I'd been too busy pissing myself to notice.

Gundy's face dropped. He blinked at me once, then twice.

"You some kinda retard, boy?" he finally barked, flinging his hands to his hips. "What job were they gonna give you back on Earth, playing a doorstop? Those machines just set a god damn trap for us down there! Did they not?"

"Well, yeah, but that's not—"

"That was rhetorical, you dumbass!"

I fidgeted with my helmet as I suddenly regretted opening my big mouth to begin with.

"I swear you maggots get stupider with each batch."

A large finger flew to point down the row of dropships. "Now quit wasting my time and go be an idiot somewhere else. You're another SLs problem now!"

Whispering a quick bye to Ness, I did just that and skedaddled. Perhaps I was ten kinds of a moron, thinking I'd be able to have a conversation with the likes of him.

I didn't quite make it to my squad, however. Not ten steps from Gundy, a certain familiar face had me slide to a stop. The witch spotted me too. Eyes flying wide, Fallon almost tripped over her own feet in surprise. The hand not clutching her helmet balled into a tight fist as one of her eyes began to twitch.

Long seconds ticked by as we stared at each other, neither one of us breaking away even as troops and medics rushed between us.

Unsure of what to do, I did the first thing that jumped to my mind. Smiling wide, I waved. What happened next was priceless. With an animalistic snarl that echoed and had people jump, Fallon whirled and stormed towards the elevators, roughly shoving past whoever was unfortunate enough to be in her way. A poor sap who wasn't quick enough even got a helmet upside the head as she barreled by.

My ear-to-ear grin remained as I basked in the remnants of the delightful interaction. The mental snapshot I had of her outburst was the best thing I'd seen all day. I was sure she'd throw more horrors my way, but I'd already thwarted two of her attempts at getting rid of me. I was more than ready to ruin her plans a third time.

Smiling and in a great mood, I helped my squad remove extra air packs from the dropship, then headed to the equipment room to return my gear. I was careful to take out my alien souvenir.

"How?" was all Hughes managed to stammer as I shoved my filthy helmet into his startled hands.

I really hoped some of the goo was still wet.

"I want this nice and shiny by the next drop." I winked at him. "And don't forget to get all that dried gunk out of the cracks. I saved some there, just for you."

The man just gaped at me in reply, jaw hanging open. Without saying another word, I turned and left, stopping only long enough to grab a handful of muscle repair gel from the bin next to the door.

Clutching the squishy packets, I headed for my room, ready to enjoy what time I had before the next drop. I was going to take a much-needed shower, get some food, then finally sleep. The first thing I did, however, was throw my alien knick-knack into my desk drawer, being careful to push it all the way towards the back and out of easy view.

Whistling a happy tune, I slammed the drawer shut. The only thing that could have improved my mood at the moment, besides never having to drop again, of course, was if I had something more to look forward to than the cool relief of the medicated salves. Such as the company of another warm body. I needed to find Wagner, but how? On a ship as big as *Venator*, finding a single person that I had no direct connection to was a task more difficult than killing droolers.

After enjoying my much-needed hot shower, while trying not to ogle the naked soapy ladies at the other showerheads, I waltzed back into my room to see that Ness had returned. She popped her head over the edge of her bunk and greeted me with a giant smirk as giggles sounded from behind her. The girl wasn't alone. Chuckling, I plopped on my chair, deciding to give them some space, and reached for the gel. Every muscle was sore and my neck stiff. The helmets weren't light and being repeatedly battered like a volleyball hadn't helped.

Just as I started to rub some of the cold goop onto my sore calves something caught my eye. I swiveled my chair like a madman to face what draped over Ness' chair, sending the opened packet of gel to fly from my grasp. On the back of the chair was a jacket, but not just any jacket. The gray camo pattern of a Space Fleet uniform greeted my eyes—here on the trooper deck. If that wasn't a sign, I didn't know what was.

Ignoring the dropped packet oozing goo onto the deck, I leaped up onto Ness' chair and popped my head over the bunk's edge. The two women didn't immediately acknowledge me, as they were busy giggling and chatting. Saying nothing, I stared at them, a big stupid grin on my face. At last, Ness' friend noticed.

Scrunching her brows, she stopped talking and slowly rotated to face me. "Is something wrong with your roommate, Ness? Did he get hit in the head or something?"

"Sure was!" I continued to grin at her like a fool. "Popped on the head plenty and electrocuted to boot."

My eyes rolled up to the ceiling in thought. "Then hit pretty much every other place, but that's not what I needed to talk to you about."

"Oookay..." she said, slowly. "What is it then?"

Ness looked around her friend to glare at me. The death lasers beaming from her eyes screamed she wanted me gone, but I pretended not to notice.

"Do you know a LT Wagner?" I asked. "And how did you get here, to this deck?"

"Ugghh!" Ness scoffed and fell back to her pillow with a squeak of her bunk.

For a moment her friend stared at me like I had a concussion, but then she slowly ventured an answer. "I walked… then took the elevator, then walked some more. And yea, I kind of know Wagner. I've seen her around here and there, but she's not in my direct chain of command."

"That's great!" I slapped the railing loudly, startling both women. "Can you give her a message for me, or ask her to meet me somewhere?"

The room went dead silent as both ladies propped themselves up on their elbows and stared at me as if my biscuit wasn't fully cooked in the center. Then, after exchanging looks, they burst out laughing. I frowned. This wasn't the reaction I had expected.

"Let me get this straight," Ness' friend said, wiping away a tear. "You want me to go up to some officer, tell her I was just chatting it up, hanging out on the trooper decks, then say, hey there's this rando who wants to meet up with you, you should go."

She fell back on the pillow laughing.

"Then afterwards…" she huffed, "she and I can braid our hair and gossip, right? Is that what you're asking?"

My face scrunched in thought. Perhaps she was right, it would be somewhat awkward for her to carry out my request. One didn't go up to a random officer, admit they were doing something they shouldn't, then play cupid between an enlisted.

However, being of a hardheaded nature, I wasn't about to give up so easily. As such, I decided to try a different approach. "Is there any way you can swipe her my info, at least?"

The friend quit chuckling to glare at me with dissatisfaction, but her tired expression told me I was slowly whittling her down. If not for anything else but to get me to leave. All I had to do was stare at her longer.

"Fine," she snapped, at last. "If that would get you to leave us alone, then sure. Go swipe your info to my phone, then I'll pass it to her like we're in high school. I'll say it's from some trooper in the hangar bay. I'll get creative."

Bingo! I jumped off the chair and lunged for her phone on Ness' desk.

"Do you know her first name by any chance?" I asked as I flicked my trooper ID off my watch to her screen.

Loud irritable sighs erupted from the bunk. The girls must've been under the impression I was now going to leave them alone.

"Taylor, I think, or Terry, maybe. One of those."

I smiled at that. Wagner kind of looked like a Taylor. Then, I frowned, considering what squad number I'd be under. Taylor wouldn't connect someone she'd just met on her transport with someone in the first squad. *Damn,* I hoped she remembered me and didn't think some random Gold Squad punk was hitting on her.

"All done!" I jumped back onto the chair and looked at the ladies.

My excitement was met with an angry glare from Ness, followed by a guttural growl.

I arched an eyebrow at her, feigning innocence. "You want some of my gel? You looked tense."

Ness didn't find that funny. Her jaw set and she looked ready to throttle me.

"It's fine," the SF woman said, sitting up. "I have to go anyway."

Giving Ness a quick peck, she climbed down from the bunk and threw on her jacket, walking out of the room with all my hopes for the immediate future shoved into her pocket.

CHAPTER
TWENTY-TWO

I was looking forward to a day of R&R since the following drop was scheduled for approximately 0200 the following morning, but once again, the Legion flushed all my expectations of rest down the toilet.

Around the ungodly hour of 0500 both Ness' and my phones and watches began to buzz. They rattled and jumped on the tables like a couple of ticks. Groaning and cursing, Ness and I did what any sleep-deprived and sore person would do. We ignored the wicked devices and buried our heads in our pillows.

I swore, right then, my next month's allotment of credits was going to a tech-savvy trooper that could install a silencing hack. Seeing as the brass wasn't keen on the idea of troops being able to silence messages and announcements, our issued devices weren't pre-installed with that luxury.

Anyone interested in obtaining that much sought-after option had to seek the services of a techie, and such services weren't cheap. With my new Gold Squad rank, I figured that wasn't going to be a problem.

Unfortunately, burying our heads in our pillows proved a futile resolution. Because then, the intercom announcements began, wishing us a good morning Legion style.

"Attention troopers of second cohort," said a young female voice, which I recognized to be that of our Prefect's aide.

"Scheduled exercises will commence at 0700 hours at the arena and continue throughout the day. Check your phones for your unit's scheduled time slot."

The message must've been prerecorded because after too brief of a silence it replayed, over and over again.

"What the hell are they thinking?" I fumed, my voice muffled by my face being buried deep in my pillow.

It hadn't even been a day since we'd been bashed like piñatas by blathering aliens, and now we had to gear up to pound each other? Which ingenious brass had somehow seen the logic in that?

"I don't know," Ness seconded my dismay from her bunk, slamming an angry fist against the wall and causing it to rattle. "This sucks! I had plans."

We spent another few minutes moaning, groaning, and complaining, neither one of us ready to embrace the suck just yet, but then we pulled it together.

Grumbling, Ness clambered down from her bunk and grabbed her phone. "Well, at least we have time to get breakfast. Fourth unit's slot is at noon, so thankfully this bullshit isn't an all-day event."

Sighing, I tried to look at the bright side. Ness was right, at least this stupid exercise wasn't an all-day thing, and that left me with time to nap after we ate, and then again after the arena nonsense. Reluctantly climbing down from my bunk, I agreed to join Ness for an early breakfast, eager to fill my stomach, then hit my pillow.

Like usual, after we ate, Ness stayed to mingle, and I found myself walking back to our room alone. I didn't mind. I whistled a happy tune, all the same. Reacquainting with my bunk was going to feel damn good here in a minute.

Then, my joy receded, and my breakfast did a flop in my gut. Loitering next to what I was certain was my door, were two MPs. The men shuffled, staring at the door as if they'd never seen one before.

Not daring to take another step, I contemplated dodging into the random room next to me and pleading for asylum. Maybe they'd hide me, but it was too late. The MPs had spotted me, and unfortunately, this wasn't my lucky day. One of them happened to be the same goon that had dragged me to the Centurion's office.

He recognized me instantly and a waving hand shot up to grab my attention.

"Hey! Adlar!" he shouted as both stormed my way with determination.

Gritting my jaw, I backed a step, still contemplating an escape. Then, I stopped with a heavy sigh. We were on a floating metal canister in the middle of nowhere and as big as *Venator* was, there were still only so many places I could go. Eventually, one way or another, I'd be dragged to wherever it was they were about to drag me to. It was probably better to get this over with now, instead of getting a charge for insubordination heaped onto the pile.

"Thanks for not running," said the familiar burly MP, whose nametag I finally decided to look at.

Something told me this wasn't going to be the last time I'd see him.

"Man, I hate to chase troopers down," Garner huffed, panting from the short sprint he'd done to get to me. I frowned at that. Fitness standards appeared to be laxed for the Fleet side.

"I mean it's not like there's anywhere to go. I always want to ask the runners, what was your plan? To hide out in the cargo bays until you die?"

He laughed, nudging his buddy who chuckled in agreement.

Cutting his laughter short, Garner flung his hands on his portly hips. "So, Mr. Popular, I don't know what you did now, but you know the drill. We're here to escort you to the Centurion's office."

Sighing, I gestured towards the hallway elevator. "Lead the way, I guess."

With that, we all made for the elevator, me reluctantly tailing behind them as they chatted away with random gossip.

"What did you just say?" I interrupted in panic as I lurched forward and pushed between them.

I could have sworn one of them had said something along the lines of a transport being shot down. Garner startled at my untimely interruption, but after a few blinks continued.

"Hard to believe, huh? It just departed, too, and just like that, gone!" He snapped his fingers.

I tried to remain calm, hoping for the best, but my heart hammered. All I could think about was Taylor.

"Which transport was it? Who was the pilot?"

I wanted to grab the man and shake him until the answers spilled out of him, but I urged myself into restraint. Both of the MPs were armed.

Exchanged what-the-hell glances, they ushered me inside the elevator, then Garner turned to me.

"I don't know which one," he said, with a twisted expression. "It's not like I can hear every detail of what the brass says from outside their door. Just bits and pieces. All I know is, it was one headed for Earth to replenish the losses from this last drop."

Garner's face suddenly changed from a snarky scowl to a big grin as he slapped his buddy's arm.

"Oh hey, I almost forgot to tell you, did you hear some *newb* survived dropping with the Gold Squad? Isn't *that* something?"

The other man whistled and replied, but I couldn't hear him. Blood rushed in my ears, and my chest tightened. What if it was Wagner's transport they were gossiping about? I reached inside my pocket and took out my phone, looking to see if I had any missed texts or calls from an unknown ID. I didn't. Only a black screen with a spinning Legion crest stared back at me. Steeling myself, I decided that after whatever this was ended and I endured the arena, I'd find a Space Fleet soldier and wrangle more info. Or better yet, I'd march up to the SF decks and look around myself. I couldn't care less if someone pitched a hissy fit as long as I got some answers.

The elevator glided to a stop at the now too familiar officer's deck, and I somberly followed the MPs out and tailed them to the Centurion's office. Just like last time, I was less than thrilled. I didn't imagine he was too excited, either. Besides perhaps the SLs, ground troops didn't normally rack up such frequent miles with their Centurions.

Cautiously, I inspected the office from the safety of the hall in search of my nemesis. Fortunately, I saw only Centurion Paxton and Braves. Paxton was perched behind his desk and Braves was busy pouring drinks.

Noticing me, Braves' face stretched into a hearty grin.

"Ahh..." he greeted. "If it isn't our newest member of first squad. Come in! Come in!"

He gestured to the chair in front of the desk.

I carefully ventured in as Braves marched to grab another empty glass from the table set by the door.

"Close the door," Centurion Paxton directed in his usual calm and level tone.

Obeying, I turned hesitantly and swiped the control panel, wondering why the Centurion had me do it when he could've sent a signal to shut the door himself. Unlike last time, he had a transmitter looped over his ear, and with it, he could control anything he wanted in his office. Maybe it was an intimidation tactic; me sealing my own demise.

As the door shut, I twisted my head around like a barn owl, giving the room a second thorough inspection. I even eyeballed the ceiling. I wanted to be damn certain Fallon wasn't hiding somewhere in the corners, stirring her cauldron, or perched on a rafter.

Braves chuckled at my antics as he filled an empty glass almost to the top and shoved into my hands as I sat. Taken aback, I eyed the liquor gingerly, then my Centurion. My mouth watered from the spicy aroma, but I was wary of drinking in front of Paxton. Especially with training coming up.

The Centurion gave me a small nod of approval, and that was all I needed. I downed the whiskey in four large gulps. It burned my throat, but I didn't care. I didn't want to leave a drop behind in case the Centurion happened to change his mind.

"So..." Centurion Paxton began when I came up for air. "I suppose you're wondering why you're here... again."

I wiped my mouth on my sleeve and set my empty glass on the table in front me. "Uh, yes, sir."

My gaze flitted between the two men as I tried to read them. The vibe in the room was pleasant enough. Centurion Paxton seemed somewhat relaxed, and Braves was just as I remembered the last time I'd seen him, drunk and happy.

"Well, let's get the official stuff over with first," Paxton said, picking up his tablet and sliding a finger over the screen. "A report has been filed by one of your squadmates claiming conduct unbecoming of a Legionnaire, against a trooper Boyer."

He paused, rolling his eyes up to stare at me. Before I could stop myself, I scoffed. Conduct unbecoming my ass. Boyer was a fucking lunatic. It wouldn't surprise me if he'd tortured kittens as a child.

Paxton didn't miss my inadvertent scoff, and his brows scrunched in suspicion.

"Would you like to shed any light on this, trooper?" he asked.

I quickly straightened my expression. As dull minded as I was, I had enough sense not to touch this with a ten-foot pole. This wasn't some random trooper we were talking about, but his son, and being so new to the ship, I had no idea of what was truly going on; what feud I'd been sucked into. Furthermore, I couldn't help but wonder what Pax would want me to do. Would he approve of me tattling to his dad behind his back? I didn't think so.

As such, I kept up my ignorant act.

"What do you mean, sir?" I asked with a few stupid blinks.

Centurion Paxton picked up his glass and took a tiny sip, studying me intently over the rim.

"I need you to tell me what happened, and where, as well as who was involved? We have an hour's worth of missing suit footage from your entire squad, while also having trooper Boyer's locator going off the grid at about the same time. On top of that, the submitted grievance is about as detailed as an empty holo-vid."

He paused to stare at me in silence. I resisted fidgeting.

"Do you have anything that can fill in these blanks, trooper Adlar?"

My mouth suddenly felt dry.

"Uh, could you tell me who filed this report?" I asked, trying to buy time as my mind reeled, thinking of how to scramble out of this one.

"Hmm," Centurion Paxton said after a few seconds, leaning back in his chair and exchanging a glance with Braves.

When Braves shrugged in reply, Paxton continued. "It was trooper Mills. Now, can you, or can you not, shed any light on this for us, Adlar?"

I shifted in my seat, my eyes darting between Paxton, Braves, and my empty glass on the table. Perhaps more whiskey would aid this awkward conversation.

"Uh, did you by any chance talk to trooper Boyer, sir?" I asked cautiously.

Paxton's stone-cold expression hardened even further at my dodge. I could tell I was pushing my luck, but I wasn't ready to piss off Pax just yet by saying something I shouldn't.

The Centurion frowned, but then decided to oblige me.

"I did talk to Boyer, yes." He took another tiny sip of his drink. "But that was about as productive as the conversation we're having right now. Trooper Boyer claimed complete ignorance of the event."

I fidgeted, no longer able to control myself. Had the room just gotten hotter? I opened my mouth, not sure what to say. I had no desire to piss off another Centurion but would running my mouth irk Pax or cause Boyer to target me next?

Thankfully, Braves came to my rescue. "Perhaps that's enough for now, Paxton." He jumped up from his chair with gusto and snagged the decanter, refilling his glass, then mine. "What'd you say we give Adlar a break? Just this once—"

He winked at me, signaling at my full glass that I should help myself. "We all know Boyer is a piss-poor excuse for a trooper, and your boy is just going to have to grow a pair and take care of that problem himself. That damn moral code he clings to, it's nonsense! There's no room for that out here. Not amongst the stars."

He raised his glass, first at Paxton, then at me, before taking a hefty swig. Centurion Paxton showed no reaction to his comment. Stoic, he continued to nurse his drink as his eyes slid to stare at one of his paintings, unfocused. I used the opportunity to grab my glass. Braves *had* hinted I should help myself. It would be rude not to.

This time, I didn't rush. It was clear Paxton had heavier things on his mind than my drinking habits. Sipping my drink slowly, I studied the two men with relief. It appeared both already knew what was going on between Pax and Boyer. Regrettably, I doubted Pax would ever handle the problem. Even if that creep had a gun to his temple, I wasn't sure Pax would turn and pull the trigger.

After the half-hearted toast, Braves didn't return to his chair but walked to stand at Paxton's shoulder, a look of gleeful anticipation glazing over his weathered eyes. He looked like a school kid who was just told he could have all the candy he wanted.

Nudging Paxton's arm excitedly, he gestured at me with his glass. "Now, ask him about that other thing."

An unexpected thing happened then. The storm clouds over Paxton's face parted, and he almost smiled. Something I'd yet to see him do. Stern and brooding appeared to be his default settings.

I found their strange enthusiasm contagious, and I felt a hint of a smile tug at my own lips. *Damn,* it was so much better when Fallon wasn't around. What the hell did Paxton see in her anyway? The ship was teeming with women, and fraternization wasn't forbidden.

My grin grew larger as I downed the last gulp of my drink. Braves hadn't been stingy with his pouring and having not had a drop in what seemed like an eternity, the booze was getting to me.

With a slow shake of his head, Paxton broke, and allowed himself a tight smirk, then gestured at me. "You may have the honors Braves. You seem to be more curious about this than I am."

"Awww, cranky." Braves chuckled, downing the rest of his liquor in one gulp.

Placing the empty glass on the table, he looked at me with a beaming grin. I grinned right back, curious to hear what mysterious question he wanted to ask.

"So, Adlar," he said, leaning forward onto the table like some Galactic Senate Rep in a vid performing an interrogation. "What I want to know is what does that crazed kangaroo of a Centurion from the fifth unit have against you? Why was she hell-bent on booting a trooper who'd *just* arrived back to Earth? What'd you do, mate, catch her with her pants around her ankles, or step on her toes? Now don't tell you did something as stupid as proposition the banshee?"

Centurion Paxton's chest bounced with a chuckle as he rubbed his forehead with weary amusement like one did when entertaining the ideas of a drunk friend going on about something ridiculous. I, on the other hand, lost my smirk quick. There was absolutely no answer that wouldn't result in me digging a grave for myself, especially since I had zero proof of what I'd seen.

If I told them the truth, Fallon would simply deny it, then put even more effort into murdering me. Then, there was the chance

Paxton might take the "kill the messenger" approach to the whole situation if some infantry grunt dared to slander another Centurion. I was sure Fallon had already filled his head with all kinds of lies. Either way, there was no good outcome for me if I talked. I was ready to put the incident behind me.

Unfortunately, the men must've picked up on my sudden change of mood because both stopped smiling and narrowed their eyes. Exchanging quick, questioning glances, they both fixated on me.

Thinking fast, I slapped my hand over my mouth in an "I'm about to puke motion" and bolted to the door and into the hall.

The last thing I needed was to get involved in the brass' personal drama.

"Hey! You need an escort!" MP Garner shouted somewhere behind me as I ran down the hall.

Not looking back, I ducked into the stairwell.

CHAPTER
TWENTY-THREE

To say I was not ready for a military exercise of any sort, or to be around weapons, was an understatement. Half-drunk, I shambled down the hall, right into a cleaning bot. The machine whirred and beeped in protest as it almost crashed to the deck, sprinkling me in the face with unsavory water. I grabbed onto its metal chassis just in time, and straightened it, then wiped my face with my sleeve. I didn't want to think about where the water had come from or been.

"All better," I mumbled, patting its metal, oval head, which tilted up to look at me.

I grimaced at my disheveled reflection in its optical lens. Cowlicks stuck out of my hair at odd angles, and I looked drowsy. Counting on going back to bed after breakfast, I hadn't bothered putting myself together. Little did I know my luck was going to strike again, and that instead of a pillow and sheets I'd be entangling with two Centurions. Seeing as there wasn't much I could do about my appearance, I haphazardly smoothed out my uniform and hair, then continued my trek.

Somehow, I finally managed to locate the equipment room and stumbled inside. This time I wasn't too busy trembling in my boots to look around. Cubbies filled with hanging heavy-gear suits took up the majority of the space. On one side of the room, the suits gleaned, shiny and pretty. On the other, not so much. They were scuffed and dirty, some even cracked. I could swear a strange, nauseating smell wafted from that direction.

Or maybe that was just me. The attendants in the room didn't seem to mind. One was even right next to one of the filthy things, studying a holographic projection of code that emanated from an open panel on the breastplate. I didn't know how he wasn't gagging from the stench, but then again, he probably hadn't just visited a bar.

The helmets were lined separate from the suits but also divided in the same fashion. One section of racks contained the spiffy shiny ones and the other, the used. Just like with the suits, it wasn't hard to tell which had returned from a romp on Atlas and which were brand new or had been fixed up and put back into service.

This time, the attendants refrained from teasing me and just stared as I lumbered over to the suits, bracing on the tables as I walked.

"Are you drunk?" Hughes asked, following me with narrowed, suspicious eyes.

For a second, I considered teaching the guy a lesson in manners—with my fists—both for his tone and for all the "*poof*" gestures he'd thrown my way. Maybe if I broke a finger or two, or his nose, he'd be warier of teasing the next newbie sent to die.

A quick glance at my watch told me I didn't have time for such pleasant distractions.

Facing him, I slapped a hand over my chest in innocence.

"No, of course not! That'd be ridiculous," I said, feigning appalment.

Swallowing a burp, I stuck out a swaying finger to point at the clean suits. The liquid burned as it made its way back down my throat.

"Now stuff me into that, I got somewhere to be."

Cavelli got up from his stool with Hughes jumping after him. I fixated on his bad leg, still confused about the injury. It didn't matter how badly a trooper was maimed, if they weren't ripped in half and still breathing, they'd be patched up and shoved right back out onto the battlefield. So, why was *he* limping?

I contemplated if it was rude to ask, but only for a microsecond. My intrigue quickly won over tact.

"Why's your leg like that?" I braced on the edge of a table so I wouldn't collapse to the floor. "And how do you get away with having a ponytail? Isn't that against regs?"

Cavelli chuckled, ambling towards the row of clean suits. "Yup, it sure is. But I don't give two shits. Nor does anyone else."

He slapped his injured leg. "The medics couldn't fix it and the Legion refuses to send me home, so they basically ignore me. It's not like I could PT or fight, so the brass lets me be."

"How come they couldn't fix it? I thought they could fix almost anything nowadays."

Cavelli shrugged nonchalantly as he disconnected a suit from a cubie and turned back to me.

"I dunno. They tried, though, many times, but it just wouldn't take. The doctors even broke my leg twice themselves trying to rebuild it, but the bone refused to reconstruct perfectly straight."

Crouching next to me, he grabbed my ankle and attempted to shove my leg into the suit. My head was woozy, and my foot kept missing the boot. He chuckled at my sloppiness, but continued his efforts, grabbing my arm to steady me. I'd swayed when I let go of the table.

"I even had to wear one of those old-fashioned casts for a while. Like what they had in the dark ages."

Hughes wasn't as patient.

"Damnit, Adlar!" He roughly jerking me straight. "Stop swaying or we'll never get this done!"

I cut the chit-chat then and did my best to cooperate. For some reason, the suit felt much heavier and tighter than I remembered. At last, the intense struggle-session came to an end, and I was suited, with a frustrated Hughes roughly shoving a helmet into my hands.

"That was worse than dressing a fucking goat!"

I cocked my head at him. "And exactly how many goats have you dressed, Hughes?"

He scoffed and twisted me around, giving me a hard shove towards the exit. "Just get the fuck out!"

Clumsily donning the helmet over my head, I synched it with my gear and tried to do just that. I didn't make it far. Distracted by the slew of flashing readouts in my HUD, I smacked into the wall next to the door instead.

"All good!" I shouted, giving my head a shake and throwing a thumbs up over my shoulder.

To the backdrop of everyone's roaring laughter, I regrouped and stumbled out. Then, resigned to the fact I was about to have the shit kicked out of me on the training field, I decided to embrace my current state instead of fighting it. I relaxed and pushed my worries out of my mind. Surely this ill-timed exercise wasn't of any significance. The troops were tired and beat as it were.

With a large grin and a pep in my step, I headed for the arena.

"What the hell do you think you're doing?" barked SL Gundy's gravelly voice as I reached inside the bin of training weapons.

I spun to face him, almost falling off my feet in the process. "Uh, getting a weapon, sir… I think?"

Gundy crossed his arms over his armored chest and glared at me. He wasn't wearing his helmet, so I got a good look at his steely eyes full of suspicion and disapproval.

"No weapons for Gold Squads," he barked. "At least not at the start. You get your blades, that's all."

A loud groan escaped me as my head flung back in dismay. I couldn't care less what Gundy thought of my tantrum. With no weapons, the chances of getting pummeled and thrown around by the explosive training rounds had gone up tenfold.

Gundy ripped into me for my outburst. "You think just because you survived one drop, you now know your ass from a hole in the ground—"

I tuned him out. Behind my visor's tint, my eyes slid to look over his head and to the main balcony overlooking the arena. Three familiar Centurions stood amongst the disinterested faces I didn't recognize. The officer turnout was shotty at best, and the balcony was mostly vacant.

Braves was no longer grinning and stood separated from the other two Centurions, while Fallon was on Paxton like a fly on shit. She looked to be adamantly trying to convince him to leave, and taking full advantage of everything the good Lord gave her to accomplish the task. Pawing at his chest and arms, she was practically climbing him like a tree. Or humping him like a horny dog. She didn't appear to give two hoots about being professional.

She wasn't the only entertainment up on that stage. Braves was a sight to behold. Glowering at Fallon's antics from the corner of his eyes, the man looked like a pufferfish, arms crossed, inflated and scowling.

I wanted to laugh at the show and keep watching, but a heavy hand slapped onto my shoulder and grabbed my attention. Expecting to find Gundy, I braced myself to give him a piece of my mind, but it was Pax's confused face that stared back at me.

His brows scrunched as he eyed me with reserve. "Everything... okay, Adlar? The exercise is about to start."

I nodded, feeling like I was swaying, even though I knew that was unlikely. My suit's stabilizers would keep me steady.

Throwing discretion out the window, I turned and looked back up at the balcony.

"Why is your dad with that Fallon chick, anyway?"

I tried not to slur my words but wasn't sure if I'd succeeded. There wasn't much the suit could do for that.

"You know, she's batshit crazy, *right*?"

I don't know if Pax simply ignored me but the man was already walking away by the time I turned back. The rest of the squad was ready to go, gathered at the staging area.

I trotted over, complaining. "Why are we doing a stupid exercise right now? So close to another drop? And why can't we have any weapons? That makes no sense?"

"We *can* have weapons," Mills corrected, raising a finger. "We just can't start off with them, and that's not the same thing. Don't worry, it won't take us long to get some. As for why we're doing this right now, don't get me started on that pile of bullshit—"

By now Pax was glaring. "Are you all done? Or are we in need of PT to help with the misplaced energy?"

Mills slammed his yap shut, and we all smartly stifled the rest of our objections. Griping wasn't how Pax ran his squad, and no one wanted to add a lengthy run to the remainder of our day. I was starting to understand that no matter how idiotic, Pax took the slightest of the brass' whims as if the high heavens themselves had spoken. Being that I wasn't as keen to kiss the ring, I found the attribute annoying.

"At least it's short, right?" I chirped enthusiastically.

I wasn't sure I had much to give. All I wanted to do was get shot and be disqualified.

Pax slowly rotated to face me and frowned.

"It's not short if we plan on *winning*," he stated with obvious disapproval.

Grimacing at my inadvertent hick-up, I shuffled and averted my gaze, thankful he couldn't see my 'yeah right' expression through my tint. There was a bullet out there with my name on it, and I was going to find it. After twenty minutes or so, that is. I didn't want Pax to catch on that I was weaseling out.

Everyone donned their helmets, and mine beeped as it synced with theirs.

"Here's the deal," Pax instructed over comms. "It's a simple one today. Clear the field. Last squad standing at the end wins. No other rules besides that."

"Why the hell are we even doing this?" Mills couldn't contain himself any longer.

He sounded ready to stomp his foot on the ground like an angry toddler. "I'm still sore from that last drop and my neck's killing me!"

"Shut it, Mills!" Pax cuffed him over his helmet. "This isn't a joke. It's our job. And every exercise matters."

Mills rubbed his helmet, grumbling quietly. "Yes, sir. I'll appreciate every second, sir."

It surprised me Pax didn't pop him again, but he let it go, probably used to Mills' antics by now. Turning away, he marched to the arena. We tailed like reluctant ducklings.

Right as our boots hit the sand, the periphery of our breastplates lit up green, and a vertical line of three glowing circles appeared on our chests. Pax sped up to a jog, leading us towards a propped-up metal wall. Dust puffed from our scuffling feet, coating the jet-black glisten of our suits. I felt myself already starting to pant.

"Are we out when we get shot?" I asked, probably way too eagerly. I prayed the answer was yes.

"When you get hit three times or slashed once with the blade, then you're out," Pax replied. "That reminds me, Adlar, make sure your blades are set to training mode, okay?"

Pax extended his own blades, toggling them to training. The blades crackled as their sizzling blue light dulled down to a whitish glow.

"Change of plans, Mills, from what we discussed earlier. Adlar's acting funny, so instead of Adlar, take Lee. You guys are on offense. Adlar, Somner, and I will play defense."

My cheeks warmed, and I was again grateful for the tint on my visor. Yup, Pax definitely suspected something was off with me. But I guess the joke was on me, because it would've been that much easier to get shot three times and be done with this if I was on the offensive with Mills. Now that I was under Pax's annoyingly vigilant eye, who knew how long it'd take to find a few bullets and run into them. Probably much longer than the initial twenty minutes I'd hoped to give this thing.

Not even ten minutes into the exercise and our entire squad had obtained weapons. I don't know what other squad we took out, but they didn't have their shit together. They only managed one shot at Lee and Mills as the duo snuck up behind them and took them all out with their blades while the rest of us kept them occupied from a distance, allowing them to use us for target practice. I considered letting myself get shot right there, but after I'd stumbled over my own two feet in the initial minutes of our plan, Pax shoved me behind a stack of barrels and told me to stay put.

Having a weapon did nothing to help me get my act together, and as the exercise went on, to Pax's escalating irritation, I found myself messing up more and more. Having to run and think fast wasn't an easy feat to accomplish after multiple shots of whiskey. Sure, I was able to provide adequate cover fire whenever Pax barked at me to do so, but being able to keep up with everyone else was another story. As we jinked between cover, with Mills and Lee tactically shooting and slicing their unsuspecting targets, I soon found myself falling behind and, frankly, just getting plain lost among the props. The haphazard collection of sand dunes, propped walls, barrels, sandbags, boulders, foxholes and ripped-up dropships was a maze.

My muscles burned as I sprinted, trying to catch up to my team for probably the twentieth time. I'd fallen behind again, and they'd all disappeared behind a mangled dropship. But before I could get to them, an unexpected barrage of bullets in front of me cut me off. A wall of murky dust billowed into the air as the rounds popped like popcorn. Veering, I dove behind a stacked collection of barrels only to cringed at my own stupidity. I should've ran into the hailstorm of fire and ended this, but instead had acted out of instinct.

"Where the hell are you, Adlar?" came Pax's irritated shout.

I could tell he was nearing the end of his patience. I considered bolting back out into the open, right into the few stray rounds still peppering the sand, but the agitation in Pax's voice made me reconsider. I rolled my eyes, resigned to participate.

With a heavy sigh, I ducked back behind the barrels and listened to the pops of fire. When they ceased, I was about to make a run for the rest of my squad, determined to get it together, but instead I froze. An odd sight loomed before me.

CHAPTER
TWENTY-FOUR

Pressed back against the barrels, I found myself face-to-face with another trooper and something about him seemed off. The large figure wore the heavy-gear of a Gold Squad trooper, but no golden emblem shined on his breastplate. Nor were there any lights on his suit. I considered he must have been disqualified, but then why was he still in the arena, and why was he lifting a weapon, aiming right at my chest?

The stranger shot me, point-blank, and since there was nowhere for me to fly when the round exploded, my squishy body ended up absorbing most of the inertia. With a pained yelp, I bounced off the barrels and dropped to a knee. My chest throbbed as I gasped for air with rasping inhales.

"What the fuck?" I shouted.

With much effort, I pushed up to my feet and faced the mysterious trooper.

"Aren't you out?" I pointed at his unlit suit with one finger as my other hand clutched my throbbing chest.

The towering stranger didn't respond. He just stood there like a block of stone, his ominous black visor facing me. Discarding his weapon to the sand, he took a methodical step in my direction, his boots slamming down in puffs of dust.

Not knowing what else to do, I shuffled back until I bonked against the barrels. My eyes darted towards the balcony to see if the

Centurion referees were catching this. To my disappointment, only unoccupied chairs greeted my eyes. The balcony was empty. I cursed under my breath as I looked back at my assailant.

"Look man," I began, raising my hands up, palms forward in surrender. "I don't want any trouble, so—"

My plea cut short when a pair of electrical blades burst out of his forearms. They crackled and buzzed, leaving tracers, as he brandished them through the air in slow, intimidating arcs. For a second, I felt a smidge of relief. Getting sliced would disqualify me. I had no idea who this psycho was, but if he wanted to kiss his squad leader's ass by getting some extra points or whatever, I was game.

Then my eyes narrowed. His blades sizzled a hot blue, not white. They weren't in training mode.

Before I could point out his error, the stranger lunged. Thankfully, the bullet to my chest had sobered me up, and I had regained my wits. My instinct didn't fail. I dodged the attack, shouting in surprise when a searing hotness chased over my torso.

I'd felt it right through my gear. Panting, I looked down at my chest just as my display flashed a damage warning. My eyes popped wide. My suit was no longer fully intact. A large diagonal gash ran across my breastplate, splitting my armor almost in two. Blue fluids leaked down my legs and decimated wiring sparked and popped. If I'd been even an inch closer, the blade would've gutted me like a fish.

"Hey!" I stumbled back.

I stuck out a finger to point at his blades. "You forgot to toggle them to training!"

At my proclamation, the man made a show of rotating his head slowly to glance at a blade, then back at me. I flung my hands to my hips, waiting for an apology. Waiting for him to correct his mistake.

But he didn't. Instead, he lunged. In a smear of blue, a blade flew down to cleave my head.

I dodged, barely managing to keep my balance.

"What the hell? What'd you doing?" I again attempted to reason with him.

As I shuffled back haphazardly, I toggled up the volume with the rest of my squad.

"Someone's after me!" I shouted, interrupting Pax's chatter.

I probably shouldn't have toggled the volume down to begin with, but I'd assumed whoever was in front of me and I were going to speak like two civilized individuals, even if it was just long enough for him to gloat he was about to disqualify me.

Unfortunately, my squad didn't have the reaction I'd hoped for. Loud laughter exploded over comms.

"Hey, everyone!" Mills mocked. "The newb is being attacked. Who would have thought something so *unimaginable* during a training exercise."

"No!" I cut in, dodging another jab from my assailant, then another.

The man was really coming at me now. His blades windmilled through the air like prop blades, missing me by mere inches.

"I mean, I'm being attacked for real! He's trying to fucking kill me!"

Everyone busted out laughing again. Well, almost everyone.

"We're all being attacked, dumbass!" came a very, very, pissed-off shout.

I winced. It was Pax, and he wasn't amused. "I don't know what the fuck is going on with you, Adlar, but it needs to stop. Deal with your contact, then get over here!"

I cursed with irritation at their complete disregard.

It was obvious they weren't going to be any help, and I was going to have to face this problem on my own. Not that I had any clue of how. The prick kept lunging at me like some wind-up toy whose winder had been pushed to the max. I dodged, skidded, and jumped, evading his deadly slashes.

Muting my squad before I had to hear any more of Mills' teasing, I turned and ran. What else could I do but that? I hightailed it like a jackrabbit from a jackal, weaving around obstacles and avoiding stray fire, then vaulted over a collection of boulders that happened to be in my path. Peeking over the bullet-pitted rocks, I scanned the field. Maybe the man had given up. The last trickles of my buzz quickly evaporated when I saw that he hadn't.

With long, determined strides, he charged my way, sending up clouds of dust and blades sizzling a deadly blue. My mind scampered for an explanation. *What the fuck did he want?* Had Boyer somehow discovered I talked with the Centurion and was now looking to end me or teach me a lesson? There was no way to know. The gargoyle of a man hadn't spoken a single word.

Heart racing, I looked around for another place to hide among the props and sand mounds, only to realize that wouldn't work. That wouldn't save me. He'd just keep coming, finding me no matter where I hid on the field. I finally concluded there was nowhere safe in the chaos of the arena. Amidst the intermittent gunfire and scampering troops, him trying to kill me simply looked like part of the exercise. If he happened to succeed, well, he'd simply claim it was an accident. That didn't sit well with me. What I had to do, was get out. I needed to reach the disqualified troopers loitering at the staging area. Then, my assailant would have no choice but to give up. He wouldn't slice me in front of witnesses.

I staggered back when my attacker suddenly hopped over the boulders in one leap, landing in a crouch in a cloud of dust. He didn't waste any time. Like some blood-thirsty beast from the holos, he charged me in a maddened frenzy, whacking his blades at me over and over again. They whizzed mere inches from my visor as I evaded. One flew across the rocks with a loud crack, leaving a charred streak on the stone's surface.

Not knowing what else to do, I spun about and fled for cover. The staging area was nowhere near me, and I had no idea how I was going to shirk the man long enough to get there.

Panting, I slid behind a propped wall, grasping at my chest. It still ached and each breath resulted in a stab of pain. As I huffed, groaned, and thought, my mood suddenly shifted. Something flipped inside of me like a switch, and all my fear evaporated in a blink. Instead, rage began to take hold. My blood boiled. *Who the fuck did this guy think he was?* In no way could I boast about actually deserving the gold emblem that gleamed on my breastplate, but no matter the circumstances behind me acquiring it, it was still there. I was fed up with people trying to kill me. Enough was enough.

With that in mind, I pushed off the wall and bounded towards a hill. My assailant changed his course as well and followed, just like I'd hoped he would. Speeding through walls of dust from aimless incoming fire, I slowed just enough to allow him to catch up. I could hear his pounding footsteps hot on my flank. Right as his blade was almost within reach, I doubled back and threw myself to the dirt. As his blade missed me, I extended my own blade and struck. A light buzz vibrated through my armored arm as the sizzling energy found its target and sliced through his leg.

A loud, guttural scream bellowed from the man as he toppled to the sand and writhed. His suit had protected his leg from being cleanly severed but judging by the amounts of blood pouring out of him, just barely. Smiling a wide smile, I set my visor to clear so the prick could see the grin in my eyes, then crouched over him. I wasn't sure he noticed though. He was too busy screaming and thrashing like a gigged frog while pointlessly clutching at his dangling leg. My smile broadened with satisfaction.

I saw nothing wrong with defending myself, and in my opinion, he'd gotten away light. He was, after all, trying to kill me. Whomever Boyer sent next was going to think twice about his assignment after talking to this wriggling asshole. Not only that, but I'd had just about enough of people thinking they could run me over like a piece of trash on the road. I was done tucking my tail.

Plus, it wasn't as if I'd get in trouble. Apparently, everything went in the Legions. We were all expendable here, and murder, if done right, was easily an offense comparable to breaking someone's lamp. *Oops*, was an acceptable excuse. Perhaps, Braves' words weren't simply the rantings of a drunk.

CHAPTER
TWENTY-FIVE

The man's bleeding gradually slowed as the suit's inner layering weaved to stem the flow. I presumed it also injected him with meds, because the screaming eased, turning into colorful, muffled swearing.

Squatting over him, I clicked on my external comms, leering. "Tell Boyer to come do his dirty work himself, next time."

The prick didn't at all appreciate my comment. Releasing an animalistic roar, he lunged, an outstretched hand aimed at my ankle.

I hopped back, laughing. "Whoa… why so feisty? An ice pack should do the trick, right?"

He lashed out again, this time with an extended blade. I hopped out of the way with ease and retreated. It turned out the psycho was one dedicated lackey. Snarling, he dragged himself in my direction, hand over hand, his mostly severed appendage snaking behind him in a trail of red. The boot was sticking toe up, despite the fact he was on his stomach. The medics were going to have a hell of a time putting him back together again.

For a second, as I retreated, easily evading the beast of a man, I considered skewering him through his back as if he was one of the droolers. Extending my blade, I eyed the crackling glow, then the snarling man. Killing him would surely teach Boyer a lesson, but would I be able to live with myself tomorrow? Reconsidering, I deactivated the blade.

Even if he deserved it, I wasn't capable of murder. Instead, filled with satisfaction of a job well done, I turned away from him and casually jogged to exit the arena, dodging a stray round here and there from the few players still participating in this pointless exercise.

Once I was off the sand, I popped my helmet off and chugged water, only to almost choke as a realization struck me. A chill ran down my spine. I remembered something important. I'd muted my squad and had never reversed the option. Worst yet, I'd left the exercise perimeter without being officially disqualified.

Wide-eyed and with water dripping down my chin, I slowly turned to face the arena. Mills' massive form bounded towards me, with Pax and the rest not far behind. Their angry gate told me they weren't coming to congratulate me on outwitting my assailant.

Mills popped off his helmet the moment one of his boots hit the staging area.

"What the fuck, Adlar?" he bellowed, flinging his arms wide to the sides. "You realize you disqualified us by running off the field like that, right?"

Getting right into my face, he shoved me hard on my chest. I stumbled back but caught my footing. My eyes drifted over his shoulder. Mills wasn't who I was worried about. Frozen like a deer-in-headlights, I watched an enraged Pax quickly close in on me. Saying nothing, Pax swung his powered fist into my jaw. I staggered back from the blow. The chatter around us ceased instantly as troops turned to eye the show with bewildered expressions.

I opened my mouth to plead my case, but quickly shut it. Pax didn't take his duties or his responsibilities to the Legion lightly, and I knew walking off the field like that reflected poorly on the entire squad. In the aftermath, I simply hadn't been thinking

Pax released a low growl, clenching his fists, and stepped forward, bringing us nose to nose. His piercing eyes bore into mine. I stood still, saying nothing. If he was going to hit me again, so be it. I deserved it. Before he could, Mills intervened. He jumped between Pax and me with outstretched arms, separating us as if we were two school kids scuffling on the playground.

"Okay, okay." He glanced between us. "Let's just save all this for the actual enemy."

As pissed as Pax appeared, he heeded Mills' advice, and stormed away from me with angry bootsteps. Though he'd momentarily glanced at my damaged, dust-caked breastplate, he didn't appear interested in *any* kind of excuses.

Throwing me disappointed looks over their shoulders, Lee and Somner rushed to tail.

"You screwed the pooch there, *newb.*" Mills shook his head, then also left, leaving me and my busted lip to our own devices.

I watched them go in silence. By now, I'd concluded that just like during Pax's attempted assassination, my visuals were going to be squeaky clean. A glitch, poor connection, whatever, there wouldn't be a crumb left for me to point a finger at.

Working my sore jaw, I then swept my gaze over the captivated audience. Some were whispering, while others had evil smirks of enjoyment plastered over their faces. Go figure, the Legion brutes relished a fight.

I winced when a familiar face caught my attention. Gundy, arms on hips, had witnessed the entire show.

"Making friends already, huh?" He barked a laugh, *tsking* in disapproval.

Feeling like absolute crap, I shoved past everyone and made for the exit. The fact that I'd let my team down was a punch to the gut.

Pissed and with a throbbing lip and chest, I decided this wasn't the best time to go search for Wagner like I had planned on doing after the exercise. Instead, after returning my suit and getting reamed by Hughes for damaging the gear, I settled for hassling every SF soldier for information as I ambled to my room. Turned out it were two male pilots that had been shot down. Feeling somewhat better, I picked up my speed, hoping to catch some shut-eye before the upcoming drop, which was now only a few hours away.

Regrettably, I only made it as far as my door. Right as I reached to open it, a grating, unwelcomed voice stabbed at my ears. A headache, which had so far been taking its time creeping in, exploded like fireworks inside of my skull.

"Well, well, well, long time no see, Adlar," MP Garner's snark echoed down the hall.

The throbbing in my head intensified. Looking over my shoulder,

I saw the familiar MP, buddy in tow, rushing towards me. He seemed as eager as ever.

"What now?" I demanded angrily, though my annoyance quickly reverted to alarm.

I had all but forgotten about my latest visit to the Centurion's office, and the troublesome question they'd thrown at me.

"You tell me, trooper," Garner said, cackling a nasty laugh as the two MPs came to stand on either side of me. "They should just assign you a room on the officers' decks or something, you're up there enough."

Garner swung his head in the direction of the elevator. "You know the drill."

Then he zeroed in on my face. "What happened? D'you lose your helmet during the exercise?"

He let out a snort, chiding his buddy. "Did it roll away from you, newbie?"

"It's nothing," I replied with a grimace, rubbing the back of my neck in annoyance.

Something about the man just didn't sit right with me. I wasn't sure how much more of him I could take.

"Hey, Garner!" I boomed, startling both MPs.

Their teasing chuckles cut short as they stared at me with dumbfounded, wide-eyed expressions.

"What's the punishment for knocking out an MP?" I asked.

The men exchanged concerned glances as the last shreds of amusement drained out of them. Garner's eyes flicked to my collar and my newly acquired insignia.

"How…" he trailed off, pointing, "are… are you that *newb* the rumors are about?"

I didn't grace him with an answer. Folding my arms over my chest, I waited for the dumbass to come to the conclusion himself. A moment later, both MPs straightened and took a careful step away from me. They brought their hands to rest on their weapons.

"Look, Adlar, we don't want any trouble, okay? We're just here to escort you, that's all," Garner said, extending a placating hand in my direction.

I snorted, giving him a disdainful look, not at all surprised by his fearful reaction. He was only a Fleet lackey, after all. It was a good bet he'd never left the ship or tasted combat. I, on the other hand, was a new arrival who'd survived dropping with the Gold Squad. We both knew who'd win if it came down to throwing fists, even if he did have a blaster.

Taking another cautious step away from me, the MPs gestured for me to move in front of them, towards the elevator. Both were now out of jokes and as alert as two lion tamers afraid to get too close.

Throwing Garner another dirty look, I decided to comply. I had bigger problems than him to worry about. Even if Braves again showered me with liquor, I doubted my disappearing act would work a second time. My mind reeled, contemplating what in the world I was going to tell them.

To my complete surprise and confusion, my escorts changed up the routine. When the elevator spat us out on the officer's deck, Garner didn't make the usual left towards Centurion Paxton's office but instead turned right.

"Uhm..." He shuffled nervously when he saw I hadn't followed.

I stood rooted in place, staring down the unknown part of the officer's hall.

"We really should get going," he said, eyeing me with caution.

He hadn't unholstered his blaster but hadn't let go of it either. His palm was still wrapped firmly around the grip. That was probably a good idea. Ground troops weren't the nicest bunch and infamous for short tempers. Scuffles were common amongst the ranks and often ended in death.

I stood still for a few more breaths, fists clenched, letting Garner sweat. The man blinked stupidly as he tightened his grip on his weapon, but he didn't draw it.

At last, with a heavy sigh, I stood down and gestured for them to lead the way. "Fine, let's get this over with."

Rushing to do just that, Garner led me to an opened door. As he stopped and knocked, my eyes traveled to a painting hanging next to the office. It was of a massive ship in front of a blue planet that had no visible land mass, maybe a gas giant or a water-world. I couldn't help but wonder where in the cosmos this mystery floated, or if the picture was just a decoration.

"Send him in," barked a female voice.

My blood ran cold, and I forgot all about the picture. With a hanging jaw, I turned to Garner. The weasel was no longer frightened.

"With pleasure, sir," he responded, grinning at me like a carnival clown.

Grabbing my arm, he roughly shoved me inside, making a point to slap the control panel and close the door behind me.

CHAPTER
TWENTY-SIX

T he door slammed shut with an ominous *clang*. Slowly, I turned to face the woman sitting behind the desk. Our eyes met, and I couldn't help but shudder under her icy glare. Breaking away from the uncomfortable eye contact, I glanced around the office. Just like Paxton's, hers too was Roman themed. Except here, the paintings weren't of battles and victorious men on horseback but of the gladiator arenas.

Piles of murdered men and beasts lay behind the gladiator victors wielding swords and spears. I couldn't help but feel that the blood-drenched men in the artwork were staring at me. Perhaps she purposefully had the art arranged in such a way, to where the soulless eyes pointed at whoever entered her lair.

"Sit!" Centurion Fallon ordered.

I hesitated, eyeing the two chairs in front of her desk with reserve. Both were too close to her for my liking. I took another few seconds to squirm uncomfortably, but then relented and ambled to a chair.

Her fingers drummed on the desk as she glowered at me. "Do you know why you're here, trooper?"

"No, sir." I shook my head.

Her fingers froze mid-tap as that one eye of hers twitched. Jumping up, she slammed both palms on the table with a thundering bang.

"Cut the shit, Adlar!" she roared. "You know what you did in the arena today, you cretin! Don't you dare play the fool and claim you had nothing to do with that!"

Jerking back in surprise, I braced my boots against the deck and tried to push my chair even a smidge further away from her. Into the hall, if possible. But the chair didn't budge. She must have had it fastened to the deck, but I didn't dare to drop my head and look.

Then, her words registered. *The arena?* My eyebrow arched as I stupidly blinked at her. Why would she be interested in that? As I recalled, she couldn't have been there for more than five minutes and that was only to pull Centurion Paxton—

Then it clicked.

My mouth fell open. My attempted assassination. That was *her* doing? Here I was, thinking it had something to do with Pax and Boyer, but instead it was all *her*, again trying to kill me.

My chest heaved as I glared. "*You* set that up? That entire pointless exercise… that psycho?"

I dug my nails into my chair's armrest, trying to contain my quickly escalating rage. Anything that would keep me from launching myself over the desk and wrapping my hands around her scrawny neck.

"What the fuck is wrong with you?" I exploded. "You tried to kill me… *again*!"

I didn't give a damn that I was currently yelling at a Centurion. In my book, all need for formalities had long gone out the window between the two of us.

Relaxing a fraction, Fallon released a loud sigh and made an off-hand gesture of disinterest. "This isn't the time to remind me of my failures, trooper."

I stared at her, blankly, in disbelief. *The lady was nuts.*

Rubbing her temples, she inhaled deeply and dropped back into her chair. "The fact remains, you're still here, scuttling about the ship like some vermin that I can't seem to exterminate."

An angry fist slammed down on the desk, causing the blaster laying to the right of her to jump and rattle. I threw a wary glance at the weapon. Was she about to shoot me dead, right here, in her office?

Not missing the inadvertent movement of my eyes, Fallon also glanced at the weapon.

"If only it was that easy. If I could just blow your brains out, I would, but unfortunately, I can't. Since you took it upon yourself to survive this last drop, Paxton has taken a certain interest in you."

She glared at me. "Too many questions and all if you suddenly happen to end up with your innards oozing over my rugs. So, this brings us here… Adlar. Now… What do you want?"

My head cocked in confusion. "What do I want… for what?"

Did I actually have to spell it out for the psycho, that I preferred not to be murdered?

"To keep your mouth shut indefinitely, you idiot! I know Centurion Paxton and that buffoon, Braves, are sniffing around, asking questions. Don't you dare deny that!"

A boney finger flew to point at me. "So, I'm asking you, what do you want to keep your damn mouth shut indefinitely about everything? Do you want to be moved back to tenth squad? Do you want your own quarters? Just tell me what the fuck you want so we could end this!"

An unexpected pang of concern stabbed at me as I absorbed her offer, and I suddenly had the urge to squirm. I controlled myself. Not two days ago I'd quivered in my boots at being part of Gold Squad, but now the mere suggestion of a transfer turned my gut. Sure, the men were currently pissed at me and probably still saw me as a burden, but that wasn't at all how I felt. I had no desire to fight by anyone else's side.

"No!" I blurted, probably much too loud since Fallon recoiled.

I quickly composed myself and straightened my face. I knew I had to play it cool before the lunatic or else she'd transfer me out of pure spite or get Centurion Paxton to do it, that is. She did have his ear, after all… and his bed.

Leaning back, I rubbed my chin in thought, making a show of contemplating her offer.

"Well…" I dragged out the word, my eyes rolling up to the ceiling. "Moving back to the tenth squad does sound appealing. I mean who wouldn't rather pick up equipment and injured instead of being dropped right in the middle of those drooling freaks, right?"

Fallon rolled her eyes, impatient. "Yes, yes, I know. You would slink away from a fight any chance you get. So, is that what you want then, to go back to tenth squad?"

I paused my thinking act to look the woman square in the eyes. Had she just called me a coward? I was sure she had. Resisting my resurfacing violent urges, I continued my act.

"Hmm... but then my own quarters would be nice too. It's impossible to get any privacy around here, you know?" I shrugged, nonchalant.

Fallon's eyes narrowed to slits and her lip curled. She bared her teeth like some rabid dog. *Damn,* the woman was in dire need of a stress ball. That, or some extra attention from Centurion Paxton.

"You're enjoying this, aren't you?" she hissed.

My hand flew over my chest in feigned ignorance and shock. "Not at all, Centurion! I'm taking the matter of coming to some sort of understanding with you very seriously, sir."

I swallowed down a smile. Truth be told, I was enjoying every delightful minute of jerking her leg, and it was all I could do to keep a straight face. How far could I push her, I wondered? Would she eventually lose it and pounce on me?

I jumped, startled, when a loud bang rang through the room. Fallon had sprang back to her feet and was now leaning over the desk, glaring at me like a crazed wolf ready to lunge. One hand clutched her blaster, which she'd slammed on the desk.

"That's it! You have thirty seconds, Adlar. Thirty seconds! Then, I'm just going to shoot you right here, damn the consequences!"

Grimacing, I threw a glance at the blaster. It wasn't aimed at me, but the fact her claws were on it made me nervous.

"Fine, fine." I held up my hands in surrender. "If you're going to be that impatient, I'll just have to throw out the first thing I think of. Give me a sec." I again scrunched my brows and glanced about the room, pretending to think.

"Okay," I said at last. "I got it. I think I know what I want."

"Well? What is it? Spit it out already. It feels like we'd been at this for hours, and I want your acrid stench out of my office."

I opted not to correct her extremely poor ability to tell time, nor to bring up the fact that I, too, had zero desire to be in her office.

Fighting a drooler buck naked would be preferable to interacting with the likes of her.

"Can you get someone on the Fleet side transferred to work on our cohort's deck? See, there's this Fleet girl, Wagner, that wanted to get out of piloting, and I owe her a favor."

I tried to play it as casually as possible. I dreaded the fact that I'd uttered Wagner's name to someone as unhinged as Fallon, but at the same time, I couldn't pass up this golden opportunity. Not after what our transport went through and hearing Garner's story about one being destroyed. Nowhere in the cosmos was completely safe, but I felt Wagner would be safer here, on *Venator*, instead of that cockpit.

A second after hearing my request, to my dismay, the spite in Fallon's eyes changed to suspicion. I could tell the gears in her head were spinning on overdrive. *Shit!* I rubbed the back of my neck which had warmed. Fallon wasn't buying my story of owing Wagner a favor.

Fallon's demeanor suddenly lightened, and she slowly glided into her chair. "So, you *like* this Wagner girl, I presume?"

"Not especially, no." I attempted to look shocked at the insinuation. "I just owe her a favor, that's all. If you must know, I prefer to keep my options open."

Fallon snorted a laugh as her hand slid over her blaster, petting it as if it was some sort of pet. "Sure, you do, Adlar. You're just a regular lady's man aren't you."

A cold chill ran down my spine, and regret filled my thoughts. Had I just thrown Wagner onto the tracks of an oncoming train?

The woman watched me sweat with a ruthless sneer on her face.

"Fine," she finally said. "I don't give a shit who you screw, so consider it done. I'll get this Wagner transferred to our deck and you keep your mouth shut. Now get the fuck out before I change my mind and put a bolt through that pretty boy face of yours."

She scowled, eyeing my busted lip where Pax had popped me.

"Or through whatever's left of it," she added with disgust.

I needed no encouragement and flew out of her office like my ass was on fire. As I shot through the door, I spun to Garner, ready to tell him that, no, he won't be playing escort, only to see the man had no interest in my goings-on. With an eager grin on his face, he slunk inside Fallon's office and shut the door behind him.

CHAPTER
TWENTY-SEVEN

The dreaded three blasts came much too soon the following morning, lurching me out of a restless sleep. Yesterday, after the conclusion of the shitty day, I couldn't wait to hit the pillow. Yet, when I made it up to my bunk, sleep didn't come. Every time I closed my eyes and tried to clear my head, a slide show of unwanted images scrolled through my mind. Death, screams, and gore plagued me incessantly.

Unlike last time when the blare of the horn reached my ears, I didn't jump out of my bed like the ship was on fire. Instead, I buried my head deeper into my pillow and listened to the damning sound repeat itself. In two hours I'd again plunge through the sky of the alien-infested planet, to face who knew what surprises the Synths had in store for us.

With a groan, I pulled myself out of my bunk just as Ness did the same. I grimaced at the sting of my busted lip, but quickly straightened my face. My grimace had reopened the wound, and I tasted blood. Sure, I could've had the annoying injury repaired in the med-bays, but I hadn't wanted to venture down to grave deck. That's where the morgues were and the auditorium that held mass services at the end of each campaign. I figured a busted lip wasn't worth the paltry sights.

Soon, I again found myself in Gold Squad's equipment room. The attendants looked as exhausted as I felt. Cups of coffee littered the tables and benches, some completely full, steaming into the air, others half-drunk and stale, a film of creamer floating on the muddy surface. The collection of damaged suits and helmets had decreased substantially since my last visit, and it wasn't hard to tell the attendants didn't get much rest during a campaign.

"What the hell happened to you, dude?" Cavelli asked, limping over to the racks of gleaming suits.

Dark circles rimmed his eyes and his disheveled ponytail had seen better days. "Did you forget to put your helmet on and walk into a wall again?"

Everyone chuckled quietly. Maybe they were too tired to tease me or maybe they could see I wasn't in the mood to be teased. The bags under my eyes and my lip didn't hide that fact.

"Let's just say the training didn't go so smoothly," I replied, donning the suit Cavelli had delivered to me.

Hughes also got up to help. "I bet," he scoffed, making his way to the helmet racks.

He disconnected one from a charging port, then shoved it into my hands. "Strange how they scheduled an exercise between drops. That's never happened before. Not that I can remember."

A frustrated hand flew to encompass the room. "It's not as if we don't have enough work to do as is, without you guys damaging gear for shits and giggles."

He shook his head then glared at me. "You know how hard it is to repair blade damage, shit-head? Do you?"

"Uh…" I shrugged. "Sorry about that. It wasn't intentional, trust me."

If only they knew the real reason behind the freakin' exercise. That it was all Fallon's doing just to kill me. At least something good came out of it, I took solace. I hated the fact that I'd inadvertently revealed my interest in Wagner to Fallon, but relished that she'd now be safe. That she wasn't going to be blown into sub-atomic particles in that merciless abyss outside our hull. Plus, I couldn't wait to see her around my deck, tools in hand, working on the dropships. That thought put a huge smile on my face. I didn't even care about my stinging lip.

A chuckle whisked me out of my daydream. I looked over to see Cavelli limping my way, charged blaster in hand.

"Never seen anyone so happy to go on a drop before," he said, handing me the weapon.

Only officers and MPs were allowed to saunter about the ship armed. Regular ground troops, like myself, were only armed before a drop and then relieved of our weapons when we returned our equipment. I supposed there was some logic to that rule. I'd been on *Venator* for only a few days and I'd already had the urge to shoot multiple people.

I say *some* logic because so far, the officers seemed to be the craziest of all, Fallon being a prime example, and everyone, especially the brass, did whatever the hell they pleased. Even the Space Fleet crews treated the Legionaries like sleeping lions and avoided us whenever possible.

"Come back safe, okay?" Cavelli said, clapping me on the arm before turning back to his work.

Ness was waiting for me outside the equipment room when I walked out. We gave each other a tight hug before splitting up to join our respective squads. The hangar bay was still empty of loose equipment such as forklifts and carts, with everything else secured to the deck with straps and magnetic clamps. Even the lift-mechs lining one of the bulkheads appeared to still be bolted down.

I figured it was going to stay as such until the end of the campaign, at which point the heavy repairs on the dropships were going to begin. So far, even though scathed, most of the ships had returned. A sight I was thankful for.

As I neared the first squad's dropship and the massive inner door which was retracted and ready for deployment, my heart rate spiked. The rest of my team was already there, checking air packs and syncing suits. I had wanted to find Pax last night to apologize and clear the air, but I hadn't had the energy after my oh-so-pleasant interaction with my personal admirer.

Mills was the first to spot me and fell silent as everyone's heads twisted to look. Diverting my eyes to the deck, I proceeded towards them, towards Pax, ready to face whatever was coming. As I approached, both Mills and Somner backed away then skedaddled to the dropship.

Steadying my breathing, I marched up to Pax and lifted my gaze to meet his. Was I about to be thrown out of the squad?

"Sorry about yesterday," I mumbled, not knowing what else to say.

Even if I dared to break my agreement with Fallon and spill the beans, I wasn't sure I could simply blurt everything out without sounding crazy myself, or worse, like I was coming up with BS excuses for my behavior.

Pax sighed, shifting his stance. To my surprise and relief, he didn't jump me. A tired, resigned expression veiled his face.

Reaching over, he clasped my forearm and pulled me closer.

"We all have our days, Adlar," he said, clanging our breastplates. "This gig isn't for the light of heart. It gets to you. As long as you don't pull that shit again, consider it forgotten. We have bigger worries."

Releasing me, he stepped back and arched an eyebrow. "Why didn't you get your lip fixed?"

I shrugged in reply, not wanting to admit I was too chicken shit to glimpse the corpses down on grave deck. Then a large grin spread over Pax's face. He extended an armored hand in my direction, palm up, his fingers grabbing at the air.

"I know you survived the last drop and all, but I can't say you exactly nailed the landing. Hand them over, fireball."

For a second, I blanked on what he meant, but then my eyes slid to the frags attached to my waist. Mills and Somner joined in on the chuckling as Pax commandeered each one. With that, the last bit of tension evaporated from our group.

"Attention on deck!" boomed a voice.

All the troops jumped to act out the practiced routine of welcoming the Centurions. Then the double blast reared its ugly head, and the Fleet pilots swarmed out of the elevator. They dispersed to wake the sleeping dropships which purred to life like a litter of kittens as they spooled up, one after the next.

Centurion Paxton rushed our way, aimed for Pax. Deciding to give them their space, I ducked inside our dropship, but I didn't make it far. I slid to an abrupt stop at the top of the ramp. A strange contraption was perched on the deck between the seats.

"Oh, hey," Lee greeted, looking up from the dog-like robot he was working on.

"What the hell is *that*?" I asked, scowling at the unfamiliar machine.

It had the form of a dog, with a swiveling camera for a head. The camera sat back and over the two large circular blades mounted to both of its shoulders. Gleaming razor-sharp daggers lined the robot's limbs, like the thorns on a rose stem, or perhaps fishhooks since the tips were slightly curved. The blades were retracted to lay flat, but that didn't render them any less daunting.

"Oh, this?" Lee pointed at the dog-thing, clicking away at an open panel on its torso. "It's a Razor. The design is old as hell, back from the Rap-Wars, but we still have some use for them. Initially, they weren't authorized for this campaign, since their low profile isn't ideal for a jungle environment, but after what happened last drop, the brass decided to throw us a bone."

His head jerked up and he bellowed a laugh. "Get it… bone."

I, however, didn't laugh. Warily eying the machine, I squeezed around it, to my usual spot—a seat towards the bow, away from the ramp.

CHAPTER
TWENTY-EIGHT

This time, I didn't scream. Not the first time nor the next our ship was hit. As the hull rumbled and the engines howled, fighting to stabilize the vessel, I gritted my teeth and braced. I pretended I was simply on one hell of a rollercoaster ride and if I held on just a little bit longer, one way or the other, it would soon come to an end.

Then, it was time. The buzzer blared, and the ramp yawned open to the roar of the wind and utter blackness. We were dropping at night, and I saw nothing past the residual bluish glow of the engines. Even though my heart pounded like a drum, I didn't need anyone to shove me forward. I fell right in with the rhythm of my teammates. Step by step, I made my way closer to the howling opening. The red emergency light near the ramp strobed over our gleaming suits and flashed its intrusive glow into the oppressive darkness that awaited us. One by one, each person in front of me vanished. Then, it was my turn. Without hesitation, I hurled myself into the void.

Strong winds slammed into me the moment I was free of the ship, and the gusts pounded against my gear. They screamed around me like angry ghosts as I fell through a sky that was aglow with streaks of blue. It was a laser maze of bolts. The deadly energy whizzed above me, under me, and all around. Some zipped so close that their massive electrical charge momentarily blinded my night vision, changing the grayscale image to a brilliant flash of white.

Terrified, and at times completely blind, I suppressed my urge to flail and forced my body into the arch position. I wanted nothing more than to imitate my teammates, who'd all plunged down in the bullet drop and were probably already on the ground, but I wasn't ready for that just yet. All I could do was hope. Hope that the lethal fire was going to miss me, and I wasn't going to be blown out of the sky in an explosion of sparks and burnt flesh. Our armor was able to withstand fire from the bots and blasters, but even a graze from the massive defensive turrets would instantly end my life.

The Synths' bubble-like shield wasn't clearly visible in the darkness, but the origin of the relentless fire was impossible to miss. Right away I could tell that we were dropping much closer than we had before. The bolts flying towards me weren't popping out of the shield from straight ahead, but instead, from about a sixty-degree angle. We were dropping practically on their doorstep.

Finally, the second part of the hellish roller coaster neared its end, and the trees rushed up to meet me. Angling myself up a fraction, I felt my suit kick in to finish the job. The jets hissed, righting my body. With a hard, upward thrust, the air pack slowed my descent just as my feet cleared the first layer of the canopy. Unfortunately, even though I managed not land on the canopy this time and made it to the actual ground, my timing was still off.

As my boots touched the ground, I toppled over and half-tumbled, half-skidded through the underbrush as the air pack finished discharging its propellant. My head slamming against a trunk brought me to my final stop. I didn't make a move to rise. Sides heaving with both panic and exertion, I just lay there, trying to catch my breath from the wild ride. I was thankful Pax had again relieved me of my frags. I dared to say, my jaunt would've damaged all of them, or worse.

My inadvertent tumble through the underbrush turned out to be a godsend though, because right as I pushed up to stand, a bright blue beam streaked over me, burning a scorched path through the trees. It slammed right where I'd initially landed in an eruption of crackling light, dirt, and shredded plants. Reconsidering standing, I dropped and ducked my head under my arms.

As soon as everything quieted, I wriggled out of my air pack while doing my best to remain as flat as possible. There was a bot in my vicinity, shooting at me, and my squad was nowhere to be seen.

"Pax!" I prompted as I disengaged the clamps and disconnected the pack from my suit. It hissed a weak bust of residual propellant as I cast it aside.

The bot fired again. Two more power-bolts streaked overhead to nail where I'd initially landed. The jungle flared white, and more saplings splintered and crashed. It was evident that this time the Synths weren't flanking our rear squads but were set up defensively next to their base, probably pissed that we dared to drop so close.

"Pax! Where are you guys?" I shouted again when I received no response.

Breathing heavy, I glanced this way and that, trying to orient. What greeted me wasn't very reassuring, nor a surprise. All my night vision showed was the outlines of stalks and leaves brushing against my suit. I was cocooned in plants.

I pulled up a locator overlay to look for my team. My heart jerked when I saw no friendlies in my vicinity. It was only me, and an empty grid. Doing my best to remain calm, I zoomed out. Relief flooded me when I glimpsed my squad, but the relief was fleeting. I'd zoomed out to a quarter of a mile. Releasing a low growl of frustration, I remembered the strong winds that had hammered me during my fall. I put two and two together. Why I was nowhere near my squad and taking fire from a bot instead of clashing with the droolers. Due to my slow fall, I must've been blown off course and the rest of my team was now at least a quarter of a mile away.

"We're a little busy, Adlar," came Pax's voice, finally.

I exhaled a slow breath, relieved they'd heard me.

"Who has eyes on the bot?" he asked.

His voice was steady and calm as usual, but his breathing was labored. I amplified my audio and listened intently. There, in the distance, I could hear a fight, and the commotion and echoing roars painted me a clear picture of the situation. Since they'd all landed before I had, the droolers had converged on their location while their master stayed behind. The bot stalking me was likely it.

"Great," I grumbled, bonking my head into the crook of my arm.

I'd bonked it quietly, too terrified to make a peep or flinch a muscle. The bot was likely scanning for me with everything it had, and even though my suit concealed my infra-red signature, I was sure it would detect movement.

"I think it's somewhere over here," I whispered into my comm.

Exactly where, I had no idea, but I wasn't about to stand up and find out the hard way. The bot didn't appear hell bent on finding me, but it still intermittently shot off a few aimless bolts, filling the jungle with rumbles, crackles, and startled squawks, audible over the maelstrom of the weather.

"Copy that," Pax replied. "We're engaging the droolers, and there's a lot of them. You need to take out the bot, Adlar."

I blinked stupidly in the privacy of my helmet as my eyebrows shot up in surprise.

"Say... what?"

Had I misheard? Or had Pax just ordered me to single-handedly take on a machine? A machine whose location was a complete mystery to me in this patchwork of leaves and trees.

"You heard me, Adlar," Pax repeated, between shouting out target locations to the rest of the team. "Take out that bot, that's an order."

My heart sank all the way to my toes. The bot had stopped aimlessly shooting and all I could hear was the howling wind battering the canopy, making it that much more difficult to pinpoint the bot's location.

Nevertheless, I had been given an order, and I knew I needed to act, and I needed to do it fast. If not for myself, then for the squad. I couldn't have the thing circle around and go after them while they were distracted by the droolers.

Heaving a sigh, I got to business. Slithering through the brush, I advanced towards what I suspected to be the origin of the blasts. I didn't attempt staying quiet and splintered fronds and cracked branches in my wake. I stopped every twenty feet or so to listen and see if the bot had heard me. I wanted it to. I needed it to start blasting so my suit could start interpolating its probable location.

As I crawled, fighting the grisly claws of claustrophobia in the black jumble of vegetation, I couldn't help but yearn for daylight. Even though my night vision displayed a perfect picture, to where I was able to see the crisp outline of every leaf, stick, and stone, the overwhelming darkness was still disorienting and pressed in on me with suffocating force.

"Adlar! Did you get it?" Pax shouted. "There's about fifteen droolers here and they're still behaving like they have a brain!"

"Not yet," I replied, through heavy pants.

I stopped crawling and clunked my head onto my arm in resignation. My passive plan wasn't working, and the bot still hadn't shot. Which meant, I had to take a more active approach. My gut cinched, and I was thankful for my extra battery.

Taking in a deep breath, I went for it. I popped straight up then dropped, right as a bolt tore past my head, turning the shrubbery behind me into a sizzling salad. Seeing as one shot wasn't enough info for my computer to calculate any kind of fix, I turned and crawled, repeating the whack-a-mole process as my display interpolated the machine's probable position. Except, on the third attempt, the bot didn't miss. In a flare of searing electricity and blinding light, I was shot. Every muscle in my body stiffened as I flew head over heels, veiled in darkness, as my armor worked to absorb the energy.

Seething with frustration, I cursed, then cursed some more. With my tumble and my HUD's glitch, all data was now useless. However, I didn't get much time to worry about that. The bot fired, missing me by inches as I vaulted aside. It must've had its own targeting computer, and to no surprise, it was better than mine. Tucking my arms close to my chest, I didn't stay put when I hit the ground. I was on an incline, and I barrel-rolled through the underbrush like a loose tire, bouncing and jarring over plants and stones as bolts peppered hot on my tail. Plants snapped under me as I crushed them, and bits of debris plinked my gear.

"Hurry the hell up, Adlar!" Mills shouted. "We're screwed over here if another formation joins in. Take it out!"

"I can't see it!" I protested.

With me toppling and rolling, the suit's targeting computer was having a hell of a time coming up with anything useful, dutifully popping up probabilities.

"I can't get close enough to get a shot. When I try to get a fix, it shoots, and I can't pin it."

I finally came to a jarring stop when I slammed into a trunk with a grunt. Scampering on my knees, I ducked behind it.

"Lee, send him the Razor," Pax ordered.

Even though his breathing was labored, his tone didn't carry a trace of unease. The man was as cool as a cucumber; prepared and ready to deal with anything that might go wrong. Such as one of his troopers completely missing the LZ. Personally, I couldn't fathom how he was so composed, not a bit unnerved by the fact everything was currently trying to kill us.

"Adlar!" Lee's voice. "I'm sending the Razor your way. It's too low to the ground for me to see anything, so I'm targeting your locator's current position. Then, I'll get it to make some noise, so I suggest you move. And you better shoot straight, the Razor won't last long once the bot spots it."

"Copy." I flipped over onto my stomach and crawled about fifty feet away.

This time, I stayed as quiet as possible, weaving around anything that might crunch. It didn't take long for my audio to pick up the approaching rustling as something beelined for my last position. Seconds later, the night lit up with a dazzling display of hot-blue fireworks.

As the bot targeted the Razor, I jutted out from behind my cover and aimed at the source. The bot was firing from both cannons, and the muzzle's flashes looked like sparklers going off in the dark. I sighted and shot, over and over again, slowly advancing, hoping that I'd pinpointed the correct location.

"You got him!" Pax announced. "You got him! One of the droolers just stumbled out, completely disoriented."

Though I heard Pax's shout of my success loud and clear, I didn't stop squeezing my trigger. I continued to let off a stream of blasts until I was looming over the sprawled, deactivated frame of the machine.

"Shit," I huffed as my fingers felt around my waist.

I had no frags to finish it off. My barrage of shots hadn't left a single scratch or char mark on its frame. Our blasters did a great job of disrupting its energy flow but were in no way a match for whatever metal its exoskeleton was constructed from.

"They're regrouping!" Pax shouted. "There must be another formation closing in and another bot taking over this one. Adlar, stay put. We'll come to you."

I jerked my blaster back up, fearful the machine was going to restart. When it didn't, I lowered my weapon. My mind raced as I eyeballed the creepy thing. It was humanoid in design, with two legs, two arms, and a head, but both the arms and the legs were disproportionately long for the compact torso. Crouching, I placed my blaster's barrel in the only vulnerable spot I saw, the slit in the middle of its head, and squeezed the trigger.

Something crackled and buzzed as its head jerked and lit up like a jack-o-lantern. Thin tendrils of smoke snaked from the slit, illuminated with a reddish hue in my display.

Smiling wide, I gloated over the thing, but my victory smirk was cut short. Out of nowhere, something massive slammed into the side of my helmet and sent me to the dirt. I didn't need to see it to know what had hit me. Assuming the drooler would follow his usual pattern and lunge, I twisted up as I fell to my back and fired. A rage-filled howl erupted as holes blew from his gut. Roaring, he whirled away from me and bounded back into the brush.

"I got one!" I shouted, triumphantly. "But it disappeared before I could finish it."

"Run!" Pax yelled in reply. "Right the fuck now, run!"

For a second, I was confused. *Weren't they coming to me?* Then I remembered Pax's warning about the beasts being connected. The drooler I'd just encountered hadn't backed off because he'd seen fit to give me a pass or was choosing to live another day instead of meeting my gun or blades. It had retreated to give away my position.

I jumped to my feet and ran. I had no idea where I was going in the all-encompassing blackness as leaf after leaf slapped over me, but I used every ounce of my suit's power to propel me away from where I'd just been. Even if I had no problem taking down one, two, or even three of the droolers myself, I stood no chance if I was swarmed by an entire formation.

"I'm coming for you, Adlar!" Pax's locator separated from the rest of the group. "Find a place to hide and hold tight."

I had every intention of following his instructions and hiding, but the universe had other ideas. Before I could look for an acceptable spot, my boot caught on something, and I pitched forward into a bush. Grunting and huffing, I twisted and squirmed like a hooked worm, trying to free myself from the leaves and the scraggly branches. At last, I flumped to the dirt and glanced behind me at what had tripped me.

My blood ran cold. Before me was a mutilated corpse of a trooper, partially lifted off the ground by the one arm that wasn't missing. My eyes jerked up to what was holding him. An incredibly surprised drooler gaped back at me. His eyeball rolled side to side in confusion as drool stringed from his sagging jaw. The beast looked just as stunned to see me as I did him.

However, unlike me, he had no weapon, and before he could peep a sound, I took him down with a single head shot. The surprised creature didn't even release the usual dying howl, but simply collapsed in a heap. My stomach twisted as I stared at the corpses. The trooper's armor was dented and ripped with jagged edges of metal and wiring sticking out in every direction. Blood, cooling gels, and other liquids trailed in the mud.

I swallowed hard. It looked as if the poor sap had been beaten to death before being torn apart. Or maybe it was the other way around. In any case, it wasn't a pretty way to go.

My wide eyes then jerked to the drooler as I wondered about the beast's intentions. Why was he dragging a corpse? A late-night snack perhaps? Now that had me gag, and I decided to drop the matter. If the drooler had seen me so had a bot. I needed to run.

Pax's pissed voice boomed in my ears the instant I started moving. "What the hell are you doing, Adlar?" he demanded.

He must've seen my locator take off.

"There was a—"

My explanation cut short as I skidded to a stop and gawked. No more than two hundred feet away from me, between the trees and brush, shimmered a glossy surface. I knew it could only be one thing —the shield. Not daring to venture further, I backed up a few steps and ducked behind a trunk.

"I'm in front of the shield," I whispered, feeling like this was a whispering-type situation.

"Shit, Adlar," Pax barked. "Stop advancing before you get yourself killed and just freaking wait!"

This time, I did as I was told and hunkered down behind the trunk. My suit scraped at the bark as I warily slid to the ground and looked around. The vegetation here wasn't as congealed and thinned towards the shield. Perhaps it was a natural occurrence, as the mountains were somewhere behind the barrier, or perhaps the Synths had cleared it out for their use.

With bated breath, I intently studied the darkness, trying to spot any sign of weapon emplacements or troops. It wasn't far-fetched that the Synths would set up a kill zone this close to their base. Yet all I saw were sparse trees and rocks jutting from the dirt. Some were just large enough to be a trip hazard and others were big enough to provide adequate cover.

Suddenly, I felt exposed, even behind the trunk. Dodging to another tree, I dove into a sprawling cluster of leaves growing at the base. They rustled back into place and fully concealed me. Slowly pushing a leaf aside, I peeked toward the shield again, my eyes widening. A formation of droolers lumbered out, trailing a bot.

There must've been at least thirty of them, and they were still coming, popping out of the glowing shield like wizards out of a portal. I couldn't help but wonder where the Synths kept all these creatures or how they cared for them. Their sharp teeth and aggressive nature pinned them as carnivores. Perhaps the aliens sustained them off the native life of whatever planet they'd infested and marshaled them only when needed.

I almost jumped out of my skin when the leaves behind me rustled and shook as a form slid next to me.

"Hell yeah!" Pax clapped me on the back. "We made it, Adlar! That's the target, right there! Now let's show those shits what we're made of!"

I quickly shook my head *no*. I guessed he hadn't spotted the droolers. "There are formations marching out."

"Oh." Pax leaned over my shoulder to look. "Well, shit… we'll just wait then. I'll tell the guys to retreat and meet up with second squad. I bet those formations are heading straight for them to set up a defensive line."

He let out a barking laugh and shook me by my shoulder in a congratulatory fashion as if we'd just won some grand award.

"Those fuckers have no idea the two of us are here, do they? And we're not leaving until we cause some damage. How did you manage to drop so off-target anyways?"

"Got... *lucky*," I deflected, knowing full well I must have screwed up one thing or another. Our computers accounted for shoddy atmospheric conditions.

Pax chuckled, again shaking my shoulder with excitement. I could practically feel his grin. I, on the other hand, scowled. There was absolutely nothing fortunate about my current situation and most certainly nothing worth celebrating. More like, about a month ago, the stars decided they hated me and wanted to kill me off, but then changed their mind and decided to play an endless cruel joke on me instead.

"Hell yeah, we got lucky!" Pax cut through my gloom.

Apparently, he hadn't caught on to my sarcasm. I blinked stupidly in reply as my stomach knotted. Pax was probably concocting some crazy stunt inside that head of his right about now, and since it was just him and me out here, smack dab amidst enemy forces, there was going to be no weaseling out. Yup... the universe was doubled over, holding its sides with laughter.

We didn't have to wait long until both Mills and second squad reported contact with multiple formations, and we figured those must be the ones we'd just seen. Pax gave it a few more minutes, then grabbed my arm and pulled me out of the leaves and towards the shield. Groaning internally, I had no choice but to follow. I had no idea what crazy plan he'd crafted, but knowing Pax, it wasn't going to be anything safe and cozy.

My heart rate spiked as we neared the dome and hunkered down behind a collection of boulders. The shield towered before us like a wall and its surface swam with faint hints of color like a soap bubble or an oil sheen. They swirled lazily, twisting and blending into each other. But the shield wasn't transparent, and we were unable to see inside.

To my right, it stretched as far as the eye could see. To my left, it curved. I didn't have a clear view past the few trees and rocks in the way, but guessed it curved to cut into the mountain.

Pax glanced around, pondering the situation. "Well… with just the two of us, we're not going to run in blind, but I have another idea. Come on. Let's get closer."

He scurried forward with me on his flank.

"Here's what we're doing," he instructed. "We'll throw in a couple of frags and bring down part of the mountain. It's not much, but it's something. With any luck, we'll bury or damage something critical."

I sucked air through my teeth, fighting my urge to protest. I was thankful Pax had opted not to blindly charge inside, screaming praises to the Legion till our very end, but still, I dreaded going closer. Every fiber of my being yearned to run in the opposite direction, away from the danger.

"You can have the honors," Pax said as we hunkered behind a group of jutting stones.

He extended an arm towards me, but I was too nervous to pay attention. We were now out of the jungle, and on the cleared area spanning the shield's perimeter. I was expecting defensive batteries or troops to light us up at any moment.

"Here!" Pax repeated, more forcefully this time.

Snagging my arm, he shoved a frag into my palm. I could practically sense his exhilaration.

"From what I understand, this is just a research outpost, so quit shitting yourself. It's unlikely anything will run out. They have no idea we're here."

My jitters eased at his words and my head and blaster stopped frantically spinning. Holstering my blaster, I succumbed to the contagious atmosphere of his excitement. Just maybe, we'd make it out of this alive while causing some actual damage, bringing this whole campaign that much closer to its end.

A smile stretched my lips as I closed my palm around the frag and my suit beeped, acknowledging the device. I squeezed it until it cracked like an egg and a blue glow emanated from the fissures. The glow intensified. Winding my arm back, I launched it with all my might at the enemy's compound, my grin widening as I watched the glowing orb arc through the air. I'd angled it to fly at the mountain once inside the shield.

My victorious smirk quickly died. Out of the corner of my eye I saw Pax hurl himself in my direction, a long "noooo" bouncing around inside of my helmet. He tackled me, right as I glimpsed my frag bounce off the shield and double-back in our direction.

Whoomp! The air itself shook and everything in my vision flared.

A force like I'd never felt before slammed into me and sent me flying. For a second, I was sure this was it. It felt as if I were being torn apart from within, and no matter how hard I tried to breathe, my lungs wouldn't inflate. Then I collided with the ground. A loud ringing erupted in my head as I tumbled and skidded, ass over feet. I finally slammed to a stop against a rock. My entire body ached and my breaths came in heaving gasps. Ignoring the pain, I pushed to my feet, right as my faltering display flickered and stabilized.

"P-Pax?" I called weakly, doubling over and bracing on my knees, white blotches flashing in my vision.

I felt like I wanted to puke.

My eyes finally found Pax's prone form and my heart squeezed. But right as I was about to full-on panic, he moved.

"*Oooh…* hell, fireball," he groaned.

Coughing, he rolled over onto his stomach and tried to rise. He almost made it but teetered and fell back to his knees. Grasping at a tree for support, he finally managed to stand.

"How… are you… still alive, man?"

He swayed when he let go of the tree, looking like he was about to fall, but then caught his footing and stumbled in my direction. Pushing off my knees, I staggered towards him.

Saying nothing, we clasped onto each other's shoulders and dropped our heads together, our helmets clanging. We burst out laughing. At first, our laughter was just a wary chuckle, an unspoken relief we'd survived, but a second later we both dropped to our knees, laughing like lunatics. I supposed nothing got the chuckles going like nearly killing yourself with your own frag.

"You have to roll it in, not throw it, you dumbass," Pax huffed, between bouts of laughter.

He grabbed the sides of my helmet and shook my head. "Didn't

Gundy teach you anything? Nothing traveling at high speeds can pass through those shields."

I stopped laughing and inhaled deeply. Hopefully, Pax's question was rhetorical because I'd hardly paid attention to Gundy. For the most part, my mind had conveniently wandered to its own world whenever he'd dove into one of his long-winded lectures. I mean, I knew bombs and other powered weapons couldn't penetrate the barrier at high speeds, but for the life of me I couldn't remember if Gundy had said anything about frags. Tenth squad wasn't armed with those.

Pax playfully shoved my helmet as he released me and pulled me to my feet. Standing arm to arm, we took a moment to heed my handiwork. The rocks we'd hunkered behind had been reduced to a large smoking crater with rubble scattered around it.

To my utter disappointment, Pax wasn't deterred. "Come on. We better hurry. They might not have strong defenses, but something was bound to have heard that."

Dragging me behind a boulder, he armed another frag, cracked it, and sent it rolling towards the shield as if it were a bowling ball. This time, the frag disappeared into the barrier. We dropped to the ground, awaiting the blast. A second later, nothing happened.

Slowly rising, we exchanged confused glances. Right as my comm clicked and Pax started to say something, a magnificent flash of white flared on the interior. We couldn't actually see the blast, but a massive section of the shield lit up as bright as a spotlight. A second later, the sound of crashing and tumbling rock told us we'd accomplished our goal.

"Ahhh… so that's how it's done," I said, squinting and blinking from the blinding light.

"Let me see some of those!" I extended an impatient hand, wiggling my fingers in a grabbing motion.

It wasn't going to be long until something rushed this spot, and I was eager to cause more damage. Chuckling, Pax handed me a bundle of frags. My suit immediately registered the devices and popped up an option to activate. I was more than ready to wreak some havoc for the alien freaks and not only because it was our mission. I yearned for an explosion. All the pent-up energy and fear roiling inside of me ached to be released in the form of mass destruction.

"Crap!" Pax suddenly shouted, right as I was about to activate the frags and take aim at the invisible bowling pins. "Something's coming. And by the sound of it, there's a lot of them. Hurry up and roll them, let's go!"

I quickly attached two of the frags to my suit in case we needed them later but activated the third and rolled it. As the frag vanished into the shield, sure enough, my audio picked up a stampede of something quickly approaching. Pax gave my arm a tug, then bolted for the jungle. I sprinted to follow but only made it a few steps before my feet slipped out from under me. Pitching forward, I bumped and tumbled down a slope.

I flopped flat with loose dirt trickling over me. Groaning, I gave my head a shake to chase off the disorientation, then looked up and around. I quickly realized what'd happened. I'd slipped on the loose gravel littering the area and had just tumbled into the crater my failed grenade toss had created.

"Adlar! Where are you?" Pax called.

Releasing a slew of profanity, I scrambled to my feet and peeked over the ledge. Pax was almost at the treeline, running full-speed, head spinning as he looked for me. Slipping on the crumbling dirt that crunched under my boots, I scrambled up the slope, ready to give chase. That was when a shower of power-bolts punched out of the jungle. In a flare of bright light and explosive crackles, two of them nailed Pax square in the chest. Sparks splashed and extinguished like embers as he flew off his feet.

Alarmed, I dropped back into the crater. The sky glowed overhead as the concealed bot continued to fire. The bolts peppered around the hole and showered me with rock and debris.

"Pax, you okay?" I shouted as a jolt of adrenaline surged through my body.

Clutching handfuls of dirt, I again scaled the slope but this time flat on my stomach. Pax's locator wasn't moving, and I had no idea how to get to him through the hailstorm of fire and exploding earth, but I had to try.

A second later, he jerked, then moved.

"Run!" he roared, jumping up and running for the trees. "Just run! I'll be fine!"

I braced, ready to make my break through the incoming fire, only to see the trees quiver and shake. A horde of droolers charged out and barreled in my direction—twenty maybe more.

I felt a flare of alarm. Following Pax was no longer an option. The droolers and the power-bolts flying out from the blackened jungle weren't going to allow it. Seeing us right next to its outpost, the bot was unloading. It didn't even give a damn that it was plowing down its own in the process. With death curdling howls and holes blown out of their backs, the droolers pitched to their faces to bleed and writhe in the dirt.

I breathed a sigh of relief as I watched Pax's locator zoom away from the chaos, but I wasn't making it in the same direction. Glancing around, I quickly deduced there was only one place I could go where I wouldn't be fried like a scrap of meat in my armor or torn apart limb by limb. Jumping out of the crater, I took four massive, lunging leaps through the barrage of fire and vaulted into the shield.

CHAPTER
TWENTY-NINE

I almost made it through the shield unscathed, but right as the swirling colors came up to meet me, a shot nailed me in the back. Screaming, I rolled like a rag doll with no control. My display fuzzed and beeped, popping out strange, fractured readings, unfinished words, and warnings.

I finally came to a stop and curled up in a shivering ball. I knew I'd been shot, but the pain that usually went with catching a bolt was ten times more intense than usual. The searing burn pulsated over my back in waves. Doing my best to push through it, I reached for my backup battery with trembling fingers. It took me a few tries to insert the thing, I was shaking so bad, but I finally managed. To my dismay, that did little to ease my suffering, nor did it fix my glitching suit. The readouts in my HUD fuzzed and crackled.

As the burn slowly subsided to something bearable, I stopped clenching my teeth and, with much effort, pulled myself up, first to my knees, then to my feet. I scanned for cover. It wasn't going to be long until the droolers and the bot came to finish the job.

After a few tries, I managed to stabilize my visor on clear. The shield gave off a greenish glow, illuminating everything in an eerie light, enough to where I could see without night vision. Which was a good thing, considering whatever energy flowed within the confines of this area was wreaking havoc on my suit. My display flickered, and my comms toggled between a hissing static and dead silence.

Scanning over the barren area, the enormity of where I was suddenly dawned on me. I was inside the Synths' encampment, and it was both exhilarating and daunting. The mountain of shiny black stone loomed in front of me, and I almost dropped to the ground when I spotted the silver cylindrical turrets dotting the slopes. They paid me no attention. With rhythmic clatters, their large barrels swiveled and fired, spewing massive bolts of electricity into the night.

The gouts of energy punched right though the shield, unhindered but for the outward roiling ripples. I almost felt as if I were underwater looking up, dizzy and listless. I wondered vaguely how the energy was able to pierce out but not inward only to quickly conclude something as advanced was beyond my comprehension. Matching energy signatures, perhaps, or intuned frequencies?

Whatever the explanation, I presumed the turrets had to be automated, or else I would've been long dead. If not by their hand, since I wasn't sure they were capable of angling down at such a steep angle, then by whomever the operators would have alerted. Yet, I was still breathing and seemingly alone.

From this side, the shield was transparent, and I squinted, trying to see into the darkness beyond. There was only blackness and intermittent splatters of light. The bot that was after me wasn't done. Bolt after bolt slammed into the shield in magnificent flashes of white. The surface of the shield rippled after each hit but remained intact.

I didn't let the momentary reprieve of having a barrier between me and the bot fool me into thinking I was safe, and I cut the sightseeing. Turning, I charged to the mountain, jumping over the crumbled rocks and debris our frags had left in their wake. I huffed and strained with exertion. Without mechanical aid, my malfunctioning suit felt like it weighed a ton.

As I ran, or to be more precise hobbled under the weight, I scanned the barren grassy area for anything I could use as cover. To my dismay, there was nothing. There were no piles of equipment or housing units, only a flat field of grass as far as the eye could see. Inspecting the mountainside, my attention drew to a dimly lit entrance. A tunnel led into the mountain.

I considered running in but scrapped the idea. I wasn't ready to face the alien den. My eyes jerked to the slopes. The stone was obsidian black and shiny but not unscalable. Some of the protrusions promised decent handholds. Hustling over, I began to climb. My heavy suit was a pain and my muscles burned, but the lower gravity assisted my ascent. I scrambled onto the first ledge large enough to contain me and stretched flat on my belly. I winced as loose pebbles clinked and clattered down the rocks. The tips of my boots dangled off the narrow ledge but there wasn't time to find anything better.

"Wha… ad… com…" crackled a broken transmission.

It may have been Pax, but I couldn't be sure. I tried answering but gave up when it became apparent he wasn't picking me up. My comms, the most basic of the suit's functions, were now useless. I exhaled a shaky breath as I pondered what would happen if I were to get shot in here. Would my suit still function enough to mitigate the electricity, or would I instantaneously sizzle like a drop of oil in a frying pan?

Lying flat and as still as possible, I watched as a group of frazzled droolers charged through the shield below me. The barrier warbled and swam with color where they'd passed but quickly stabilized. Skidding to a stop, they spun in frantic circles as they looked around. Their chests heaved, and madness flashed in their swiveling eyes. Upon not seeing me, the horde seemed to calm. The arms they had extended outwards in anticipation of grabbing me dropped and their eyes quit jumping. They began to lumber about aimlessly, sniffing, scratching, grunting, and at times even bumping into each other. Some dropped to all fours. Some sat.

Then, I saw something truly strange. As if a switch had been flipped, the droolers froze, then rushed into a formation. Not a growl, chomp, or sniff could be heard. It was a prelude to their master's arrival.

A single bot strode through the shield, red light shining like a beacon out of the slit in its head. It circumvented the droolers and proceeded to walk towards the tunnel, its head turning mechanically as it scanned the area. Muttering a slew of panicked curses, I didn't dare twitch a muscle. I lay glacially still, hoping the thing wouldn't look up or perform some kind of scan and discover a Leege clinging to the rocks like a freaking spider.

Stopping at the entrance, the bot fixed its slit of an eye on the opening. I could only guess what it was doing, but it didn't venture inside. Spinning about, it marched back out of the shield. The droolers tailed, two abreast and in step with each other as if marching to a cadence. Not a hint of their animalistic tendencies remained.

I allowed myself to breathe a long sigh of relief when the last lumbering back disappeared into the darkness. My mind reeled, debating how to proceed. What if, unlike me, they had the ability to see through their own shield, and if I moved too soon, I'd be toast. At the same time, I didn't want to be in here a moment longer.

Ultimately, the decision was easy. Tension wracked my every nerve. It was time to go.

Accordingly, I swung myself over the ledge and shimmied down. I grumbled and stewed as I went. How was it that I kept landing in one mess after another? While all the experienced troops were out *there*, out in the jungle, here I was, shimmying down a freaking cliff at the alien's doorstep.

Suit scraping and clattering on the rocks, I at last reached the ground. I braced on my knees to pant, drenched in sweat in my cumbersome gear. Without power I might as well have been cocooned in an oven. Figuring sweaty and out of breath was better than dead, I quickly composed myself and turned to run, but a distant silver structure on the mountain slopes caught my eye.

At first, I thought it was another turret, but it was too tall and too large. It resembled a lighthouse that stuck out of the rock and reached all the way up to the shield, tapering as it went. It glowed a faint blue towards the top. Taking a few cautious steps back for a broader view, I allowed my eyes to glide to its highest point. Circles of electricity pulsed out of it and flowed over the shield in rhythmic waves. I quickly realized what it was. This had to be a power source, a generator of sorts, forming this section of the shield.

Anxiously, I took stock of my surroundings. It was still and quiet. Not a blade of grass moved and not a sound peeped. A voice in the back of my head screamed at me to run while I still could. Yet, my boots remained rooted in place. Something else beckoned me. Something deeper told me running wasn't what had to be done. A strange and very unexpected sense of duty pulled at my mind. After all, whether I liked it or not, I was now a Leege, and I couldn't simply walk away.

A second later, my mind was made up. I was going to take a closer look. The bot had already searched here and was now probably busy trying to kill my teammates. It wasn't coming back any time soon, and the turrets high above me still paid me no attention.

I made it all of one step when movement flashed on my left. My heart skipped, and I spun to face it, blaster trained on the scattered boulders near the tunnel's entrance. I tightened my grip, finger on my trigger. Something had flitted out and hid, I was sure of it.

Fearing it might be a bot, as it hadn't been big enough for a drooler, I threw myself flat against the mountain for cover, but that proved hopeless. Not enough stones protruded to be of use. Before I could search for something better, two creatures slowly edged from behind a boulder. My blaster lowered fractionally as I blinked at them in surprise.

Two lanky, humanoid aliens, dressed in white, stared at me with giant black eyes. They were roughly four feet tall and appeared as surprised as I was. Surprised and curious. They chatted away with clicks and chitters, throwing me intermittent glances. They were discussing me, I was certain.

Cautiously, I edged closer. The beings didn't startle at my movement, nor did they run. They continued to chatter as they curiously gaped, their clueless eyes roving over my person as if *I* were the anomaly. A zoo exhibit of sorts. I supposed I was. To them, *I* was the alien.

I scanned them for weapons. Neither appeared armed. In fact, they seemed helpless and fragile. I was sure I could easily break them with my bare hands if I needed to. My heart squeezed. I knew both were Synths, but it didn't take more than a second's glance to know that they were noncombatants. Like any other species, the Synths had civilian personnel.

As I edged closer, I tried to find a way out of what I had to do. Yet there wasn't one. If I didn't kill them, I'd never reach the generator. As intrigued and befuddled as they were by the novel, alien primate slinking about their doorstep, I was sure they'd snap out of it and sound an alarm, and I couldn't let that happen.

I slowly raised my weapon.

Holding my breath, I pulled the trigger. Oddly, nothing happened. No blue bolt shot out to accompany the click of the trigger. Confused, I glanced at the side of my blaster. The power bar flickered begrudgingly.

"Damn," I mouthed.

The shield was messing with it, just like it was with my armor. Reluctantly, I took aim once more. As I did, I wished the beings would run, but they didn't. They seemed to have no idea of what was pointed at them. They stared up at me like dumbfounded children, cocking their heads and chittering. Neither appeared to comprehend the danger before them.

A lump formed in my throat as I again squeezed my trigger, the heavy *click* piercing the surrounding stillness. Again, nothing happened, and the two fools still didn't run. Gritting my teeth, I repeatedly squeezed. At the tenth *click*, my blaster finally fired. With a gruesome, wet cracking sound, a Synth's head exploded. Chunks of meat and blue watery blood showered the rocks, my boots, and his startled buddy.

The other Synth jumped, chittering and clicking like a panicked monkey. Yet, he still didn't run. Instead, when the headless corpse crashed to the ground, he darted to its side. The human-like behavior sent an unexpected pang through my chest, the likes of which surprised me. They were Synths, the *enemy*. Yet...

With delicate, twiggy fingers the alien grappled at his companion, and his chitters and clicks changed to whines. He let go of the body and looked up at me with black eyes full of ignorance and confusion. Swallowing hard, I again squeezed my trigger repeatedly, until he too fell to the dirt.

CHAPTER
THIRTY

Trying to shake off the elephant-sized weight on my chest, I turned away from the two dead Synths and rushed towards my target. I tried not to dwell on what I had done. The bottom line was, it had been them or me, so I had killed them first. I had done what needed doing, what the Legion needed me to do, and that was that. I didn't have time for distractions.

Since I still hadn't been shot and appeared to be alone, I deemed the two Synths hadn't alerted anyone prior to their demise, but that didn't mean something else wasn't about to venture in. Not only that, but it was getting more unbearable inside my suit by the second. I wasn't sure how much longer I'd last. My armor had now given up trying to recirculate my air and opened the vents. I could feel the steady rise in temperature and humidity as my helmet filled with an acrid electrical smell that clung to my nostrils.

Huffing and struggling to breathe the thin, muggy atmosphere, I half-ran, half-hobbled along the mountain until I was right under the generator. The silver cylindrical pole stuck out of the rocks about forty feet above me. Scanning the slopes for the best place to climb, I settled on some jutting stones.

Seeing how I was in no way a professional rock climber, and no longer had mechanical aid, the going was rough. More than once my boots and gloves slipped, sending rocks and pebbles clattering to the ground, but eventually, I managed to reach my target. What I assumed to be the shield generator was much larger up close than what it had appeared to be from down below. The thing was at least as wide around as an air-car, and that was just the part I was next to. Peeking through the two-inch gap between the structure and the rock, I could see it widened further as it extended down into the mountain.

Since I was strapped for time and struggling to breathe, I decided to skip any kind of investigative pursuits. Unintelligible symbols similar to ancient hieroglyphics with extra dots and strange lines were etched into the metal, but I didn't see myself memorizing enough of them to be of use. Nor was my glitching suit in any state to document. That meant there was only one other thing I could do to make my side-trip into the Synth lair of any use—I needed to destroy the thing.

Grabbing the two frags from my waist, I attempted to activate them. To no surprise, it took a few tries, but finally, the signal got through, and the explosives in my hands were no longer fancy paper-weights. I quickly clambered my way to the back of the generator, sliding and tripping on the jagged stone. The humidity had layered them with moisture and my boots were having a hell of a time getting traction.

As I reached the back of the generator, I glanced at the frag in my palm. A very unsavory premonition occurred to me. It told me that I could die, right here, right now. That this might be it. If I went through with my plan, I stood no chance of escaping the blast radius, and my armor wasn't going to protect me.

Do it, whispered a distant voice from the shadows of my mind. *For the Legion.* I took a moment to blink at the frag, considering my potential demise. *I could always run,* I argued with myself. No one would blame me. No one would even know. Yet, some unknown force told me that taking down the generator was more important than my life. It screamed at me to throw myself onto the knife—for the Legion. *Son-ova-bitch!*

No, not for the Legion, I corrected the pesky, distant whisper. I'd fucked around and cowered long enough, pissing off my squad and disappointing Pax in the process. Disappointing him was what stung the most. For whatever irritating reason, a part of me yearned for his approval. I wanted him to see that I belonged in Gold Squad, that I wasn't just some *poof* or bait.

"For Gold Squad," I whispered, slowly closing my palm around the frag.

It cracked, radiating warmth. I rushed to shove it in the gap between the rock and generator. Sure, I'd die for Gold Squad if I had to, but that wasn't the preferred outcome. Hustling to the front next, I repeated the process, jamming the second frag between the rock and metal. Then, I jumped.

I was midair, or maybe almost to the ground, when the frags went off.

"*Whoomp, whoomp*" and suddenly the grass was no longer rushing up at me.

My world became a blur as I flew ass over feet, with the blast force trying to rip me apart into a million pieces. I landed hard. Not Gundy punching me in the gut hard, but being struck by a train hard. I groaned as my head pounded and coughed, choking on blood. As if that wasn't bad enough, a new sensation stabbed at me. A searing pain erupted over the right side of my body. Clenching my teeth with determination, I tried to rise, but all I managed was a twitch.

Even with my mind in a cloudy haze of disorientation, I didn't need a medic to know I hadn't fared well. I couldn't tell the severity of my injuries, but it was apparent I wasn't going anywhere. I could barely breathe and even that was a chore.

The realization this was it dawned on me. Wheezing out a painful exhale, I let my head drop onto the crumbled dirt and fixated on the shimmering shield above me. Had I succeeded? I wanted to look at the generator also, but it hurt too much to turn my head. My eyelids fluttered at the flickering colors as the shield destabilized. They sparkled like crackling fireworks—red, green, yellow, blue. I couldn't hear much through the numb ringing that filled my head but figured there were pops and zaps.

I took a shuddering breath, waiting for my life to flash before my eyes like the colors, trying not to think about what was next. My success was a comfort for sure, but I was still terrified to die. If it wasn't for the fear, I suspected I might have laughed. I lasted all of what, a couple of days in the Legion. *Damn*, what an embarrassment.

Unfortunately, I got no slideshow of my childhood or good times with friends. All that hit me was an increased pounding in my head and blurred vision.

Resigned to the inevitable, I closed my eyes and released a lengthy exhale. One that I assumed to be my last before I drifted off into oblivion. To my surprise, the world didn't go black. Instead, a sudden, deep sting stabbed at the base of my skull. At first, I was too out of it to care, but then my heart squeezed and jerked as if a hand had punched into my chest and grabbed hold of it. A jolt of drugs surged through my veins, and my eyes flew wide, darting whichever way.

I panted, feeling blood rushing in my ears in rhythm with my pounding heart as I attempted to make sense of everything. Then it came to me. With the generator destroyed, my armor's functions had been restored, and it had injected me with meds. By the feel of it, a whole heap of them. My aches receded, and the fog in my mind cleared.

Coherent again, I twisted my head around like a mad man, taking stock of my situation. Rocks and debris were scattered around me, and the carnival of colors overhead was now replaced by a carpet of twinkling stars. A smile tugged at my lips. I'd done it. I'd disarmed a section of the shield.

Overjoyed, I tried to get up again, and failed. Confused, I let my head roll to the side, grimacing when my eyes landed on why. A massive boulder pinned my arm. Fluids from the suit and blood oozed from underneath, mixing into a tie-dye pattern of blue and red that painted the stone and grass. I sucked in a strained breath at the gory sight, fighting back clamoring panic. Now that my pain was a distant afterthought, and my mind clear, I wanted to live.

Taking a moment to count my blessings that the boulder hadn't fallen a foot to the left to crush my skull, I pondered how to escape. As my eyes darted, a new realization dawned on me. My display had stabilized. It beeped incessantly, popping out a slew of warnings and messages as if I wasn't aware of the gruesome damage. As if I couldn't see that my arm had been pancaked.

Ignoring the distant, yet stomach-churning sensation of my muscles pulling and tearing, I wriggled like an animal in a snare. The drugs had relieved me of pain, but there wasn't much they could do about the feel of my own broken bones grinding against each other. It churned my gut, but I kept yanking and thrashing, nonetheless.

"Pax!" I shouted as I squirmed.

Twisting up, I slammed my boots against the stone, and shoved, hoping to roll it off.

"No way!" crackled a familiar voice.

It was music to my ears.

"Is that really you, Adlar? Your locator just vanished. We thought you were dead for sure."

"Close," I huffed, slamming my boots against the rock a second time while pulling my arm. "Not dead yet, but close."

Begrudgingly, the rock finally rolled off. I sucked in a shuddering breath as I eyeballed the damage. I couldn't feel it, but the fact I couldn't see where the suit ended and my arm began, didn't fill me with confidence. It took me a few tries, but I at last pushed to my feet, the remnants of my arm dangling limply by my side. Whatever the suit had injected me with had cut the sensation of pain to my entire body and everything felt numb. I was thankful for that.

After I stood up, I teetered. "The shield. I blew up the shield."

I felt woozy as I took my first steps. There wasn't much the suit could do for the blood loss.

"The section... where I'm at. It's gone!"

"Did you hit your head or something, Adlar?" Mills snarked in reply. "Because I swear, I just heard you say you took down part of the shield."

"I did," I rasped, stumbling away from the mess.

I stopped and turned, scanning the destruction with my helmet. Now that it was operational again, I'd be able to transmit the footage. Not only had I blown up a decent chunk of the mountain, but I'd completely demolished the generator. The thing was torn in half, the upper portion dangling by scraps of metal which looked to be barely holding. A decimated mess of wires and whatnot sparked and crackled into the darkness.

I veered away and headed for the squad.

"Check the… helmet cam," I panted as I did my best to run.

It wasn't going to be long until the Synths reacted, and I was in no shape to fight.

"No freaking way!" Pax said after a pause. "You weren't kidding, fireball. You really did it!"

Smiling with pure satisfaction, I picked up my pace, ignoring my injuries. I did my best not to glance at my arm. Even though I couldn't feel it, I knew there wasn't much of it left. Splintered pieces of plastic and metal jutted out at odd angles, and the overpowering flavor of blood filled my mouth.

"I transmitted the footage to the brass," Pax huffed.

By their locator's zagging movements and their panting, I could tell they were still in the middle of chopping droolers.

"We're breaking off and heading your way, just keep coming towards us, Adlar. We got you."

I toggled the suit to inject me with another stim as whatever energy I had left waned. Then, mostly delirious, I shambled towards my teammates, relying on my suit to do most of the work. Relief swept over me when a collection of heavy-geared forms burst out of the plants like wavering ghosts, a blur in my vision. Arms reached out for me and propped me up. I was about to collapse. Then, everything grew even murkier, and I had very little recollection of what happened next, how we made it back to the dropship. Somewhere along the way, I passed out.

A loud voice jolted me back to awareness as my helmet was ripped off my head and cold air stabbed at my sweaty face. Shivering from the sudden drop in temperature, I blinked in confusion and looked around. I was back on the dropship with everyone staring at me.

My head lolled to one side, then the other. No matter how hard I tried, I couldn't focus.

"I did good, huh?" I slurred, as the suit stabbed me with yet another injection. This time in my thigh.

I groaned, trying to massage where the needle had poked, but neither arm moved.

Pax grabbed my knee and gave it a firm shake. "You sure did, buddy, you sure did. Now, stay awake, okay."

Savoring the praise, I managed a partial thumbs up on my good hand. That earned me another reaffirming pat from Pax before he turned back to the rest of the squad. They chatted, basking in the success, taking turns asking me questions and punching me to keep me awake. I was too out of it to answer or protest.

CHAPTER
THIRTY-ONE

I was expecting a medical team and a hover-gurney to be the first thing I saw when we docked on *Venator*, but to my disappointment, that wasn't what greeted us. Instead, as the ramp lowered and the hangar's bright lights hit me square in the eyes, the silhouettes of three suited Centurions slowly revealed themselves. By the look of their gore-stained suits, they hadn't taken the time to clean up and had instead waited for our arrival. Through a haze, I wondered what was so important.

Before I could inquire about the unprecedented greeting, medics rushed into the ship and began sticking me with needles and spraying my arm with coagulants. At first, I tried to bat them away, but then whatever they gave me started to work. My heart again kicked into overdrive, and the tingles of pain that were beginning to creep back in swept away. As the pain dulled, my vision blurred, and I had the strangest urge to break out with laughter.

"Enjoying the meds, huh?" Mills chuckled as he helped the medics unbuckle me, pull me to my feet, and hand me over to a couple of Fleet guys.

They grabbed me under my good arm and around my waist and proceeded to haul me behind the now moving collection of brass.

"Where… where are we… going?" I mumbled at last.

After a ride up on the elevator, we had exited onto an officer's deck, I could tell that much, but which one, I had no idea. Nor was this the way to the med-bays.

"Just following orders, trooper. You'll see when we get there," one of the Fleet pukes choked out through his panting.

Both were huffing and grimacing, having a hell of a time keeping me upright. I wasn't so light in my armor.

I didn't much appreciate his dismissive tone, but seeing as at the moment I had the strength of a newborn kitten, there wasn't much I could do about it. I had no choice but to let them drag me. We entered some sort of a large conference room with an oval table in the middle, surrounded by plushy chairs. Most looked to be occupied by Legion or Fleet brass. Centurion, Primus, and Prefect ranks glimmered on the collars of unfamiliar faces.

I probably should've been more nervous since a situation such as this called for a trooper to be on his best behavior, but I found myself not giving a damn. I gave the room a slow once over with a huge sloppy grin on my face.

With grunts of exertion, my assistants dragged me to Centurion Paxton and finally released me. Scurrying a few steps back, both immediately doubled over and wiped at sweat.

Face ridged, Paxton gave me an appraising scan as I did my best not to teeter, then pulled out a chair and shoved me into it.

"Thanks, Pax!" I said loudly, thinking of how my SL was basically a duplicate of his old man.

Centurion Paxton frowned but didn't comment. I then slumped forward in my chair, dropping my good arm on top of the table while my mangled one swung limply by my side. I tried to move it, but with no luck. I couldn't even twitch a finger. My mind wondered what it was going to feel like when it was time to remove the suit from my arm or my arm from the suit. I wasn't exactly sure which at this point. It was all a congealed mess of jutting plastic, metal, and flesh. Hopefully, there'd be more meds.

I think my good arm hit the table a bit too hard, because the room swept into sudden silence and everyone glared at me. Not heeding the ornery stares, I turned to the head of the table.

"Heeeyy…" I slurred, stretching over the surface, towards the bald, dark-skinned man sitting there. "Aren't you the damn Tribune?"

My vision was on the blurry side, but I swear the man only a few seats away from me was Tribune Gallus, himself, the man in charge of every Legionnaire aboard *Venator* and whose pictures were splattered all over the Legion's recruitment site. He somehow looked even more important in person.

As I grinned at the high commander, stretched over the table, I glimpsed a scowling face. Centurion Fallon was to the right of Paxton and glowering at me as if she'd discovered a new kind of turd. Forgetting all about the Tribune, I leaned around Paxton and opened my mouth to give the psycho a piece of my mind—a whole speech, if need be—when a hard slap landed on my injured arm.

I yelped and jerked straight as a jolt of pain traveled all the way up to my head. Damn, the meds were wearing off.

Looking down, I saw Centurion Paxton's hand reeling back for another blow, his face wearing a quickly deepening frown. Squeaking out a whimper, I dragged all my appendages off the table and leaned back into my chair, ready to behave.

Fallon suddenly popped straight up.

"On behalf of second cohort, I apologize for this trooper's behavior," she bellowed, turning to look at the Tribune and the sharp-faced Prefect Neero who had walked up to stand at his elbow. "Perhaps we should get started since we all have preparations to make before—"

That was as far as I made it to listening to her annoying blather. My eyes and mind drifted, melting into whatever meds still coursed through my veins. I couldn't care less what someone like her had to say, anyways.

With a crooked grin and a bit of drool on my chin, I scanned the concerned faces of the people around me. I found my grin involuntarily widening whenever my eyes landed on the cute Fleet ladies that happened to be in the room. Most were tapping away at their tablets. Even though I earned myself more than one surly frown, I gawked at them, nonetheless. I couldn't help but wonder if Ness' friend ever got around to giving Wagner my info, or when the witchy Fallon would finally hold up her end of our bargain and transfer Wagner to our deck.

"Trooper Adlar… trooper Adlar!" Centurion Paxton's voice lurched me from my daydream.

"Present!" I shouted, my head spinning.

I suddenly had no idea where I was. This didn't look like a muster or drill, so why was Centurion Paxton calling me? His disgruntled face quickly reminded me of the unpleasant situation—I'd been dragged to some sort of meeting. Paxton shook his head in disapproval, but this time didn't slap my arm. I was grateful for that.

"Can you walk us through how you were able to single-handedly dismantle a section of the Synth shield?" he asked.

Everyone's head turned to stare at me. Even the cute ladies momentarily paused tapping on their tablets to look.

"Well sir, it went like this," I stated in a matter-of-fact tone, acting out my words with my good arm. "I shimmied up some rocks, then it basically went *boom*, sir!"

I forcefully slammed my gauntleted hand down for emphasis, sending a vibration over the table and causing the brass to jerk back in surprise. Water bottles and coffee cups jostled as hands darted to steady them.

"And then I flew and smashed!" I finished with another loud bang. "Then there was a rock! Lots of them. Big ones!"

Silence followed, and mouths fell open. However, I couldn't help but notice that some of the ladies I'd previously eyeballed were trying hard to suppress their smiles. I grinned back, wholeheartedly, figuring they were what mattered.

Unfortunately, nobody was satisfied with my very direct, yet accurate, recounting of events, and since there was no recovered camera footage prior to the shield going down, I was then interrogated ten ways to Sunday.

"Okay, okay," Centurion Paxton finally said, cutting off some red-faced Primus grilling me for details.

Apparently, Paxton had enough of trying to translate my incoherent responses. Releasing a terse sigh, he stood and glanced down at the decent-sized puddle of blood that had now formed under my dangling arm. The coagulants must've missed some of the nooks and crannies.

"Let's get this trooper some medical attention before the next drop. We can reconvene later, if need be."

Turning, he waved over the Fleet guys that had assisted me earlier.

I paused, stunned, then bolted straight up in my seat as if I'd been prodded in the ass.

"The what? I'm going to have to drop? After this?"

Naturally, nobody bothered offering my very reasonable protests an explanation and without as much as a word, my two Fleet nannies hauled me to my feet and into the hall.

CHAPTER
THIRTY-TWO

As loopy as I was, I was still coherent enough to bombard my two SF lackeys with questions as they lugged me through a web of passageways and into an elevator. Surely, I wasn't going to have to drop again? In my condition? Unfortunately, my attendants weren't the chatty type. That, or they themselves hadn't been informed of my fate.

I finally shut up when I realized what deck we were on. The sterile-looking hall was freezing, and a thick smell of antiseptic and something acrid hung in the air. I didn't want to hypothesize about what the unfamiliar smell was, but it sure wasn't daisies.

I was on grave deck. Countless doors were labeled 'MORGUE,' and a floor-to-ceiling holographic legion crest glimmered on a wall. It was an inverted sword with a vine wrapped around it, in front of a golden shield. "*Ad Victoriam*" read the large banner that shimmered above it. I recognized the words to be Latin, a language from a distant time in Earth's past the Galactic Senate seemed to embrace.

"Couldn't they just fix me up in one of the med-rooms on the upper decks?" I whined. "I'm sure some more coagulants and skin patches would do the trick."

One of the men threw a glance at my dangling arm, scrunching his face.

"Uhm… I don't think skin patches will help with what you've got going on there, bud. Especially if they need you back in action so quick."

"So you do know something!" I twisted to face him as he groaned and looked away.

I opened my mouth to bombard him with more questions and even contemplated digging my heels into the deck, but then noticed a figure rushing towards us. A large grin spread over my face. I recognized the familiar short hair bob that bounced with each one of her steps.

"Wagner!" I dug my heels into the deck to the protest of my two assistants. "Is that really you?"

She rushed to stand in front of us as the SF lackeys grumbled and tried to nudge me forward.

"Are you okay?" she asked in a breathy tone. "A Specialist swiped me your info and I meant to contact you, but then the strangest thing happened. Out of nowhere, I was transferred to ship maintenance for the second cohort, and I got busy dealing with the transfer."

"That is strange, isn't it?" I smiled widely, enjoying the concerned look painted on her pretty face.

"Yeah!" She arched an eyebrow and gave her head a shake. "The transfer was weird for sure. Transport pilots moving to maintenance without a medical reason? It's almost unheard of."

She hesitated as her eyes darted to my arm, then back at me and her voice lowered. "I searched for you when your cohort returned, but then someone told me you were injured and probably down on grave deck. I had to find you. For a minute, I thought you—"

She trailed off breathing heavily, then looked up at me with glistening eyes.

"I was worried I'd find you in the morgue, Jake," she finished in almost a whisper.

Grimacing, she reached for my arm but pulled back. "Is your arm going to be okay? Are *you* going to be okay?"

"Oh, this." I glanced at the jigsaw puzzle of flesh and suit.

My sensation was slowly returning, and I could tell I was still bleeding. The warm liquid trickled down and dripped to the floor.

"It's just a scratch. I'll be good as new here in a bit."

"That is if we ever make it to the med-bay," chirped one of Fleet flunkeys.

The men again tried to shove me forward, but I didn't budge. My boots remained firmly planted on the deck as I continued to grin at Wagner, savoring every minute of this encounter and her genuine worry. Here I was, thinking the girl didn't remember me, or the fact that we'd met, when instead, she knew exactly who I was, and even bothered to seek me out. Not only that, but she seemed almost frightened at the idea I might have died. Now if that didn't mean she was into me, I didn't know what did.

Wagner cocked her head and looked up at me with a quizzical smile, her somber demeanor shifting. "So, I heard you took down a part of the shield? All by yourself?"

"Oh, for crying out loud—" the SF guy on my right groaned, throwing his head back in exasperation.

He again tried to push me forward. "That's it, we're dragging you, if that's what it takes."

He wasn't kidding. The two men proceeded to haul me across the deck like a sack of potatoes. I slumped in their hold, refusing to walk, but had no energy to put up any meaningful resistance.

"Hey, Wagner!" I called over my shoulder. Turning my head was about all I could do. "Once I get this scratch fixed, how about dinner? Galley? Two hours?"

"Sounds great," she called back, smiling. "And it's Taylor."

A few passersby threw us quizzical glances and sneered, but I didn't care. Beaming from ear to ear, I stopped trying to resist, and allowed the two Fleet oafs to haul me into the reconstruction room.

CHAPTER
THIRTY-THREE

"How… much… longer?" I finally managed to ask the nurse, between the grimaces and the embarrassing high-pitched yelps that I couldn't seem to control.

She was hunched over my arm, plucking out shards of suit and stringy wiring. It wasn't a pleasant experience. The jagged pieces scraped at my bone and made a gruesome wet sucking sound as they released from my flesh. Worse, the disinterested, grumpy nurse was moving at the speed of a three-legged turtle.

Pursing her lips, she gave me a dirty look. "If you keep wriggling like an infant, it will take all night."

She glanced at my two SF babysitters who were loitering near the exit. They must've been given orders to monitor me throughout the procedure because the disdainful, tired looks on their faces didn't scream they were hanging around to keep me company.

"Can't you guys hold him down or something?" she asked.

Both men groaned but reluctantly shuffled over to the reclined dentist-like chair I was in and pinned me down. One pushed on my shoulder so I wouldn't move my arm, while the other slapped a grubby hand onto my chest. I scowled at them but knew I didn't have the strength to contest.

Then, an idea popped into my head. Would this nurse perhaps be as enthralled by my exploits on Atlas as Taylor had appeared to be?

In any case, it was worth a try. Otherwise, I might still be here this time next week.

Plastering on one of my most genuine, poster-perfect smiles, I turned my attention to her.

"Haven't I seen you around before?" I asked, trapping her eyes the best I could as I was still woozy. "I haven't caught your name, but I meant to. *Been* meaning to. Then the drop happened, and *this*—"

I glanced at my arm, wincing. "Worth it though. What's a tiny scuff when compared to dismantling part of the Synths' shield all by myself. If anything, I should be thankful I walked away at all, right?"

I would have thrown in a hapless shrug to complete the act, but the unpleasant male hands over me made that impossible. It wasn't needed, however. The woman's demeanor lightened almost instantly as she paused her work to study me with newfound intrigue.

"That was you? The Gold Squad trooper everyone's talking about?"

"Yes ma'am, sure was. Jake Adlar, at your service." I kept up the charm even as my cheeks warmed.

In my book, I hadn't done anything special, nothing anyone else wouldn't have done. Nor was I proud of popping the civilians. Yet, at the moment, I was willing to try just about anything to make my date with Taylor.

Fortunately, my posturing appeared to have done the trick. A twinkle had entered the nurse's eyes.

"Well, I'm Janice," she said, reaching over and gently moving a clump of sweaty hair off my forehead, smoothing it out, "and nice to meet you, Jake. You're kind of famous, you know. Usually, it takes the cohorts a while to make such progress."

"Ehh… it was nothing. Just doing my job, that's all."

The Fleet oafs rolled their eyes and mumbled insults, but Janice ignored them, concentrating only on me. I could tell she was impressed. Edging closer to my chair, she studied my face with a gentle expression.

"What'd you say we take care of that lip while you're here?"

"Uh…" I hesitated, not sure if I wanted to be prodded any further.

The swelling had gone from where Pax had punched me, but it had yet to fully heal.

I was about to politely refuse, figuring I'd been medicated enough for the day, but then a thought occurred to me. What if my date with Taylor went well. It wouldn't be a bad idea to have my face back in shape, especially my lips. Just in case.

"Sure." I beamed at Janice. "That's mighty nice of you. You know, not many are so considerate of us, grunts. But if there's any way to speed all this up, I'd sure appreciate it, ma'am."

The SF lackey with his paws on my chest released a loud snort. "Yes, please. Just knock him out already, so we can leave."

Janice ignored him. With a coy smile, she popped open a drawer under my chair and pulled out a tube of nu-skin.

"I'll set the reconstructor to speed over economy. That way, it'll only take about an hour," she said, unscrewing the tube and leaning over me. "Now this might sting a bit."

"Nothin' I can't handle." I smirked, appreciating her ample chest, which was now only inches away from me, the low v-neck leaving little to the imagination.

I'd had plenty of experience with nu-skin, at least on most parts of my body. Not so much on the face, as I was careful with that commodity. A second later, I forgot all about Janice's buxom cleavage. She hadn't been kidding. Even with all the pain meds coursing through my veins, the stuff bit into my lip like a venomous viper as she layered it on. Clenching my teeth, I feverishly blinked away the sting in my eyes.

"There, that should do it," Janice stated, putting the tube away and sitting back down next to my arm. "Your face should be good as new here in a minute."

"Thank… you," I squeaked out, turning my head away from her to the muffled snickers of the SF men.

My macho warrior routine wasn't going to hold up if I started crying.

She chuckled and squeezed my shoulder. "It's all right not to play tough *all* the time, trooper. I know there's more to you, Legion boys, than that."

I wanted very much to protest her very accurate observation and claim that I'd felt nothing, but I was too busy biting the inside of my cheek to keep my eyes from watering.

With that, Janice returned to work on my arm, but this time, without treating me like a pin cushion or moving like a zombie. She expertly removed a few more metal shards and a long piece of wire that released with a gruesome slurp. She checked on me between each yank, periodically offering me more meds.

"All done," she finally announced.

Brushing my sweaty hair off my forehead again, she then wheeled over the reconstruction box and swung it open like a briefcase. I cringed. The interior was filled with a greenish gel and inch-long needles.

"You won't feel a thing," Janice assured, noting my concern.

Gently lifting what was left of my arm, she plopped it in. As if alive, the cold goop immediately stirred into motion and began to consume my arm. My skin prickled at the repulsive sensation, and I yearned to pull away, but the SF brutes held me steady. I turned my head from the sight as Janice closed the box, leaving my arm sealed up to the shoulder in the machine.

Taking a step back, Janice flung her hands to her shapely hips and gave me a pointed stare.

"Normally, it's up to the trooper if they want more meds for this part, but with *you* I'm not going to make it an option." Her flirty tone was all but gone.

With purposeful steps, she grabbed an injector off a table, then marched my way. Even though it was obvious I'd piqued her interest, at least as far as I could tell, she appeared eager to get her job over with. My interrogation by the brass had delayed my treatment and I was one of the last men still in the room.

I opened my mouth to protest, disdainfully eying the silver cylinder in her hand. I wanted to be lucid for my first date with Taylor, and not drooling like one of the cyclops, but Janice didn't give me much of a choice. She stabbed me. My head slumped, and my mind floated to the clouds. With strange gurgling and slurping sounds, the machine set to work.

The first thing I did when my eyes flew open, and I regained lucidity, was glance at the time display flickering on the wall. I breathed a sigh of relief. My trip to la-la land had only lasted about an hour. The next thing I did was resist the very strong urge to yank my arm. It felt whole again but was still shoulder deep inside the machine, which gurgled and splooshed. I waggled my fingers experimentally and frowned. Thick icy sludge hindered their movement. I winced. Apparently, the machine wasn't done, and now that the meds had worn off, I felt the jab of each tiny needle.

Suppressing my urge to pull my arm out, I looked for the nurse. All the other chairs were now empty and the reconstructors lined in neat rows against the walls. There was a slew of arm-sized ones, just like the one slurping at me, and a decent collection of larger ones, probably for the legs. For anything more serious, I knew there were also body-sized machines and tubs, but those were in a different room.

After glancing around the empty room, I paused and scrunched my brows in confusion. Why *was* I the last one here? I strained to think. The last thing I remembered clearly was stuffing frags into the generator. Everything after that was a haze.

My mind flashed with images of a crowded room. Someone had interrogated me, I was sure of it. Centurion Paxton and Fallon, perhaps? I tried to think back to who else was there, but their faces were a corrupted vid-file as far as my brain was concerned. All I remembered was that they were brass.

I rubbed my chin in thought, concerned about what I might've possibly said in my altered state. A few blinks later, I shrugged it off. My ass was no stranger to the chair before Paxton's desk, so what if I warmed it for yet another time.

I returned my attention to what mattered. Aside from being blown up, there was another thing I remembered as clear as day. A much-anticipated date awaited me, and I needed to get out of here if I was going to make it.

"Nurse!" I shouted, just as a series of needles jabbed into my bicep, then around my elbow.

Sucking in a quick gulp of air and hissing, I again resisted the urge to free myself and shouted for the nurse, louder this time. If I hurried, I'd be able to snag a shower. I wasn't going to make a great impression showing up with a slimy arm and my funky post-armor stench.

When I received no reply, I reached to open the machine myself but froze when my eyes landed on my flashing watch. I heaved a sigh. Apparently, while I was floating away on meds, I'd missed a message—or ten. Anticipating they were nothing good, I had half a mind to ignore them and claim I'd been passed out, but then I thought of Pax. Had my inadvertent success with the generator made up for the arena mishap? I didn't know but decided I didn't want to push my luck.

Bringing my arm up, I reluctantly tapped the screen with my nose. An announcement popped up, the first of many.

A loud groan escaped me as I read. The last minute or so of my dance with the brass floated back to me. Now that I'd disarmed a section of the enemy's defenses, the Legion was going to make a push. All the cohorts were dropping. In fact, according to the announcement, they'd already started. Both the first and third cohorts were currently on the ground. Second was to follow. We were to report to the hangar in a matter of hours.

"Nurse!" I hollered.

"Calm down, calm down!" came a shout, as a vaguely familiar lady popped out of a side door.

Janice, I think. She was curvy with a dolled-up face, and in scrubs that hugged her body just a tad too tight. I'd missed all those details while I was drugged, but now I couldn't help but glide my eyes over her shapely form.

"I need to get out of here!" I focused on her face.

With both the humans and Synths throwing everything they had at each other, I could only imagine what fresh hell awaited me on Atlas, and if that was to be my fate, I wasn't going to miss seeing Taylor.

I sat up, reaching for the box, as Janice's footsteps rushed my way.

"Stop it!" she hissed, whacking my arm away.

I relented and anxiously eyeballed her painstakingly slow work of opening the machine and pulling the stray needles out of me. I silently willed her to hurry up. Finally, she plucked out the last inch-long needle, clattering it into a metal bowl with the rest of them. She ripped open an alcohol wipe and reached for my freshly remade arm. The slime-covered skin glowed bright pink and tingled. Swatting her away, I jumped out of the chair.

"Hey!" she protested loudly. "I still need to clean and examine it."

But she was shouting to my back. I was already almost to the door.

"It's all good," I assured her over my shoulder, flinging my hand high as proof, opening and closing my fist.

The skin felt tight, but everything seemed to be working fine.

Rushing into the empty hall, I looked around, calculating which path would get me to my room the fastest. With a groan, I realized it was the one past the morgues. The rooms lined the hall on either side, each labeled with a black projection plaque that read "MORGUE" in golden letters. Shrugging off a cold shiver, I decided to pull up my big boy pants and started walking.

Not twenty steps into my march, a door I was passing flashed open with no warning. I jumped a foot in the air and nearly pissed myself.

"Dammit!" I shouted trying to keep my cool.

Grave deck was creepy. Retreating a step, I glanced at the door to see who had opened it, hoping it was just some nurse or Fleet guy trying to do their job, anything but a ghost, or a maimed trooper come back from the dead.

However, it was no nurse, medic, or ghost that greeted my eyes with an expression of utter shock and surprise. The person who had startled me was none other than MP Garner, and his face went as white as a sheet at the sight of me. At first, I almost didn't recognize the guy since he was out of uniform, dressed in civvies, but the confusion was fleeting. By now, his freckled mug was seared into my retinas.

I quickly scanned him up and down in search of weapons, but I didn't see any.

"A-Adlar?" he stuttered out nervously, placing a hand on the edge of the door so it wouldn't shut.

His head spun, searching the hall as he panted. For whatever reason, the man looked like I'd just walked in on him in the shower.

He focused back on me. "Wha… what are you doing here?"

"Getting a brand-new arm," I said, raising my slime-covered appendage as proof. Some of the after fluids were beginning to dry, making it itch. "What the hell are *you* doing here? And why are you gallivanting in civvies?"

Instead of his usual uniform, Garner was in jeans and a roughed-up t-shirt of a band I didn't recognize. The man looked to be at a loss for words, his mouth opening and closing stupidly as if he were a fish. I think he stammered some sort of explanation, but I missed it. I was too busy trying to see what he was attempting to hide behind his butt.

Leaning around, my eyes landed on a hover-cart.

"What'd you got in *there*?" I stretched my neck further, trying to see inside, but a white sheet was draped over it.

I knew I was short on time and needed to go, but everything about the situation struck me as odd. What was a Fleet lackey, such as Garner, dressed in civvies, doing in a morgue? And what was he retrieving that required a whole damn hover-cart?

"N-nothing," Garner stammered.

He shuffled over a few inches, trying to block me from seeing around him. Unfortunately for him, that move only fueled my curiosity.

"It's nothing. You should leave, Adlar. Just go!"

I contemplated his request, since I did have somewhere important to be, but then decided against it. I just couldn't wrap my mind around what he could possibly be doing down here.

"Naahh…" I said, stretching a casual arm in his direction.

I slapped it on the door so it wouldn't close, then took a methodical step closer to Garner.

"I think I want to see what you have in the cart instead."

Garner's eyes flew wide in panic as he shuffled back.

He shook his head, throwing a hurried glance at his watch. "Trust me, Adlar, you don't. Now get out of my way, I don't have much time."

Releasing a heavy sigh, I was about to relent. As entertaining as it was watching him fidget, I wasn't about to miss my date with Taylor for the likes of him. But then, the hover-cart made a noise, and it wasn't the mechanical equipment kind. It was more like a groan.

CHAPTER
THIRTY-FOUR

"Uhm… uhm…" Garner stammered like a glitching vid as his eyeballs darted between my shocked face, the hover-cart, and the room behind him.

He looked like a trapped fox caught in the hen house.

To my surprise, instead of attempting an explanation, the man lunged. He shoved me hard on my chest. Since I was unprepared for that move, I lost my balance and pitched to my butt. Garner used that opportunity to grab the hover-cart and bolt for the elevators.

Any inkling I might've had about dropping the matter disappeared in a flash. Heat flowed into my cheeks. The scumbag had made the mistake of his life putting his dirty mitts on me. Not only was I beyond done taking shit from everyone, but he should've known better than to mess with a ground trooper who'd just spent the day killing droolers, being interrogated, and prodded.

With a surge of adrenaline, I jumped to my feet and sprinted after him.

"Oh, hell no!" I boomed, my voice echoing down the sterile hall.

Garner glanced over his shoulder, eyes as wide as saucers, and tried to pick up his pace, but it didn't do him much good. Not only was I in much better shape, but not many could match my stride. In seconds, I was on top of him, grabbing a fistful of his shirt and yanking him back.

Not bothering to give him a chance to spew some BS apology, I flung him to the wall. The skin on my new arm felt tight and itched, but as my fist flew towards his face, everything seemed to be functioning fine. A gruesome crack sounded as I popped him right in the nose.

"Stop it!" he shrieked, feebly trying to fight me off.

Releasing a growl, I was about to go for another swing, but my thoughts jumped to Taylor. I didn't have time for this. If I hurried, I might still make our date. I'd have to fabricate an excuse for being late, but that wasn't anything I hadn't done before.

I leaned closer to Garner.

"Just try messing with me again," I hissed into his ear, then roughly shoved him away.

Determined to make my date, I turned to sprint to the elevator when an unexpected sound froze me dead in my tracks. Garner's hover-cart moaned. With how hot I'd gotten, I'd all but forgotten about the thing. Befuddled, I approached it with careful steps. As I did, it moaned again, then whimpered. There was no mistaking it. Something inside was alive.

Both intrigued and concerned, I reached for the sheet and yanked. Then, I just stood there, blinking. I wasn't sure what I had expected to find, but it certainly wasn't what met my eyes. There was no injured trooper or illegal pet or drone inside the four-foot deep rectangular bin, but instead, a nurse. She was scrunched in a fetal position on the bottom of the cart. I quickly scanned her body for injuries but didn't see any. Her eyelids fluttered as she whimpered weakly, struggling to regain consciousness.

"It's not what you think... it's not!" Garner pleaded from somewhere behind me.

I was past listening. Giving my head a slow shake, I bared all my teeth at once—he wasn't about to get away with whatever sick, twisted thing this was.

Wheeling on him, I snagged him by his scruff right as he tried to run. I flung him against the wall, pummeling at his face, gut, and whatever else my fist found. My mind went mad as I thought about what he'd intended to do with the helpless nurse.

"St-stop-it—" he gurgled, coughing up spurts of bloody drool.

Ignoring his pleas, I continued to punch him, my knuckles sliding on his bloodied face. At last winded, I let go of him. The moment I did, he fell to the floor in a heap. I pulled back my leg about to go in for a kick when he stretched up a quivering arm in my direction.

"It's not… what… you think," he rasped, between bouts of coughing.

He twitched and gasped. I considered not following through with my kick but then changed my mind and nailed him right in the stomach, figuring he deserved every blow. I mean here we all were, the only humans hundreds of light-years away from Earth, and instead of protecting each other, this guy was in the middle of abducting a helpless nurse for who only knew what heinous intent. That just wasn't going to fly with me.

"Oh, yeah?" I exclaimed. "Why don't you explain it to me then? Let's hear it. Come on!"

Garner clutched his stomach as more bloody drool stringed to the floor.

"He-here…" he rasped, reaching into his pocket and pulling out a plastic card.

It almost slipped out of his trembling hands, but he thrust it towards me.

I had half a mind to kick him again, but instead grabbed the card. It was an access badge. The kind I'd seen carried around by aids or troops running errands for the brass. Our watches were capable of opening any door that one had clearance to, but sometimes personnel needed additional access, depending on their duties. In that case, they were swiped clearance to their watches or issued a badge by whoever needed them to carry out their assignment.

"What's this?" I asked, wiping blood off the card on my pants.

"Airlock 71. In the storage holds. Go there."

I glanced at my watch in frustration, then back at the access badge. I knew I'd already spent way too long dealing with this freak, but I couldn't let this go. I had to break up whatever disgusting crap this was. Taylor would understand me showing up in dirty clothes and with a crusty arm covered in peeling film after I told her about what I'd just seen and stopped.

Leaving Garner moaning and twitching on the floor like the shriveled rat that he was, I scooped up the semi-conscious nurse from the cart and, using the access badge, rushed her into a med-bay. I placed the woman on one of the reclined chairs, hoping she wouldn't remember what just happened to her, then hurried out the door. I made sure it clicked shut behind me so Garner wouldn't be able to get back in.

Cursing, but feeling I had no choice but to investigate the matter further, I sprinted through the labyrinths of passageways to the storage holds. Even though I hadn't had the chance to explore even the unrestricted parts of the ship, since that could easily take weeks, I'd familiarized myself with the decks. I knew where the holds were. Unfortunately, they were nowhere near my current location.

The storage holds, which housed old and unused equipment, among other things, were famous for all kinds of shady activities, ranging from gambling to lovers trying to find some privacy. So, I wasn't at all surprised that's where Garner was trying to take the abducted nurse.

That sick fuck! I seethed to myself as I ran. I should have killed him. There was no place in this universe for men like him.

At last, huffing and winded, I reached the holds, deep in *Venator's* bowls. Slowing my steps, I carefully weaved through the hauntingly quiet bays. I never thought it possible to hear such complete silence on a ship crammed to the brim with people, but now that I was here, I knew I'd been wrong. A blanket of dust layered the metal crates, and an uneasy stillness hung in the air. It was so still, in fact, I felt like I could both hear and feel the hull vibrate with a gentle thrum.

Gingerly making my way through the maze of compartments, I eyeballed the numbers labeling each hold. Finally, there it was. At the end of the passage, on a garage-sized door, large white print read "Airlock 71."

My cheeks flushed with anger as I stormed towards the door with long determined strides, and I tightened my grip on the crowbar I had dislodged from behind one of the desolate crates. I was ready to give whoever was there a beating deserving of their crimes, and I didn't plan on showing mercy.

Scanning the card on the control panel, I fidgeted with impatience as I waited for the door to open. With a loud metallic clang that dissipated eerily down the passage, the door began to retract. I braced, ready, but as the cold air from the airlock hit my face, I didn't lunge. Instead, my jaw dropped in disbelief.

CHAPTER
THIRTY-FIVE

It hadn't occurred to me to stop and look for anything more substantial than the crowbar in my hands, as I'd been all too sure all I'd find were a few dudes in need of a beating. Boy, did I suddenly regret that decision. Not only was the person before me armed, but they regained their composure much faster than I. Before I could turn to run, a blaster was trained at my head.

"What the hell are you doing here?" Centurion Fallon roared as my pathetic crowbar slipped from my hands and clattered to the deck.

She stretched her neck to look around me, down the hall. "And where the fuck is Garner?"

My hands shot high in surrender.

"Uh…" I said, blinking stupidly and my eyes flitting between her reddened face and the blaster.

My mind raced. What was Fallon doing here?

Fallon returned her attention to me, baring her teeth. "You have to be shitting me! How is it always you? How the fuck are you always popping out of nowhere like some damn roach from the cracks!"

I remained silent, hands raised, my heart pounding in my throat. The bat-shit crazy woman already thirsted for my blood, and if she was going to kill me anywhere, this was the place to do it. Not only were we alone, but we were standing right smack dab in the best body disposal system on the entire ship—an airlock.

"Where's Garner, and where's the body?" Fallon demanded.

"The... what?" I finally managed.

Fallon's eyes darted to her watch in panic, then back to me. They glimmered with feral madness in the dim overhead lights.

"The body. Where's the fucking body? There's not much time left, you fool!"

"You mean... the nurse Garner had in his hover-cart?"

I was still having a hell of a time digesting that the two were somehow connected, but if it quacked like a duck... what else could it be?

"I don't care if it was a nurse or the damn Legate, herself!" Fallon shouted, waving that blaster at me. "Don't test me, you fuck! I'll blow your brains out, right here, right now! Where is he?"

Not providing her with an answer, I let out a slow breath and stepped towards her. I wasn't exactly sure what I planned on doing, but I noticed that the hand holding the blaster trembled. Plus, for whatever reason, she still hadn't shot, and she'd had plenty of time. Perhaps, if I got her to flip out some more in her usual fashion, I'd get a chance to disarm her.

"Why were you abducting someone?" I narrowed my eyes.

Was this what Garner was doing in her office earlier, hashing out whatever nefarious scheme this was?

Fallon narrowed her eyes right back at me. To my dismay, instead of further losing her cool like I'd hoped, she straightened, and her lips curled up in a thin, wicked smile.

"Hmm..." She rubbed her chin, eying me in contemplation. "It looks like it's your lucky day, Adlar, being that you're a man... at least on the outside."

"Huh?" I stopped my advance, hesitating.

The wheels in her foul head looked to be turning, and I didn't like that.

Casting a glance at her watch, Fallon's smile broadened. "You have thirty minutes, trooper."

"What?" My face scrunched in confusion. "Thirty minutes... for what?"

Fallon chuckled. It was a wicked sound.

"Well, it's not to get me a fucking sandwich, you moron. To bring me a body, of course. Anyone, as long as it's female. If not... well—"

She feigned a nonchalant expression. "That Wagner girl you had me transfer to our deck, she'll be next on the menu."

My mouth fell open.

"Now, hold on a second!" I protested. "She has nothing to do with this!" I looked around the empty airlock. "Whatever this is."

I silently kicked myself. How could I have been so stupid? So careless as to mention Wagner's name to someone as unhinged as Fallon?

"Doesn't matter now, does it?" she spat. "Bring me a body, or that Fleet pilot is next. And don't get any funny ideas while you're at it. I have eyes and ears everywhere."

I took a moment to stare at her as a chill traveled down my spine. My every brain cell was riling on overdrive registering the enormity of her demand. When it at last sank in, I felt sick to my stomach. She wanted me to bring her an actual *person,* and she wasn't kidding.

"I-I can't—" I shook my head.

I had no clue what twisted thing I'd just stumbled upon, but I had enough sense to know that a trip into this airlock was a one-way ticket for the victims.

Appearing amused by my rebuttal, Fallon nodded a slow *yes.*

I again shook my head. As daunting as her threat was, I didn't have it in me to murder anyone.

Fallon's expression darkened.

"Fine!" she snapped. "Get me a corpse then. We don't have time to fuck this up any more than it already has been, so a corpse will do."

"Fucking Garner. That moron," she added under her breath, rubbing her forehead. "As dumb as a Havarian shrew, and those forget they're climbing and plummet to their death."

As she seethed about some planet I'd never heard of, I just stood there, speechless. There was no doubt in my mind her threat held weight. If I didn't deliver her a corpse, she'd go after Taylor.

Jerking her attention back to me, Fallon rotated her watch in my direction.

"Tick, tock," she purred. "Twenty-five minutes, trooper."

CHAPTER
THIRTY-SIX

Now I had found myself in some very strange and terrifying situations in the last few days and had even been on death's door a time or two. Yet, this was the most terrified I'd felt thus far. Fallon, with her crazed eyes and tight wicked smile, scared me more than any drop, bot, or drooler. Even though it was freezing inside the airlock, sweat beaded my forehead. If I didn't do what she asked, she'd kill me, then Taylor—I had twenty-five minutes to get her a corpse.

Saying nothing else, I turned and ran, bouncing off bulkheads, sliding around corners, and taking the stairs three steps at a time, back to grave deck. Back to where the morgues were. What I was about to do twisted my gut, but I wasn't about to call Fallon's bluff. After all, what was an already dead trooper's corpse when weighed against Taylor's life?

When I at last reached grave deck, I was relieved to see that it was as empty as I had left it. Two cleaning bots hummed at the far end of the hall, but I knew unless there was something suspicious, no one was going to scour through their visuals. First and third cohorts were both deployed, and the medical staff were resting while they could. All that worked in my favor.

I quickly hustled to the smeared blood Garner had left behind. Even though he'd slunk away by now, his hover-cart was still there, aimlessly floating in the middle of the hall. Grabbing it, I veered towards the morgue and scanned my access badge on the panel. I bounced on my toes as I did. I had no idea if the card was still active or had expired. Most were only good for a day or two, some for mere hours. But since I'd just acquired it, I hoped it still worked.

The screen beeped, flashing green. I burst through the retracting door, only to freeze after two steps. With a flick of my hand, I shoved my tailing cart back into the hall. A cold chill enveloped me, and it wasn't due to the frigid air. Unlike the hall, the morgue wasn't empty. Two confused faces of a man and a woman popped up from their tablets to look at me. I didn't recognize the man, but the woman was Janice.

Breathing hard, I covertly slid the badge I wasn't authorized to have into my back pocket. An uncomfortable silence lingered as we all stared at each other with baffled expressions.

"Can we help you?" the man finally asked. "And how did you get in here?"

His eyes jumped to the door then back to me as his face scrunched in bewilderment. My mind raced. What excuse could I possibly give them? Troopers weren't allowed in the morgues, and by all accounts, the SOPs called for me to be detained.

Both stared at me expectantly, waiting for an explanation.

"Is something wrong with your arm?" Janice broke the silence, her expression changing from one of surprise and confusion to one of concern.

"My arm?" I echoed.

I glanced down at my now fully functional appendage.

"Ahh, yeah, my arm!"

Reaching over, I methodically peeled off a thin, dried layer of film, trying to buy time to figure out how to get rid of the male nurse. An idea brewed in the recesses of my mind, or at least the beginning of one, and I had a very strong sense my scheme would go over smoother without the guy in the room.

"*Is* something wrong?" Janice repeated. "Does it hurt? Are you having mobility issues?"

Dropping the tablet from her hands, she rushed to me and grabbed my arm. She gently prodded, frowning when her gaze landed on my battered knuckles. The skin was raw from where I'd turned Garner's face into hamburger.

"What happened?"

"Uh… nothing." I yanked away.

"Nothing at all, see." I waved my arm around, opening and closing my hand. "Just like new."

I shuffled, throwing a bashful glance at the deck and fidgeted for effect. "I'm actually here for another reason. I came to talk to you. I just, uh… wanted to apologize for running out earlier, and my impatient behavior in general."

I shrugged sheepishly. "You were just trying to do your job, and I was rude."

Janice's concerned expression changed to a playful kind of smirk. "Well, aren't you just the sweetest."

My muscles untensed. Just maybe, this was going to work. Now, I just needed to get rid of the guy. His slitted eyes screamed that he wasn't at all buying my crap, that I was here for an apology, and one of his fingers was hovering dangerously close to his watch. I could tell he was itching to sound the alarm.

"And there was something I wanted to ask," I rushed to add.

I threw an obvious glance at the male nurse. "But it would be better if we were alone if that's okay?"

The man's squinted eyes narrowed even further as they darted between Janice and me with suspicion. He opened his mouth to protest, but Janice stuck up an eager hand to cut him off.

"It's okay, Mike. Give us a minute."

"But—" He blinked, gesturing at the door with one hand. "How did he even—"

"You heard the lady!" I loudly cut him off before he got any funny ideas about asking more questions. "Now let us have a minute, sheesh."

The man blinked a few more times in shock, glancing between Janice and me, but then, relented. With a disdainful snort, he exited the room. I breathed a silent sigh of relief at both the fact that he was gone, and that he'd used the side door for his exit, instead of the door leading into the hall. The hover-cart was still there, not to mention the bloodied wall and deck.

Once we were alone, Janice glanced up at me with a flirty smile. "I suspected you might be back. So go on, ask."

I took a step closer, almost right up against her, doing my best not to drop my gaze below her chin. As panicked as I was, I just couldn't help it. Janice didn't back away, staring up at me with eager eyes.

"I… I wanted to ask you a *favor*…" I said, gauging her reaction as I spoke.

Unfortunately, it wasn't what I had hoped for. Her posture stiffened and her smile waned, very dangerously edging towards a frown.

"A *favor*? That's it?" Her fists flew to her hips.

Fuck! My mind reeled. Sure, the hope that she'd go for my friendly 'favor' routine was a long shot, but it was still hard not to be disappointed. Her batting eyelashes weren't hiding the fact 'friends' wasn't what she was after.

Seeing no other way, I quickly rushed to amend my request before my scheme spiraled down the drain.

"*And* a date, of course! Maybe we can hang out sometime?"

Janice's smile sprang back to her face like the sun's rays after a storm. She practically glowed.

"Now that's *much* better, trooper," she approved, twirling a strand of brown hair around her finger and licking her shimmering lips flirty-like as if she were about to kiss me right here on the spot. *Damnation!* The girl wasn't shy.

I forced a strained grin back at her. Any other time, I would've jumped at the tantalizing opportunity—the woman was nothing to scoff at—but then, there was Taylor. Even though *Venator* was massive, rumors spread like wildfire.

Inching closer to be right under my chin, Janice gently caressed the side of my arm and gazed up at me.

"Now, what was that favor you needed?" she cooed, her breath tickling my neck.

Blinking down at her, I almost lost my train of thought. She smelled of lavender or some such under the antiseptic, and her body was warm against mine. The enticing combination had certain thoughts spinning rampant in my inattentive brain.

Giving my head a shake, I snapped out of it. The clock was ticking. By my accounting, I had eighteen minutes left, if that.

I dropped my eyes to the deck plates, dejected, and got on with my plan.

"Well, you see, a few of my friends... well... they didn't make it in this last drop," I lied, "the one where I was injured."

I glanced at the medical gurneys lining one side of the room and the sheet-covered bodies on top of them, then back at her. She was now wide-eyed with concern, and looked like she wanted nothing more than to fling her arms around me in a hug. I no longer had to fake looking bashful. Not only was I about to steal a Leege's body, but I was manipulating an innocent woman to do so.

Seeing as there was no going back, I threw another glance at the tables and kept at it.

"I know I'm not supposed to be down here and there's going to be a service and all, but I just wanted to have a moment with them in private. Before the next drop."

Janice could no longer contain herself. Flinging her arms around my waist, she wrapped me in a tight hug, letting her head drop onto my chest. I awkwardly reciprocated her embrace with a few pats on her back.

"Of course, you can," she whispered softly. "Whatever you need, Jake. I'm really sorry about them. What were their names? I can check if they're on the gurneys or—"

She trailed off as her eyes slid to the refrigeration drawers lining the back of the room.

I swallowed hard. "Uh..."

Thinking quick, I aimed a finger at the sheet-covered bodies. "That's them. I-I checked with another nurse earlier. He directed me here."

"Oh..." For a second Janice looked confused but didn't press the matter.

"Well, okay," she said, breaking our hug.

She stepped back, holding me at arm's length. "Take all the time you need."

With that, she turned and exited the room, thankfully using the side door just like her buddy had. Grimacing, I shoved down the guilt lingering in my throat and got to work. I was doing this to save Taylor, right? These troops were already dead, so what did it matter what happened with their corpses?

First thing I did was pull my hover-cart in from the hall. Then, instead of walking to the sheet-covered bodies on the metal gurneys, I rushed to the freezer drawers. My gut flip-flopped as I searched for one with a woman's name beaming on the e-tag then pulled it open. The drawer squeaked as it slid. I cringed, doing my best not to think of the corpse as an actual person.

Reluctantly, I stuck my hands in. Cold spongy flesh greeted my fingers. I almost gagged but forced myself to stay on task. Trying not to look at the woman's face, I rolled the body into the hover-cart which I'd placed next to the open drawer. It plopped in with a heavy thunk and the cart sank an inch from the weight. I then circled around it, shoving the dangling limbs inside, to where nothing was sticking out. Next, I snagged a sheet, and draped it over the cart. At last ready, I pushed my plunder to the door and out into the hall.

A heavy sigh escaped me as I glanced up and down the empty passageway. Garner's bloodstains were now gone and so were the cleaning bots. I wanted to run right then but feared that would be too suspicious. What if Janice decided to go search for me, or worse, report me? After all, hurt feelings could make a woman to lash out in countless evil ways.

Deciding to play it safe, I reluctantly stepped back into the morgue, but I didn't feel good about it. Not only had I now missed my date with Taylor, but I was about to confirm a date with someone else.

Heaving a sigh, I turned and made for the door Janice had vanished through, only for it to gust open as I came near it. I could now see this room was connected to yet another morgue. Refrigerated storage drawers lined a wall and there were more sheet-covered bodies on gurneys. I noted that most of the remains didn't look complete, judging by how small the lumps were.

Janice stood framed in the doorway, pity and concern painted over her face. She opened her arms to go in for another hug right as my watch buzzed and flashed red. I hopped back, making a show of glancing at my wrist.

"I have to go," I said, without actually reading the message. "but thank you for letting me do this, I really appreciate it."

I swallowed down a grin, never before so thankful for a priority message. Naturally, they were never anything good, but at the moment it was a godsend. I didn't have time for drawn out farewells.

Janice looked disappointed, but not so much so. Shooting up a finger into the air to halt my hasty departure, as I'd already spun to the door, she darted to a table and grabbed a transmitter, looping it over her ear. I guessed one of the holo-cubes littering the desk was her personal one.

She rushed back to me with a big smile on her face and grabbed onto my hand, lifting it up.

"You almost forgot my info, silly."

My watch paused flashing red and beeped, accepting whatever it was she'd sent. Chuckling nervously, I gave her a parting nod, then pulled free and rushed to the door.

CHAPTER
THIRTY-SEVEN

Fortunately, Janice didn't follow me into the hall, and I was able to grab the hover-cart and bolt.

I had no idea why Fallon needed a corpse, but the fact that she did was enough to light a fire under my ass. I didn't want to imagine what the crazy woman would do if I failed.

At the thought, my eyes darted up and around. Was Fallon watching me this very instant? Had she sent some tiny spy drone hot on my heels to make sure I stayed in line? I had no idea, but the possibility was unnerving.

Resolved not to test her insanity, I gave up searching the air for spyware and glanced at my watch. I wondered what Janice had sent me and what I was going to do about the situation, if anything. As dim witted as I was, I fathomed that going on a date with her wasn't the best of ideas. Not if I wanted any kind of chance with Taylor. However, it was one thing to ditch a girl that worked on the fleet decks and completely another to stand someone up who worked in critical areas like the med-bays. I had no doubt I'd see her again, and probably sooner than later. Likely after this next drop.

Furthermore, would ditching her arouse suspicion? As far as I knew, the majority of the ship wasn't under surveillance, but most equipment had optical recordings. I had no idea what had been in the morgue, or what stray drones had been buzzing around. Would standing her up cause her itchy, pissed fingers to dive deep into a cleaning bot's visuals to see what I had been up to?

Lost in thought, I sped right past the elevator and stairwell. Realizing my mistake, I doubled back. My boots squeaked and my jostling hover-cart almost plowed down some passersby. This part of grave deck was busier, and more than a few heads turned in my wake. Evidently, a stampeding infantry man with a crusty arm and a bouncing hover-cart wasn't a regular occurrence. Thankfully, since most Leeges were on a drop, or getting ready to drop, the personnel here were all civilians and SF soldiers. None dared to get in my way.

I rubbed the back of my neck, thinking, as I glanced at my watch. I had ten minutes left to deliver the body. Which meant I had to risk the elevator, even if that chanced ending up in a confined space with a corpse and some Legion brass. Unlike the SF personnel and civilians, they sure as hell would question my dealings.

I fidgeted, nervously chewing my freshly patched lip as I waited for the elevator. Just maybe, the universe would cut me a break and it would be empty.

The universe had no such intentions. The doors slid open to an SF soldier lounging in a corner. We stared at each other, neither one of us moving. After about ten seconds his eyebrows popped high on his forehead.

"Getting on or what?" he asked in a snooty tone.

"Yeah!" I snapped back to reality.

Shoving the cart forward, I stepped in behind it and selected the lower decks. The man's face scrunched at my selection as he proceeded to give me a slow once over, momentarily pausing on my arm. It looked as if I was shedding reptilian skin. Layers of dried film were flanking off. Scowling, he turned away, but not before throwing me a disgusted headshake for good measure.

My jaw gritted, but I controlled any kind of outburst. Mere hours ago, I'd almost died, and I didn't much appreciate this prim punk, who likely spent his days in a cushy office, glowering at me as if I were no better than dog shit. He probably even possessed that favorite coffee mug that I had coveted for my own snuffed out future.

As a distraction, I poked at my watch, deciding to see what

priority message had saved me from yet another awkward hug from nurse Janice.

I suppressed an audible groan as my eyes perused over the text. Even though I had yet to come up with an adequate excuse for missing our date, I had intended to find Taylor after getting done with whatever sick, twisted thing this was to profusely apologize. I figured the sooner I got to groveling the better. Now, it looked like that wasn't going to happen. According to my watch, second cohort was dropping in less than three hours. That left no time for side trips after I got through quenching Centurion Fallon's psychotic desires.

Two floors down, the elevator glided to its first stop, and the SF man disembarked. He did so with a peeved expression and eyeballed my cart with gusto. Not wanting curious Nancy to get any ideas, I returned his prying look with a grin and a polite nod, silently willing him to hurry up and be on his way.

"Whatever," he grumbled, at last, stepping past the threshold and allowing the doors to close.

"A bunch of ruffians. Damn Leeges." His gripes echoed down the hall.

I couldn't care less about the insults. Now that I was alone, I was free to panic. To act as freaked out on the outside as I felt on the inside. I immediately doubled over and braced on my knees, breathing in shallow pants. Not only was I pushing a dead, naked woman in a hover-cart, but making it to the airlock in time was looking iffy. Would Fallon go through with her threats if I was late?

The elevator slid to a stop and before the doors had a chance to fully open, I flew out like a bat out of hell. I again skidded around corners and bounced off walls, torpedoing towards Airlock 71.

"Hurry up!" echoed Centurion Fallon's annoying screech the moment I rounded the last corner and she saw me running in her direction. She was no longer inside the airlock but right outside the sealed room frantically waving me over.

"Finally," she hissed as I slid to a squealing stop next to her, my boots digging into the deck.

I shoved the hover-cart towards her.

"Here," I panted, trying to catch my breath.

Fallon glowered at me in disgust as her eyes flicked between me and the cart. Using two careful fingers, she snagged one corner of the sheet and lifted it to inspect the cargo.

"Acceptable, I suppose," she stated, nonchalant, and released the sheet to drape back into place. "They wanted a live one, but this will have to do."

I glanced at her sidelong, still hunched on my knees and panting. I couldn't help but notice her hands right then. Her fists were pressed firmly on her narrow hips and no longer clutching a blaster. The weapon was now holstered. The idea of knocking her out, right here, right now, and throwing her out of the airlock, flashed through my mind. All this woman had done so far was cause me a slew of problems. Not only that, but she herself appeared to have no issue with murder, so getting ejected out of an airlock was a fitting demise.

Right as I was about to talk myself into actually going through with it, the airlock whooshed with the sound of escaping air. I jerked up in a panic and lunged to the small porthole in the door. Had she already thrown some poor sap in there and was about to space them?

However, it wasn't a person that greeted my eyes, but a settling ship. A strange one. I didn't recognize the streamlined design, and the hull itself was odd. The jet-black metal gleamed in the dimmed lights and swam with tinges of purple. Not a scorch mark or speck of dust marred its flawlessly smooth exterior.

In a practiced manner, the ship lowered three landing legs and settled onto the deck.

Slack-jawed, I turned to Fallon. Was this from the European sector? Russian perhaps? Or some top-secret model the Galactic Senate was keeping under wraps?

Instead of answers, I only received more questions. Not saying a word, the woman reached into her pocket and extracted a small, round metallic device. I immediately recognized the trinket. The one in her hands was somewhat larger than the transmitter lounging on the bottom of my drawer, the one I'd claimed as a souvenir, but there was no mistaking it, the two were basically identical.

Then, things got even weirder. Reaching up, Fallon jammed the transmitter onto her temple, right where it had been on the drooler. She yelped in pain and grimaced, bracing against the wall with an extended arm. A few seconds later whatever ailed her seemed to pass and she straightened, feverishly massaging her forehead.

"What is that?" I asked, pointing at her head.

I'd had no idea the devices could be used by any species. Except, for what?

Again, Fallon didn't appear interested in quenching my curiosity.

"Just shut up!" she snapped, reaching for the panel to open the airlock. "Don't talk and do exactly as you're told."

She turned to glare at me. "And don't you dare think about doing anything stupid. Or that Fleet plaything of yours is as good as dead!"

A shiver trembled my body. The feral gleam in Fallon's eyes told me she wasn't kidding. Ever so slightly, I turned to eye the dimmed hall behind me. A bunch of the lights on the storage decks were out, and sections of the hall were shrouded in an eerie darkness. Others weakly flickered, strobing the bulkheads as if in a haunted house or some murder mystery vid. It oddly fit this strange circumstance, I supposed.

Part of me wanted to run, right then. To get away from whatever perverse crap Fallon had going. That was the smart thing to do. It was unlikely she'd bother shooting me in the back. Not completely out of her character, but a safe bet. One that I should've probably taken.

However, both intrigue and worry held my boots rooted in place. I wanted to be damned sure the lunatic didn't go after Taylor, but at the same time, I also wanted to learn the identity of the mysterious vessel, and what we were doing here in the first place.

With an ominous clang, the airlock door began to retract, slowly revealing the ship. The hull was most certainly *different*, like something from a futuristic sci-fi vid where crafts were constructed of metals we'd yet to discover, create, or purchase. Nor was there a single marking. No labels hinted at its origin and not a single scorch mark evidenced atmospheric re-entry or participation in combat.

Glancing at Fallon, I was surprised to see a change in the woman's demeanor. She was no longer all snark and hatred, but nervous and twitchy. Smoothing her uniform with trembling hands, she visibly swallowed, then took a moment to stare at the deck before striding inside.

Not knowing what else to do, I followed.

She threw me a furious glance over her shoulder. "Get the cart, you moron!"

"Oh." I rushed to retrieve the cart and pulled it behind me as I joined Fallon in approaching the mysterious vessel.

Questions piled up on the tip of my tongue. Before I could ask, a crack of bright wintery light appeared on the side of the ship, growing larger as a door lowered and clunked onto the deck. Steps lifted from the surface. Curiously, my eyes trained on the opening. A creature stood framed in the light, and I gasped at the sight.

CHAPTER
THIRTY-EIGHT

" **S** o that's why the bot didn't shoot you!" I blurted before I could catch myself.

I'd all but dismissed the odd encounter I witnessed in the jungle, figuring I'd mis-seen or misinterpreted, but now it clicked. Standing tall before us, framed by the ship's bright interior lights, wasn't a person of a different nationality at all. In fact, it wasn't even human. Sure, the lanky, white-fleshed being had a humanoid form, but there was no mistaking what it was.

An honest-to-god Synth stood before us, and not one of the ignorant lackey models like the civilians I'd encountered on the planet, but the real deal. The big kahuna. The brains behind their species' operations, the ones that had eternal life and controlled the bots and all their other high-tech gadgets through the neural interphases. Even though the majority of the Legion, Earth-Gov, and Galactic Senate dealings were classified, for the most part, Rap-Wars weren't. That dark time in Earth's history, our first encounter with an alien race, was available to the public and even taught in school.

"You're some kind of traitor, aren't you?" I accused Fallon in a harsh whisper. "Some turncoat. A spy—"

"Shh…" Fallon shushed me, absentminded. I wasn't sure she'd even processed my ill-timed commentary. Both of us were busy eyeballing the Synth.

He was at least seven feet tall, or maybe it was a she. There was no way to tell the gender. Its white skin appeared delicate and thin, like rice paper, and smattered with metallic patches. Those spots swam with a glimmer of colors. I recalled one teacher or another discussing the dalmatian-like appearance. The creature before us was an ancient being. Unlike the norm of jumping from clone to clone, some amongst their species preferred to use one body for lengthy periods of time. They kept said bodies kicking with nanites and other advanced juju that visibly altered their biology over the countless centuries. The Synths were as much machine as flesh and blood beings.

The bald head was just as creepy as the patchy skin. It housed two oversized black eyes with no pupils, two small angled slits for a nose, and one for a mouth.

I couldn't help but shuffle back a step when I inadvertently locked eyes with the being. The hairs on my arms prickled, and I shivered involuntarily. It was almost as if I could feel its biomechanical coldness. I glanced away quickly but sensed that its icy gaze was still upon me.

I spun to Fallon in alarm. I wasn't sure whether I should run or try to grab her blaster and shoot the Synth. For a split second, I even considered grabbing Fallon herself and chucking her at the alien while I ran for my life. In my wildest nightmares, I couldn't have imagined encountering one of these creatures in person or being this close. Most humans never had. Their advanced models abstained from showing themselves, using machines or their lower-level kind to do their bidding. In fact, following the initial invasion, it took Earth many years to sight one of the bigwigs.

Fallon caught my panicked glance from the corner of her eyes and scowled without turning my way. She remained fixed on the Synth as the creature continued to observe me.

Suddenly, my watch buzzed. In the silence of the airlock, the noise might've as well been a bullhorn. Both Fallon and I jumped a foot in the air.

"Dammit, Adlar!" she hissed through gritted teeth as I frantically tapped on my watch to silence it.

I didn't bother reading the message, I just needed it to shut up.

Unlike us, the Synth didn't startle. Only its large unblinking eyes moved, gliding between Fallon and me. A moment later, its gaze froze on Fallon, and it proceeded to chitter and click, talking to her in a strange language I couldn't understand.

Fallon nodded slowly, acknowledging it as if the thing was speaking plain English.

"Right here," she responded, pushing the hover-cart towards the ship with an outstretched arm while keeping her distance. "No, it's not alive. But the body is intact."

A small smile tugged at my lips. Fallon's demeanor had reverted to that of a cowering wretch, and her eyes, which usually burned with rage and evil, brimmed with fear. Guess it took an advanced alien being to knock her down a peg.

A microsecond later, I stiffened as a realization struck me like a brick upside the head. I remembered that it was supposed to be a *living* person within the cart. At least, until I'd intervened. My jaw tightened and my heart raced. The psycho wasn't just some sort of a spy, but something a thousand times worse. She was handing living people to the Synths. I yearned to punch her right there, damn the consequences.

The Synth chittered at Fallon as she fidgeted.

"I know, I know," she pleaded, throwing a nervous glance at the hover-cart which floated next to the ship's stairs.

The Synth made no move to retrieve it.

"But you must understand, that with such a short notice, there was only so much I could do. Please send my apologies to Rea, and—"

The Synth cut her off with an angry squawk, followed by rushed gibberish. It glared at her with deadened black eyes as bottomless and hollow as the cosmos.

Fallon squirmed. "I… I apologize. I meant to say please send my apology to the *queen* and plead for her mercy on my behalf."

As she cowered, Fallon's eyes intermittently darted to me. Pure hate permeated her glance. I did everything in my power not to look at her. Hell could freeze over before I felt bad for rescuing the nurse, even if it did ruin whatever unholy scheme she had going. With any luck, the Synth would be so pissed he'd put her down himself. I could only hope for such a fortunate outcome.

The alien chattered and clicked at Fallon, and I didn't need to understand its language to know the thing was livid. When, at last, it silenced, it retreated back into the ship as something silver flashed to take its place.

The frame of a bot loomed in the doorway. Alarmed, I jumped back and spun to Fallon. Was it about to shoot the *both* of us?

"Shut up!" Fallon snapped at me before I had a chance to comment.

I closed my mouth. The bot's weaponized forearms weren't raised, but that did little to calm me. This machine had hunted us down like rats and was responsible for the slew of corpses lying in the morgue and the dead Leege crumpled at the bottom of the cart.

Despite the tight blanket of fear and confusion wrapped around me, I was sure of one thing—I wasn't okay with any of this. I opened my mouth again to protest only for her to cut me off with a hiss.

"Shut! Up!"

Glowering, Fallon jabbed a skinny finger in the direction of the hover-cart, and feverishly gestured for me to move it towards the bot. I hesitated, furrowing my brows. *Was she serious?* One glance at her frazzled eyes told me she was.

I frowned, but then stepped gingerly to the cart and nudged it forward. The faster we got this over with, the faster the thing would leave. With a gentle hum of repulsors, the cart glided up the stairs. I pushed it up until it was a few feet from the bot, then quickly retreated.

The machine didn't budge.

"Take the sheet off," Fallon growled.

Begrudgingly, I obliged and again approached. I leaned over, trying to keep my distance, as my fingers grabbed at the sheet and snagged a corner.

As soon as I ripped it off, the bot came to life. With one arm, it yanked out the lifeless corpse by a leg, as if it were as light as a feather, and dragged the naked woman into the ship. The head bonked and brown hair spilled over the steps. I shuddered and glanced away, not wanting to witness any of it.

Not waiting for instructions, as soon as the bot and corpse vanished, I pulled the hover-cart away from the alien craft. I let go after a few steps, startled by a loud buzz. It was my watch again.

Panicked, I jabbed at the screen with gusto as Fallon squirmed and glared. The Synth reappeared to chatter at Fallon angrily for a final time then retreated into the ship and closed the door behind it.

"Go, go!" Fallon ushered, grabbing me and shoving me out of the airlock.

I eagerly obliged and we both hustled out, closing the inner airlock door behind us. At the same time, the outer door retracted, and the Synth's vessel vanished into the darkness of space. As soon as it was gone, my hands balled into fists. Part of me was still numb from what I'd just witnessed, but another part of me ignited with rage.

"What the fuck was—" I rounded on Fallon only to freeze.

Har blaster's muzzle was two inches away from my head. I could hear the faint hum of primed energy and heat tickled my forehead.

Fallon's expression was again that of a feral coon's. My hands flew up in surrender. Was this it? Were my brains about to decorate the bulkheads?

Keeping her weapon trained on me, Fallon used her other hand to peel the transmitter off her temple.

She bared her teeth in pain as she pulled. As the device released and she squeaked, the arm holding the blaster faltered. I took full advantage of the opportunity. With one swift swipe, I knocked the weapon out of her hand and charged her. Unfortunately, and to my complete surprise, the woman was a lot quicker than I'd anticipated. As the blaster clattered to the deck and skidded, she dodged my attempted tackle, nailing me with a knee to the gut and a blow to the back of my head. Hissing, I pitched to the deck plates.

Pushing through the throbbing, I jumped back to my feet and took on a fighting stance.

"What the fuck are you doing?" Fallon roared.

"What was that?" I jabbed a finger at the closed airlock. "What the fuck, Fallon! I knew you were crazy, but this? Humans? You're giving humans to the god-damn Synths! How—"

I was momentarily rendered speechless, my finger aimed at the airlock.

"That's fucking treason, Fallon!"

Instead of providing me with an answer like a sane human being, an animalistic howl barreled out of the woman, and she charged me like a wild bull. Before I knew what was happening, kicks and punches slammed into me from all directions. I tried to fight back, to get a few licks in myself, but I quickly realized I had gravely underestimated my opponent. I'd initially figured that since I had a good amount of weight on her, I'd easily overpower her.

Turns out, I was wrong. Very wrong.

Within seconds, Fallon had me pinned, face down, on the deck, with her knee painfully digging into the back of my neck as she twisted up on my arm.

"Okay, okay. I give up," I pleaded.

My lip again stung and by the feel of my throbbing cheek, she'd gotten me there too. With one last frustrated exhale and a quick painful jerk on my arm, Fallon released me. Panting, she walked to collect her blaster while I staggered to my feet and wiped my bloodied nose.

"Just tell me what just happened!" I demanded. "Why? Why are you giving *humans* to the Synths? Was that what happened to the man I saw you with on the stairs? That's why you wanted me off the ship, isn't it?"

"*Ughhh!*" Fallon exhaled sharply in disgust and holstered her blaster. "The less you know, the better. Trust me on that, you prick."

I stared at her for a few seconds, mouth hanging open. I blinked. I didn't want to know *any* of this, but now I was involved.

"Fallon!" I practically shouted, again gesturing at the airlock. "What we just did, that's treason! Punishable by death! On top of just being… despicable."

"Ha!" Fallon barked a loud laugh as if I'd just told some sort of joke.

"*Despicable*," she mimicked me in a whiny tone. "Oh, *please*. You think ethics matter out here?"

She flung her arms wide, gesturing at the bulkheads, and spun in a circle. "We've slaughtered our way through almost every known species without blinking an eye—*and* been slaughtered. Another death hardly matters. Unless it's your OWN!"

She'd shouted the last into my face. I staggered back from the beast. I'd heard tales of Leeges simply losing it. Was this the case?

With a huff, Fallon jabbed her boney fists into her hips and glared at me. "We all have something over our heads, you fool, and I'm going to do whatever it takes to keep myself breathing. I suggest you do the same. All that righteous morality bullshit, do yourself a favor and throw it out the airlock. There's no room for that out here."

My mouth was still hanging open, as I'd planned on wrangling answers out of her, even at the expense of another beating, but I slammed it shut with a clank of my teeth. My brows furrowed. Something about her last statement ate at me. Her words had a familiar ring to them. Hadn't Centurion Braves said something similar?

"The deal we made," Fallon was still going. "It stands. You breathe a word to anyone and you're dead. So is your Fleet pilot. Do you understand?"

I nodded, noncommittally, only semi-paying attention. My mind spun. How many other officers were involved? Was Braves? Was Centurion Paxton?

My watch buzzed, vibrating my wrist and startling me.

Crap! This was now the third time I'd been paged. I rushed to read the message. So far, I'd been swiping them away without heeding the text. My gut sank as I absorbed the words. All had been from Pax, ordering me to report to Gold Squad's equipment room, and judging by the escalation of certain words in each consecutive one, he wasn't happy. With my recent antics at the arena, ignoring a summons wasn't at all what I needed. Without another word to Fallon, I turned and ran.

CHAPTER
THIRTY-NINE

For the fourth time in the span of hours, I found myself sprinting down *Venator's* halls like I'd been caught bedding the sheriff's daughter. Pax had now summoned me three times, and I had ignored each and every one of his messages. As I skidded around corners and bounced off walls, I knew I should be concocting excuses, but that's not what my brain was fixated on. All I could think about was Fallon. That lunatic might be desensitized to murder and treason, but I wasn't. Furthermore, was I now an accomplice?

My stomach cinched at the realization that I was. By Legion code, I was now as culpable as her. One was expected to fall on their sword before ceding to the enemy in any shape, way, or form.

My mind quickly scrolled through who I could possibly confide in to get me out of this. Unfortunately, I came up blank. Pax was the obvious option, but right off I knew that was foolish. Even if Pax agreed to keep this to himself instead of addressing it head on, like I suspected he would, I'd still be endangering his life just by telling him. It was bad enough both Taylor and I were in Fallon's sights, I didn't need to add more people to that tally. Plus, I had no idea if he'd even believe me.

Not being able to tell Pax immediately excluded telling my other squadmates. They'd run straight to him. That left me with Centurion Paxton or Braves, but both were a no-go. Even though Fallon had been dead set on keeping her late night escapades from them, and even willing to kill me to keep the secret, there was still a possibility they were involved. There was just something about Fallon's last statement that ate at me. She'd sounded almost like Braves. And sure, both of them might just be two seasoned Leeges, marred by constant war and death, who had lost their marbles, but that would be one hell of a convenient coincidence. I didn't believe in those.

I skidded into the equipment room panting like a racehorse, with absolutely no good excuse for my tardiness.

"Where were you?" Pax glared at me.

His eyes narrowed even further when they focused on my face. I had taken a minute to duck into a bathroom and clean up the best I could, figuring it wouldn't do to show up late, looking like I'd just been in a bar brawl, but that had only helped so much. The blood under my nose was gone, but there was nothing I could do about the faint hints of purplish bruising and the cuts over my cheekbone. I had a nagging suspicion I wouldn't retain my poster-perfect face after the Legion was through with me.

Begrudgingly, I wondered if *that* was included in the initial contract, in the tiny print, shoved somewhere between the paragraph detailing how my life now belonged to the Senate, and the one stating I was to be an officer's punching bag whenever they damned well pleased.

Wiping sweat off my brows, I reluctantly met Pax's glare and sucked in a deep breath in preparation to spout some BS excuse.

"Uh…" I began, scratching my head.

That was as far as I got. Jumping over Pax's shoulder, my eyes landed on an unexpected gathering—a strange one. If I didn't know any better, it almost looked like a square off. On one side were Centurion Paxton, Prefect Neero, and Tribune Gallus, and on the other a collection of jittery civilian scientists. One elderly man stood apart from the rest, facing the Legion brass squarely. He had thinning gray hair, sunken cheeks, and an ornery expression and hostile stance that had me frown.

Unnerved, Prefect Neero eyed him right back, arms crossed over his chest. Whatever was going on here was more important than my tardiness. Swallowing my excuses, I slunk to join my squad in silence.

I bunched up next to Mills. The squad wasn't at ease. Everyone was stiff, neatly lined in parade rest, facing the gathering. The atmosphere in the room was as thick and heavy as molasses. The lab-coats were irked, the brass exasperated, and somehow my squad was involved. The unnerving fact sent a chill down my spine. Even Cavelli and the rest of the attendants were making themselves scarce and had all abandoned their stations. I glimpsed them working, or pretending to work, on the suits that were out of direct view of the brass.

"Is this yet another one of your troopers tasked with protecting us?" scoffed the gaunt, elderly scientist, jabbing a crooked finger in my direction. "He barely looks old enough to operate a vehicle, if that! It's unacceptable!"

The rest of his frowning posse rushed to nod their agreement, all eyeing us with disdain.

I scowled at the unwarranted hostility but decided it wouldn't be wise to voice a rebuttal. I was starting to understand a little something about this outfit. Just about every department viewed the infantry as no better than trash. Swallowing my irritation, I bore his condemnation in silence, like the rest of my teammates.

"I assure you, Dr. Sholtz," the Prefect replied through his teeth. "These men are all highly experienced and more than capable of providing adequate security."

The man whom the Prefect had just called Dr. Sholtz scrunched his nose in displeasure, not appearing convinced. By the Prefect's restrained frustration and the doctor's frazzled demeanor, I guessed this tete-a-tete had been going on for some time prior to my arrival.

Seeming to have had enough of Neero, the doctor threw his hands high in frustration and spun to Centurion Paxton, pointing.

"You! I demand troopers like you, the ones of higher rank. You at least look as if you've had your tenth birthday and a modicum of training. I will not put my life in the hands of children!"

Sholtz shuffled, smacking his papery lips. "Yes, yes. If we are being given no choice but to do this, I want Centurions and above as escorts, not those."

He waved a dismissive hand at my squad. My scowl deepened. Insulting us was one thing, but insulting the Prefect was another. I'd never witnessed anyone dismiss Neero so brashly. I didn't think anyone would dare. Didn't the lab-coat know he was playing with fire?

Centurion Paxton stiffened upon the spotlight being cast on him, but if he was unnerved, he didn't show it. His expression remained as stoic as ever. Nor did he dare to speak.

"I just don't think this is a good idea at all," Sholtz continued. "We should wait until the area has been cleared and rendered safe. Then we could venture down and prod. Trekking into hostile territory is outside our purview!"

His voice grew higher in pitch as he frantically gestured at his co-workers. "We're not here to swing guns this way and that! We're not militants!"

A smallish lady who stood a few steps behind Sholtz, raised a finger, vying for attention.

"Maybe the troopers could retrieve the Synth technology themselves," she offered, meekly. "Then we can study it here, in our labs."

The Prefect's face twitched in reply. This wasn't at all what he was used to. Normally, troops fell over themselves in a rush to carry out his orders.

Taking a step towards Sholtz, Neero reinserted himself into the conversation, his tone dangerous and low.

"That's not how this is going to go," he said. "We have reports that the Synths are evacuating. We don't know how many of them are left or the expanse of the tunnels under that mountain, and if we wait any longer anything of value might be gone. We don't have the time to train infantry personal on what that might be—"

"A vid-link!" Sholz interrupted. "We'll tell them what's important or not."

Neero showed him all his teeth. "You propose my men turn over every trinket as you stare at a screen? Ridiculous! There are too many unknown variables for such a drawn out endeavor, the locals for one, or the Synths. The scum might blow the whole place by then. We need to get down there before that happens."

A murmur of disbelief erupted from the scientists, and their eyes seemed to pop even further out of their sockets. The wheels in my head turned as I began to catch on. The brass wanted to retrieve themselves some alien tech, but the infantry wouldn't know their ass from a hole in the ground when it came to alien gadgets. That meant someone smarter had to do the sifting, and the collection of disrespectful lab-coats before me were the lucky volunteers. They were about to experience Atlas first-hand. I smiled. Maybe that'd teach them some manners.

Then, my smirk vanished. I did another quick scan of the room. Besides the attendants, the lab-coats, and the brass, we were the only squad here. Groaning internally, I realized why. We were the only ones chosen to be their escort.

"So now there's a chance of explosions?" Sholtz raged in alarm.

It appeared he had the spokesman role for the group. The rest of the lab-coats squawked in agreement, heatedly protesting such a danger. A low growl escaped the Prefect. Rubbing his forehead, he took a methodical step back from the scientists as one of his hands got to work. The lab-coats were too busy flustering to notice. I, however, noticed as did every other Leege in the room.

The Prefect's hand had wrapped around his blaster. The Tribune, who'd so far been perched leisurely on the ledge of a projection table, letting Neero handle the situation, straightened and loudly cleared his throat. The room went as silent as a graveyard as everyone's gaze snapped to him.

Neero wasn't fazed. His mouth twisted with displeasure at the Tribune's sudden involvement, but he didn't let go of his weapon.

"Wha—" Sholtz huffed, at last heeding the Prefect's action. Wide eyed, he hopped back to merge with the other scientist.

They all huddled together like scared ducklings. heads jerking between the Tribune and the Prefect, their eyes pleading for an intervention.

The Tribune took a step towards Neero and raised a placating hand. "Stand down. We don't need a blood bath in the equipment room. The men here have enough to do as it is."

Neero frowned, but then deemed it best to comply and let go of his blaster. Though not before an obvious hesitation.

Satisfied, Tribune Gallus moved to tower over Sholtz. "I think I've had about just enough of this, so let me make this simple, doctor."

He jabbed a finger into Sholtz's chest. "You are going to go down to that planet and retrieve anything of value. You can walk or you can be dragged onto a dropship, your choice."

"B-but... you can't do that!" Sholtz sputtered. "I'm... I'm not part of your Legion! I'm a civilian! Selected by Earth Government for this position and employed by the Galactic Senate, itself! You have no authority over my department!"

The corners of the Tribune's face twisted up in a wry smile. "In that case, doctor, it appears I do, as I too serve the Senate. But if it behooves you, you are more than welcome to file a complaint, with Earth, with the Senate, with whoever, *after* we get this done."

Sholtz blinked stupidly, growing pale. "Th-this is absurd!" Yet some of the wind had been swept from under him at the mention of the Senate. If this order came from that high up, none of us had a choice.

Turning towards the two MP's standing at the door, the Tribune signaled them over. "Escort these scientists to gather their equipment, then back here to be suited."

He turned back to the sputtering lab-coats who were all as white as paper. "You have twenty minutes. If you're not back in time to get suited then you will be going down with what's on your back, and let me assure you doctor, then you will truly have something to complain about."

Whispers and chatter of 'can he do that?' and 'unbelievable' erupted among the scientists, but none dared to test the threat. With a stern look on his face, the Tribune took a moment to eye everyone coldly, then, saying nothing more, he turned and strode out of the room. Neero and Centurion Paxton rushed to follow.

Once the brass departed, the MPs jumped into action and quickly ushered out the griping scientists. I waited for what felt like the appropriate number of seconds before speaking, allowing the heavy tension in the room to at least partially dissipate, then turned to Pax.

"Are they going to drop with us?" I asked, recalling my unpleasant ordeal with the air tunnel. It didn't look like any of the lab-coats even knew where it was, much less received any form of training.

"No." Pax shook his head. "That's why I called you all in here early, to have a briefing. Thank you for finally joining us by the way, Adlar."

All heads spun to me. Even Cavelli's and Hughes' curious eyeballs poked out from behind the racks. I chuckled nervously and picked at my nails.

Sighing, Pax continued. "We're going to leave before the rest of the units and land in a safe zone. Then make our way towards the compound. That way, we should get within range around the same time our cohort drops. They'll occupy any remaining contacts, while we carry out our objective, which is to get the scientists to the mountain and back."

Mills groaned loudly, throwing his head back in a childish fit. "We're going to have to babysit them *that* long? All the way from a safe zone? That's like five miles, SL! Do any of them even know how to shoot? Is it even safe to arm them?"

Pax didn't reprimand Mills' tantrum. He probably felt the same way. Not that he was going to show it. Just like our Centurion, Pax was all business.

"Yes," he replied flatly. "They'll be armed with the standard blasters. As far as whether they know how to use them, for our safety, we have to assume they don't."

Mills groaned again then muttered. "Figures we're the ones who get stuck babysitting."

Pax allowed himself a tiny smirk. "That's the orders, Mills. You know the drill. We do what we're told. We're to keep the lab-coats alive, get them inside the compound, and retrieve any tech they deem useful."

With a sigh Mills relented, falling in line with Pax's wishes like we all knew he would. He then turned to me with a large, stupid grin on his face. I resisted rolling my eyes, not at all in the mood for his shit.

"So, what's her name?" Mills said, thumping me on the back.

I stared at him with a dumbfounded expression. I'd been all too sure he was about to hassle me for my tardiness, but this was a surprise. I had no idea what he was talking about.

"The girl you must've been with." Mills stared at me expectantly. "Isn't that the reason you were late? It's not like you could've slept through *that*."

A meaty finger pointed at my watch, implying the racket that accompanied each priority message, one I was all too familiar with.

"What the fuck else could've kept you so busy around here," Mills added.

Catching on, I rushed to nod, thankful for the convenient excuse. For once, the brute-of-a-man happened to be useful. It was better that everyone thought I'd been with some girl than handing human corpses to the Synths.

Plastering on a partial smirk on my face, I stuck my hands into my pockets and shrugged nonchalantly as if snagging women was just another day in the office.

Mills let out a hearty chuckle and a low whistle. "You dog, look at you. Only been here a few days and already working your way through the ship."

He gave my back another hard slap as I acted out a slow "*hell yeah*" nod in reply.

CHAPTER
FORTY

Every single scientist made it to the equipment room with time to spare. None wanted to test the Tribune, and I couldn't blame them. There was no question in anyone's mind that the man would throw them onto a dropship when it was time to go, whether they were suited or not. Even though the Tribune didn't want a bloody shootout in the equipment room, to me, it didn't appear as if he was overly concerned with their comfort or wellbeing.

What he cared about was getting the job done. This whole hasty expedition probably wasn't his idea to begin with. From the way he'd spoken, the Senate itself had assigned the task, and they weren't an entity to be disobeyed.

As Cavelli and the rest of the attendants wrestled the disgruntled scientists into their suits, my thoughts jumped back to my own experience. Only a few days ago, the struggling, stumbling newbie had been me. My mind labored to comprehend that.

I couldn't help but wonder right then, if I stayed alive, endlessly hacking away at the creatures that littered this stellar dark, in time, would I evolve into someone resembling Pax… or Fallon. Ice gripped me at that morbid prospect.

My ponderings were cut short by the mayhem around me. The equipment room had transformed into a war zone of its own as the attendants feverishly argued with the scientists. Some had the gall to complain about having to remove their coats to get into the suits, while others whined about having to keep their armor and helmets on for the entire duration of the trip.

"That's it!" Cavelli shouted as he flung a helmet onto the deck.

It clattered, bounced a few times, then rolled under a table.

"Fuck you, fuck you, and fuck you!" He jabbed a finger at each lab-coat in turn. "I've had enough! If you don't want to wear your helmets, then fucking don't! I don't care if your heads get ripped off your shoulders."

Throwing his arms up in defeat, he stomped away to assist Mills, who was next to the weapon racks, beaming like a fat kid with a milkshake. Even though this had started out as a green campaign, somehow, rads were now authorized, and Mills, being our heavy specialist, was meticulously inspecting his beamer. The RPG-style weapon seemed heavy and clunky, but the man looked more excited than bothered by the burden.

His grin widened with pure ecstasy as the weapon thrummed and powered up with a low whine under his touch, clicking rhythmically as it ran diagnostics.

"Now this is what I'm talking about!" he boomed, slapping the yellow rad-packs Cavelli was handing him onto his suit.

Each bone and skull-marked cartridge provided the weapon with a five-second beam of deadly energy.

"I love myself a good barbeque."

Sholtz glowered at Mills in disgust. "Imbeciles, all imbeciles. I'm going to report this, all of this! You can be sure of that!"

Annoyed, and having had just about enough of the man and his insults, I turned away from him, to Pax. A new concern had entered my mind.

"Are their blades deactivated?" I asked.

All the scientists were gearing up in Gold Squad kits, with the only difference being that the gold earth emblems shimmering on their breastplates had been covered up with white diamonds. I worried one of them might accidentally toggle on their blades and kill one of us, or each other.

Pax frowned as he checked his suit.

"Nope," he grumbled. "Maybe when a drooler is on top of them, they'll suddenly grow a pair. Or, at least, we can hope."

"Yeah, maybe," I agreed, halfheartedly, as I double-checked my own suit. Since we weren't dropping, Pax hadn't relieved me of my frags, and I checked that each one was snugly secured.

Pax would never complain outright, but I could tell he was less than thrilled about being responsible for a bunch of untrained brainiacs.

Hughes and the other attendant apparently had more patience than Cavelli, because somehow, they finally succeeded in gearing the scientists. As soon as the last helmet was thrust into a pair of trembling, disgruntled hands, we were all shoved out of the equipment room and sent on our way.

Ladened with two full hover-carts of sciensie gadgets, we headed for the hangar bay.

"Do we really need all this shit?" Mills frowned at the sagging carts, then at Sholtz. Both carts were loaded to the brim. "This is a lot of stuff to lug. We're not going for a stroll in the park down there, you know. It's a hot zone."

Sholtz didn't miss a beat. "Why do you think we have you, buffoons?"

A dumbfounded expression flashed across Mills' face, but quickly gave way to rage. One side of his face kind of twitched as he fractionally raised his beamer. I didn't know what he planned on doing, but before he got around to it, Pax grabbed him by the arm and shoved him back, next to me. A move I was *absolutely* thankful for.

"You think anyone will mind if I fry one of those fucks by accident?" Mills whispered, glowering at Sholtz's back. "The targeting systems on these things get finicky, everyone knows that."

He patted his beamer's long cannon, then nudged me in a conspiratorial fashion. "You distract Pax, and I'll start dusting them, one by one."

I sighed, wanting to get the man off my back. Which wasn't going to happen since Somner and Lee were behind us and Pax was in front, strategically positioned between Mills and the lab-coats.

"So, what'd you think? Are we doing this, or what?" He nudged me again. "It'll be fun, right? You can even take out a few if you want. We'll tell Pax it was an accident, or just throw the bodies to the droolers before he notices."

I took a second to study him out of the corner of my eyes with a quickly deepening scowl. The man wasn't kidding—he wanted to kill them. My skin crawled at the thought. Sure, Sholtz was like a rash on stims, but the rest of them didn't seem so bad. Your run-of-the-mill civilians. What you'd see in any lab or office back on Earth. Yet, murder burned in Mills' psychotic eyes.

"No thanks, man." I waved him off, hoping to end the unpleasant conversation.

My mind was already somewhere else. Now that Taylor's transfer had gone through, I wondered if she was going to be in the hangar bay.

"Pfft. Whatever, man," he scoffed. "But let me know if you change your mind, okay?"

Thankfully, I didn't have to put up with him for much longer, as we soon entered the hangar. The scientists wobbled in their suits like toddlers learning to walk, and our bootsteps and their shuffling feet echoed in the heavy stillness. The rest of the cohort still had some time before they deployed, so hardly anyone was around. The lined ships sat desolate, like an armada of boats on an ocean of calm awaiting the storm. Their scarred hulls glinted in the dull light, each charred streak depicting what was to come.

I stretched my neck, looking for Taylor but didn't see her. Frowning, I glanced up at the control room. Both the Tribune and the Prefect were there, following our group with unforgiving expressions. I diverted my attention to the airlock. One lone dropship sat in the middle, already humming with life. Two Fleet guys buzzed around it, completing their inspection and re-securing panels.

"So, what's the plan? Are there any reports from the ground?" Mills asked, nudging up to Pax who was helping the lab-coats don their helmets, although *helping* was an overstatement.

One by one, he yanked their helmets out of their hands and slapped them onto their heads as they huffed and shuffled. I scowled as my suit synched with theirs. We truly were herding toddlers.

"No detailed plan, just the objective," Pax replied. "We get these people into the tunnels, then get them back. As far as the reports from the ground, they're in our favor. Third cohort took down another section of the shield so it's looking promising down there. They might even have the entire area cleared by the time we make it to the mountain."

Mills snorted dismissively. "Sure, because it's always that easy." Making it a point to turn away from Pax, he then went back to grumbling about the long hike.

One of the diamond-marked ladies suddenly yelped and stumbled back into me. Her suit clanged against mine. Reflexively, I grabbed my blaster and braced. My head spun in alarm. A second later, I breathed with relief. No ravenous foe had sprouted in our midst. The lady had been spooked by Lee, or more precisely, his companion.

She shrunk back, pressing up tighter against me and pointing a shaky finger. "What *is* that?"

"A Razor." I frowned. "Shouldn't you scientists know that? Didn't you guys help design them?"

"No, no." She shook her head. "I'm a biologist. I have nothing to do with weapons. I *despise* violence."

I pried her off me and rolled my eyes. Here she was, on a troop carrier, working for the Senate of all entities, and yet she disliked violence—the sole purpose of the Legions and the one and only reason we were here. Go figure. However, being the gentleman that I was, I decided to explain the Razor to her. How the bot provided surveillance or played bait, if need be, instead of one of us, meat-bags, getting stuck with the job.

I hoped to alleviate her fear, if only a fraction, but quickly saw that was too tall of an order. Stammered something incoherently, she bolted for one of her colleagues.

I shrugged it off and followed everyone up the ramp and into the dropship.

"Comm check," Pax called, once we were all seated and strapped in, bunched together uncomfortably.

The dropship wasn't designed for eleven people, a Razor, and two full hover-carts of equipment. Warily, the scientists acknowledged Pax with quivering voices, all sounding as skittish as cats.

With a muffled clang, the inner airlock door slammed shut and the air whooshed, after which, the ship took flight. I smiled to myself, grateful for the one ray of sunshine amidst this tedious gig—we weren't dropping. I wasn't going to have to plummet through thousands of feet of atmo, only to possibly splat like a bug on a windshield at the end. Because it happened, more than the Legion liked to admit, and sometimes to the best of the Leeges. Equipment malfunctioned, troops made mistakes, and at those speeds, even a small glitch or delay was fatal.

"Can we perhaps gather a live alien specimen from the planet?" Sholtz suddenly broke the silence.

We were all in helmets with our visors on tint so we couldn't see each other's expressions, but I suspected everyone looked as stunned as I felt. In unison, all heads turned to Sholtz.

"Ha!" Mills bellowed. "Do you want a drooler or one of the bots? Feel free to try and snare either one, buddy, just don't expect us to help."

"No, you oaf!" Sholtz shot back. "I'm obviously referring to a moth. Such a specimen would make a wonderful addition to my research. We know very little about them."

A low growl emanated from Mills, and I sensed the man coil up in preparation to strike, but Pax intervened. He halted him with a raised hand, then leaned forward in his seat to stare Sholtz in the face.

"The locals have nothing to do with our mission. And know this, Sholtz, if you even think about doing anything stupid to jeopardize our ultimate goal, I'll shoot you myself. You got that?"

Sholtz scoffed, mumbling under his breath about our squad's lack of foresight and brains, but then wound down. His silence was music to my ears. The man's snobbish voice was worse than nails on a hull. I had no idea how Pax was managing to keep his cool.

Twenty minutes later, after an uneventful flight and without the ship doing a single whirling dance, we touched down on Atlas. As the ramp lowered, and the bright light and heat swamped the cabin, I leaned my head back and closed my eyes. I tried to calm my breathing. Since we'd landed a good distance from the Synths' compound, I wasn't as frazzled as I'd been on the last two drops, but my heart still pounded too fast for my liking. Nothing good ever happened on Atlas.

Disembarking, we corralled the lab-coats and their equipment into a tight group in a grove of leafy things. The massive, purple-veined leaves swept over our heads providing a semblance of cover.

"Listen up!" Pax clapped his gauntleted hands together loudly, trying to get their attention.

The scientists were busy spinning whichever way as they took in the alien environment.

"This isn't a sight-seeing tour," Pax instructed. "Do exactly as we say and stay with the group. Keep your eyes open and blasters ready. You have enough charge in your suits to protect you from approximately three shots then you will have to change the battery. Don't forget that."

All the scientists stopped looking around and began inspecting their suits for the extra battery.

"And don't fucking shoot any of us!" Mills boomed. "Unless you want to give me a reason to shoot back." He raised his beamer, swinging it in wide arcs. "And mine's bigger."

I imagined I wasn't the only one who rolled my eyes.

Not a single lab-coat heeded Pax, and not one unholstered their blaster. I couldn't help but wonder if that was a good thing or not. On one hand, that would prevent any accidental slips of the trigger fingers, but on the other, how were the five of us supposed to watch our backs and theirs? The droolers might look bulky and slow, but I'd learned the hard way that they weren't.

Turned out, arming themselves wasn't the only thing the scientists missed in Pax's speech. That, or they were simply choosing to be a pain in the ass by refusing to recognize our authority Our trudge towards the mountains started out well enough. They clustered and stayed as close to us as possible, jumping at every sound and every moving leaf. That didn't last. After about half an hour of no enemy contacts, they decided that the whole thing was simply a safari and began wandering off to inspect the plants and stopping to take samples.

Our progress slowed substantially after that as we had to halt to retrieve the stragglers. We heatedly reiterated that we couldn't protect them if they dispersed, only for them to counter with the importance of every specimen. They collected bugs, bark, leaves, and even pebbles, bouncing away like hyped-up rabbits.

Mills sure wasn't as patient as Pax. He shoved them left and right, cursing up a storm every time one slinked away. As for myself, I didn't worry too much about the wandering explorers, at least not as much as I worried about Sholtz. I had a bad vibe about the sleazy man, and a nagging inkling he'd be the first to do something stupid. So, as everyone else darted around like frazzled chickens, I made sure to keep an eye on Sholtz as he marveled at every tree, leaf, and rock.

When I dared to take a moment to glance away from him, I ground to a halt. Only five diamond-marked suits roved amongst my stressed-out squadmates.

"Shouldn't there be one more?" I said, looking about the area in bewilderment, and seeing only swaying plants.

After an hour of walking, our herding skills had slacked. If it weren't for Pax's constant hassling about keeping track of them, we would have long given up and left the unruly bunch to their own much-deserved devices.

Pax stretched his neck to look over the group. "Crap! You're right. One's missing."

His displeasure was echoed by the rest of us as we checked our HUDs. Not only had someone ventured off, but they were surrounded by blips. I guessed the contacts to be the moths coming to investigate the fighting that was taking place. We were now only a mile or so away from the Synths' base.

"Hey, Beeson!" Pax shouted. "Don't move. We're coming."

"It's fine," the lady chirped back on squad-chat. She even had the nerve to chuckle. "They aren't hurting me."

Unlike her, none of us were amused, and we rushed towards her position. My heart hammered as I zigzagged between trees and the mega-ferns. Unlike the unsuspecting lab-coat, I knew that danger lurked just about anywhere on this planet, even if we couldn't see it. At any moment, a drooler could jump out and nab her, and she'd be helpless as it ripped her apart.

Lee reached her position first, skidding to an abrupt stop in front of me.

"Wow..." he said as I rushed up behind him.

A whole swarm of moths encircled Beeson. There were so many that the chorus of their fluttering wings sounded like a collection of flags flapping in the wind. On top of that, all of them were talking in piercing whines and chitters. The hairs on my arms prickled at their grating dialect. It was almost on a different wavelength, like that annoying high-pitched electrical tone that one can never find the source of. I lowered my incoming audio a notch, grimacing at the unpleasant sounds.

Beeson, on the other hand, showed no discomfort, nor any indication of understanding the danger she was in. She reached towards the cat-sized bugs wonderingly as if trying to touch fireflies.

"Beeson," Pax huffed, taking a cautious step forward while signaling us to hold back.

He extended Beeson an arm, his tone grave but patient. "Back away slowly. Back towards us."

Now one would think she'd heed the mood, but that wasn't to be. Looking over her shoulder at us, the girl *giggled*. "It's fine. There's no indication the locals are hostile. They won't hurt me. How amazing is this."

"Shit, Beeson!" Pax barked, his composure cracking. "Everything on this planet wants to hurt us. Now back away slowly, towards us. Now!"

"Want me to fry them?" Mills offered, eagerly, priming his beamer.

Pax shook his head, still signaling us to stay back with an outstretched arm. "Everyone, holster your weapons Those things might understand what we're holding."

Every inch of me brimmed with tension, but I did as ordered and holstered my blaster. I sucked in a strained breath, remembering how Boyer had shot down two moths in cold blood. Even though the beings didn't appear advanced enough to venture into the cosmos, their behavior suggested they were intelligent. What had seemed like aimless buzzing at first had become organized. The bugs had divided into groups, each group taking a turn to swirl around Beeson, then retreating to confer.

Just like that, my unease grew. I was sure the moths Boyer had killed hadn't gone unnoticed, and the rest of the hive had found the corpses. Maybe that's why they were here, following our squad.

Pax shuffled irritably when Beeson didn't heed his order. She remained planted in place as if she were in the eye of a tornado as the moths swirled around her.

"Don't be stupid!" Pax's tone grew hotter. "Walk back towards us, right now! If you don't—"

I stopped listening when something streaked behind me. Turning, my eyes popped wide.

"Mills!" I slapped the side of his arm and pointed.

Thirty feet away from us was Sholtz, and just as I'd feared, the old coot was up to no good. Held tight in his hands was some sort of boxy contraption with a wide mouth on one end and a grip and trigger on the other. He was lifting it towards a moth that hovered before him.

"No!" I shouted, sprinting in his direction, but I was too late.

A whirr sounded and Sholtz sucked up the moth.

CHAPTER
FORTY-ONE

Time appeared to move in slow motion as we rushed Sholtz, but the mirage didn't last. The moths attacked. Letting out a unified high-pitched shriek, they swarmed Beeson and engulfed her from head to toe with their wriggling bodies.

I had to lower my incoming audio as she shrieked at the top of her lungs, stumbling about and flailing. Veering away from Sholtz, we all charged Beeson instead, only to slide to a stop. None of us knew what to do. Even Pax was at a loss. His blaster was trained at the swarming mass, but he didn't fire. None of us did. We had no idea if shooting them would harm Beeson or *worse*, draw them to us.

"Get them off! Get them off!" Beeson squealed, stumbling about haphazardly and thrashing, cocooned in bugs. I had no idea how she was managing not to smack into a tree.

"Stop running!" I shouted at her. "They can't get through your armor, now stand still."

"O-ok-ay," she stammered and stopped.

Holstering my blaster, I marched over and thrust my hands into the pile of squirming insects and closed my fingers around a squishy body. My skin crawled. It was as if a massive caterpillar was wriggling in my palms.

"Get them off… get them off," Beeson kept at it with a trembling voice. "Get them off!"

Gently pulling up on the moth, I saw how it was attached. Razor-sharp barbs covered its legs and dug into the suit.

"They're not coming off," I informed Pax over my shoulder.

It was like dealing with a pissed off monkey. No sooner did I free one leg then another clamped on with a deathly determination, and the moths were screaming bloody murder to boot. Their piercing whines stabbed at my ears, and it was all I could do not to pop the one in my hands out of pure annoyance.

"Want me to fry them?" Mills offered again, all too eager to use his toy.

I wasn't sure how he was going to do that without killing Beeson, but I doubted he cared.

Pax took a second to glance around in a controlled kind of panic. I could hear him breathing heavy in his comm.

"I have a better idea," he said, rounding on Sholtz.

The man saw him coming and turned to run, but didn't make it two steps before Pax tackled him to the ground. The vacuum box flew from his grip and vanished into a bush. The lid must've released because a disoriented bug shot out of the leaves a moment later, zigzagging and spiraling like a damaged plane. Quickly regaining its bearings, it beelined to rejoin its buddies.

"This is unacceptable!" Sholtz raved, scampering back to his feet and jabbing a finger at the roiling mob of insects. "Procuring a specimen of this novel species would be invaluable!"

None of us heeded his gripes, busy watching Beeson in tense anticipation. I was about to let go of the moth in my grip when I felt all the legs release at once.

"Argh…" I flung the thing away from me and staggered back.

A wave of repulsion shuddered my body. Smaller insects gave me the creeps, much less ones as big as cats. One by one, the moths fluttered off Beeson, but to our dismay they didn't leave. Coming together into a cloud of chittering bodies, they loitered in the trees. Too many scrutinizing eyeballs to count glared in our direction. I got a funny feeling. It felt as if the bugs were passing judgment, and I could swear some of their antennas were pointing.

Ignoring the audience and the still griping Sholtz, Pax charged Beeson.

"What the hell were you thinking?" he roared, grabbing the woman by the arm and pulling her to be right under his nose.

"I-I don't know… I'm sorry." She cowered in on herself.

I was all too sure Pax was about to punch her, but he didn't. Roughly shoving her away, he rejoined us.

"We need to move. Every stray formation for miles is going to be heading our way now."

"You got that right, SL," Lee chimed. "The Razor just picked up a formation of droolers on our three. Want me to sacrifice it and see if I can lead them away?"

Since the Razors were unable to see over the tall brush, they weren't the most useful for Atlas' environment. However, they did provide a great diversion for the droolers, sending the beasts into a frenzy as they all converged on the Razor instead of us.

"Not yet," Pax instructed. "We might need it later. We'll try outrunning them first."

"Okay," Lee replied. "I'll auto pilot it to follow us then."

"Let's go!" Pax waved an arm. "Time to stretch our legs!"

We took off into the jungle. At first, the panicked scientists almost managed to keep up with us, the fear of being torn to shreds being a great motivator and all, but not even fifteen minutes later they started lagging. I wasn't surprised. Thinking back to the equipment room, I recalled plenty of white hair and wrinkled brows.

"Let the suit do the running!" Mills shouted as he veered to retrieve yet another straggling scientist.

I knew he would've gladly left them to their own devices, but as pissed as Pax was, he continued to track each and every one of them. I was glad for that. My skin prickled at the idea of a helpless civilians having their heads ripped off by the carnivorous beasts.

It didn't take long for us to realize that we wouldn't be able to outrun the droolers. The Razor's surveillance showed they were steadily gaining on us, while the scientists slowed with every minute. Some even had to stop, bracing against trunks on outstretched arms to pant. Not only that, but the hoard of locals had tailed us and was continuously giving away our position.

"We're going to have to make a stand," Pax concluded at last, with an unnerving casualness that had me grimace.

Heeding his command, we bunched the scientists into a tight group and pushed them ahead, placing ourselves between them and the approaching droolers. It was now inevitable the formation was going to catch up. The brush on our heels rumbled, and fronds squeaked and snapped under massive trampling feet.

Unfortunately, not as soon as we had the lab-coats clustered, one of them shrieked and bolted away. This, of course, spooked the rest. In a din of shouts, they scattered for the trees.

We all skidded to a baffled stop.

"What the... why—" Somner began but cut short.

We were stunned into silence. For a group of supposed brainiacs, they were *idiots*. The droolers were going to pick them off one by one.

Throwing a glance at what had spooked the lab-coat, I groaned. A drooler's maimed corpse lay crumpled in a pool of rotting entrails. The lower half looked to be eaten away. Insects buzzed around it, and chunks of worm-filled meat littered the grass. Those saber-toothed pigs were growing fat off this war.

"Now what?" I asked, glancing around.

Pax threw his head back in exasperation and allowed himself a curse. It appeared even he had his limits.

Composing himself, he turned to us, voice firm. "Look, I know we're all frustrated, but we can't fault them for this. They're civilians. We're the soldiers. It's our job to keep them safe. So, let's get it together and gather them back and do a better job monitoring . Adlar, you're on Beeson, Mills—"

I bolted into the trees. Beeson's locator had stopped moving away and was now darting around haphazardly in one spot.

"Don't move!" I instructed as I aimed for her locator. "Stay where you're at, I'm coming to get you."

As hard as it was, I saw Pax's point. Fear had a certain way of scrambling even the smartest minds. Who was I to talk? I'd frozen plenty, and I hardly had anything rattling up there.

Unsurprisingly, Beeson ignored my instructions. Shrieking, she darted towards me.

"They're almost here!" came Lee's shout.

I cursed, picking up speed, and soon spotted flashes of her black suit bouncing through the green. Not slowing as she approached, she almost knocked me off my feet as she plowed into me and threw her arms around my waist.

"I heard something! Over there!" She pointed a shaky finger behind her.

With a resigned sigh, I resisted the urge to shove her away. I could tell the woman was terrified.

"Whatever it is, we can handle it," I assured, giving her an awkward pat on the shoulder.

I pried her off after that, figuring *handling it* would be much easier if I didn't have anyone sticking to me like a piece of lint.

Following the direction of her trembling finger, I scanned the shrubs and mega-ferns with my blaster, but all I saw were gently swaying leaves. Leaves... and a bug. We weren't alone. A single moth hovered about thirty feet away from us. It didn't chitter or whine, but neither was it attempting to conceal itself. It was as if it wanted me to know it was watching. A chill traveled down my spine. I was certain there was more to these bugs than met the eye.

"Any second now!" Pax's shout tore me away from the moth and its three probing eyeballs. "Hopefully, it's just one formation and it'll be quick."

A panicked hand grabbed my arm. "We're going to fight them?" Beeson squeaked. "Shouldn't we run instead?"

I resisted rolling my eyes at *that* hell of an idea, opting not to mention that's exactly what we had attempted to do.

"Running's not an option anymore," I stated, throwing one last glance at where she'd claimed she'd heard something.

Seeing nothing, I turned away. "Come on. Let's get back with the group."

Beeson didn't protest, and we set off towards everyone else. As we jogged, the moth followed. My suit calculated it to be at a distance of thirty feet. Exactly thirty feet. Occasionally, the number flickered up or down a point two or three, but only momentarily as the moth corrected. The consistency was unnatural and unnerving. Perhaps the lab-nerds had not only underestimated their intelligence, but also their technical capabilities. Sure, they weren't constructing jump-drives, at least as far as we knew, but something told me they were way past discovering fire and tinkering with sticks and stones.

Thunderous *booms* overhead tore me from my thoughts. Yelping, Beeson slammed into my side like a retracting yo-yo with a clang of armor. I sucked in a strained breath, resisting the urge to snap at her. I now understood why Mills had hassled my hollering.

Craning my neck, I squinted through the canopy. *There!* Flashes of black streaked through the sky. A wide grin stretched my face. Second cohort was dropping. However, as the Leeges filled the sky, so did enemy fire. My grin broadened at its inadequacy. There was one aimless bolt per second, if that. None hit anything. Perhaps the shield generators also powered the automated turrets and taking them down had disabled the firepower.

"Trooper!" Beeson suddenly yanked on my arm with impressive force for her small stature, enough to pull me around.

I whirled, but not fast enough to train my blaster on the charging drooler. Arms wide open, he tackled us to the ground.

Beeson continued to shriek at the top of her lungs as we all scrabbled in a tangled mass of arms and legs, with the beast's massive fists pummeling away at our suits. The force of his punches wasn't anything debilitating, but his weight on top of me had me strain for breath.

"For the love of everything, stop screaming!" I pleaded as I activated my blades and swiped to meet the paws flying at my helmet.

With a crackle, I sliced both arms clean off, sending dark blood over my visor. The beast reared up, howling and roaring in pain. My next slash gutted it open. Beeson again screamed bloody murder as drooler guts spilled onto our armor.

Shoving the carcass off me with a heave, I flipped over onto my stomach, practically on top of Beeson.

My hands gripped her helmet.

"You're okay, we're okay," I reassured, smearing a glove through the black blood coating her visor to wipe it off.

Beeson stopped screaming but shook. I could feel her trembling through my suit.

"Wh-wh-how, that-," she stammered incoherently.

I figured she was in shock. Deciding to try something, I set my visor to clear and brought my face up to hers.

"Hey, Beeson. How do you know your date with a Viper pilot is halfway over?"

The incoherent stammering ceased. "Huh?"

"He says, enough about me, let me tell you about my ship."

Silence lingered, then Beeson rasped a laugh. It was weak and mirthless, but still, better than the hollering. Grinning, I let go of her helmet, relieved she seemed to have pulled it together. My audio still picked up her frantic breathing, but she no longer trembled.

"You okay?"

"No!" she shot back matter-of-factly. "I'm very much the *opposite* of okay. I'm pretty sure we both just almost died. That *thing*, it... it came out of nowhere."

A weary chuckle escaped me as I dropped my head onto her shoulder in resignation. Both of us were still stretched out on the ground, Beeson on her back, and me on my belly with a protective arm around her.

"Tell me about it," I said. "You get used to it, though. If that helps."

By the disgruntled snort that came out of her in reply, I guessed it didn't. She gently squirmed from underneath me and rose, looking over her gore-covered suit.

"So gross," she mumbled, swiping some chunky bits off her breastplate.

I too hopped to my feet, smiling as I thought of the disgusted expression she probably had behind that tinted visor. I couldn't help but wonder what she looked like under that exoskeleton of a suit. Blonde, brunette, red head? I knew this wasn't the time or place for that, but I felt a tingle. I found a certain excitement in the rush of adrenaline and the close call.

"I'm considering another sample," Beeson's voice cut through my pondering. I was busy thinking back to the equipment room and the lady scientists that had been in the group.

Taking a step towards the drooler carcass, Beeson leaned in to inspect the seeping fluids and entrails.

She quickly jerked away and edged to me. "Never mind. The lab has plenty of samples."

She then looked up at me, right through my still clear visor. Hers was on tint, but I sensed she was looking me in the eyes. I presumed she liked what she saw because she continued staring.

"Thanks for not letting me be ripped to shreds. I know you guys can't stand us," she said, stepping closer, almost pressing up against me. "And you're... Adlar, right? That's what that other man called you."

Sucking in a sharp breath, I reverted my visor back to tint, and spun away to look for my blaster. Her voice was now all friendly and whispery, tugging at parts of me that had no business being tugged at.

"We have to go," I interrupted her chatter, at last spotting my blaster next to one of the severed paw-hands. "Now that this bastard saw us, they all know where we are."

Grabbing my weapon, I spun to retrieve Beeson, only to smash into her instead. The girl had followed me. She chuckled as our suits loudly clanged, sending an irritable, yet enticing shiver down my spine. This time, I didn't push her away. Instead, with our chests pressed together, I reached over and slowly glided my hand down her thigh. She startled but didn't retreat.

Wrapping my fingers around her blaster's grip, I pulled it out, then shoved it into her very surprised and reluctant hands. I don't know what she was expecting, with us encased in armor and all, but her incoherent mousy stammer told me a blaster wasn't it.

"Here. Just point and shoot," I instructed, suppressing a smile.

Bishop hadn't been kidding, the ladies swooned for a man in blood-drenched armor. Even my comedic skills seemed to have miraculously improved. Hopefully, the same applied to Taylor.

Deciding I'd worry about my personal life later, I twisted Beeson around and gave her a firm push towards everyone else. My display showed the lab-coats huddled in a tight group and encircled by my squadmates' locators.

The droolers had caught up.

CHAPTER
FORTY-TWO

S hoving Beeson with the rest of her colleagues, I jumped into the fight. The squad had fanned out to encircle the lab-coats.

We had the upper hand—at first—shooting and slicing the charging droolers with ease. Even the scientists held their own. A few of the brave ones were aiming their blasters, while the rest bunched together next to their precious hover-carts. With shaky hands and intermittent shouts and yelps, the lab-coats shot any drooler that managed to get past us. Not that many droolers achieved the feat. With Mills' beamer, we mowed most down before they got anywhere near us.

"Get some!" Mills bellowed as he swung the beamer in a steady ark like a fireman dousing flames.

The blinding beam of lethal white plasma annihilated everything in its path. With hellish screams, the droolers toppled. Even enormous trunks were cleanly sliced and the trees thundered to the ground.

Yet the droolers kept coming. Howling madness, they stampeded over the scorched land and smoking carcasses. Pax's hopes had been for naught. There was no way this was only one formation. Maybe three, or possibly more. That immediately had me wonder about how many trigger-happy bots were currently lurking in hiding. observing this slaughter.

"You want more?" Mills boomed, discarding a spent rad-pack at his feet.

The field was now littered with the yellow skull and bone marked casings. Releasing an animalistic roar of his own, Mills clicked in yet another rad-pack and let loose on the new wave of barreling monsters. He mowed them down with one swipe. Most were dead before they even hit the ground, their flesh smoking and bubbling from the plasma.

Then our luck ran out. The bots decided they wanted to add humans to the tally of slaughtered—and the things were smart. They didn't go after us, but instead, after what we were protecting.

Shrill screams, both male and female, erupted over comms. I whirled to see the lab-coats twitching and writhing on the ground like a pile of worms.

"Where did those shots come from?" Pax shouted, sending a volley of aimless fire into the surrounding trees.

"Lee! Does the Razor have a fix?"

"No, sir," Lee panted, working with Somner on finishing off a pair of yowling droolers. "They must not be moving, and the Razor can't pin them."

The bots had the same, or even better, sensor-scrambling tech as their blathering troops. Without a visual, or them causing an actual physical disturbance, drones and Razors were useless in pinpointing their location.

"Shit!" Pax barked as he cracked a frag and hurled it into the trees. "We need to go. Get the lab-coats."

Most had stopped screaming and were now huffing and whimpering, trying to get back to their feet. They didn't make it far. A slew of well-aimed power-bolts shot out from north-east of us and nailed each scientist with mechanical precision. This time, the bots didn't stop with them. As the lab-coats again cluttered the comms with their screams, the machines aimed for us.

"Looks like it might be just one bot, Pax," Lee said as Somner and he intercepted a drooler that was barreling towards the downed scientists.

Somner skewered the beast through the chest as Lee decapitated him cleanly from behind.

"At least that's all that the Razor's estimating from that wave of fire. Maybe the Synths evacuated most of them."

"G-get us… out of here!" came a cackle.

It was Sholtz. "You're going to kill us with this amount of radiation!"

Sholtz wasn't completely wrong. A red skull and bone symbol, signifying unsafe levels in the vicinity, had begun to flash in the corner of my display. It even came with a piercing *breep, breep,* but I'd muted that two minutes ago. A pang of concern hit me as I wondered about the locals. There was a good chance they had the capacity to understand that we'd just irradiated a good chunk of their jungle.

Fortunately, there was only one bot—there just wasn't enough fire streaking from the trees to be any more—and as always it seemed intent on preserving its own existence and remained hidden. Both Pax and Mills managed to make it to the lab-coats without getting shot and rushed them into the trees. However, Somner, Lee and I weren't so lucky.

No more than ten steps away from the running group, I was shot in the back and knocked off my feet. My skin erupted in fire. Somner went down in front of me and Lee on my right.

"Adlar" came a panicked cry.

Gritting my teeth, I jumped back up, right as a lab-coat veered in my direction. It was Beeson.

"Noo..." I shouted, but it was too late.

A blue beam punched into her chest, sending her to vanish into the waist-high grass.

"Get us out of here! Now!" Sholtz shrieked on repeat, not at all helping the situation.

His shrill voice only added to the maelstrom of chaos.

"Everyone, grab a lab-coat," Pax instructed.

Grinning, I rushed towards Beeson. I suspected I knew Pax's intentions. We were about to hunt the son-of-a-bitch bot and obliterate it to scrap metal. Which was exactly what it deserved for shooting us from cover like the coward that it was.

Finding Beeson, I ushered her behind a bushel of feathered leaves. The girl had reverted back to panic mode and practically climbed me as I urged her down and out of view.

"Stay down." I pried her off and shoved her flat onto her stomach.

I had half a mind to pin her with a knee but decided to take the chance that she'd actually listen.

I crouched next to her, blaster in hand, awaiting Pax's instructions. Were we going to slowly encircle the bot and push inward? Or did he have something else in mind?

"I'll trade you," sounded Mills' voice over private chat.

My face scrunched in confusion, having no clue what he was going on about.

He cleared it up for me.

"How the hell are you getting all the chicks, anyways?" he complained.

I couldn't help but laugh. At least the guy had the decency to use private chat for his idiotic comments.

"Who do you h—"

Something crawled onto my leg. My heart jumped into my throat. I didn't know if this planet had snakes, but that was the first thing that popped into my head, and I almost shot straight up with panic. Subduing the urge for a more logical approach, I stayed put and glanced down instead.

I froze and blinked. It wasn't a squirmy python crawling up my thigh, but Beeson. Her gloved hand had slunk onto my leg as she scooted closer.

"Sorry," she chuckled nervously but didn't let go. "It's just that this whole thing... it's nuts. Us on a hostile planet. It really *is* in our contracts that we wouldn't be venturing into combat zones. None of us ever had—"

"Who do you think?" Mills' voice cut over Beeson in my helmet.

I was grateful for that. Maybe if I bantered with that ass-hat, I'd be able to distract my errant mind from the illicit ideas churning within it. Had this been any other circumstance, I would have already acquired Beeson's number, her lab-coat ID, whatever, and made plans to see her tonight. I chewed my lip, urging myself into restraint.

"Just don't kill him and blame it on the bot," I stated, over Beeson's rambling.

She was still going on about something. I wanted to pull away, but the very noticeable tremble in her voice held me put. I could tell the girl was trying to be brave, trying to hide her fear. Placing a hand on her shoulder, I gave her a reassuring squeeze.

At last, Pax came on over squad-chat. "Here's the plan. Second squad is coming our way to handle the bot. Lee, have the Razor make some noise, then send it to them and patch over control to their tech. I'll send you his ID. As soon as they engage, we move. Until then, everyone stay put."

I sucked air through my teeth. With the pressure relaying strands in my armor, I felt every twitch of Beeson's probing fingers. Something I didn't think she was aware of. If she were, I doubted her hand would be lingering where it was.

"Where are you from, Adlar?" Beeson asked, with an obvious hint of flirtation. "Is Adlar your first name or last?"

Muffled snickers accompanied her question. She hadn't switched to private chat. I didn't think she knew how. I would have done it for her, to save myself from Mills' future hassling, but I had no way of tapping into her HUD.

I hesitated but then decided to oblige her. Who knew, maybe I'd see her around the ship. "It's Jake," I answered, making sure I was on private, "and I'm from southern North America sector, Texas."

Before I could ask her name in return, Mills' annoying voice hopped into the chat.

"Awww… come on, man! Switch yours back from private, I wanna hear. Did you answer or what? Ask her name. Where you from, Beeson? Are you seeing—"

Mills suddenly cut off. I stiffened in concern, tightening my grip on my blaster and straightened, but then saw it was Pax who'd shut him up. He'd overridden his comms with his own. Being the SL, he had the power to commandeer the comms.

"Not the time, Mills," Pax snapped. "And get ready to run. Second squad's almost here. Ready, Lee?"

I quietly chuckled to myself, imagining the storm Mills was cursing up inside his helmet right about now. I wondered if I buddied up with the equipment guys if they'd slip that option into my kit. Maybe I'd offer them some credits to just give me the ability to override Mills.

"All set," Lee reported. "Sending the Razor now."

At that, Beeson's chest heave against my thigh with newfound gusto. I gave her shoulder another reassuring squeeze, though I also tensed.

"We'll finish our talk later," I assured, making sure to keep my tone level.

Who knew what awaited us at the mountain—we weren't that far —but I didn't want to worry.

My audio picked up a loud rustling as the Razor began its task of seeking attention. I didn't know if Lee had the machine doing circles in the shrubs but whatever it was sure made plenty of noise. Branches snapped with loud cracks and leaves rustled and ripped.

A breath later, the bot took the bait and the Razor's antics were joined by pops and zaps, which quickly receded into the distance. The bot had given chase and was unloading, trailing the Razor right into second squad's grasp.

"Let's go," Pax said.

I pulled Beeson up and we all clustered into a tight group, with us encircling the lab-coats. This time the scientists didn't split up whenever we swerved around corpses. Even Sholtz became somewhat more docile and stayed in line, clutching his gadget-filled hover-cart as if his life depended on it. I guess the zapping he'd taken had done him some good.

As we ran, cringe-worthy thoughts of Fallon impinged on my mind. She was the last thing I wanted to think about, but as I eyeballed the area, I couldn't help myself. We were now less than half a mile from the Synths' base and skewered, burned, and torn drooler carcasses littered the underbrush. Even a few decimated bot frames glistened in the sparse sunlight that pierced through the canopy. But where were the Leeges? I wholeheartedly wished there hadn't been casualties, but I knew that was a pipedream.

Maybe tenth squad had done a thorough job retrieving the dead, I hypnotized, but that, too, seemed implausible. Not unless more squads had helped or they'd done multiple passes, and they wouldn't have had the time. My skin prickled and I felt unnerved. Back when I'd caught the drooler dragging the leftovers of a trooper, I'd figured it was for an easy meal, but now that I knew what unholy deeds Fallon was up to, I wasn't so sure.

CHAPTER
FORTY-THREE

About thirty minutes later, just as Sholtz began complaining for a break, the surrounding greenery thinned, and the black mountain came into view. We stopped at the treeline and surveyed the cleared strip of dirt and grass that ran the perimeter. The last time Pax and I had the misfortune of being here, we hadn't gleaned any heavy weapon emplacements, but who knew what had changed since then.

I slowly scanned the devastation before me and exhaled with relief. We had certainly given their lawn a good tilling, but as far as fire-power went, not much was different. Their main defenses remained to be the turrets. I wasn't worried about those. With the generator destroyed, they were now mere decoration, bejeweling the slopes with glimmering silver.

I gave my head a slow shake and snorted. For an advanced race that had ruled this sector of the cosmos unopposed for eons, their setup was weak. Maybe that's why this whole campaign was rushed, with new troops receiving so little training. Hadn't Neero said something about exterminating them before they'd taken root? I had no complaints about that. Dealing with taking down heavy weaponry wasn't exactly on my Christmas wish list.

Breaking away from eyeballing the turrets, I blinked feverishly to chase away the tracers swimming in my eyes. Without the shield, Atlas' hot sun turned each one into a blinding beacon. I regarded the dirt skirting the mountain instead. The crater-pocked zone looked like a cross between an unfinished construction project and the scene of a massacre, littered with both drooler carcasses and chunks of bots.

I grinned with pride. We'd shattered the Synths' defensive perimeter in a matter of days, and now we were slaughtering what remained of them. Atlas was practically ours.

"Looks clear," Pax stated, somewhat uncertain.

We truly had no idea what we were about to walk into. Giving the area one last scan, he spun to the lab-coats and spoke in a hard tone that conveyed he meant business.

"Get in a group and stay *together*."

The lab-coats nodded hurriedly, and all rushed to comply. Encircling them and their junk in a protective wall of armored bodies, we then slowly approached the tunnel. The dim white light I'd previously seen emanating from the entrance was now gone, and the interior looked dark and foreboding.

Somehow, I ended up on point. I warily eyed the area, my throat tightening when my gaze landed on where I'd shot the two civilians. There wasn't much left of them underneath the rubble and debris, but the shreds of whitish flesh and the splatters of blue blood were discernible.

Turning away, I strode into the tunnel with purpose. I had long weighed my actions and accepted them. I had done what needed to be done. I wasn't going to pout about it.

My HUD automatically toggled to night vision after we rounded the first bend and drew further away from natural light. Soon, the darkness swallowed us up completely. Without my night vision, I knew I wouldn't be able to see my own hand in front of my face, but my display painted me a vivid grayscale picture clear as day. As far as I could tell, this wasn't unlike a mining tunnel back on Earth. Jutting stones made up the walls and gravel layered the floor.

Running an investigative finger over the rock, I frowned. There was no evidence of boring nor any piles of discarded rubble or bracing to suggest that the tunnel was freshly blasted. That led me to believe it was of a natural design. That, or this complex had been constructed ages ago. How long exactly, I couldn't tell, but it was long enough for moss to have claimed most of the stones. It felt slimy and soft under my fingertip.

I wondered how the Synths had come to settle here. Had they simply sniffed it out or was it something darker? After all, this was a prime piece of real estate for any entity seeking seclusion for their ill-intentioned deeds.

The gravel crunched under our boots as we strode forward. The echoes of our steps carried down ahead of us to eerily dissipate in the distance. My audio picked up the rhythmic plops of what might have been dripping water, but I couldn't be sure. However it came to be here or however old it was, the place was creepy. The tunnel weaved deeper and deeper into the mountain, twisting and turning like a snake. Even though the temperature here was drastically cooler than outside, my palms grew clammy as I tightened my grip on my blaster. Every time I turned a blind corner, I braced for an attack from some unknown alien beast.

We walked in silence, our tension palpable. Even Mills held back his usual smart-ass commentary. We pulled to a stop when a white glow flickered from around the next bend.

"What'd you think that is?" Mills ventured carefully.

"Let's check it out," Pax said. "Everyone else, stay put."

"Copy," Mills replied.

He fidgeted with his beamer as it again hummed to life and primed. In the confines of this labyrinth, its mechanical clicks and whines sounded that much louder.

As Mills and Pax broke away and advanced to investigate the light, something touched my arm. Startled, I almost jumped out of my skin for probably the millionth time. Before I could shuffle back, a familiar voice greeted my ears.

"What do you think we're going to find in there?" Beeson asked.

I calmed my breathing then turned to her. "That's a good way to get shot, sneaking up like that?" I glanced around. "In a place like this."

"Ehh…" She sheepishly shrugged. "I didn't think you'd shoot me."

I scowled, knowing I wouldn't.

"You think there's anything worthwhile in there?"

"I don't know, but you better get back with the group."

"But—"

Mills' snark cut her off. "All right love birds, coast is clear. It's just overhead lighting. There must still be a working generator somewhere out there."

Nudging Beeson back, I guided everyone forward, seeing what Mills was talking about. Pliable tubing was attached overhead, emanating an icy glow and casting everything in a dreary light. Right as we were about to round the next bend, movement flashed in front of us. The scientists immediately rushed back and jammed the comms with racket.

For my part, I jerked my blaster up at what had skittered out. Three flustered Synths gaped back at me. I recognized the short humanoid creatures. They were the same kind I'd previously shot. Just like before, none of them appeared to be armed or even aware of what we were. They all froze statue-still. White film flashed over their black eyes as they blinked and chattered incoherently. I had no idea what to do and stood frozen, just like them, blaster trained.

"Grab one!" Sholtz shouted, darting past his colleagues to stand at my back.

He shoved me forward roughly. "Don't just stand there, you fool! Apprehend one of them!"

My jaw clenched. I didn't much appreciate being shoved and was about to turn around and let him know when Pax shouldered past both of us. Without hesitation, one by one, he shot each Synth in the head. He paused between each pull of the trigger to watch the corpse crumple at his feet. I shuddered. It was almost as if he'd enjoyed it, savored it even. I couldn't see Pax's face through his visor, but suspected he was smirking.

"Are you insane?" Sholtz screamed in outrage as he dashed towards the aliens, only to slam into Pax's broad chest as he stepped to block him.

Roughly grabbing the stammering man by his arm, Pax twisted him around and flung him towards the rest of the lab-coats. Sholtz yelped in surprise as he lost his footing and tumbled to the ground.

It was my turn to shuffle back, unnerved. I'd yet to see this side of Pax. Mills, sure, he'd roughed up the lab-coats plenty, but not Pax.

"Unbelievable!" Sholtz barked as he huffed and puffed trying to scramble back to his feet, slipping on the pebbles. "What we can learn from capturing one of those models alive is—"

"File a complaint," Pax snapped, pointing at the rest of the lab-coats with his blaster to the backdrop of Mills' snickers. "Now get!"

Pax's mood had certainly darkened.

Sholtz sensed this. Ceasing his protests, he hustled closer to the other scientists. Closer, but not into the group. He made it a point to stay a few feet apart from them. I doubted he was doing the smart thing by baiting Pax, but it was his funeral. Ignoring him, Pax signaled us to continue. This time, he stepped in front of me, taking point.

Ten steps later, my private chat lit up.

It was Pax. "What was that?"

I frowned, confused.

"Uh…" I said, unsure how to proceed, but getting a sinking sensation.

Pax's tone was glacial, like I'd done something wrong. Except, I wasn't sure what. Nor did I know why we were speaking on private.

"What was what, SL?"

"Back there, why did you hesitate… again? I thought we were past this?"

I cringed, realizing what he was referring to—when I'd failed to shoot the charging drooler. Now I'd done it again. My brows scrunched as I considered the situation. To me, the two incidents weren't the same. Not at all. Back then, I hadn't shot because I'd frozen out of fear whereas here, I wasn't sure the Synths needed to be shot. None had been armed and they weren't a threat. We gained nothing by murdering them.

Something told me Pax didn't share in my opinion.

"They… looked like civilians," I said. "Maybe scientists, if I had to guess. Aren't there some regs about—"

"That's not going to fly, Adlar," Pax interrupted. "Not in this squad. There's no such thing as civilians out here as far as I'm concerned. If it's not human, we kill it. We kill them all. Is that clear?"

I hesitated but knew there was only one answer he was going to accept. "Yes, sir."

Pax dropped it at that, but I shivered. I wasn't sure I'd ever understand him. In my opinion, he was devoted to humanity to a fault. He wouldn't pull the trigger on a scumbag like Boyer, even when the punk was trying to kill him, for the simple fact he was human. Yet, he didn't hesitate to kill other creatures for the fact they weren't. Not only that, but he enjoyed it.

I wasn't sure what to make of that.

CHAPTER
FORTY-FOUR

Three bends later, the tunnel stopped snaking, and we found ourselves staring down a dim, straight hall with a series of door-sized openings on the left. The light tubing overhead flickered, accompanied by distant rumbles. The walls around us shook as a shuddering tremble passed through the mountain and the light further down suddenly extinguished. I smiled as pebbles rained over me and clattered to the ground. Invictus was still causing havoc.

Clicking on my helmet light, I sent a bright beam into the absolute darkness that now consumed the far end of the passage. I made out nothing of interest, just ghostly sheets of dust drifting through my light. Others had the same idea and additional beams joined mine.

"Let's get on with it," Pax instructed.

Taking a step forward, he strobed his light over the uninviting entrances. Some were pitch-black, while others emanated a dim glow. We all shuffled with unease, tightening our grips on our weapons. I don't know about everyone else, but I again felt my palms grow clammy. This place gave me creeps. It was like some sort of damp dungeon from the vids full of who knew what ghastly nightmares.

"Hey! Hey!" came a shout.

As one, we all audibly sighed at the familiar voice.

"What is it now, Sholtz?" Pax snapped.

"What is it now?" Sholtz's head twisted between Pax and Mills.

Or more precisely between Pax and the bulky item in Mill's grasp. "Do you want to kill us all before the Synths do?"

Pax remained silent for a second, thinking, then figured out Sholtz's gripe. "Oh. Yeah." He turned to Mill. "Switch to a blaster for now."

Mills hesitated, momentarily clutching his beamer tighter to his chest like it was some precious heirloom, but then obeyed.

"Yeah, yeah... okay," he mumbled.

Unslinging it, he carefully placed the weapon into a hover-carts, jamming it in just right, to where it wouldn't fall out. He then drew his blaster. We clicked off our lights and Pax took point, leading us past the first few rooms which were cast in darkness. We tried to walk as quietly as possible but occasionally the pebbles crunched under our boots, piercing the overwhelming silence. I winced whenever that happened.

Fortunately, Pax led us past the blackened rooms. I was grateful for that. It was going to be bad enough having to go into one with the ominous, haunted-house-like light glowing out of it, without having to step into one that was stark black.

Stopping before the first room that still had functional lights, Pax signaled the lab-coats back and for us to stack the entrance. He motioned for Somner and me to take up positions across from him.

"On three," he said.

My hairs stood on end as I raised my blaster and steadied my breaths.

"Three, two, one—"

We moved. I swung into the room, blaster at the ready. This time, I didn't hesitate. Right as a Synth jerked up from a thin, glassy device in its hands to look at us, I shot it straight through the head. The flash of my muzzle momentarily illuminated the gloom. In a twisting spin, the alien crumbled to the floor. The device flew from its hands and shattered into a thousand glimmering pieces.

However, I'd picked the wrong target and everyone else was just a microsecond too slow. They fired at the bot behind the Synth, nailing it center mass, but not before it got off three shots of its own.

I was shot in the chest and thrown off my feet.

"Get the aliens alive!" Sholtz shouted from the entrance.

He must've heard the commotion and seen the flashes of blaster fire. I gritted my teeth as I struggled back up, swaying, panting, and hissing from the burn. My hand not holding a blaster curled into an angry fist.

"Fuck!" Mills roared, pushing himself up. "I'm so tired of this shit! I hate getting shot!"

He stomped over to the crumbled Synth.

"*Bzzt, bzzt, bzzt,*" echoed around us as he filled it with holes, sending blue blood and meat chunks to spray over his boots.

He glanced at the downed bot next which was partially slumped over its master's smoking carcass. "Can I use a frag in here?"

"I'll get it," I chimed, walking over to the machine.

A final shudder passed through me as I shook off the last bit of tingling from my skin. Pressing my blaster's barrel against the slit in the bot's head, I squeezed the trigger. The head jerked, crackled, and sparked, then lay still, wafting a string of smoke.

"Why in the world—" Sholtz shouted.

I turned to see the man charge into the room, his head spinning feverishly over the mess.

"These are all valuable speci—"

Sholtz cut off, frozen. Pax was up, his blaster aimed.

"Just try asking to keep another alien alive," Pax spoke in a dangerous tone. "I dare you."

My nerves buzzed. It wasn't so much that I worried Pax would pull the trigger, I knew he wouldn't, but something inside of him had rattled, and I had no idea what. I made a mental note to ask Somner about it later.

Sholtz staggered back a step, hands raised.

"Fine, fine," he huffed.

Circumventing Pax, he ran to the dead Synth and dropped to his knees. He then noticed the glimmering pieces of whatever the alien had been holding. Even though the thing had shattered, the tiny fragments still swam with radiant reds, oranges, and yellows. Muttering a slew of insults under his breath, Sholtz began picking the pieces out of the gravel.

Pax ignored him and quickly ushered the other scientists into the room. "Get to work. Don't make this trip a complete waste."

The lab-coats heeded and jumped into action. We watched, stunned, as they pulled out two additional folded hover-carts from underneath their equipment and activated them. The repulsors glowed and hummed as they unfurled and transformed into bins.

"You have to be kidding me…" Somner voiced what the rest of us were thinking.

When folded, the carts were the size of a briefcase. We had no idea they'd brought more. The scientists didn't waste any time and dispersed like eager children in a toy store, tossing whatever their hands landed on into the carts.

Quickly running out of loose items to pillage, they moved on to investigate the few sheet-thin, glassy screens that still remained in the room. It wasn't hard to tell that most everything had been removed or destroyed prior to our arrival. Shredded tubing littered the floor, and I could see where, at one point, it had run along the crease of the wall. Bits of it were still there, ripped at the ends and leaking a whitish liquid.

Pax ordered us to keep watch, but since nothing had charged out after all the commotion, I guessed the space to be clear. Having nothing better to do while the lab-coats poked around, I decided to explore. I squatted over the tubing and inspected the white puddle of ooze underneath. Specks of silver glimmered within. I reached a finger towards it, only to yank back with a grimace. The specks moved, darting about like tadpoles.

Reconsidering sticking my finger into alien goop, I stood and eyeballed what was left of the tubing. It ran the length of the wall. Wondering where it led, I followed it. It disappeared into a dark opening on the opposite side of the room. Another entrance, perhaps.

I threw a cautious glance over my shoulder. The lab-coats were now trying to pry open some kind of drawers, and my teammates had dispersed to stand watch. They didn't seem interested in exploring. Making sure no one was looking my way, I quietly stepped through the narrow entrance.

Darkness again engulfed me, prompting my night vision to activate. The place was a cavern and a complete mess. At the far end stood large cylindrical vats but they were too far to make out details. To my left was a jumbled heap of wheeled metallic gurneys, similar to the ones used at the morgue. Some were knocked over while others were pushed together into haphazard piles. I grimaced when I saw the thick straps hanging from their sides. They looked like restraints. More screens hung above them. Some had crashed to the ground and shattered while others dangled, mid-air, suspended by partially torn tubing.

I shuddered. The scene reminded me of an abandoned asylum, demented, eerie, and dank.

Glancing behind me, at the lit room, I reconsidered venturing further. Maybe something was still alive down here. Or maybe a bot was hiding somewhere, waiting for an easy kill.

Against my better judgment, I opted not to retreat. Toggling on my helmet light, I scanned the cavern and over the stony walls, glimmering with condensation. There were more shredded cables and broken stuff. Perhaps this babysitting gig was, in fact, a waste of time. Everything of use appeared to have been removed or broken.

I stopped when my beam illuminated a row of metallic stands. They were concave like bowls and as big around as trees. Intrigued, I crouched next to one and ran my gloved hand over the raised alien symbols on the exterior, only to quickly pull away. What if the Synths had rigged something to blow like Neero had posed? It was obvious they'd anticipated we'd make our way in here. Then again, they might have plans to return once the Legion departed. Unfortunately, that was a common enough occurrence. Like a persistent parasite, the Synths regrew. The Senate had no way of monitoring the entirety of the galaxy, nor the resources or manpower to station a force in every system.

A pang hit me as I considered how pointless our presence here might be. That so many had died, and were dying, for nothing. Hadn't Rap-Wars been enough? All to chase the Synths off Earth and away from our solar system. Which we had. Yet, many decades later, here I was. So were a few thousand other people, floating in Atlas' orbit. I couldn't fathom what the Senate saw in this backwater planet.

I snapped out of my stewing and shook my head like a wet dog, trying to clear my mind. My thoughts were pointless anyway. As a ground trooper, I wasn't here to think.

Standing, I made my way down the wall, my boots crunching on broken glass and other crud littering the ground. It was obvious the metal stands were meant to hold something, and I wanted to see what.

At last, my light hit the shimmer of glass. The stands were no longer empty. An eight-foot-tall cylindrical capsule stood in each.

Cautiously approaching one, I wiped the condensation and debris off its cracked glass and peeked inside, wondering what the pods were used for. Judging by their size and width, the only creepy conclusion I could come up with was that they were intended for bodies. Whether for Synths or some other species, I had no idea.

Figuring this might be more useful than stray gadgets, I reached out to Pax.

"Hey, I might have something over here."

"What is it?" Sholtz piped as a beam of bouncing light rushed into the cavern.

He immediately noticed what I was talking about and dropped to his knees, grabbing on to a capsule base.

"Make yourself useful and come help," he huffed, trying to pry it off with grunts of exertion.

I considered his demand for all of one second, then decided to do the more pleasant thing and ignored the man. He had no actual authority over me.

Reverting my attention back to the darkness, I decided to investigate the mysterious vats. Now that I was closer, I could see they were made of glass and were filled with a greenish liquid like thick, dirty pond water.

Frowning, I fractionally raised my blaster as I approached. Some of the liquid was gently sloshing. I had no idea why considering everything else was as still as a graveyard. Shining my light, I edged closer, but the beam failed to penetrate through the sludge. If something was floating in there, I wasn't going to get a visual, and I sure as hell wasn't curious enough to attempt climbing to the top. With my luck, I'd end up going for a swim.

Sholtz continued to whine for help, cluttering the comms. I lowered my volume as I studied the rest of the tanks, noticing one with a busted glass. Greenish liquid dribbled down the side and pooled around it. I approached it until I reached the edge of the puddle. Then I hesitated, eyeing the suspicious goo. Was it dangerous on top of disgusting?

Figuring that since my suit was encapsulating and pressurized the stuff wasn't going to actually touch me, I placed one foot into the muck, then waited. It felt slimy under my boot but nothing crazy happened. No warnings popped up in my display and nothing beeped.

Growing braver, I ventured forward, waddling through the sludge with careful steps. The floor under me was no longer loose gravel, but something comparable to concrete, and I could feel my boots occasionally lose their traction. At last reaching the broken glass, I clutched the jagged edges for balance and stuck my head inside. I was thankful that my armor recycled the air. I didn't want to imagine the stench.

The tank turned out to be empty, but for a few inches of lapping sludge. I again found the liquid's disturbed state odd but didn't glean anything of interest. Maybe these tanks were the last thing the Synth had messed with before I shot him dead.

Deciding it ultimately didn't matter, I pulled my head out. It was time to rejoin the group. Turning, I made it all of one step. My swinging light flashed over something green and bulky laying behind the tank.

"Hmm…" I squinted, trying to make it out as I waddled closer.

When it became clear, panic shot through my every nerve, and I lurched back, forgetting about the goo under my feet. I slipped and crashed to the floor with a splash.

Working my legs frantically, I scooted back, sliding on my butt through the slime. I was breathing hard, and my eyes were wide. What I had found was a corpse—a human one. Or what was left of it. The entire lower half of the body was missing, severed at the hips. It must've spilled out of the broken tank and now lay face down, wet and slimy, in the pool of liquid.

"Everything all right, Adlar?" came Pax's concerned voice. "Why'd you yell?"

I grimaced, realizing I'd yelped when I'd fallen.

"He probably saw a spider," Mills snickered.

"Yeah, uhuh... that's what it was," I rushed to reply. My alarm had given way to paralyzing fear, and not just at sighting the corpse.

A whole heap of things was coming together in my mind—the gurneys, the drooler dragging a trooper's carcass, Fallon. This research outpost in the darkest corners of the nether was to experiment on *humans*. We were lab rats. Were they building a bioweapon, I instantly thought?

I suddenly felt sick as I stared at the corpse before me in a numb-like trance. Was this some poor sap off the battlefield, or one of Fallon's victims? The woman I'd nabbed from the morgue or the man I'd caught her dragging?

Mills' loud snickers jerked me back to reality.

"Did a horde of vicious butterflies get ya?" he chided. "Or did you stub your toe? Do we need to call an evac?"

"I just slipped, that's all," I rushed to placate. "I'm fine."

I didn't want them coming to investigate. Why? I wasn't certain. Perhaps I was in shock. All I could think about was that icy airlock and the crime I'd committed. Treason was not a forgivable offence.

Ignoring Mills' teasing, I holstered my blaster and crawled towards the human remains. I had no idea what I was hoping to find, but I reached for it, nonetheless, and flipped it over. It splashed onto its back as the lifeless head lolled to the side. With my stomach in a knot, I scanned it with my light. My beam illuminated slimy flesh and a skull with empty sockets. The head had been skinned with only a few tattered pieces hanging on.

Gagging, I pulled away. Not only was the victim missing their eyes, but they'd been mutilated. Precision-cut holes dotted the body.

I felt like I wanted to hurl. Why the hell was Fallon doing this? Credits? Something else?

"Adlar!" Pax boomed, concern evident in his voice. "Are you okay? What's happening? Your suit's vitals are off the charts? I'm sending Somner."

"No, no," I rushed to reply, spinning away from the corpse.

I exhaled a shaky breath, willing my heart rate to stabilize. "I just got spooked when I fell, that's all."

"You sure?"

"Yeah, I'm sure. I'm fine. You guys just finish what you're doing. It's all clear over here."

The moment their comms clicked off, I turned my light off and allowed the darkness to envelop me. My mind spun with thoughts. Fallon had sworn me to secrecy. Was this the horror that awaited Taylor if I dared to cross her?

I tensed. I knew what I had to do. No matter what came of it, I needed to confront the crow, and the sooner the better. Right after returning to the ship. I'd force her to tell me *why*, even if it meant having my ass handed to me in the process, then lie, threaten, and coarse her into stopping this. Surely no amount of credits could be worth sentencing your own to such a dismal fate.

"Adlar!" came a crackled boom of external speakers behind me.

I jumped up from the sludge, shuddering at the unpleasant sensation of the thick goop running down my legs to drip back into the puddle. I clicked my light on and turned. A suited figure briskly approached.

"Stop!" I shouted, illuminating the green goop with my beam. "It's slippery. Very slippery."

I couldn't have Somner come any closer. Shoving my Fallon problems to the back of my mind, I waddled in his direction. He'd stopped short of the puddle, strobing his beam over the glassy surface.

"I know you said you were fine, but Pax sent me anyways. Did you find something?"

"Nah. Just lost my footing in this damn swamp."

Somner ran his light over my slime-covered suit as I approached.

"Did you... try swimming in it too?" he asked with both disgust and amusement.

He edged away from the mess. "We gotta go, man. The place is going to blow soon, so hurry up."

I then noticed that the initial room we'd entered was now dark. In fact, everything around me was now pitch-black with only the clustered suit lights providing any illumination. All the generators must've been taken down and the Legion was getting ready to blow the place. The Synths might've desired to move back in, thus not rigging the caves to blow, but we had a different idea. We were going to make sure they never took root in this exact location again.

Part of me was relieved. The sooner we buried this slaughterhouse in rock, the better.

"There you are," Pax greeted, when Somner and I rejoined everyone next to the row of pod stands.

His light swung my way and froze.

"What happened?" he asked only to shake his head dismissively. "Never mind, let's just go."

Mills instantly cozied up to me, flinging a heavy arm over my shoulders. "After battling that vicious butterfly, did you fall into some alien snot? A spa treatment for that pretty boy complexion of yours?"

He cackled at his own stupid teasing. I shoved him away, not in the mood for his shit. Scanning over the group, I saw that almost everyone was ready to go. The lab-coats were clustered next to Pax, all four of their hover-carts filled to capacity. They sagged low to the ground, the struggling repulsors casting a bluish glow over the pebbles and debris. One cart hovered lower than the rest.

"I'll be damned." I eyed the cargo, shaking my head in disbelief.

Somehow, Sholtz had managed to pry off the pod base and it now rested sideways in the cart. Pax loudly cleared his throat, grabbing the squad's attention as the lab-coats continued to chatter in hushed tones while pointing at their loot. I could tell they were chomping at the bit to get everything back to the lab and dive in to investigate.

I lowered their volume, seeing that Pax was on squad-chat and blocking them out.

"The shield's down, and the tunnels are next. They're about to start blowing them, but don't tell the lab-coats. I don't want them griping or scattering like rats again."

His voice was again calm and level. I was glad for that. Whatever had bitten him seemed to have passed. Confirming we understood, we proceeded to herd the scientists towards the exit. Wanting to hurry up and get away from the corpse-filled tanks, I rushed into the first room, ready to gather anyone still there.

"Time to go!" I said, walking briskly towards the two lab-coats elbows deep in some bin.

They'd made quick work of the room. Most drawers were hanging open with their edges smoking from the cutting torches, and odd gadgets littered the floor. I presumed those were the things they'd deemed useless.

Both scientists ignored me. Frustrated, I had every intention of physically grabbing and dragging them, if need be, when instead, I found myself pitching forward to sprawl flat on my stomach.

Cursing, I shined my light behind me to see what had tripped me. My beam roamed over the disabled bot, sprawled over his master's tattered corpse. Both lay in a puddle of blue blood, which I too was now covered in. Pushing up from the dirt, I groaned in disgust as I looked over myself. I was starting to look like a damn painting—or a carnival clown. Throw a honking nose on me and I'd be ready for the stage.

"Dammit," I hissed, kicking at the bot's metal frame, putting all my suppressed anger and frustration behind the kick.

Seeing as I had plenty, my boot slammed into the bot with some serious force. It teetered, then slid off the Synth with a squishy slurp. More blood seeped from the corpse. Grimacing, I was about to walk away when I saw a shimmer.

Intrigued, I edged closer to the Synth and ran my beam over what remained of its head and the slop that had drained out of it. My light illuminated something silver amidst the gore. Crouching, I used one careful finger to turn its head. A familiar trinket greeted my eyes. Wedged under the alien's tattered flesh was a transmitter, just like the one Fallon had used. Unlike with the drooler, this one wasn't simply attached to the temple, but looked to be embedded under the alien's skin as if it had fit into the skull itself. Seeing as this Synth was one of the advanced models, the same as I'd encountered in the airlock, I decided the transmitter might be of use.

Looking this way and that, I inspected my immediate vicinity. To no surprise, the two lab-coats who I'd tried to retrieve and was risking my life to protect, had completely ignored my fall and were both still huddled over the bin. The rest of the squad was busy ushering out a complaining Sholtz. Satisfied there were no witnesses,

I reached for the corpse and slid two uneasy fingers under the alien's skin. I tried not to gag as my fingers scraped bone, or whatever a Synth's skull was made of. *Damn those pressure relaying threads.* They sure weren't an asset when it came to poking around a carcass. At last managing to snag the device, I pulled it free. Grinning, I took a moment to study it with reverence, then pocketed the souvenir.

CHAPTER
FORTY-FIVE

Wrangling the lab-coats into a tight group, we ushered them out of the room. Since they were already spooked enough, and we didn't want them tripping over their own feet, the squad had the honor of dragging their gadget-filled carts full of strange techie items and one massive pod stand.

I couldn't help but feel claustrophobic as we snaked through the stifling darkness. Sure, I had a grayscale image in my display, but it still felt like the air itself was pressing in on me. I didn't even mind when Beeson broke away from her group to walk beside me. She didn't chat in her usual manner, probably too unnerved to do so, but I appreciated the company.

When we were a few twists and turns from the exit, the explosions started. The ground shuddered under our feet as massive *booms* sent quaking rumbles down the tunnel. Even though they were a good way behind us, my nerves rattled. It was hard not to envision the whole place crashing down on top of us.

Just like Pax had suspected, the scientists freaked. Shouting in panic, they dashed ahead like roaches from a light, with zero consideration of what else could be lurking in the tunnel or what awaited them at the entrance or in the jungle. Given that the Synths tucked tail and ran in a rush, who knew how many bloodthirsty slaves they'd abandoned to their own devices?

None of the lab-coats seemed to consider those facts, however.

"Fine!" Mills shouted to their backs. "I don't care if you get eaten out there. And sure, we'll take care of pushing all this junk for you!"

Not a single lab-coat had made a move to help us with the hover-carts before bolting. The realization they might encounter a drooler, without us around to protect them, had them quickly reconsider. They all rounded back, only for most to topple as another rumbling detonation quaked the tunnel and everything around us shook and trembled.

"We better hurry," Pax said in a matter-of-fact tone as he pushed off the wall he'd used to steady himself.

He had a point. We didn't want this place to be our tomb. As soon as the ground stopped shuddering, we ran for the exit, dragging the lab-coats to their feet along the way. We didn't stop until we saw the faint beams of natural light from the tunnel's entrance flickering around the upcoming bend.

Pax halted us. "Everyone, change batteries. Help the lab-coats."

Beeson was the closest lab-coat within my reach. Without saying a word, I pulled her closer and quickly changed out her battery, then mine. I felt that she was again trembling in her suit.

"This is almost over, right?" she whispered.

"I really hope so," I replied, wholeheartedly, to the backdrop of Mills' mocking cooing.

I wanted nothing more than an uneventful walk back to the safe zone, but so far, nothing had been uneventful or easy. Such terminology didn't exist in Legion Invictus. I did a quick scan of my HUD while zooming out.

To my dismay, I didn't see what I was hoping to find.

"Pax," I prompted. "Where's our safe zone?"

With this complex destroyed, were we going to be spared the long trek, or did that just mean the droolers were now able to venture further, having nothing left to protect and fewer, if any, bots to organize them?

Before Pax could answer, Sholtz's annoying voice cluttered the comms. He'd made it a point to be a pain and ventured towards the exit all by himself but was now sprinting back like he'd been prodded in the ass. Shoving Mills out of the way, he squeezed himself into the middle of the clustered lab-coats and pointed a shaking finger at the entrance.

"There's a whole swarm of them out there! A whole swarm! You better get us out of here alive, you hear me!"

Pax immediately tensed, looking over the group.

"Get behind us," he instructed the scientists as the squad exchanged worried glances.

We had a fairly good idea of what Sholtz was blathering on about. Holstering his blaster, Mills reached inside a cart and withdrew his beamer. He gently patted the weapon with admiration as he activated it and discarded the spent rad-pack to clatter to the gravel. The weapon thrummed to life at his meticulous touch and hummed as it primed.

Clicking in a fresh rad-pack, Mills turned to Pax.

"I only have three left, SL," he said in a somber tone.

My eyes roved over his suit to see he'd spoken the truth. Only three yellow skull and bones cartridges remained on his breastplate. Fifteen seconds of the deadly plasma was all we had left to get us through. I wasn't sure that was enough.

Pax gave his head a slow shake and shrugged. "What we have on us, is all we've got, Mills."

With that, he pushed the lab-coats behind us, and signaled us to approach the bend. I did so with my stomach in a knot. The daylight flickered and danced on the other side in an unnatural fashion. Leaning out, we peered at the exit. Curses followed as we sucked air through their teeth. For the first time ever, I was disappointed not to see a pack of droolers—ten, twenty, whatever.

They would have been preferable to what was before us, and I now understood why the daylight flickered. Moths swarmed around the entrance like pissed-off hornets. Their flapping wings sounded like a thunderstorm, competing with their piercing chatter. I lowered the volume on my incoming audio and accessed my display, pulling up a target overlay onto my visor—they were everywhere. Contacts overlapped contacts, blurring into a blob.

"Do something!" Sholtz whined, from the safety of our backs. "Get us out of here!"

The swarm grew thicker by the second, cutting off most of the natural light, and the tunnel around us dimmed. I cleared my display and glanced at Pax. Being the SL, and still breathing, he was the only one in contact with the brass, or any of the other squads who weren't in our immediate vicinity. Since my HUD wasn't popping up any friendlies, and the tunnel around us had stopped quaking, I figured everyone else had evaced.

"Soo... about that safe zone?" I reminded Pax of my previous question. "Can our dropship pick us up here?"

Fifteen seconds of Mills' rad-laced fire wasn't going to get us through this, and popping the moths off with blasters, one by one, was unrealistic.

Pax sighed. "Already checked on that option. The ship can't chance landing in a mess like this. The Fleet agreed on a closer pick-up but only after we're clear of that swarm."

We all nodded somberly in understanding, allowing the heavy silence to linger. Out here, light-years away from Earth and ship-yards, re-supplying wasn't an easy task. It was much easier to cram human bodies onto a transport to replenish the ranks than procure a shipment of dropships or other vessels. Since delivering them one at a time was simply uneconomical, each re-supply carrier required an entire battle group for an escort. That, unfortunately, meant each precious ship was worth more than our lives.

Mills broke the grim silence as he took another peek around the bend.

"They looked pissed, man." He tightened his grip on the beamer.

Pax sucked in a strained breath, loudly. "Yeah, about that..."

All our heads whipped around to look at him, even the lab-coats.

"...they're probably going to be irked even more in a minute."

"And... why's that, SL?" Mills ventured, cautiously, without a hint of his usual bravado. We all knew we weren't armed near well enough to get past what awaited us at the entrance.

"Well..." Pax paused.

"Yeeees..."

"We're ordered to blow this tunnel after we're out, just like the other squads had done."

Sholtz gasped, pushing past everyone to Pax. "That's absurd!"

He waved a hand at the flickering entrance. "Those moths will target us immediately! Why can't the Legion buffoons just bomb this place from orbit after we're safe? I know for a fact, *Venator* has the capability!"

Pax shook his head. "Then you should also know something like that would need the Senate's approval, and we don't have it. So now get your ass back with your group and let us handle this."

Sholtz hesitated at the mention of the Senate, but unfortunately, he wasn't done. "What about all of this priceless technology? It's imperative we get this back to our labs!"

Pax snorted. "Oh, it'll make it back, don't you worry, but we don't need to be alive for that, do we, doc? We push the carts out of the tunnel, and they'll be retrieved after the moths get bored and disperse."

Sholtz flustered. "That... that is—"

"A fact," Pax helped him out, tone hardening as he made a show of glancing over his blaster. "Now, unless you have something useful to add, I suggest you don't make me repeat myself."

I allowed myself a tight smirk. Sure, Pax was only blowing smoke, but I understood the logic. Sholtz's utter disregard for our authority was going to get someone killed.

Sholtz did the smart thing after that. Throwing up his hands with a sardonic scoff, he retreated, muttering insults under his breath.

"Whelp! Let's do this, then!" Mills piped, as always ready to follow Pax down to hell if need be. "What's the plan, SL?"

Pax turned towards the group of lab-coats. "Mills, Somner, and Lee, take them and their junk. Mills, you're on point, but *don't* use your beamer unless you have to. I'm sure the moths are ready to be rid of us, so maybe they'll let you pass unhindered. Once you're clear, Adlar and I will blow this place then catch up."

"What?" Beeson let out a low whisper, looking up at me. "But—"

"It'll be fine." I gave her hand a reassuring squeeze.

During the discussion, she'd nudged up to me and looped a nervous hand around my arm. Seeing as I didn't mind one bit, I'd let her. "Don't worry. Just stay safe, yourself, okay?"

Gently prying her off, I encouraged her towards the rest of her colleagues, right as my private chat clicked on.

"Look at you, still working your magic. I promise I won't tell whomever you were with just a few hours ago." Mills paused. "On second thought, I *will*. That'd be *way* more fun."

"Eat shit, Mills." I flipped him off, out of Pax's line of sight.

Cackling, Mills returned my one finger salute, then reverted his attention to herding the lab-coats. He corralled them into a tight group and ushered them to the exit where they sprang out of the cave and vanished into the swarm of moths. Screams and curses rang out, but I didn't see the beamer's blinding flash. That was a good sign.

Pax and I watched the churning swarm for another minute, giving the others time, then holstered our blasters. I yanked two frags off my waist and activated them. Pax's were already in his hands.

"You clear, Mills?" Pax asked, when the screams quelled to disgruntled grumbles, Sholtz's being the most prevalent.

"Yeah. We're in the trees. We're clear. They didn't stick to us, they just bounced off our suits like freaking torpedoes. It was weird, man. They're squishy as—"

"Great!" Pax interrupted. "But don't stop. Keep running. I have a feeling they're going to change their minds about letting us go once we pop these frags. The dropship's position is marked in your HUD. Make sure the scientists and that junk gets on. That's an order."

For a second, the comms were dead silent and not a locators budged. Mills was hesitating at the idea of leaving Pax.

Pax didn't miss a beat, nor did he acknowledge Mills' concern. "Somner, take point."

"Copy," Somner replied.

A kick in the guts for Mills, but right away the locators moved. Taking in a steadying breath, I slowly closed my palms around the frags as my eyes cast to the daunting entrance. My heart accelerated. There were so many of them. The swarm blocked out the natural light, and I could hardly see any green past their bodies. I glanced at Pax, wanting nothing more than to protest, but knew that was pointless.

"Ready?" he asked.

I shook my head *no*.

"That's the spirit, fireball." Pax chuckled, nudging me with an elbow. "Just follow my lead."

Cracking his frags, he hurled them behind us, then bolted fcr the entrance and vanished into the soup of moths. Blood pounding in my ears, I mimicked.

CHAPTER
FORTY-SIX

My world plunged into darkness as I was engulfed by insects. I tried to push through the swarm as everyone else had, but it wasn't happening. Bug upon bug hindered my progress.

Right then, the ground rumbled and heaved as the frags went off at our backs, and an overpowering *boom* shook the air. Next thing I knew, I was flying, then tumbling ass over tea kettle in a shower of dirt. At least, it earned me a momentary reprieve from the moths as they scattered off me, screeching. I was sure I'd pancaked more than a few of them as I rolled. The bugs didn't appreciate that very much.

No sooner had Pax and I scrambled back to our feet, then they regrouped. This time with a vengeance. Torpedoing into me, they stuck, their legs slashing and scrabbling at my armor in a maddened frenzy. I was cocooned by their pissed, writhing bodies.

They weighed me down with sheer numbers.

My legs buckled, and I fell to my knees. My display clicked between clear and night vision attempting to compensate for the situation, but that did little good as my head was engulfed. My stomach twisted, and I could no longer contain myself. I howled and hissed, attempting to escape the living nightmare. With the pressure relaying tech, it felt as if the bugs were on my bare skin, wriggling over my arms, my legs, my back, and every inch of me.

All coherent thoughts left me then. I thrashed, rolled, and

hollered, trying to knock them off. I envisioned being entombed. Through the haze of my all-consuming hysteria, there came another sound. Pax bellowed over comms. His voice jerked me back. I remembered where I was, what'd happened, and that I wasn't alone. I couldn't see Pax—I couldn't see anything—but I knew he was near.

"Adlar! Adlar! Shut the fuck up, man. And stop thrashing. Crawl towards me."

I slammed my mouth shut, my heart hammering in my throat. Perhaps Pax had a plan, and I really, really wanted to live. Taken out by a mass of insects wasn't at all how I imagined myself going out.

Even though every muscle screamed at me to keep flopping, I stopped and concentrated on Pax's locator. Grunting, I rolled onto my stomach and wormed towards him, hand over hand. I could feel the bugs popping under my breastplate as I dragged myself over the dirt.

Somehow, Pax and I managed to push through the vermin, and I felt his hand slide onto my helmet. He gave my head a reassuring shake.

"I'm going to shoot you, okay?" he said in a voice that I considered much too calm for this hell of a situation. "Be ready to shoot back. You have a fresh battery, right?"

"Ugh, ugh." I tried to nod but wasn't sure if my head actually moved under the mound of bugs.

I shuddered. Now that I was no longer fighting the moths, my body jerked as they scrabbled over me unhindered and slashed and sawed with their thorny legs. It was a repulsive sensation. If I didn't know any better, it felt as if they were trying to cut into the armor.

Giving my helmet a parting pat, Pax's hand vanished. I had no idea how he managed to get to his weapon through the mass of creatures, much less raise it and aim, but somehow, he did, and multiple power-bolts nailed my head.

Thankfully, the moths' bodies had formed a decent enough barrier against the electrical shock, and I was only mildly stunned. As the electricity dissipated over my suit, the moths shrieked as if lit on fire, then released and scattered in a giant swarm. Sunlight stabbed my eyes, and I was able to see again. I didn't waste a precious second. Grabbing my blaster, I fired at the churning mob consuming Pax.

"Run!" Pax shouted the moment he was free and staggering to his feet.

Together, we sprinted for the trees. I looked over my suit as I ran, shocked by the damage. Glinting silver scratches crisscrossed my armor. Some closely resembled gashes. The evidence spoke for itself. The moths *had* been trying to saw through, trying to get to the squishy center that was me.

Those fucks! I fumed. If we'd been engulfed even a moment longer, I was sure they would have succeeded. I didn't want to imagine what would have came next.

Turned out, the assholes had no intention of letting us off the hook. Not twenty steps into the trees a billowing thundercloud of bodies caught up to us. I was sure we were about to be swarmed again, but to my complete surprise, we weren't. Instead, the moths opted for a pummeling approach. One after the next, they torpedoed into us then darted away. They screamed bloody murder all the while. I couldn't understand their language, but I suspected they weren't paying us compliments.

Neither Pax nor I bothered with our weapons. There were just too many of them. The only thing we could do was keep going, stumbling and correcting our course as they played pinball with our bodies.

"Why did you stop?" Pax shouted all of sudden, his words prompting me to check my HUD.

Sure enough, for whatever reason, the squad had halted. Squinting at my display some more, I recognized why. They'd dispersed into a familiar pattern. Each trooper had grabbed a scientist or two and slightly separated from the others, motionless and likely hiding.

"I think it's a formation, but we haven't spotted the bot yet." Somner reported. "We'll flush 'em out."

It surprised me that it wasn't Mills who'd spoken, always the first to jump at Pax's every whim, but then I remembered Somner had been put in charge. Now that had me smile. Mills was probably pouting like a baby.

Extending a hand to slow me down, Pax began to reply, but a walrus of a moth slammed into his visor, almost taking him off his feet. The fat bastard looked big enough to have eaten a few of his buddies. The bug vanished almost as fast as he'd appeared, but I blinked in his wake. I could've sworn he'd been wearing something silver and shiny.

"Pax, I think that bug was—"

A hand grabbed me and pulled me down into a thicket of plants. I hit the dirt next to Pax, my thoughts chased away. What did it matter what the bug was wearing. I was sure by now everyone had arrived at the conclusion they weren't simple, primitive insects.

The bugs tried to get us even then, but they weren't fans of slamming into the foliage—or our boots. We kicked at a few and swatted at the rest. With angry chitters, they retreated to blanket the sky above us instead.

"Negative, Somner," Pax finally had a chance to speak. "Every squad has evaced. It's just us out here. Don't draw attention to yourself, or else everything in this jungle is going to converge on you."

He glanced up at the furious locals above us. "You should see the shit following us now."

The bugs were still chittering and whining, cursing us out if I had to guess.

"What?" Sholtz jumped into the conversation, uninvited as per usual. "They just left us here, in this jungle? With just you? This is unacceptable! Demand the officers send us reinforcements this instant!"

Pax snorted a laugh. "I'll get right on that, Sholtz. Now please, shut up."

"This is—" Sholtz abruptly silenced as Pax overrode his comm.

I was grateful for that. I was sure Pax was doing some serious thinking right about now and Sholtz's croaking wasn't helping. We all knew that the only help we were getting was the evac ship, and that was only if we were able to reach it.

I chuckled as a realization came to me. Even though the lab-coats were suited in high-tech Gold Squad gear, the Tribune had made sure to limit their comms, not allowing Sholtz a direct connection to *Venator*. I could just imagine the Tribune thinking ahead on how to avoid a headache for himself by leaving the paltry task of dealing with Sholtz to Pax and the rest of us.

"Here's the plan," Pax said. "I talked to Fleet Ops, and the drop-ship has been approved to do a hot pickup. It's heading our way now, so all we have to do is hold out until it arrives. Somner, get everyone back together and hide."

"Copy," Somner replied as someone in the background whistled in awe.

I joined in the surprise. A hot pickup wasn't so easy to swing. The Fleet had mandated regulations on the use of their vessels when working with the Legions, and they weren't easily swayed to go above and beyond. Unlike ships, troops were a dime a dozen as far as they were concerned, and if some happened not to make it to a desig-nated safe zone, or one was overrun before they could board, well, that was that. The troops were on their own until a new location was set up and another ship deployed.

I thanked my lucky stars right then that Pax was with us, suspecting that Centurion Paxton had pulled every string at his disposal. I doubted any of the Space Fleet brass or even the Tribune himself cared enough about the scientists or our squad to authorize such an action. Pax hadn't been kidding back in the tunnel. The alien trinkets would be retrieved weather we lived or died.

Pax and I settled onto our backs to wait and stared up at the riled cloud of insects above us. I received a surprise. Instead of an impene-trable mishmash of bodies, traces of purple sky were now visible through the moths. It appeared a good chunk of them had dispersed.

"Maybe we can make a run for it?" I asked, yearning to rejoin the squad.

Pax nodded in approval. Jumping up, we hightailed for the squad. I threw intermittent glances over my shoulder as we went, at the twenty or so moths hot on our tail. None of them swarmed, but unfortunately, nor did they leave.

CHAPTER
FORTY-SEVEN

B efore we could make it to the rest of the group, we were attacked, but not in the way we were expecting. The droolers didn't strategically ambush us in their usual fashion, but instead, five of the beasts barreled out of the brush as one and charged us like unhinged bears. We shot them down mercilessly before they got anywhere close.

As we weaved around the carcasses, Pax fired a shot into each head just to be sure. The heads jostled, sprayed blood, then oozed.

"I think we just put down the group that was after you, Somner," he said on squad chat. "And they definitely weren't under a bot's control. I doubt there are any bots left."

Mills let out a whistle, then chimed in. "Not gonna complain about that. I'll take hordes of idiot slaves over a bot any day. But since we don't have to worry about getting our asses zapped, what'd you think about making a run for it, SL? After you and the newb rejoin us."

My jaw clenched as did my fists.

Pax shook his head as we jogged. "Not yet, Mills. The ship still has a good fifteen minutes before it gets to you. Just keep cover for now. Even if there's no bots, we can't fight off all the droolers if they swarm us, even if they're disorganized."

Unfortunately, the decision of whether to wait the fifteen minutes or push forward was taken out of Pax's hands almost immediately after he'd spoken. Perhaps it was the roars and wails of the droolers we'd just slaughtered which gave us away, or perhaps they'd tracked us long before that, but whatever the cause, they attacked.

"Crap!" Somner suddenly shouted as everyone's locators came alive with movement.

"They're rushing us!" Somner reported, barely audible over the lab-coats' terrified shrieks. "There's a whole hoard of them!"

Picking up our pace, Pax and I soon jumped into the midst of the fight, doing our best to keep the riled beast away from the scientists. By the looks of the charred plants and bubbling carcasses littering the area, Mills had used up his rad-packs prior to our arrival. That left us with blasters, blades, and whatever frags we had left.

The droolers lacked all coordination. Swinging their massive fists at anything in their path, they charged recklessly right into our line of fire, only to crumple in wailing heaps. Yet, there was a lot of them, and they kept coming. As soon as our torrent of energy put down one rushing wave, another roiled forth to replace the fallen. We shot down as many as we could, but they closed in, trampling over their dead. We switched to blades as they overran us, and still, more came.

It was as if all the droolers that had been abandoned to aimlessly wander the juggle without a masters, had suddenly become reinvigorated. I didn't have a visual of the lab-coats, but I hoped that at least some of them had the brains and balls to pull out their blasters and activate blades.

"We have to move!" Pax shouted over the din of screams, roars, and dying yawls. "A dropship won't be able to land in this."

With a roar of my own, I skewered a lunging drooler clean through his bottom jaw, my blade piercing his skull with no resistance. I kicked him in the gut as I yanked my blade out, splitting his head in half and sending the carcass sprawling. Pax was right. With no bots to blast us, we were holding our own against the unarmed creatures whose biological flesh stood no chance against our weaponry, but a ship wasn't pulling off a landing amidst the mess. The droolers would overrun it in seconds.

"We gotta go!" Pax repeated. "Break off and let's try to lose them."

Mills rounded on the huddle of cowering lab-coats, shouting.

"You know your suits have blades and those things in your holsters are guns, you know that, right?"

He rushed towards them, swinging one of his blades in a wide arc to spill a drooler's guts to the grass. The lab-coats shrieked as a spray of black showered over them.

Mills' complaint went unheard. Only one scientist grabbed his weapon, and he wasn't going to be much help. His arms trembled as he tried to aim, and the blaster jerked about as if with a mind of its own. If anything, he was more likely to shoot one of us instead of the droolers.

Our opportunity to run came when the droolers lapsed into momentary confusion. A charging group tripped over the piled corpses littering the ground, and their high-pitched howls and yelps of surprise completely threw off the rest of them. As one, they went placid and milled about in a stupor. They truly weren't the brightest of species. If they weren't attacking in an uncontrolled, animalistic rage, they easily became disoriented. We took full advantage of the reprieve and set off into the trees.

Suddenly Sholtz let out a guttural shriek. My first thought was that he'd been skewered by one of his own colleagues or snagged by a drooler, but unfortunately, that wasn't it.

"Where's the cart with the capsule base?" he raved, sliding to a stop and spinning in frantic circles. "Where is it? Which one of you idiots left it behind!"

Before anyone could utter a word, he broke away from the group and bounded to retrace our steps.

"Sholtz!" Somner called as the man sprinted past him.

He tried to grab him but missed. Spinning about, Somner gave chase, shouting for the man to return.

I was in the lead with Mills, but broke off, figuring Somner was going to need backup dealing with that sleazebag of a lab-coat.

"We got 'em!" I said, weaving around maimed droolers and the few remaining trees that were still standing. There was no need for everyone to be thrown off track. Somner and I were capable of wrestling Sholtz back if we had to.

I almost caught up, when a sight had my heart jerk and my blood run cold. There, in the distance, was the hover-cart, hovering dutifully right where it was left, above the blood-drenched grass and scattered carcasses. Sholtz was galloping towards it, fixated on the cart and nothing else. He was completely oblivious to the goliath of a cyclops that had popped out from the brush to charge him. The thing was *huge*. Twice the size of the regular droolers if not more—a horse to a donkey.

"Sholtz! Somner!" I shouted. "On your four!"

I was about to veer towards the monster myself but missed a drooler coming at me. Before I knew it, I was tackled to the ground with huge paws grappling at my helmet with murderous intent. I made quick work of the beast. Thrusting both blades into his torso, I tore him in half. Yowling, he still managed to grab my head, but his pull was weak, and I chunked the heap of spilling entrails off me with one quick twist.

I jumped back to my feet, just in time to see that Sholtz had ignored my warning. He skidded to a stop next to the hover-cart, oblivious to the monster charging his flank.

"Sholtz!" Somner screamed, rushing toward him. "On your right, Sholtz!"

Heart pounding, I sprinted with everything I had, even though I knew I wasn't going to make it in time. The drooler was going to reach him first. Sholtz let out an ear-piercing shriek when he finally noticed the barreling monster. Before the thing could close its massive arms around Sholtz, Somner tackled him out of the way. The man screamed as he cartwheeled over the hover-cart and flew to the ground.

In a flash, the goliath's trunk-like arms bear-hugged Somner instead. The air trembled as it roared with feral rage, spinning him in wild circles. Somner flailed, bicycled the air, and thrashed, attempting to break free, but he was a rag doll in the behemoth's grip. His blades were activated, but of no help. His arms were pinned to his sides and neither blade was able to reach the drooler.

My legs felt like rubber, and it was hard to breathe, but I kept running. I ripped out my blaster, taking aim. Even if I shot Somner, the electrical shock would get the drooler to release, but it was too late.

Snaps and pops of splintering metal reached my ears along with a scream no living being should ever make. Somner was being crushed like a tin can. A sound comparable to an explosion of crackling fireworks came next as Somner's armor caved. His screams lessened, changing to drowning gurgles.

"Sh-sho-oot," he stammered, coughing and choking as his body crumpled along with his armor.

A numb ringing filled my head as I slid to a stop, and my breath caught in my chest. My finger was on the trigger, but I couldn't squeeze. Somner's damaged armor wouldn't protect him.

He wheezed, sucking in wet inhales and choking.

"Sh-sh-shoo—" he rasped.

My eyes stung and my vision blurred. I bit down on my lip with enough force to draw blood as my mind reeled. Everything was happening in a blink of an eye.

I pulled the trigger.

One more stifled rasp escaped Somner, and his locator flashed to red. The goliath drooler didn't heed my shot, nor the chunk my blaster-bolt had taken out of its arm, and continued to roar and thrash, squeezing Somner's now lifeless body. With all my might I tackled the howling monster and hacked, my hot blue blades fueled by rage. I didn't stop until there was nothing left but fist-sized chunks of meat and heaps of gore.

At last, when my blades were throwing up sparks and dirt, I stopped and pitched to my knees.

"What happened? Somner flashed to KIA," Pax demanded.

I didn't answer. Wiping blood off my visor, I fixated on Somner's battered body in a trance. Had *I* just killed him?

"Somner," I whispered, reaching for him with a trembling hand.

I pulled on his arm gently only to jerk away as it slid off his torso to drop lifelessly onto the grass. Shards of plastic and metal jutted out of his chest at odd angles with blue and red fluids bubbling around them. They formed a small pool on his shattered breastplate before slowly trickling to the ground. The lump in my throat grew. I knew Leeges died. They died by the hundreds. Only hours ago, I'd flopped a dead corpse into a hover-cart. Yet, my chest squeezed like never before and tears stung my eyes.

"What the hell is going on, Adlar?" Pax bellowed in my comms with burning rage. "What happened to Somner, and why aren't you moving? Answer me for fuck's sake!"

I didn't. I remained quiet, my mind numb. I blankly stared at the corpse, then at the swaying green and purplish leaves around me. In any other circumstance this place would be considered a paradise, a prime location for mansions and high-end vacations. Was that why this campaign was originally designated green? Did the Senate want Atlas for themselves, after all fighting concluded?

I could've sat there forever, berating myself—how could I have been that stupid, that slow, and why had I shot? If I would have gotten Somner to the med-bays, just maybe…

A human screech pierced through my morbid thoughts as someone slammed into me from behind and violently shook me by my shoulders.

"There's another one, there's another one!" Sholtz screamed, pointing at the shaking trees, from which a drooler charged.

Shoving Sholtz out of the way, I jumped to my feet with lethal intent. My eyes were wide and my mind brimming with murderous urges. On my first drop, I told myself I would never freeze again and I intended to keep the promise. Lunging, I met the attacking beast without hesitation, savoring the vibrations that ran up my arm as my blades carried out their deadly task. With three slashes, the drooler collapsed at my feet.

"Adlar?" Pax prompted, yet again. "I don't know what's going on with you, but the dropship is almost here. Get your shit together. Now!"

I didn't acknowledge him. Both pissed and numb of mind, I grabbed Sholtz by his arm and swiftly brought my blade to be right under his chin. He gasped, trying weasel out of my grasp.

"Wha-what are you—" he stammered incoherently.

I held on, watching him squirm. I wanted nothing more than to thrust my blade through his head. After all, who would know? No one was around but us.

"SL Paxton! SL Paxton!" he shrieked.

With a sigh of disgust, I shoved him away from me and deactivated my blade. To the song of his outraged protest, I then began trying to wrestle the alien base out of the hover-cart. I needed a way to carry Somner to the dropship.

"Paxton! Paxton!" Sholtz wasn't letting up. "Your buffoon is attempting to discard the alien technology!"

"What the hell is going on, Adlar? Answer me! I swear, I'm about to send you straight to the arena—"

"Somner!" I interrupted. "He's dead, Pax. He's dead. I need the hover-cart to bring him back."

Dread squeezed my chest with the weight of an anvil. Shoving it down, I continued to struggle with the heavy base. The thing wasn't budging. I momentarily considered simply chunking Somner on top of it but judging by how low to the ground the cart already was, that wasn't going to work. I finally decided it would be easier to deactivate it, then tip it and roll out the stand.

Right as I reached for the repulsors, Pax spoke, his voice heavy but stern. "No, Adlar. Bring back the tech… that's the mission."

I froze in disbelief.

"W-what?" I stammered, speechless.

Somner didn't deserve that. To be left to rot or devoured by some alien pigs. He deserved a proper send off. One befitting his life of service and worthy of a Leege—amongst his squadmates. If not for him, then for the rest of us. That was more important than this junk.

Pax let out a heavy exhale. "You heard me, Adlar. Get Sholtz and the tech to us, now. The dropship isn't going to wait. You have five minutes."

Gritting my teeth, I considered telling Pax to go fuck himself. Who was he trying to impress? His dad? The Tribune? He could send me to the arena ten times over if he wanted. Any damage done to my body would be repaired.

Sholtz slammed into me with a grunt and yanked the cart out of my grasp. "You heard him! Now get us out of here!"

My fists balled as I contemplated knocking him out, but instead, I answered Pax. My body would heal after a flogging or bolts, but Pax still had the power to boot me from Gold Squad.

"Copy," I confirmed in a low growl, not bothering to hide my disdain for the ridiculous order I had no choice but to follow.

The thought of slinging Somner over my shoulders crossed my

mind next, but then, how would I fight? Pax was right, the ship wasn't going to wait. It was going to load up whoever was there when it landed and take off before it was overrun by the droolers or the locals. The wretched moths were still hovering in our vicinity, watching our every move from the safety of the trees.

"You heard your squad leader! We need to go!" Sholtz bleated, wisely keeping his distance from me.

Ignoring him, I dropped to my knees, next to Somner. Various liquids and blood still seeped out of the broken suit, and a puddle of sickening colors had formed around the body. It slowly soaked into the alien soil. I reached to remove his helmet to say goodbye but froze when my gaze landed on the red splattered over the inside of his visor. I reconsidered, not wanting to see the dead, pain-filled eyes that surely awaited. That wasn't how I wanted to remember him. I pulled back and gripped his forearm instead, squeezing it tight with numb fingers.

"To victory," I whispered.

CHAPTER
FORTY-EIGHT

I was stark mad as I guided Sholtz to rejoin the squad, but I kept placing one foot in front of the other. He deserved a blade through the chest and to be left to the will of the droolers and pigs just like Somner had been, but I knew Pax wouldn't give me a pass. Not even if I delivered the tech.

"Hurry up, Adlar," Pax shouted in my comm. "Our ride's here."

I roughly shoved Sholtz forward, urging him to pick up his pace. The man grunted as my hand slammed into his back but didn't spout insults in his usual manner. I guess he was smart enough to deduce his survival depended on my mood, and my mood was a sour one. The droolers weren't giving up and charged us at random. None were organized, and I cut them down with ease.

We rejoined the squad just in time to see our ride cast a shadow over the canopy. The repulsors screamed like wild banshees as they incinerated the treetops in plumes of fire and smoke. Rocking and swaying, the ship sluggishly descended through the whirling clouds of charred debris. I watched it with a nervous eye. It was too slow, and too loud. The jungle around us echoed with the ship's piercing wail as trunks scorched and sizzled, then crumpled to ash.

The dropships weren't designed for stealth, nor could they simply crash down through the thick foliage without taking damage.

With a resounding "*thud*," the ship finally settled onto the ground, expelling a cloud of charred brush and smoke from underneath.

The tension among us was palpable. Without a word, we drew apart to encircle the scientists and their precious tech. Between the din of the crackling fire that whipped about on the burning trees and the whining engines, our audio picked up another sound. The jungle rumbled.

A wave of droolers erupted from the brush as one. The ground trembled as they charged through the swirling smoke, their combined roar louder than an accelerating ship trying to break atmo. It no longer mattered that they didn't have a master. After the ruckus that had just ensued, every drooler within a mile's radius now had a mission—to kill us.

Blasters whined and bolts pierced through the plumes of smoke as we cut them down. We used our blades for any that got close. However, not all attacked our squad. Some charged the ship and threw themselves at the hull like enraged apes. They shrieked and howled in pain as the pulsing repulsors set them ablaze like kindling.

In a matter of minutes, the area became pure chaos, and carcasses piled up amidst the burning jungle.

"Get on!" came a shout over everyone's comms.

Not recognizing the voice, I spun to the dropship and the lowering ramp. An SF man burst out of the gap, blaster rifle shouldered, and hopped to the ground. He immediately began blasting the beasts that were pounding on the hull. The blaster rifle plowed them down like a weed eater, blowing chunks out of their bodies in sprays of gore.

"Go, go, go!" the man bellowed, discarding the spent charge pack and reloading.

"Adlar. Load the lab-coats!" Pax roared. "We'll hold them off!"

Wiping blood off my visor, I pulled Beeson toward the ship, shouting for the rest of them to follow. I didn't wait for the ramp to finish lowering. Snatching Beeson up by her waist, I flung her inside the cabin. Turning, I reached for another lab-coat only to see two howling droolers hook their palms on the ramp's ledge and scrabble to climb inside.

With terrified screams, the rest of the lab-coats scattered. Swiping my blade, I cut down the dangling droolers with ease, sending them to the ground. That was when the ramp finished opening and slammed on top of them in a spray of innards. I hardly noticed. Spinning about, I chased after the scattering lab-coats as they ducked behind trees, ferns, and any other semblance of cover.

"What the fuck are you doing? Get on the ship!" I shouted after them, my boots crunching over the spent charge packs that littered the area.

The blaster rifle to my right thundered as the SF man mowed down the beasts attacking the vessel.

Yet the droolers kept coming.

The squad had dispersed to surround the ship, but there weren't enough of us to protect a 360-degree perimeter, and now the lab-coats were gone.

"Get on the ship! Now!" I continued shouting, hoping they'd heed my order.

I didn't want to venture too far from the ramp and leave it unprotected.

Thankfully, the scientists listened, and I didn't have to. They turned and ran back, but two were too slow. Screams rang out as droolers tackled them, face down, into the dirt.

Seeing this, the SF man veered, but I stopped him with an extended arm and sprinted towards them instead.

"Everyone, on the ship, now!" Pax boomed.

My muscles burned as I sped up, not wanting to abandon the lab-coats. Sholtz might've been a piece of shit, but the rest weren't bad. They didn't deserve to be left here to be torn apart. Roaring and feeling like a monster myself, I lunged at the two droolers on top of the squirming scientists.

I skewered the first one through his skull, savoring the now too familiar vibration of my blade as it made a kill, then lunged at the second. Neither had seen me coming. My blade sliced through its back just as the lab-coat's helmet wrenched off with a shriek of metal. With his helmet off, the man's screams no longer rang over comms, but I saw his mouth gape wide in shock as a gush of cyclopean blood showered over him.

The elderly man sputtered and shrieked, frantically pawing his gloved hands over his bloodied face and hair as if trying to clean off a swarm of spiders. I kicked the corpse off of him and yanked him to his feet.

"Run!" My voice thundered over external speakers as I shoved him towards the ship.

The man staggered back, windmilling his arms for balance, and gaped at me with bulging eyeballs.

"Go!" I roared again when he didn't budge, jabbing a finger at the ship.

Managing to compose himself, he ran. I followed with long strides, throwing a glance over my shoulder to make sure we were still in the clear. Right as my head spun forward again, something struck my helmet and almost knocked me over.

Stumbling, I glanced around to see what had hit me.

"Not this shit again." I angrily swiped at a pesky month.

I'd all but forgotten about them. Apparently, they hadn't forgotten about us. A churning cloud swarmed out of the jungle and headed for the ship, veering around the droolers like water around stones in a raging river. Not one touched a single beast.

"What the—" the SF man by the dropship shouted in utter surprise.

He momentarily paused blasting, eyes growing wide at the sight of the approaching swarm.

"Adlar! Get down!" Pax's voice.

A jolt of adrenaline hit me at his warning, and instinct took over. I dropped like a log, twisting to land on my back, blades up and ready. I figured a drooler was about to nab me. Yet no beast pounced on top of me, nor was I the intended target. The carpet of moths that had been on my flank, streaked over me, skirting around my blades with mechanical precision. They swarmed the helmetless lab-coat instead.

The man screamed and flailed as they enveloped him mercilessly —both his suit and his exposed head.

Furious, I jumped to my feet and tackled the scientist to the ground, sending the moths erupting off of him in a flock of bodies. The ones that hadn't been squished between our suits, that is. Those bastards were now pancaked flat.

Turning to run, I pulled the man along with me by his arm, only for his mass to jerked me back like an anchor. I rounded on him, ready to rip him a new one, only to startle. Not all the moths had scattered. His armored body was free of the bugs, but not his exposed head. It was engulfed.

Pissed as hell, I dropped next to him and grabbed onto a mushy torso. If I had to pop them like ticks, one by one, so be it. I was determined to save the guy. To my surprise, there was no resistance as I pulled up on the bug. It released with ease—but so did the man's skin. A piece of bloodied flesh hung off the moth's black spiky legs like tattered fabric. Screaming, I jumped back and flung the thing to the ground. It wriggled and chittered as it hungrily devoured the skin.

My chest tightened and my breaths turned ragged. Slowly, I dared to look at the scientist, terrified of what I was about to see. The man no longer had a face, and his head was a giant puffed up balloon, drenched in blood. The creatures had injected him with something, and his skin bubbled and oozed like a haunted swamp. His outstretched hands feebly clawed at the grass as his body twitched intermittently in a deathly silence.

One by one the moths fell off his head and neck, feasting on his flesh, but as soon as one released, another beelined to take its spot. The rest seemed to have forgotten about the dropship. They hovered a few feet away, patiently awaiting their turn for the buffet. Every ravenous eyeball was trained on the scientist.

"Oh, hell no! Hell no!" a shout broke me out of my trance.

I turned to see the SF man toss his blaster rifle to Pax then vanish into the cabin.

"Leave him, Adlar," Pax ordered. "Let's go!"

The squad was still shooting and cutting down droolers, but more flooded forth with an unnerving determination. The corpses littering the field slowed them down some as they tripped and lost their focus, but still, none appeared interested in giving up. I wasn't sure they were capable of comprehending the concept. It seemed they were acting on instinct, like sharks drawn to blood, and they were, after all, bred for the sole purpose of killing.

I wanted to scream again and never stop when I hazarded one last glance at the man being devoured alive. The moths were peeling him like a fruit at ghastly speed, and I could see the white of his skull. But

I clamped my mouth shut and ran towards the dropship. Every fiber of my being burned with the desire to get off this hellish planet. To fly away and never return.

Once inside, I threw myself into an empty seat between two other suited figures, and before I was even secured, or the ramp closed, the ship lurched up, buckling and teetering as hollow *thumps* shuddered the hull. The droolers were throwing themselves onto the vessel, trying to bring it down. Their frenzied roars muffled as the ramp slammed shut and sealed us inside.

Engines screeching, the ship spun like an out-of-control air-car, fighting to gain altitude, plowing through both droolers and trees with jostling bumps. We all rattled about in our restraints in a nervous silence. We didn't know if we were going to make it or be pulled down by the weight.

With an ear-piercing electrical whine and a sharp fishtail, the vessel finally broke free and my stomach plunged toward the deck as it shot into the air.

When the ship finally leveled, my lungs were on fire. I exhaled loudly then gasped for air. I hadn't realized I'd held my breath the entire time. When I no longer felt like I was drowning, I let my head fall back against the bulkhead, and melted into the ship's thrum as it pulsed through my armor. It wasn't exactly the crashing of the ocean, but I still found some semblance of comfort in the rhythmic vibrations. We'd survived. At least most of us.

The sensation of a gentle hand gliding over my leg grabbed my attention. Even though startled, I didn't jump. I had no energy left to do so. Every inch of me ached. My calves, my thighs, my back, my entire body screamed with pain. Seeing as my neck was too sore to turn my head, I used my HUD to check who it was.

The designator flashed *Beeson*. No surprise there. I doubted any of the men would be cozying up to me to give my thigh a gentle caress. I sighed with mild irritation, but didn't remove her hand. At the moment, I welcomed her feminine touch, even if it was through a layer of armor.

"Thank you," she whispered. "For getting us out of there."

She squeezed my leg. "And I'm sorry about your friend, your teammate."

I placed my hand over hers and gently played with her fingers. "I'm glad you're okay. That *most* of you are okay."

That was all I had the energy to say but I wholeheartedly meant the words. What those moths had done to that lab-coat I wouldn't wish upon my worst enemy. My hand remained over Beeson's in a trance, too tired to move, until the pilot announced we were clear of Atlas' atmosphere and free to remove our helmets. I eagerly yanked mine off and savored the cool air that enveloped my sweaty head. I immediately wiped at my eyes and cheeks.

Mills, who was sitting across from me, opened his dumbass mouth as if to comment, but paused when he met my gaze. It conveyed this wasn't the time to mess with me, but also dared him to give it a shot. Nothing would've made me happier. Lashing out sounded damn good right about now and Mills was the perfect target.

With a bashful expression, Mills reconsidered hassling me and turned away, ruffling his matted hair. I watched the man with laser focus, trying to fathom how he could be so nonchalant. How all of them seemed so relaxed, so dismissive. Sure, Pax and Lee looked glum and weren't chatting in their usual manner, but no one mentioned Somner. Pax hadn't even asked me what happened.

Leaning forward, I was about to break the heavy silence, but Mills leaned forward just as quick, shaking his head *no*. Now I'm no genius, far from it, in fact, but I inferred his expression with ease. For whatever reason, he didn't want me to bring up Somner. His reaction baffled me, but I shut my mouth and straightened back into my seat. Who was I to question how they dealt with loss? They'd just lost three men on the last campaign.

Besides, perhaps I should be grateful for the lack of questions. I had no idea what to say. Ultimately, Somner had died by my hand. I'd fired the final blow. If I could have gotten him back to the ship, back to the med-bays, then just maybe—

My eyes dropped to the deck as the nagging ghosts of 'should have' swarmed about me. I should've been faster, I should've been more aware, I should've been… something.

I closed my eyes, trying to clear my head.

"Uhm… Jake," a soft female voice snapped my eyes open.

Wandering how she knew my first name, I turned to Beeson and blinked at her as if seeing the girl for the first time. Which in actuality, I was. Up until now, all I'd seen of her was her armor.

My mindset towards her softened as I took her in, her tousled wavy black hair and cheeks smeared with dried tears and mascara. It was obvious she'd taken the time to put on make-up this morning, prior to going to the 'office,' but now it was all a mess. The mascara lines ran all the way down to her jaw line. Then, I met her gaze, and the last shreds of rage and irritation about how annoying and useless the lab-coats were, vanished. Large fear-filled brown eyes stared back at me. She looked like a child's VR companion. The ones made to look cute, with the oversized eyes that were seemingly always on the verge of a meltdown.

"Are you okay?" she asked with genuine concern. "If you ever need to talk, back on the ship…"

She squeezed my hand. "I'm here." Her eyes were full of hope.

I smiled a genuine smile back at her, no longer feeling even a hint of annoyance, then turned to Mills. He was now on the edge of his seat with anticipation, eyes darting between Beeson and me as if watching some five-star reality vid.

Reaching over, I gave Mill's knee a friendly slap. "Have you met my friend, Mills, here? You should hear the stories he has about some of the aliens he's encountered and all the people he'd saved."

Mills straightened, eyes growing wide, then fidgeted like an excited puppy about to be taken for a walk. I swear, if he had a tail, it would be wagging hard enough to knock things over.

Beeson extended a hand towards Mills and gave him a shy smile. "I'm Carla."

Mills hesitated and looked to me as if asking for approval or instructions on how to proceed. I shrugged. Taking my shrug as a thumbs up, he slowly extended his hand towards Carla's, for some reason moving as if he was reaching for a venomous spider. I resisted an eye roll. Go figure. The man had no problem facing beasts twice his size but put a pretty girl in front of him and he turned into a confused pile of goop.

"I'm Thomas," he said, slowly, wrapping his large paw around Carla's dainty palm.

He gave her an awkward shake.

I stifled a chuckle. "Thomas? Really?" I just couldn't help myself. Thomas sounded like an accountant or some kind of appliance salesman, not an asshole killer like him. Not a day ago he'd wanted to see me slaughtered for shits and giggles.

He glowered at me. "Shut up, newb."

Biting my lip, I resisted teasing him further and leaned back into my seat. I figured I'd let them chat in peace. I had other things on my mind. A tornado of thoughts. How was I going to apologize to Taylor? What was I going to do about Fallon? And what the hell just happened on Atlas?

Why had the moths only attacked us humans? If they were carnivores, and had the ability to kill so quickly and with such ease, why hadn't they been feasting on the droolers all along? Were they afraid of the bots? Or was it something uglier? The moths were more advanced than we'd given them credit for, I was sure of it, but were they perhaps also landlords? Were they okay with the Synths being on their planet? After all, it wasn't the Synths who'd wreaked havoc. They weren't the ones who'd irradiated the land and instigated firefight after firefight, littering Atlas with corpses. Nor was it the Synths who'd blasted a mile-long section of their mountains.

Maybe the moths were in league with the Synths? But then why wasn't the campaign marked red? Why hadn't *Venator* been cleared to blast the alien's base from orbit after the shield collapsed, or a couple of Destroyers ordered to assist? I didn't think it was because the Senate had suddenly grown a heart. So, what were they really interested in on Atlas?

CHAPTER
FORTY-NINE

We were the last dropship to return to *Venator*. That didn't surprise me, but it was still strange to see the hangar mostly devoid of troops and rushing medics. In their place were bustling SF personnel and the rumbling and clangs of equipment. The SF personnel hadn't wasted any time. Panels had been removed from the dropships and diagnostics projected into the air. Some were head deep inside disassembled engine pods and thruster jets with their tools clanging away as they worked.

A drawn-out sigh escaped me when I made it down the ramp and took my first step onto *Venator's* deck. The ship thrummed under my boots as if it were the breaths of a living being, and a pungent odor of electrical burn, charred metal, and rotting entrails stung my nostrils. I welcomed the sensation and the familiar stench. Both symbolized that the drop was over. That I'd made it and was still alive, albeit with more grizzly images to add to my bank of nightmares.

Composing myself, I turned to study our dropship. It was an eyesore amongst the rest. The droolers' claws and teeth had done a number so had the massive fists. The hull was gashed and dented.

I didn't get to study the battle-worn vessel for too long, however, as a herd of gasping SF mechanics crowded me out of the way. They joined the disembarked pilot in walking around the ship, mumbling and shaking their heads in awe and disapproval. They threw the squad venomous glances as if this was somehow our fault. As if we'd asked to be rushed by hordes of murderous beasts.

"You know how hard it is to requisition a new dropship?" a burly mechanic grumbled as he shouldered past me with a hover-cart full of tools.

I frowned in reply. Everyone seemed more concerned with the ship than with the fact we'd survived, or didn't. *Priorities, right?*

Scowling, I turned away from the gaggle of irked mechanics, my attention grabbed by a stampede of approaching boots. A massive wave of brass had spilled out of an elevator and was rushing towards us as if we were celebrities arriving for a show. Tribune Gallus was in the lead, closely flanked by Prefect Neero, Centurion Paxton, and their aides.

Tailing a few steps behind them were a slew of Primus and Prefect ranks, accompanied by SF personnel. Some were chatting while others tapped away at their tablets, but all marched towards us with purpose.

Sholtz didn't wait for the posse to reach us and made a mad dash for the Tribune. I clenched my fists tight as the desire to skewer him rekindled. Somner had given his life for him, and he'd yet to show a shred of gratitude. It wasn't right.

"Tribune… Tribune!" He rushed towards the group.

Completely ignoring him, the Tribune sidestepped the frazzled lab-coat without as much as a glance and continued towards the squad. Sholtz twisted about, sputtering. He then, quickly and smartly, took note of the fact he was now in Prefect Neeros' direct path and jumped out of the way. Unlike Gallus, Neero took the time to notice him. He made it a point to do so, glaring at him, teeth bared, as he marched by.

Sholtz opened and closed his mouth like he was gasping for air but smartly reconsidered speaking. Huffing in frustration, he corralled the lab-coats and the hover-carts, then ushered them to the elevators.

Beeson gave Mills a flirtatious wave over her shoulder as she was pulled away. Mills eagerly reciprocated, practically drooling at the mouth. I hadn't caught anything they'd chatted about on the ship, but I don't think they'd stopped talking the whole way back. Apparently, both had found *something* in each other. That, or both were lonely and bored.

I barked a laugh at Mills' blush, making a show of it.

"Shut up." He glowered, thumping a meaty fist into my arm.

I opted not to retaliate, too busy thinking of Taylor and my forthcoming apology. I figured if I had time, I'd go down to the ship's store to see what they had. With my new Gold Squad rank, I had plenty of credits.

Tribune Gallus hardly glanced at what was in the hover-carts when the lab-coats rushed past him, instead directing all his attention to us. We were quite a sight, dried sweat matting our hair, and our suits grimed. The Tribune frowned as he scanned our forms and opened his mouth to speak, but before he could, Neero jumped around him to stand under Pax's nose.

He jabbed a finger into Pax's chest. "You seem to be missing a *man, SL.*"

The unexpected hostility radiating from the Prefect sent a shiver down my spine. I wondered if I should speak up and take responsibility for Somners' death. After all, Pax hadn't even been there. I opened my mouth, but Centurion Paxton's arrival diverted my attention. Taking two large steps, he moved to stand at the Tribune's shoulder. Paxton seemed troubled, whereas the Tribune had closed his mouth, seemingly not bothered by Neero's rage-filled interruption.

"Somner didn't make it, sir," Pax said, averting his gaze.

"I can see that!" Neero practically shouted into his face as his own grew a shade of red.

He appeared livid and barely managing to keep his cool in the presence of the other officers and aids. Throwing them a measured glance, he opted to turn his sunshine of a personality on us.

"Are you miscreants on leave?" he boomed in our direction.

I frowned, confused. A strange vibe hung in the air and prickled my skin. Something told me this wasn't just about Somner.

"Fall in," Pax ordered, his face expressionless.

I cursed the spindly wicker-stick of a man, but complied and fell in next to Mills and Lee as we all formed a neat line a few steps behind Pax. All I wanted was a hot shower, a meal, and sleep, but instead here I was doing a dog and pony show for the brass.

Turning back to Neero, Pax stood at attention, chin held high.

"I completed the mission, *sir*. We kept the scientists alive and retrieved the alien tech," he said, lowering his head to meet the shorter man's eyes squarely.

A scowl crossed my face as I took in the strange interaction. I had no idea why Neero had a stick up his ass more than usual, but what was Pax's problem?

"Yes, yes. You did complete *a* mission, didn't you, trooper?" Neero hissed, matching Pax's gaze.

The two had a stare off then, right in the bay, to the backdrop of everyone else's confusion. Faces scrunched, shoulders shrugged, and the chatter died. No one knew what to make of this, but neither Pax or Neero cared.

Long seconds passed, until at last, a loud cough grabbed everyone's eyeballs. Tribune Gallus had deemed it was time to get involved. With one determined step, he edged Neero out of the way.

"SL Paxton, you will be debriefed about trooper Somner at a later time. As for now, have your men clean up, then report to the officers' briefing room. We have important matters to discuss with your squad. Have them there in an hour."

A wave of disappointment crashed over me at his words, and I almost flung my head back and groaned. This was a kick to the 'nads. How was I supposed to apologize to Taylor or confront Fallon in a mere hour? I was sure the complex we'd demolished was a mere hickup in whatever ill-intentioned agenda the Synths harbored for us. They likely had more labs on other planets. I had to get Fallon to see reason. That her vile action, whatever the cause, weren't only treasonous, but were possibly dooming the entirety of the human race.

Pax nodded to the Tribune. "Yes, sir. One hour, sir."

He then dismissed us, relaying the Tribune's orders as if we hadn't just heard the wretched words ourselves. As he did, for a reason I couldn't fathom, his eyes lingered on me for an extra breath.

"*One* hour, Adlar," he reiterated.

Resisting a scowl, I gave him a terse nod. With that, the Tribune signaled his entourage of suck-ups to follow him out of the bay. Centurion Paxton was the only one that remained. Rushing to Pax, he proceeded to berate him in a harsh whisper. Apparently not agreeing with his dad's probably sage advice, Pax remained chest squared, eyes full of defiance. With a heavy shake of the head, Centurion Paxton dropped the matter and hustled after the rest of the brass.

As Pax and Lee departed, I sidled up to Mills, eager for answers.

"What was that about?" I asked.

Mills gave our vicinity a quick scan, making sure the coast was clear, then leaned towards me in a conspiratorial fashion. I resisted pulling away as the stench of sweat hit my nose.

"Sholtz wasn't supposed to come back, man," he said. "Neero ordered Pax to kill him, but Pax didn't."

My brows scrunched in thought. That certainly would explain the hostility. No one spoke to Neero the way Sholtz had, not even the Tribune, and Neero wasn't someone who let things go.

I eyed Mills questioningly. "How'd *you* know?"

Mills shrugged, picking at some dried gunk of who knew what on his helmet's visor.

"Just sounds like Neero, that's all. Plus, Pax specifically ordered me *not* to kill Sholtz on our ride down, so there's *that*. I guess he figured Neero might get to me when he saw Pax wasn't going to carry out his orders. Hell, I wish Neero would've come to me. I'd end Sholtz in a heartbeat."

I nodded. "But you wouldn't if Pax ordered you not to, no matter what Neero wanted, right?"

He shuffled like a scolded child and threw a bashful glance at the deck. "Probably not."

Pulling himself together, he slammed his helmet into my gut. "But this isn't good, man. Neero isn't Boyer. He's much more dangerous. Like *really* dangerous. And there's only so much Pax's dad can do to protect him, even after," he paused, hesitating. "The reason Pax despises aliens—" Mills trailed off.

"After what?" I pressed, wanting him to finish.

My curiosity strings were practicality making me tap dance. Whatever this was had started prior to my arrival to *Venator* and I wanted to know. I suspected it would also explain Pax's odd behavior in those tunnels.

Mills studied the deck for a moment and appeared to be doing some serious thinking. Unfortunately, the cards didn't fall in my favor. When he at last looked up at me, his hardened expression wasn't promising.

"Don't worry about it, man," he said, waving his helmet about dismissively. "Pax blames himself for something that wasn't his fault, but it's not my story to tell, and not my place to talk about his family. So, if you want to know more, ask him. Now we better go clean up before our next grand appearance with the brass. Let's see who we can piss off next, right?"

He barked a laugh, punching his helmet into my breastplate. "But watch Pax's back, all right?"

I resisted the urge to whack his helmet away and nodded a silent confirmation. Mills appeared resigned in his decision, his loyalty to Pax outweighing his desire to run his mouth, which I could tell he had been raring to do.

Satisfied, Mills lumbered towards the equipment room. I sighed, watching him go. As curious as I was, it was probably best not to know the details. I didn't want to get sucked into yet another mess. At least now I understood why Centurion Paxton looked like he'd stepped on a live electrical wire when he'd watched the square off.

Sucking in a deep breath, I decided to stop worrying about everyone else's problems and concentrate on my own. I wasn't going to have enough time to confront Fallon before the meeting, but just maybe, if my shower was quick, I'd be able to apologize to Taylor. I really wanted to do it in person, but at this point a text might have to do.

With that hopeful thought, I rushed to the equipment room, being careful to remove my newest addition to my contraband collection of alien souvenirs before returning my gear. I tossed everything at the attendants in a whirlwind of dropped helmets, blasters, and armor then rushed to my room and phone. There was no time to waste when it came to apologizing and fabricating excuses, and the sooner I got to it, the better.

CHAPTER
FIFTY

A pang of both worry and excitement shot through me when I saw who was sitting in my room, swiveling in circles on my chair and chatting with Ness. It was Taylor. I'd spent the entire jog through the halls crafting the perfect apology text, one with just the right amounts of groveling and excuses, to now come face to face with the girl. I was going to have to think on my feet.

Ness jumped out of her chair the moment I burst through the door and rushed to greet me.

"Jake!" She flung her arms around me in a tight hug. "Damn, I'm glad you made it. I wasn't ready for a new roommate just yet."

I chuckled in reply. "That makes two of us."

She broke away with a goofy smirk on her face as her eyes darted between Taylor and me in a knowing fashion. "I think I'll give you guys a minute."

Wiggling her eyebrows, she headed for the door, throwing me a concealed thumbs up as she passed. Then, just like that, she was gone, leaving me alone with Taylor, and possibly a couple of dust balls. I wasn't much for cleaning.

Forcing a partial smirk, I faced the girl. Taylor looked as beautiful as ever, perfect face, perfect hair, and those eyes. I took a long whiff of her pleasant flowery perfume that now filled the room and fidgeted, not sure what to expect. Most of the Legion women had a hint of feral to them. Did that extend to the Fleet ladies? Was Taylor going to yell at me, throw something?

She did neither, and nothing could've prepared me for what *did* happen. Jumping up from her chair, she charged me. My breath caught as I braced for a slap or a power kick to the gut. Neither came. Instead, Taylor flung her arms around me and pulled me into a hug.

As confused as I was, I lit up with a grin and eagerly reciprocated.

"Hi to you too," I said.

What must've been a full minute passed as we held each other, then Taylor finally spoke. "I'm so glad you're okay. When your squad didn't return with the rest of your unit, I was so worried. They don't tell us anything, you know. I had to ask practically every Fleet soldier and returning trooper for information. Then, finally, I heard a dropship was being spun up for a hot pick up of a squad on some special assignment, and I just knew it was you."

Pushing away, she held me at arm's length, looking up at me with wide eyes full of concern. My heart tripped, both at her genuine gaze and her close proximity. I wanted nothing more than to kiss her right then, but I opted to just smile.

"So, you were worried, huh?" I gently moved some hair off her cheek.

"Oh, shut up."

"So… you're not mad then?"

"Mad? Mad about what?" She blinked at me in confusion.

"Uh…" My eyes darted away from her. I wasn't sure if it was the best play to remind her of my infraction, in case she'd miraculously forgotten. "You know, about me not…uh…" I trailed off with a shrug.

To my surprise, she giggled. "Not showing up?"

"Oh… yeah, that." I grimaced. Was this the part where she chewed me out?

I was again slammed with a surprise. Before my wriggling tongue had the chance to dig my grave any deeper, Taylor jumped in with a '*mehh*,' and a shrug. "I know how it is around here. Especially when it comes to last-minute ops. They probably dragged you off in a heartbeat for whatever it was. I'm just relieved you're okay."

My eyebrows shot up as I did a double take of her fire face. The girl really didn't appear mad one bit. In fact, the twinkle in her eyes suggested she was anything but.

I jumped to accept my good fortune. It was about time some of it came my way.

"Yeah! That's exactly what happened. I was on my way to meet you, after the med-bay," I held up my arm for emphasis, "but my SL grabbed me. It all happened so fast. He didn't even let me go back to my room to tell Ness."

I glanced down at my watch and scowled. "You know what? I need to find a techie to hack this. Then we can talk whenever."

The suggestion earned me another hug.

"That sounds like a plan, Jake," Taylor said, her cheek on my chest and hair tickling my chin. Her voice was now almost a whisper, sultry and inviting.

I couldn't contain myself any longer. With my heart jackhammering at my ribs, I was about to kiss her when, instead, she made the initial move. Before I knew it, my face was cupped in her hands and her soft lips pressed tightly against mine. She gently caressed the back of my neck, giving me goosebumps.

Stunned, I forgot to breathe. *This was really happening.* Ever since I'd laid eyes on her, I wanted nothing more than to have her in my arms—and my bed—and here she was, kissing me with a passion that promised more.

I quickly snapped out of my dumbstruck stupor and embraced the moment. Gently, I encouraged Taylor toward my bunk. Chairs rolled and clattered as we shambled through the room, but we didn't care.

We had a great time then, tangled up in my sheets, and each and every one of my worries vanished.

Afterward, I could've lay there forever, but just as our lips again touched and our hands began to move with minds of their own, a loud buzz cut through our heavy breaths. My wrist vibrated as my watch vied for attention. Groaning, I reluctantly slid my wrist under my nose.

The message was from Pax, telling me in a not-so-polite way that I'd better be on time. My head slumped onto the pillow in defeat. All chances of round two were thwarted.

"You have to go, don't you?" Taylor asked, running her hand over my back in a playful manner. Her tone was still breathy and entrapping, making me shiver.

I huffed in frustration, breaking away.

"Unfortunately," I grumbled, clambering over her and rushing down the ladder. Certain thoughts were again bouncing in my one-track mind, and I was only a touch away from losing to temptation.

"I was actually worried about you, too," I said as I rushed about the room, collecting my dirty clothes off the floor and wriggling into a fresh uniform.

A shower would have to wait, but I had plenty of body spray and Ness' hair goop for the cowlicks on my head. That would have to do, even if it meant smelling like a bowl of fruit.

Taylor climbed down and narrowed her eyes at me. "Why were you worried about *me*?"

"You know, about your reassignment to a Legion deck and all."

"Oh," she mumbled, pulling on her shirt. I frowned as I watched. I liked it better when the clothes were going the other way.

"It's not so bad." She shrugged. "I actually like working on the trooper decks. It's a lot more grotesque seeing all those injured men, the blood, and the broken suit parts with *no* men—"

She grimaced. "But at least now, there are actual ships to fix. Back on the transports, between pick-ups, it was pre-flight check after pre-flight check, and maybe a maintenance flight here and there. I like piloting sure, even with the constant danger, but I also like working with my hands—"

With a stupid grin on my face, I nodded absently to her words. I wasn't actually catching anything she was saying, but that didn't matter. I was enjoying the company. However, when my eyes cast to my watch, my grin changed to a frown.

With a sense of urgency, I snagged Taylor into my arms as she finished putting on her jacket and pulled her close.

"I have to go," I whispered, trapping her gaze. "You have no idea how much I don't want to, but I have to. That pig Neero won't hesitate to send me to the arena if I'm late—"

I paused, remembering my antics during the training exercise and my tardiness to the briefing with the scientists.

"*And* my SL would probably do the same at this point," I finished.

I wasn't sure what Pax's limit was when it came to my shenanigans, but I was sure his patience wasn't bottomless.

"But hopefully, I'll see you soon, if that's okay?"

"Of course," Taylor answered me with a flirty smile. "Now that this campaign is over, we'll have plenty of time. Who knows how far our next destination is. And it's not like I'm going on any more transport runs."

Stretching tall on her tippy toes, she cupped my cheek and whispered into my ear. "I swiped my info to your phone, so just text me when you're available, and I'll meet you anywhere, anytime."

"Ha!" I chuckled nervously as my skin again prickled with goosebumps from the tickle of her warm breath. "I'll have to take you up on that."

I then chewed my lip with some serious force as I watched her rear glide out of my door. It was a fine sight to behold. I again contemplated blowing off the infernal meeting. After all, it wasn't anything I hadn't done back on Earth plenty.

Yet this wasn't Earth, and the fear of being flogged or shot had my balls cinch tight, and I jumped to business. Rummaging through my uniform, I extracted my new alien souvenir and chucked it into my drawer with the other one.

I went to close the drawer but paused. My stomach flipped.

There, towards the very front, was the frameless picture of my parents, their smiling faces beaming up at me. The e-paper shined with color in sharp contrast to the bare silver drawer and the cold metal room around me. My mind was instantaneously transported back to my old life. A life that was now hundreds, maybe thousands of light-years away. I wondered what my folks and Reeds were up to these days. It had to be near November back home and the holidays coming up.

I had no way of finding out. Deep-link transmissions cost some serious credits and nothing even a Gold Squad trooper was able to afford. Nor were we allowed access. On deployment, we were secluded. Just like the warriors of the distant past, battling it out with oceans between them and their native land.

With a heavy sigh and one last glance at the picture, I flipped it over. Perhaps, just like those long-gone warriors, I'd one day make it back across the expanse to the tiny blue and green ball that I called home, but for now, my life was here. With my squad and the Legion.

CHAPTER
FIFTY-ONE

I made it to the briefing room with a minute to spare, and yet, I was greeted by sour faces. It looked like all the lucky participants of this get-together were already here, some seated around a large oval table, littered with coffee cups and tablets, and others gathered around the room's periphery.

Tribune Gallus stood at the head of the table and paused scrolling over his tablet to give me a slow once-over, then frown. I had the urge to squirm but controlled myself.

Sucking in a strained breath, I decided to ignore everyone's scrutinizing stares and searched the collection of heads for my squad. The room was packed. Not only were all of second cohort's Centurions present, but also a slew of other Centurions, Primus, and Prefects I didn't recognize, probably from first and third. Besides them, there was also a good bit of SF personnel, aides, and even a cluster of lab-coats and other civilians at one end of the room. I frowned noting the amount of gold on most everyone's collars. This gathering was *way* above my paygrade.

So, what were a group of grunts doing here?

Alarmed, my head snapped to the battle-screen in the middle of the table. Was the brass about to send us on yet another off-book mission? I had a sinking sense that was a common honor bestowed on the first squad. To my relief the screen was off—a good bet this wasn't a tactical briefing.

Feeling somewhat better, though not any less confused, I pinpointed my squad and ambled towards them. They were bunched together at the opposite end of the room from the Tribune. A spot I also found more preferable than anywhere near him. If this wasn't about some half-cocked mission, had we done something wrong?

A forced cough sounded at my back as I shouldered past bodies, attempting not to elbow heads or stomp on unsuspecting feet. The room swept into silence.

"Now that the man of the hour has seen fit to join us, we can begin," intoned the Tribune's stern voice.

I cringed. The hint of disapproval was unmistakable. Worse yet, I'd been the last to walk into the room. Now, I was no genius, but was his snippy remark meant for me? Concerned, I shot a puzzled glance over my shoulder. My concern intensified. Leery expressions followed me as I went, so did shady whispers.

I shrugged it off, bunching up next to Mills. Ornery looks and scowls, I was growing used to. Ultimately, it didn't matter why we were here. What mattered was what came after. I thought of Taylor, silently willing this shindig to conclude. The Tribune was already rambling.

"I'm going to make this quick since I don't have much time and won't be taking questions. If someone does have any pressing concerns, address them to your Primus' or Prefects."

My smile broadened at his blissful words. The probability of round two with Taylor was growing brighter by the second.

Heads nodded as the Tribune continued. "As we speak, Legate Maldovi is on her way to *Venator*."

The room erupted in a unified explosion of muffled chatter. Heads spun, eyes widened, and gasps sounded. Gallus scowled and clenched his jaw, having no choice but to halt his speech due to the outburst.

Perplexed by the sudden uproar, I broke my front-and-center gaze to scan the crowd in search of an explanation.

Regrettably, the only thing I spotted was that even my cohort's Centurions weren't thrilled with the announcement. Fallon's cheeks flushed, while Paxton rubbed his forehead as if fighting off a headache. Even Braves was possibly upset, but he was a hard man to read. He wasn't wearing his customary grin, but that might've been because he was missing his usual accessory. A cold cup of untouched coffee was all that sat before his dissatisfied expression.

"Shut up!" shouted a voice as a loud bang pierced the chatter.

Prefect Neero had moved to stand at the Tribune's elbow and had slammed his tablet on the table.

"What's going on here?" he barked, scanning over the room.

All chatter ceased instantly as people sank lower in their seats and heads snapped to the front. Satisfied, Neero gave Gallus a nod of approval. He'd been the only Prefect who'd dared to cut into the Tribune's presentation, but the much larger and higher-ranked man didn't seem to mind.

"As I was saying," the Tribune proceeded, now in a room as silent as a tomb. "The Legate is on her way to *Venator* and should arrive within the next hour or two. She is coming to congratulate us on our record time victory on Atlas, and it goes without saying she is expecting everyone and everything to be up to Legion Invictus' standards. I know the campaign hasn't fully concluded yet, and some of our ninth and tenth squads are still busy cleaning up on the surface, but I expect every department to be in top shape. You may have your SF adjuncts requisition extra personnel from the Fleet if you need them."

He gave a curt nod to the row of SF brass lining a wall, then continued. "We will welcome the Legate with a small group, followed by a short debriefing. People who are on the welcoming committee know who you are, and you are to be present when the Legate's transport arrives."

With a wide sweep of his hand, the Tribune then gestured towards our squad. "I would also like to recognize second cohort's first squad for the instrumental part they played in taking down that initial section of the enemy's shielding, paving the way for our sweeping victory. The Legate is eager to offer her congratulations personally."

At that, my eyes popped wide, but at the same time I exhaled with relief. This wasn't about us fudging one thing or another. On the contrary, we were being recognized.

A chorus of weak applause was our ovation. Some forced half-hearted smiles, but most didn't bother hiding their disdain. No one seemed excited for their boss to come and poke around.

"That will be all," the Tribune said after the pathetic show of gratitude for all our troubles extinguished. "Everyone except for second cohort's field officers and trooper Adlar is dismissed."

Now that had me startle. Had I misheard? Unfortunately, judging by my squad's pointed stares, I deemed I hadn't. I quickly mulled over my situation. Why had I been singled out? I came up blank.

Turning to me, Pax was the first to break the squad's befuddled silence.

"Well, good luck," he said, clapping a cheerful hand on to my shoulder, only for his expression to darken.

He squeezed my shoulder, hard. "Behave. Don't do anything I'll be hearing about later. Got it?"

His stern words sounded as both an order and a threat. Wincing under his forceful grip, I nodded in confirmation. I couldn't fault the man's concern. I wouldn't trust myself amidst the brass.

Mills, on the other hand, was all mirth.

"Way to go, Adlar!" He elbowed me in the ribs as his other hand rubbed his chest dramatically. "I hope they stick you with some blaster bolts. That'll get it nice and smooth for all those ladies you're seeing."

Too stupefied to retaliate, all I could do was watch as Pax ushered everyone to the blissful exit. I stared, feeling left behind. What could the Tribune possibly want from me? If anything, shouldn't Pax be the one staying behind on behalf of our squad?

As the room cleared, my mouth grew dry with nerves. Was Mills just being an ass or was I about to be punished for who knew what. I truly couldn't recall getting into any recent mischief and had even arrived to this gathering on time, but I knew none of that meant squat. The Senate ran the Legions like the armies of the distant past and more often than not, *actual* guilt hardly mattered.

Soon, second cohort's Centurions, the Prefect, the Tribune, and I were the only people in the room. The space seemed to expand tenfold with just the six of us. I fidgeted, remaining at parade rest, too unnerved to relax a single muscle.

The Tribune pulled out a chair, gesturing for me to sit. "At ease, trooper."

Hesitating, I eyed the chair with suspicion as if it were lined with spikes—a trap, right smack dab amidst the clustered officers. When everyone else began shifting out of their seats to move closer to the head of the table and the Tribune, I had no choice but to follow suit.

As my butt hit the cushion and I dared to relax, the strongest sensation of déjà vu overcame me. I felt as if I'd been in this room before, but I couldn't place it. Had I attended another officer briefing, I wondered? Surely, I would have remembered that. Then again, I had been beat six ways to Sunday over the last few days, so I was bound to forget a thing or two.

When everyone was seated, the Tribune strutted to the head of the table and dropped into his chair. It was a throne-like affair, high-backed and much plushier than the rest.

"Here's the deal," he said with a heavy exhale. "The Legate insists on meeting Adlar *personally* when she lands."

He accentuated the word "personally" as his gaze drifted over each of the brass in turn. Now that everyone was gone, he'd dropped his stern demeanor and appeared relaxed.

Unlike him, no one else seemed at ease. Everyone jerked back in shock as if they'd just been slapped across the face, then turned to glare at me. I side-eyed them in return with unease. My eyes were squinched and my face twisted. I was as confused as them.

With forces spread wide throughout the endless expanse of the galaxy, a Legion's Legate was more like a myth or a legend, or perhaps a god as far as the underlings were concerned, and certainly not someone a lowly grunt ever met in person. But now... she was coming here. The mythical tyrant of so much gossip, none of which was good, and most exaggerated to the point of her having horns or inhuman powers, wanted to meet *me*.

I slumped lower into my seat in defeat and rubbed my forehead, feeling the initial twinges of a headache. Centurion Paxton cleared his throat, breaking the tense silence.

He leaned forward on the table, towards the Tribune. "Sir, do you think that's a good idea? Perhaps we should reconsider allowing this to happen."

His eyes scanned over the rest of the brass for support.

"Yes, yes," Neero chirped with a jolt.

He'd been staring at the Tribune in disbelief as if he'd just seen a ghost. "There's a reason ground troops don't interact with the Legate, not personally at least."

He threw me a venomous look. "*We* are going to be accountable for his behavior, and I don't foresee that going well. There's a very high chance the night will end with him embarrassing us, or worse—"

Neero trailed off as a hushed tension fell over the room.

Fallon snorted loudly, prompting everyone to look at her. "It's not a *chance* that he will embarrass us, Prefect, it's a *guarantee*. You can be sure of that. By the end of the night, all of us are going to be in the brig, waiting to pay for his antics."

My eyes narrowed at the woman. She was one to talk about *antics*. Seeing as that was neither here nor there in the present company, I turned away from her and debated voicing a rebuttal to their unfounded accusations. I wasn't a diplomat by any stretch of the imagination, but I hadn't been raised in a barn. I had *some* manners.

I glanced at the Tribune, wondering if he shared in their concern. He didn't. The man was at ease, casually slumped onto an armrest, placating everyone's protests with slow nods and a bemused expression. It was obvious he didn't give two shits about their opinions.

"Nonsense." He waved a dismissive hand. "We should all view this visit in a positive light, in fact. The Legate has the ear of the Imperator and in turn, the Senate. With them comes resources and possible funds. More sought-after campaigns, perhaps. No more losing half a cohort to the marshes of Isyria, or whole squadrons of ships to the hellish atmosphere of the Gadus System"

"*Yes,*" he drew out the word, nodding to no one in particular. "We need to take full advantage of the Legate's visit."

As he spoke, an actual smile inched onto his face, growing with each word, and his gaze drew unfocused, almost dreamlike. I arched an eyebrow at that. Sure, I'd seen the man throw out plenty of orders and send people hopping, but it had always been with an air of disconnect. If anything, Neero usually held the reins while the Tribune did the backseat driving. Until someone needed a kick in the ass, that is. His word was, after all, law for every Legionnaire on the ship, and most of the Fleet pukes to boot.

But not now. Gallus seemed on the edge of his seat with anticipation and plain disinterested in what anyone else had to say.

I caught Neero roll his eyes out of Gallus' line of view. "Sir, the issue is not the Legate's visit, we welcome her of course, it's the trooper. We all know the Legate's *temperament*—"

He hesitated, gauging the Tribune.

"How quick to *judgment* she can be," he finished carefully, shooting the Centurions a telling glance.

Catching on, they jumped to agree. Well, Centurion Paxton and Fallon did. Braves seemed as unconcerned as the Tribune and almost just as amused. The room again filled with disgruntled voices and disparaging comments heaped my way. I thought I heard someone suggest Pax go in my stead.

Straightening in my chair, I raised my hand in an attempt to garner their attention. They were flinging insults about like chimps with shit, and I wanted to put their minds at ease. Personally, I had no desire to die in some ghoulish marshes or burn up in a dropship like a piece of meat. If the Tribune needed me to do some schmoozing, I was game. Surely, I'd manage a handshake and some pleasantries. How difficult could it be?

A moment later, I slumped back, dejected. No one was paying me any mind. They all chattered over each other as if I wasn't even in the room. Apparently, they hadn't caught on to the fact none of us were being given a choice in this matter, and Neero plowed on like a broken record. Ignoring his fervent blathering, intermixed with insults, I went back to daydreaming. I bit down on my lip as blissful images of Taylor's naked body swirled through my mind.

A slap landed on the back of my head causing me to jump straight up in surprise. Lost in my promiscuous fantasy, I'd forgotten where I was. Everyone was glowering at me, and judging by Centurion Paxton's scowl, I must've zoned out for longer than I'd intended. The wide smirk I had on my face also probably wasn't helping matters.

The Tribune chuckled, then glanced between Neeros' and Fallon's disgruntled faces with pure amusement dancing in his eyes. "Now that you've got the bitching out of your system, everyone's dismissed."

With that, he rose, and headed for the door, but right before exiting, he turned to Centurion Paxton. "I trust the trooper will be on time, Centurion?"

All heads spun to Paxton as if he were just called out for his child's bad behavior.

"With bells on, sir. With bells on."

CHAPTER
FIFTY-TWO

Having provided Centurion Paxton his instructions, Gallus strutted out of the room, the rest of the brass hot on his heels. I impatiently waited for Neero to disappear, not wanting to dart past him without being dismissed. Seeing as he was keen on solving issues using his trigger finger, ending up alone with him in the hall probably wasn't the smartest of ideas.

A full minute after he stormed out, I made my move. Exploding out of my chair, I rushed for the exit, thoughts of Taylor swirling through my mind. Us, up in my bunk, my hands—

"Where do you think you're going, Adlar?" Paxton's booming bark cut through my daydream.

I ground to a halt as a vice tightened around my chest. Slowly, I turned to face the Centurion. He was reclined in his chair, studying me with a stony expression. I'd been completely oblivious to the fact he hadn't followed everyone out.

"Uh… my room, sir?" I offered hesitantly, though I suspected he didn't *actually* care about my plans.

He frowned, eyeing me as if I'd lost my mind.

"That's… hilarious, trooper, and I appreciate the comedic touch, but you heard the Tribune. I'm responsible for delivering you to the Legate, front and center, and that's exactly what I'm going to do. So, until then, you're with me."

Rising, he proceeded to the door and crooked a finger at me to follow.

My head almost flung back in a fit, but I caught myself and straightened. As disheartening as this was, I had to remember I was before a Centurion.

My irked expression earned me a reprimanding narrow-eyed glance as we walked into the hall, but Paxton didn't comment further. I was thankful for that. Still, my shoulders slumped in defeat. I wasn't getting out of this.

Soon, I found myself on the now too familiar officer's deck.

"Were you aware, trooper," the Centurion spoke as we walked shoulder to shoulder. "That the Senate has a contract with Earth-gov, allowing them to commandeer a certain number of troops from Earth's militaries? For protecting Earth as much as Mars."

I gave it a moment's thought.

"No, sir," I answered, furtively. I wasn't sure if the question had been rhetorical.

From the corner of my eye, I saw him nod. "I suspected as such. That fine print is inconspicuous as could be. As intended."

Halting, he spun to face me. "I looked up your records, you know. Minor reprimands of insubordination, nothing glaring, but neither had you placed much effort to excel."

"Uh...." My eyes dropped to my boots as I controlled my urge to fidget. The man had me pinned.

"And now you're here, an add-on from the Force. One of those *fortunates* sent to bolster our ranks on Earth's behalf."

I shrugged in reply. When he didn't continue speaking, I looked up to see the Centurion studying me closely. Perhaps waiting for me to gripe and protest the injustice of it all, plead to be sent back to Earth. I did no such thing. I didn't see the point. No amount of sniveling was going to get me out of the decade of service I had left, and I was smart enough to know no officer wanted to hear such frivolous drivel.

With a hint of a smile on his face, as rigid as it was, the Centurion finally turned away from me and continued down the hall. I tailed cautiously, certain I had just underwent some kind of an evaluation. I dared to think that I passed.

To my surprise, when we reached his office, he walked right by the closed door and led us a few rooms further. Without bothering to knock, he strode in.

"Ahh, if it isn't the famous fireball, himself!" exclaimed the cheerful voice of Centurion Braves. "So the Legate wants to meet you personally, ehh? How'd you feel about that?"

My brows momentarily shot up as I wondered how Braves knew about my joke of a nickname. Word sure got around here fast. Not feeling particularly chatty, I answered Braves' jubilant greeting with a half-hearted shrug. Having to spend the next hour or so being babysat just had a way of putting one in a sour mood.

Braves waggled a finger in my direction, grinning, and sipping on his drink. "You might want to work on that enthusiasm a bit more, mate. Not sure that attitude will fly with Legate Maldovi. She likes to make an entrance so to speak, and you don't want to end up the prime highlight of the evening, believe me."

I again shrugged with indifference as my eyes scanned his office. It wasn't anything like Paxton's or Fallon's, missing all the opulence. A plain metal desk, almost bare, stood across from the door with two chairs before it. To the left was a practical couch. It didn't appear overly comfortable. On the other side of the room was a cabinet, also almost devoid of contents, with only a few holo-cubes, a transmitter, and a couple of empty glasses scattered on one shelf.

Unlike in the other Centurion's offices, no lavish paintings adorned the walls. The only decoration was a small flickering e-picture of a lone, scraggly tree sticking out amidst a sandy desert at sunset. The pixels on the vacant image wavered, but just barely, to where if you stared long enough, you'd think there was a slight breeze nudging what stubby leaves remained.

I shuddered and looked away. Something about the room gave me a chill. Something about it was even more odd than the carnage Fallon had splashed over her walls—something hollow.

As Paxton marched purposefully towards the couch and the decanter on the glass table to pour himself a drink, my gaze wandered longingly to the open door behind me. I wanted nothing more than to leave. I jerked back at what greeted me in a corner previously out of my view.

"What the—" My eyes widened as I walked closer to the anomaly.

An honest-to-god stuffed *kangaroo* loomed before me complete with fur, ears, legs, and everything else I figured a kangaroo had. It was here on the ship, in *space*. On a troop carrier, of all places. I couldn't help but stroke a finger over its soft fur, wondering how Braves had whisked something like this onboard.

Braves noticed me marveling at the animal.

"That, right there, is Billy," he said, pridefully. "He and I shared many a sunset together, back on Earth. The mate just showed up one day and that was that."

I was about to ask how he got the thing all the way out here, but then noticed something odd on the kangaroo's massive head, something that I was sure its species didn't organically come with—a bullet hole. I studied the small puncture, caused by a pistol if I had to guess.

Puzzled, I turned to Braves. "Is that what I think it is?"

Braves bellowed a hearty laugh. "Well, of course! I could hardly bring him out here alive, could I now? And a blaster bolt would've done too much damage. Bam!"

He slammed a palm down onto his table loudly, making me flinch in surprise. "Would've splattered him just like that! Had to take the old-fashioned route instead."

His voice changed to reminiscent. "A baretta it was. An antique! I'm a collector, you see. I have everything from ancient revolvers to the shiny auto-cannons, straight from the darkest corners of the Tau Ceti system!"

Braves sounded mighty proud, whereas I glimpsed Paxton frown. I was starting to get my Centurion didn't have an errant bone in his body.

For my part, I felt a surge of nerves. Braves was one hard man to pin. One minute I would almost think him to be sane, at least when compared to everyone else, but the next, I'd see something like this. He didn't seem at all fazed about killing his pet.

Walking up to me, Braves gave the stuffed thing a scratch behind the ear, praising it under his breath as if it were still alive and kicking.

"Here," he said, shoving a whiskey-filled glass into my hands. "Take a load off, mate. We have some time."

Seeing as he wasn't giving me an option about accepting the glass, and having no desire whatsoever to decline his generosity, I eagerly grabbed the drink. This time, I didn't wait for anyone's approval before taking a satisfying gulp. If I was forced to be here, I was going to make the best of it. The liquid burned just right as it made its way down my throat, and it momentarily quenched my irritation.

Braves chuckled at my obvious enjoyment of the drink. "Go, sit. Relax. You're making me dizzy with all this tension."

I obliged, savoring the oaky and spicy flavors permeating my mouth. Perhaps Braves had a point. It was time to unwind, to see the glass as half-full. The campaign on Atlas was over, and I was still breathing. Better yet, even if I couldn't see Taylor tonight, her and I had plenty of time coming our way as *Venator* headed to whatever hellhole awaited us next.

In hopes of relaxing, I meandered to a chair, but right as my butt was about to hit the padding and the glass my lips, an unmistakable, grating voice stabbed at my head.

All my tension instantaneously flooded back.

"Can you believe Gallus, that piece of—" Centurion Fallon stormed into the room, cutting off abruptly when her flaming gaze landed on me.

"What is this? What is *he* doing here?" She circled on Paxton, chest heaving. "Is there anywhere on this massive ship where I can be rid of him?"

My eyes went wide as I blinked at her. With my upcoming theatrics with the Legate, my resolution to confront her had been pushed to the back of my mind. That infernal task was something to be dealt with later. Except now that she was right here, in front of me, all I could think about was the mutilated corpse I'd found under that mountain.

"Aww, now," Braves mused. "Give the kid a break. We are, after all, celebrating the Legion's success. Here, have a drink."

He got up and poured another glass, shoving it at Fallon. "Give the kid another month and he'll have the Imperator, herself, heading this way."

Teeth bared, Fallon slapped Braves' offering away rudely, sending whiskey splashing to the floor.

"That's *exactly* what I'm afraid of," she spat as she stormed to Braves' bar.

Glass clinked and liquid poured, at the end of which Fallon spun back to us with something pink clutched in her claws. A sweet scent hit me as she marched to the couch.

She extended the concoction in my direction with false exuberance. "Congratulations, trooper. On behalf of the entire ship, I would like to thank you for bringing this burden to our doorstep. Everyone is just *overjoyed* with this honor."

Taking a wallop of a swallow, she plopped down practically on top of Paxton, and leaned her head back with a loud sigh.

"I swear, Adlar, why can't you just fight and die like any other trooper."

The other two Centurions barked an amused laugh at what I assumed was supposed to be a joke, then went to chatting, pretty much ignoring me after that. The only one to periodically half-acknowledge my presence was Braves, and that was only to refill my glass. Every time I finished it, I placed it on the table, giving it a little suggestive nudge in his direction. He obliged me each and every time, refilling it without pausing his conversation.

Bit by bit, with each additional gulp, my mood improved, and I stopped side-eying Fallon. I'd deal with her later.

Relaxing into my chair, I marveled at my situation to the backdrop of the Centurions' casual chatter. I'd been all too sure my send-off to the Legions had been a death sentence, but not only had I survived my first campaign, but here I was, amidst the brass, waiting for a personal congratulations from the ruler of Legion Invictus herself. Somehow, I had beaten the odds and then some.

As I sat there, deep in reflective thoughts, I must've still had a disgruntled look on my face, because Centurion Paxton noticed. I caught the man studying me with a patient expression.

After a full minute, he spoke. "Do you know much about the ancients, Adlar?"

I frowned in confusion. "Just what they taught in school, sir, and the bits I heard around the ship."

"So, nothing then."

I shrugged. It was common knowledge that some higher beings

scurried somewhere out there in the cosmos, and that they were our overlords, but hardly any concrete information was available.

The Centurion scoffed, rising from the couch. "Makes sense. Humanity prefers to keep its head in the sand, too consumed by our petty squabbles to step back and see the bigger picture."

Grabbing the decanter off the table, Paxton refilled his glass then mine.

"Well, allow me to fill you in," he continued. "They are the real enemy, everyone's enemy. They rule the Galactic Empire, but to them, most species are no better than vermin. They'd like nothing more than to exterminate all of us. Purge the Milky Way clean."

My frown deepened as I processed his statement.

"Why don't they, then?" I asked, thinking back to the little I did know about these species. "Aren't they all-powerful, or something like it?"

Paxton huffed. "Ascended is what they call it. And it's their muddled belief of universal connection that keeps them at bay, at least that's what we surmise from how they present themselves through their agents, the sleeks."

Methodically swirling the drink in his glass, he walked to study the scraggly tree on Braves' wall, unfocused. "So, they exist in the shadows, unseen, keeping a balance amongst the species through proxy. Deciding which tech is proprietary and curbing advancement or autonomy when they see fit. Through the sleeks and likely through many other diplomats."

He paused in thought. "Hence the law banning mass annihilation. No species may simply exterminate another member of the Empire. The skirmishes, the perpetual conflicts of their slaves, they don't much care about. Especially not humanities. We're insignificant. A piece of lint on their sleeves. They rule thousands, you see. Perhaps millions. Species we'd yet to meet."

I took a second to dart my eyes away from him in thought. The galaxy teemed with countless species, and in the grander picture, humanity truly was of no importance. An infant race just starting to venture out.

When I looked back at the Centurion, he met my eyes. "But the ancients won't be in the shadows forever, trooper. They'll resurface. Might not be in our generation, or the next, but they *will* come."

Braves smacked his lips to the backdrop of clinking glass.

"Time is of no concern to them," he piped in as he refilled his drink to the top. I didn't know how the man was still standing. 'But I daresay the drums of war beat on the horizon, mate. I can feel them."

Paxton nodded sagely in agreement, then turned to me.

A finger flew into the air. "Exactly. There's no telling what will break the camel's back. Perhaps they grow bored, or perhaps one of us, *bacterium*, tips the scales too far one way or the other, discovers or acquires something we shouldn't, but whatever sparks the onslaught, do you know who's going to be first on the chopping block, trooper? First to be expunged?"

I shook my head saying nothing.

"The weakest," he informed me, matter of factly. "What I'm getting at, Adlar, is that every victory counts. Our combined strength matters. Mars, Earth, that's irrelevant. One day the Legion will again fight for all humanity. Just as we did during Rap-Wars."

His glass came up to gesture at me. "What you did on Atlas, the crucial part you played, matters."

I felt my cheeks flush at the praise but only for a moment. Besides my drug-hazed interrogation, much of which was a blur, no one had asked me for further details, and I hadn't offered.

Resigned, I decided that the particulars of how I ended up within the shield, butterfingers and all, didn't matter. I was just glad I'd made the choice that I had. The Centurion's words were hitting home and, oddly, providing me comfort regarding my situation. The idea of becoming a mindless killer hadn't sat well with me, but we were more than that. We weren't out here fighting to merely elevate the Senate's status, quenching their lust for power as I'd previously thought, at least not under the surface. Not when it came to the bigger picture. We were out here fighting for all humanity. *I* was out here fighting for all humanity. For my family, for my friends back home. We couldn't allow mankind to be mere pawns on the gameboard when the real match began.

Centurion Paxton's sudden laugh snapped me out of my reflections. I looked up to see him spin to Fallon, an actual grin on his face.

He shook a mirthic finger at her. "When you demanded he be transferred to Gold Squad, I was skeptical, to say the least, but I stand corrected. You saw that something in him, didn't you?"

Fallon jerked back in confusion at Paxton's impromptu declaration, but after a few blinks, she caught on. Her eyes flew wide as the fingers wrapped around her glass turned white. I wasn't sure if she was about to squeeze it into shards or throw it.

I silently hoped she'd do either. Her blowing up right now would be one hell of a cherry to top the cake.

Unfortunately, Fallon managed to control herself.

She forced out a smile as she hissed her concession. "Yes, I did. How fortunate for us all."

Paxton chuckled in reply, his melancholy demeanor all but forgotten.

He raised his glass high, first to Fallon, then to me. "Well done, trooper. My unit, the entire Legion for that matter, will need men like you."

He toasted Braves next. "There'll be plenty of woe in days to come, I'm sure of it. But for now, let's get back to celebrating. To us, and to Legion Invictus! To Victory!"

Neither Fallon nor I reciprocated his salutations right away. We were too busy locking glares behind his back. The only difference was she now looked like she'd swallowed a turd and I had a smirk as large as the cosmos. One that I wasn't bothering to hide. Not only had her murderous scheme failed, but it had completely backfired.

Breaking away from Fallon, I decided to take the Centurion's words to heart. My arm flew up high to raise my glass. His pride in the Legion's success and the part I played was palpable, and I couldn't help but succumb to the emotion.

"To the Legion, sir," I stated boldly.

"Cheers!" Braves seconded.

Fallon was the only one left pouting, her face growing crimson as she slumped lower on the couch.

I ignored the witch. I had no idea what the upcoming days held in store for us, what shithole of a planet we'd be killing on next, or what nonsense the mythical Legate was going to bring with her, but for the moment, those worries vanished.

Smiling, I up-turned my whiskey and gulped it down.

———

The story continues in Payback!

THANK YOU FOR READING GOLD SQUAD

We hope you enjoyed it as much as we enjoyed bringing it to you. We just wanted to take a moment to encourage you to review the book. Follow this link: **Gold Squad** to be directed to the book's Amazon product page to leave your review.

Every review helps further the author's reach and, ultimately, helps them continue writing fantastic books for us all to enjoy.

———

Also in Series:
Gold Squad
Payback
Turning Point

———

Want to discuss our books with other readers and even the authors? Join our Discord server today and be a part of the Aethon community.

Facebook | Instagram | Twitter | Website

You can also join our non-spam mailing list by visiting www. subscribepage.com/AethonReadersGroup and never miss out on future releases. You'll also receive three full books completely Free as our thanks to you.

Looking for more great Science Fiction books?

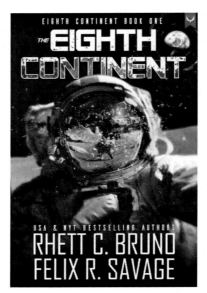

"This stellar near-future tale masterfully fuses SF thrills with an enthralling mystery." —**Kirkus Review A lowly construction worker on the Moon is Earth's only chance…** Nick Morrison always wanted to be an astronaut. When a startup company recruits him to build a lunar launch system at the Moon's south pole, Nick gladly leaves behind his troubled life on Earth—but Nick doesn't know that the company is in financial and legal trouble. Deprived of support from Earth, the team on the Moon must figure out how to survive on their own. Worse yet, there's another base at the lunar south pole, run by a ruthless contractor who has big plans for the Moon… and for Earth. Nick's team just so happen to be in the way. **Join them in their mission to stop the conquest of the Moon and Earth in this new Science Fiction Survival Thriller from Nebula Award Nominated author Rhett C. Bruno and NYT bestselling author Felix R. Savage. It's perfect for fans of** *The Martian, Artemis,* **and** *For all Mankind.*

Get The Eighth Continent Now!

———

Created to defeat the invaders. Forgotten in victory. They will rise again... We were outnumbered, outfought. Mankind was about to fall to the alien Flock. Our only chance was a desperate gamble, transforming Tier One SpecOps agents into deadly super soldiers. In the end, we won the war, but we lost the peace. The Flock surrendered and spent the next two hundred years making reparations, indentured to humanity, doing everything humans did not want to do. And the evolved super soldiers were consigned to an endless sleep. Ready if ever needed, but in time they became myths. Abandoned and forgotten. And then, when we were content in our dominance, the Flock revolted against all of humanity across the whole of the galaxy. We fell in a single day. Which is when the dreams began. People across the settled worlds began dreaming of the Sleepers. The evolved saviors. Acts of rebellion and terrorism swept the galaxy, and in response the Flock ground us under heel. Lexi Chow, descendant of a hero of the Flock War, believes the Sleepers are real, and are humanity's only chance against the alien conquerors. With a crew of misfits, criminals, and believers she sets out to wake the Sleepers. Hoping they will once more save us. If the betrayed Sleepers are willing. If the Sleepers are even human. If the Sleepers are on our side at all... **SLEEPERS: ALPHA WAVE by NY Times bestseller Jonathan Maberry and master storyteller Weston Ochse launches a new sprawling Military Science Fiction adventure that will span the whole of a galaxy at war!**

Get Alpha Wave Now!

They must learn to trust each other or humanity will fall. On a distant planet outside the reach of the Confederation, Garret Cushing finds himself in dire straits. Struggling with a guilty conscience, and his life in the balance, he decides to do the unthinkable; turn himself over to the Confederation in exchange for protection. As a witness to a decades-long conspiracy, he could save millions of lives, but first, he has to get off Bastia alive. There's only one way; with the aid of the Confederation, the organization that wants him dead. Enemies are forced to trust one another as they fight their way across the galaxy in an attempt to stop a devastating war. If they die, then humanity's hope for a future within the Galactic Confederation will end. **Conspiracies and intrigue run rampant in this first installment of The Confederation Saga, a military space opera adventure for fans of *Dark Matter* and *The Expanse.***

Get Oblivion's Dawn Now!

For all our Science Fiction books, check out https://aethonbooks. com/science-fiction/ or scan the code below!

Manufactured by Amazon.ca
Acheson, AB

13058186R00229